PRAISE FOR ROBIN
VICTORIAN MYSTERIES

"I read it with enjoyment ... I found myself burning for the injustice of it, and caring what happened to the people"—*Anne Perry*

"I couldn't put it down"—*Murder & Mayhem*

"An intriguing mystery ... Skillfuly unravelled"
—Jean Hager, author of *Blooming Murder*

"Absolutely riveting ... An extremely articulate, genuine mystery, with well-drawn, compelling character"
—*Meritorious Mysteries*

"An absolutely charming book ... An adventure worth reading ... You're sure to enjoy it"—*Romantic Times*

The Victorian Mystery Series by Robin Paige

Death At Bishop's Keep
Death At Gallow's Green
Death At Daisy's Folly
Death At Devil's Bridge
Death At Rottingdean
Death At Whitechapel
Death At Epsom Downs
Death At Dartmoor
Death At Glamis Castle
Death In Hyde Park
Death At Blenheim Palace
Death On The Lizard

*(written by Susan Wittig Albert with
her husband, Bill Albert, writing as Robin Paige)*

China Bayles Mysteries by Susan Wittig Albert

Thyme Of Death
Witches' Bane
Hangman's Root
Rosemary Remembered
Rueful Death
Love Lies Bleeding
Chile Death
Lavender Lies
Mistletoe Man
Bloodroot
Indigo Dying
A Dilly Of A Death
Dead Man's Bones
Bleeding Hearts

THE *Victorian Mystery* SERIES
5

Death at ROTTINGDEAN

ROBIN PAIGE

SOUTH DOWNS CRIME & MYSTERY

First published in the UK in 2016
by South Downs CRIME & MYSTERY,
an imprint of The Crime & Mystery Club Ltd,
PO Box 394, Harpenden,
Herts, AL5 1XJ, UK

www.crimeandmystery.club

ISBN
978-0-85730-021-8 (print)
978-0-85730-022-5 (epub)

Typeset in 11pt Palatino
by Avocet Typeset, Somerton, Somerset TA11 6RT

Printed and bound by CPI Group (UK) Ltd, Croydon, CR0 4YY

ACKNOWLEDGMENTS
Grateful thanks are due to Michael Smith, Honorary
Secretary of the Kipling Society at Rottingdean, who
provided access to the Society's archives and many helpful
insights into the history of Rottingdean, to Colonel John
Albert, USAF, for access to his historical reference library,
and to Phyllis Callf and her late husband, Leslie, for first
acquainting us with the charm of England's south coast
and for providing warm hospitality during our visits
there.

Robin Paige
a.k.a. Bill and Susan Albert

CAST OF CHARACTERS

Lord Charles Sheridan, *Baron of Somersworth*

Lady Kathryn Ardleigh Sheridan, *Baroness of Somersworth and mistress of Bishop's Keep*

Lawrence Quibbley, *manservant to Lord Sheridan*

Amelia Quibbley, *personal maid to Lady Sheridan*

Rottingdean's Residents and Visitors

Rudyard Kipling, *novelist and poet*

Caroline Kipling, *wife of Rudyard Kipling*

Lady Georgiana Burne-Jones, *wife of the painter Edward Burne-Jones*

Jack (Fat Jack) Woodhouse, *constable of Rottingdean*

Captain Reynold Smith, *coast guard commander*

Harry Tudwell, *stablemaster, Hawkham Stables*

Patrick, *an eleven-year-old boy*

John Landsdowne, *village chemist*

Trunky Thomas, *owner of bathing machines and fishing skiffs*

Mrs. Portney, *cook-housekeeper at Seabrooke House*

Mrs. Howard, *proprietress of Ladies' Fashions for Fashionable Ladies*

Mrs. Radford, widow of George Radford, *Black Rock coast guard*

Professor Waldemar Hertling, *antiquarian*

Photographer

BRIGHTON'S RESIDENTS AND VISITORS

His Royal Highness, the Prince of Wales

Arthur Sassoon, *banker and member of the Marlborough House set*

Count Ludwig Hauptmann, *Cultural Representative of the Kaiser*

Captain Pierre Gostarde, *French Navy*

Sir Robert Pinckney, *Chief Constable, Brighton*

Dr. Paul Barriston, *surgeon and Queen's coroner*

Reginald Wright Barker, *gun shop proprietor*

Mr. Maurice Burke, *tobacconist*

A Smuggler's Song

If you wake at midnight, and hear a horse's feet,
Don't go drawing back the blind, or looking in the street.
Them that asks no questions isn't told a lie.
Watch the wall, my darling, while the Gentlemen go by!
Five and twenty ponies,
Trotting through the dark—
Brandy for the Parson,
'Baccy for the Clerk;
Laces for a lady, letters for a spy,
And watch the wall, my darling, while the Gentlemen go by!

If you see the stable-door setting open wide;
If you see a tired horse lying down inside;
If your mother mends a coat cut about and tore;
If the lining's wet and warm—don't you ask no more!
If you do as you've been told, likely there's a chance,
You'll be give a dainty doll, all the way from France,
With a cap of Valenciennes, and a velvet hood—
A present from the Gentlemen, along o' being good!
Five and twenty ponies,
Trotting through the dark—
Brandy for the Parson,
'Baccy for the Clerk.
Them that asks no questions isn't told a lie—
Watch the wall, my darling, while the Gentlemen go by!

—RUDYARD KIPLING
Puck of Pook's Hill

1

"Smuggling is the chief support of the inhabitants at which they are very Dext'rous—for which innocent and beneficial practice (sad to relate) Captain Dunk the Butcher paid £500 and ten of his worthy friends were lodged in Hawsham Gaol or in their elegant language were sent for a month to colledge to improve their manners."

Old History of Rottingdean

THE SALT BREEZE was fresh against the boy's face and the waves broke with a soft chuckle and a foamy fizz on the shingle beach at his feet. On very calm days, when there was no breeze at all, the water lapped gently against the rounded flint pebbles, as it might do at the edge of a millpond. But Patrick had spent his entire eleven years on the south coast of England, and he was not taken in by the Channel's deceptive tranquillity. Autumn conjured up angry sou'westers, whose giant crashing waves scooped up the flint pebbles and flung them at the great chalk cliff a few yards behind him, undermining the soft, flint-studded rock until great slabs gave way and collapsed into the maelstrom, pulling down sections of the Brighton-to-Rottingdean road and bits of wall and even a few hapless cottages. The furious waves would pound road and rock and walls and roof to nothing, leaving only the indestructible nodules of gray flint, strewn on the beach to be used as the waves' ammunition for the next attack against the cliff.

Patrick walked for a few feet eastward, studying the shiny flint pebbles, but they gave no clue to what he had seen last midnight from the hazardous margin of the cliff above. Frowning, he raised his eyes and scanned the heaving horizon, but the fishing boats far out in the Channel seemed to be going about their ordinary business. He turned and looked back at the cliff. Nothing there, either, except for a pile of recently fallen chalk whose collapse had carved out a shallow cave a dozen feet up the rock wall, typical of the shallow caves that pocked the white cliffs eastward from Rottingdean and westward nearly to Brighton. All that was left of what he had seen was the shadowy image in his mind: a figure in black oilskins hauling a skiff onto the shingle at this very point, then dragging something heavy from the base of the cliff back to the skiff. The waning moon was draped with clouds and its light had been shuttered and fitful, like a flickering lantern in a high wind. Patrick could not see the boatman's face, but there was something in his movements and bearing that made the boy think he knew him, and he was sure he recognized the skiff. Once his burden was loaded, the man had pushed off and rowed out to sea.

Patrick had watched, his heart beating fast, until the thin moon flickered out and darkness extinguished man and boat and mysterious cargo. When there was no more to be seen, not even the glimmer of a turned oar, he hurried along the path below Beacon Hill and past the great dark windmill to Mrs. Higgs's dilapidated cottage. With the sureness of long practice, he climbed the apple tree and scrambled nimbly through the loft window to drop feet-first onto his bed, where he pulled the scratchy blanket to his chin, squeezed his eyes shut, and pondered. The longer he thought, the more vague and ghostly and dreamlike was the remembered scene, until he drifted into sleep and it actually *was* a dream, the boatman throwing off his hood to reveal a terrible face with huge holes for eyes, and the cargo a dead man.

A dead man. Well, why not? With a shiver that was half excitement and half apprehension, Patrick shoved his hands into the pockets of his ragged corduroy trousers and set off toward the Gap, where the metal pier jutted out into the sea and a row of red-and-white-striped bathing machines were lined up like miniature circus tents under the cliff. This beach had seen its share of dead men, drowned sailors washed up like bloated cod from Channel shipwrecks and smugglers killed in the pursuit of their hazardous occupation. Smugglers' Village, Rottingdean was called by some, in honor of its role in the contraband trade. There must have been dozens of smugglers caught between the coast guard and the cliffs, or trapped like rats in the maze of tunnels that lay under the streets and houses. Patrick pushed his lips in and out, his fertile imagination summoning up a disagreement, a violent struggle, a shot fired in anger. A dead man on the beach below the cliff's crumbling edge? A natural event, to any who knew the history of Smugglers' Village.

To an observer of the late 1890s, Rottingdean appeared to be a peaceful hamlet of some twelve hundred kind and law-abiding souls, where little enough happened from year to year. Its chief distinctions were its proximity to bustling, brassy Brighton, a scant three miles to the west, and its quiet streets, quaint appearance, and fresh sea air, which attracted a few wealthy London families who enjoyed summering in a seaside village. The racing on White Hawk Down brought in a different kind of visitor, who was likely to stay at the White Horse Inn and employ the village boys—among whom Patrick made himself most convenient and willing—to execute various urgent commissions.

Yes, the beach had seen its share of brutal murder. Settled in Neolithic times, the village owed its existence to the Gap, a narrow breach in the cliff that guards the south coast of England like a fortress wall. The Gap was opened eons before by a stream that cut through the soft chalk on its way to the sea and vanished before the area became a Roman outpost, and then (by subsequent violent overthrow) a Saxon territory and a Norman settlement. From time to time over the centuries, marauding raiders and foreign invaders stormed through this inviting opening into the Sussex uplands, killing and burning and destroying. Once the invasion had ended, the folk who survived (and some of them always did) returned to their peaceful pursuits: growing corn in the arable meadows and grazing sheep on the gently rolling downs.

But by the seventeenth and eighteenth centuries, the villagers, a wily, opportunistic lot who were steeled by their encounters with this harsh land, had discovered that a different sort of traffic through the Gap might be used to benefit the village. This was the period when punitive excise made smuggling both into and out of England a gainful occupation, and most of Rottingdean's citizens were in one way or another engaged in it. The cellars under the houses—chiefly those around the Green—were linked to one another and to the beach by a labyrinth of tunnels dug through the soft chalk. Bales of fleeces (wool was the chief illicit export) were stored in the cellars, then trundled through the tunnels to the beach and loaded onto ships bound for distant ports. Boxes of tea and tobacco, barrels of spirits, and bundles of lace—products that the rich people in the great houses and cities to the north wanted and were willing to pay for (without the duty, of course)—came in the other direction, being unloaded from the ships, hauled in through the tunnels, stored in the cellars, and freighted under cover of darkness in the direction of Falmer and Lewes, for further transport to London. It was altogether a profitable business, considered by the villagers to be a legitimate, if illegal, perquisite of their coastal residence.

In an attempt to halt this brisk commerce, the government built a customs house in the village and three stations along the cliff's edge, where armed coast guards made regular nightly patrols from Black Rock eastward through Rottingdean to Saltdean. But whether it was because the coast guards were lazy or stupid or dishonest (or all three), the smugglers continued to ply their trade with the regularity of the moon and the tides until the excise laws were dismantled in the 1840s and the business ceased to return a profit. That, at least, was what the high government officials thought. But Patrick, whose sharp eyes and ears and quick wit made him privy to most of the village secrets, knew otherwise.

And now he knew about the dead man on the beach. He raised his head, frowning. Should he tell what he had seen? On the whole, he thought not, with the shrewdness of a boy who knows that it may be dangerous to share secrets with men. But what if he himself had been seen watching from his clifftop vantage point and was thought to be an accomplice, a lookout? He could protest his innocence but he could not prove it, which would lead to difficulties with the officials, who would go straightaway to Mrs. Higgs, the woman who looked after him, who would shut up the window and bar the attic door at night and make it difficult for him to come and go as he pleased.

Patrick hunched his shoulders against the wind. He should tell someone what he had seen, before he was accused of complicity. But whom should he tell? If it had been any other matter, he would have gone directly to Harry Tudwell, the stablemaster and his friend and benefactor. But something made him think that Mr. Tudwell already knew about this particular happening, and that telling him might complicate the matter. The village constable, a fat, lazy man whom Patrick held in contempt, was a great friend of Mrs. Higgs's, and telling him would be the same as telling her. He might tell Lady Burne-Jones, who lived at North End House and employed Mrs. Higgs as a laundress. She was a bit of a busybody but she had befriended him, insisting that he call her Aunt Georgie and giving him copies of *Treasure Island, The Jungle Books*, and several of Conan Doyle's detective stories, which he enjoyed a great deal. But Lady Burne-Jones was a member of the Parish Council and considered herself the guardian of everyone's welfare. She would certainly ask discomforting questions, such as what he was doing at the cliff's edge at midnight. And there was no guarantee that she would not tell Mrs. Higgs about his nocturnal adventures.

Patrick looked up and caught sight of a dark-haired man clad in a canvas jacket and carrying a fishing rod and bucket, descending from the Quarter Deck—the cobbled area on the cliff above the beach—to the pier. The man waved at him, and Patrick waved back. The fisherman was Mr. Kipling, Lady Burne-Jones's famous nephew, who had come to Rottingdean on Derby day to take The Elms, the walled house at the far end of the Green. Patrick had already read the adventures of Mowgli before he met their author in Aunt Georgie's back garden and discovered to his great delight that Mr. Kipling was full of even more wonderful stories. The tales of bazaar life and wandering lamas in India, where Mr. Kipling had once lived, excited him wildly, but the teller had intrigued him even more. Patrick had met all sorts of men on his various errands and considered himself a fair judge of character. An excellent judge, come to that, as Harry Tudwell the stablemaster would attest, or Trunky Thomas, the proprietor of the bathing machines, both of whom relied on Patrick's reports concerning the visitors who stayed at the White Horse Inn. But Mr. Kipling, who was said to earn a fine living by spinning tales, was entirely new to the boy's experience. He had a worldliness born of wide travel, sharpened by an enormous curiosity about the workings of ordinary things and softened by a warm friendliness toward children, whom he treated with thoughtful respect. Patrick meant to learn more about this man, and hear as many more of Mr. Kipling's stories as he might be willing to tell.

Patrick reached into his pocket and pulled out the bent cigarette for which he had traded his friend Ernie Shepherd a striped peppermint humbug. He turned his back against the wind to light it expertly, and squatted down on the shingle to smoke and think as he watched Mr. Kipling walk jauntily out to the end of the pier and settle down to an hour's fishing, as he did almost every day. After a few minutes, the boy stood and extinguished his cigarette, saving what was left for a later smoke.

Yes, if he should tell anyone the story of what he had seen on the beach, it should be Mr. Kipling. But not just now. Just now, the story was a thin one, only a beginning, with no middle and no end, hardly worthy to be heard by Mowgli's creator. So he would not tell, not yet. He would wait and use his eyes and his ears and see what else he might learn.

2

"The principal 'Green Properties' are *The Elms*, the flint wall of which now forms the northern boundary of the Green; *The Dene* on the South, and ... *North End House* to the West. Each is a house with a history, and each was once the home of some of Rottingdean's most illustrious and remarkable characters. Writers and poets, painters and Prime Ministers, judges and politicians, actors, racehorse trainers, country squires and eccentrics—all have lived round the Green at one time or another, and some still do."

—HENRY BLYTH
Smugglers' Village: The Story of Rottingdean

"I MUST SAY, my lord, you have the makings of a first-rate motorcar mechanic."

From the driver's seat, Kate smiled down at her husband, who, stripped to his shirtsleeves in the noonday sun, knelt by the front wheel, patiently repairing yet another tire. "But you really must speak with the Home Secretary about the shocking state of these Sussex roads," she added archly.

Charles pushed back a shock of brown hair with a dirty

hand. "What was that about the Home Secretary?"

"Nails," Kate said succinctly. "In the roads. Can't someone *do* something? This is the third flat tire we've had this morning!"

"These roads collected horseshoe nails for centuries before anyone thought of a pneumatic tire," Charles said. "I daresay it will be a few more years before all of them have been retrieved. In the interim, it's not the Home Secretary but the Parish Council that—" The last few words were drowned out by a loud hiss.

Kate smiled as she watched the tire swell to its proper size and seat itself on the rim. Instead of using the frightfully inefficient hand pump, Charles inflated flat tires from a metal cylinder formerly filled with the oxygen he used to power the limelight for his photography, now filled with compressed air—a device that demonstrated his inventive turn of mind. Few gentlemen of her husband's social rank—he was the Baron of Somersworth—turned a hand to anything of practical merit, or demeaned themselves with physical labor, or did anything *real*. But Charles quite astoundingly did all three, and she loved him for it.

While her husband put away his tools, Kate adjusted her hat and motoring veil, smiling to herself. Despite the tires that went flat with maddening frequency and the necessity of carrying a supply of extra petrol, she was delighted with her new Panhard, a truly revolutionary automobile with its engine in front and a wheel for steering, instead of a tiller. The French automobile had been obtained for her by Charlie Rolls, who raced it in publicity competitions. She had met Mr. Rolls during such a competition the previous year, when she commandeered his automobile—stole it, according to one journalist's account of the event—to drive to Charles's rescue, a terrible trip of fifteen miles at speeds of nearly twenty miles an hour. The feat, an unusually reckless one for a lady, had given her a certain celebrity in motoring circles. With this reputation, Mr. Rolls had not found it difficult to convince the manufacturer of the marketing advantages to be had by equipping Lady Sheridan with their most modern machine—and so Kate had received her first automobile. Charles could hardly say no.

Charles shrugged into his long duster and settled his goggles over his eyes. "Brighton is only a mile or so, and I thought we might have lunch at The Old Ship. I asked Lawrence to meet us there so we could go on to Rottingdean together." He started the engine, then climbed into the passenger seat and touched his fingers to the brim of his cap. "Shall we soldier on, my dear? Our seaside holiday awaits!"

Steering the motorcar toward Brighton and a quiet lunch, Kate thought how good it was to see her husband smile. When she agreed to become his wife, she'd known that their marriage would be difficult. She was an American, and Irish, old enough to have lived her own life and independent enough to insist on her freedoms; he was the son of a wealthy and aristocratic British family that seemed bound to the past by every imaginable tradition. The best she could hope for was that their love for one another—a love that had grown and deepened in the eighteen months of their marriage—would help to ease the worst of the inevitable bumps in the road ahead.

And so it had, for a time. Charles's mother, the Dowager Lady Somersworth, had been bitterly opposed to her son's marriage and made no secret of her dislike for her Irish-American daughter-in-law. The newlywed couple had taken up residence at Bishop's Keep, the Essex manor Kate had inherited, and avoided visiting Charles's family. Now, Kate looked back on that quiet and happy time with a regretful pleasure, for a momentous change had overtaken them, testing their love and making the past nine months desperately difficult.

At Christmas of the year before, Charles's brother Robert, the fourth Baron of Somersworth, had died. The elder brother's death was not unexpected, and it finally visited upon Charles the obligations of the peerage, which both he and Kate had anticipated with dread. Charles's new responsibilities opened a new era in their marriage. From then on, Kate felt, nothing had been the same.

Now the fifth Baron of Somersworth, Charles seemed determined to do his duty. He saw to his brother's funeral and assumed the management of the estates, both in England and Ireland. When Parliament sat in late January, he moved to the family's large London mansion and took his seat in the House of Lords. Because Kate felt it was her duty to be with Charles, she went with him, and tried as best she could to play her role in Society. London in the season, with money to spend, a splendid home, and nothing to do but enjoy herself—what more could she want?

But it hadn't been a happy time. Charles was remote, occupied with meetings all day and sessions in the House at night. London was dirty and noisy, and Kate pined for the easy freedoms of her rural life at Bishop's Keep, where she had tended her gardens, managed her own household, and ridden her bicycle to the village. The London house was a mausoleum—immense, uninviting, and efficiently managed by a housekeeper who made it chillingly plain to the new baroness that she wasn't welcome belowstairs. While Kate had enjoyed vigorous health in the country, she was quickly exhausted by the interminable whirlwind of London social life: morning rides in Hyde Park, afternoons spent shopping and making calls, evening soirees and dinners, glittering balls that went on until three in the morning. She had also tried hard to keep up with her writing, for Kate had already published a number of fictions and wanted to do more. And on top of that there was the work she had undertaken for the Countess of Warwick, who had asked her to see to the problems of the orphanage in the parish of George the Martyr.

Kate sighed to herself, thinking back over the hectic spring and early summer. Perhaps it was the exhaustion that had led to their great tragedy. If only she'd had the sense to take better care of herself! If she had gone home to Bishop's Keep in April when she learned she was pregnant, instead of agreeing to help the Countess with yet another of her impractical schemes to improve the lives of slum children—

"I hope," Charles said loudly, over the clatter of the engine, "that you will like Rottingdean. It is a very little village, after all, with only a few families."

"I'm sure I don't care," Kate said, "as long as you are there. In fact, I shall be glad for some time alone together." It would be such a relief to have no luncheon appointments, no dinner engagements, no balls or parties—not even any servants, except for their own Amelia and Lawrence. She might even be able to get back to the book she had started writing so many months before, which was fearfully overdue at her publishers.

Charles nodded and went on. "But they *are* interesting families. The Burne-Joneses have a house on one side of the Green—the painter, you know, and his wife. She is quite an independent woman, I understand, with a great many ideas of her own. Stanley and Lucy Baldwin—you've met them both—visit Lucy's parents, the Ridsdales, who live on another corner of the Green. And the Kiplings have taken a house nearby. Rudyard's wife is an American; Caroline, her name is." He paused. "Perhaps, while we are there, we should host a dinner or evening's entertainment."

Kate's heart sank. She admired the painting of Edward Burne-Jones, who was associated with the Pre-Raphaelite Brotherhood. She had planned to take some time to study the stained glass windows that he and his fellow artist, William Morris, had created for the parish church. She would like, as well, to meet Lady Burne-Jones, about whom she had already heard a great deal. But as for a dinner or a party—

"We didn't come to Rottingdean for company," she protested. "We were to have a private holiday, with time to walk on the beach and among the downs." They were to have time, she hoped, to recapture the pleasure in one another's company that had seemed to elude them in London—to return, perhaps, to the charm of the early days of their marriage, when all seemed so right and full of promise.

"Yes, of course," Charles said. "But I'm sure you and Caroline Kipling would get on famously. She has a new baby, a boy, I understand, just over a month old."

And then he stopped and turned to her, stricken, and she saw in his sherry-brown eyes what she knew was in his heart: an overwhelming sadness at the loss of their own child, and at the awful knowledge that there could never be a son, at least not *her* son, to fulfill the obligations of his lineage.

3

"At Brighton, the lanes remain much as they were in the eighteenth century, when goods were landed on the beach and carried straight up for sale and distribution from shops and inns among the winding alleys and narrow courtyards. The Old Ship Hotel nearby has changed little since the days of George IV's coronation in 1821, when it was the scene of an admirable bit of smuggling opportunism. While the town celebrated elsewhere, the free-traders took advantage of the empty streets and moved tubs of spirits out of the pub stables completely unobserved. Today it's one of the town's better hotels, with an air more of smugness than smugglers."

—RICHARD PLATT
Smugglers' Britain

CHARLES TURNED AWAY from Kate with an inward groan, cursing himself for his thoughtlessness. What a way to begin their holiday—by reminding her of her terrible loss, the very loss he had brought her here to forget! Kate had been wonderfully brave in the months since her illness and miscarriage, but he knew she needed to be away from everything—away from that huge, cold London house, even away from Bishop's Keep, where they had dreamed together of the children they would have.

Now that dream was dead, and to ease Kate's heart, he had arranged this month-long holiday in a peaceful village on the south coast of England, where he could spend every moment with her, helping her forget, helping her heal the loss for which she seemed to carry such a dreadful burden of responsibility and guilt.

These were topics he found difficult to discuss. But then, Charles, like most of the men he knew, could not speak easily about the things that were closest to him. On their wedding night, Kate had run her finger over one of the wide scars on his bare chest. When she asked about it, he said only that he had been in a tight spot in the Sudan, and gently silenced her. She had understood that it was a matter he did not wish to discuss, and though they slept in each other's arms every night, she never mentioned the scars again. The moment never arose when he could tell her how it was that he had lived and all of his men had died, that he had been rewarded with a knighthood for his bravery, while their courage was forgotten, and how sad he still felt about these things. In fact, he had been in India to convey his condolences to the parents of his young sergeant, when Rudyard Kipling, then the eager new assistant editor of the *Civil and Military Gazette*, had heard a rumor of the affair and sought him out. He could not talk of it to Kipling, either.

They now were entering Brighton. It was Saturday, and the bright autumn sunshine, as always, had lured hundreds of daytrippers from the city on the London, Brighton, and South Coast Railway. Working class families dressed in their best, they came to listen to a concert on the lawns near the Metropole Hotels, or stroll along the seafront promenade and laugh at the banjo-playing blackface minstrels in their striped blazers and straw boaters. They joined the crowds visiting West Pier and the Aquarium and the new Palace Pier, scheduled to open the next year. Or they rode in horse-drawn buses to the neighboring seaside resorts of Rottingdean and Hove, or boarded a paddlewheeled pleasure-steamer for a trip to the Isle of Wight. Brighton had its own fine Society, of course, led by the Duchess of Fife (who was frequently visited by her father, the Prince of Wales) and the two wealthy Sassoon brothers, both bankers. The Brighton season began in October and lasted through March, with the theater, the opera, and the hunt providing abundant entertainment. The pleasure city might not be the brilliant social center it had been when the monarchy came regularly to town, but it still had plenty of life—and far too much traffic.

"Be careful, Kate!" Charles cried, as a horse-drawn brewer's wagon pulled out directly in front of them. Momentarily distracted from her driving, Kate had turned her head to stare at a bizarre cluster of buildings on the right, with a gaudy Oriental façade, Moorish trellises, fantastic onion-shaped domes, and dozens of minarets. Now, she braked hard, and Charles pitched forward.

"I'm sorry," she said. "Are you all right?" But she was beginning to giggle. "Is *that* the Royal Pavilion? It looks like something out of *The Arabian Nights*."

"That's it," Charles said, resetting his goggles. "Quite something, isn't it?"

"Words can't begin to describe it," Kate said wonderingly. "Whoever built it must have been crazy—and very rich."

"Yes to both. I've always thought of the damn thing as a monument to royal excess. Now, the place belongs to the town of Brighton. It's the first stop for daytrippers just off the train." He pointed to a heedless and noisy crowd crossing the cobbled street in front of them and pausing to stare at the motorcar. "Watch out for that lot."

Kate frowned through the heavy veil that swathed her face. "Would you care to take the wheel, my lord?"

Charles smiled and shook his head. To tell the truth, he was quite proud of the fact that she was a better driver than he was—and certainly a fearless one, with a calm, even temperament that enabled her to meet every vehicular crisis with aplomb. He would change the tires, add petrol when necessary, and lend a shoulder when they found themselves stuck in the mud, but he was content to let her drive when they went somewhere together.

"Thank you, no, my dear," he said mildly. "You are managing very well. Forgive me if I seemed critical. The Old Ship is only a little farther."

They arrived without further incident at the hotel, one of the oldest in the city, and were shown to a table in the elegantly appointed dining room. After they ordered, Charles excused himself and went in search of his manservant, Lawrence, whom he found sitting over a steak-and-kidney pie in the taproom with his wife, Amelia, Kate's personal maid. The two servants had come down on the train with the boxes and cases, and Lawrence had hired a gig for the three-mile drive east along the coast to Rottingdean, to the house they had taken for the month.

Charles arranged with Lawrence and Amelia to leave for Rottingdean after lunch, and returned to Kate, taking a moment to stand in the dining room doorway and admire her. She was gazing out the window beside the table, her chin propped on her hand, her shining russet hair gathered into a loosely coiled mass beneath her wide-brimmed hat. Her face, which was too firm-featured to be thought beautiful, was quiet and reflective, and Charles was glad to see that the color in her cheeks was brighter than it had been in some time. The bodice of her dark blue motoring dress fit neatly, showing firm, rounded breasts, and her waist was slim enough, in spite of her refusal to submit to what she called the "torture of the corset." In fact, his wife held rather firm opinions about rational dress and delighted in scandalizing people with her split cycling skirts and the knee-length costume in which she played at tennis.

Charles pulled out his chair and sat down. "You're pensive," he said, and took her gloved hand in his.

She turned to him with a bright smile. "I was just thinking how wonderful it will be to have you all to myself, my dear, after the turmoil of the last few months. We have been so little together, and I have missed you." She squeezed his hand. "Dreadfully."

"I had not known that Parliament would take so much of my time," Charles said. "I believed myself well informed about matters of government, but I found it very hard to untangle all that business about the Voluntary Schools Bill." He sighed. "No one else seemed to have difficulty understanding it."

"That's because none of the other lords was paying attention," Kate said tartly. "And it *was* a very vexed matter, all tangled up with local and Church politics and—"

She was interrupted by a tall, slender man with a mustache and a neat salt-and-pepper beard, wearing gray kid gloves, an impeccable gray coat, and striped tie. He saluted Charles.

"Hello, Sheridan," the man said, bowing over his hat. "How delightful to see you here. I hope you have come to stay for a while."

"Arthur Sassoon!" Charles exclaimed, standing, and introduced him to Kate. The Sassoon brothers— Arthur and Reuben—were among Brighton's wealthiest residents, and Arthur, who lived in Hove, just to the west of Brighton proper, had been a close friend of the Prince of Wales for many years. They were both members of the notorious Marlborough House set, sometimes called the Marlborough *banditti* because of their high jinks.

Sassoon bowed to Kate. "Where in Brighton are you staying, Lady Sheridan?"

"We are not in Brighton," Kate said. "We are in Rottingdean." She gestured to an empty chair. "Won't you please join us?"

"Thank you, no," Sassoon said regretfully. "My carriage is waiting. I'm on my way to call on the duchess. You will be in Rottingdean for some time?"

"Three weeks," Charles said. "We've come for a quiet seaside holiday. The last few months have been wearing."

"Ah, yes, quaint little Rottingdean." Sassoon raised one eyebrow, amused. "Quite a rustic retreat, most attractive, and most relaxing, known for the innocent charms of the downs and the seashore. You shall find few temptations there, I promise you, and even less excitement." He smiled. "But I trust you can make the time for an evening at my home in King's Gardens, Lord Charles. The Prince will be there Tuesday next, and I should be most gratified if you will agree to attend our party." He bowed apologetically to Kate. "A men's evening, quite informal, with cards and general revelry." To Charles, he added, "Rudyard Kipling has agreed to join us. You know, do you, that he is staying in Rottingdean?"

"Thank you for the invitation," Charles said. "It is very kind of you to include me. But I have promised my wife that this holiday—"

Kate put out her hand, stopping him. "Of course you will accept," she said firmly. "What is one evening, when we have so many lovely ones waiting for us?"

Sassoon smiled. "Generously spoken, Lady Sheridan. So it's settled. Tuesday next, then, at seven. And remember, we are very informal. His Royal Highness insists." He bowed again. "Since you are in search of quiet, I am sure you will enjoy your stay at Rottingdean. Nothing ever happens there."

4

"Try as he will, no man breaks wholly loose
From his first love, no matter who she be.
Oh, was there ever sailor free to choose,
That didn't settle somewhere near the sea?"

—RUDYARD KIPLING

IT WAS A cool, crisp morning, and the sweet call of St. Margaret's bell summoned the Rottingdean parishioners, who were an upright and churchgoing lot, to Sunday worship. But Rudyard Kipling, always a renegade soul, was offering thanks to his deity in another fashion. He was seated on an overturned bucket at the end of the iron pier with his twelve-ounce St. John's trout rod in his hand—lighter than he liked for Channel fishing, but adequate until he found something heavier.

On the whole, Kipling had much to be grateful for. It had been a good plan, returning to Rottingdean, with the grassy downs at its back and the great, gray sea all before it. He had spent a happy time here with the Beloved Aunt and Uncle—Georgiana and Edward Burne-Jones—in August of '82. He had been a boisterous lad fresh from his last term at Westward Ho!, importantly decorated with his first side-whiskers and excited about his journey to India, where his father had arranged his first employment as a journalist with the daily *Civil and Military Gazette* in Lahore. He had spent nearly seven years as an apprentice writer there, producing not only the newspaper stories he was hired to write, but dozens of other well-received stories and poems. When he came back to England in '89, still a very young man, he was ready to embark on a serious career as a writer.

And after that, it seemed, success had come so easily that he could later imagine those days only as a kind of waking dream, where he took, as a matter of course, the fantastic cards that Fate was pleased to deal him. In 1892, in the thick of an influenza epidemic, he married an American woman, Caroline Balestier, and the two of them went on a Cook's tour around the world. They settled for a few years in Vermont, where he wrote *The Jungle Books* and *Captains Courageous* and Josephine and Elsie were born, and then came home again to England, first to Torquay, then—full circle, it seemed—to Rottingdean beside the sea, where last month Carrie had triumphantly given birth to John, a black-haired, beetle-browed boy who snorted like a whale and fed like a ravenous calf.

Fifteen years, a solicitous wife, three healthy children, and too many pages to count. It was something a man could appreciate, if hardly comprehend, Kipling thought, as he stared out at the heaving sea. But while there had been happy days, those years had not been unceasingly bright. Although he could hardly say so, even to himself, he had married Carrie perhaps less out of love for her than out of a desperate grief for her brother and his much-loved friend Walcott, who had died suddenly of typhoid.

As marriages go, his to Carrie had been happy enough. She certainly looked out for his welfare, although she had a strongly proprietary attitude and could not seem to understand that he might want to go off by himself occasionally. But the time in Vermont, where he'd intended them to spend their lives, had come to a bitter end in a public feud with Carrie's brother Beatty. Illness and depression had plagued him since, and he suffered from an impotent anger at the American publishers who shamelessly pirated his books, publishing them without permission or payment. The days in Torquay had concluded in a blackness of mind and sorrow of heart, and he and Carrie had almost fled to Rottingdean.

There was peace in this little smugglers' village, which had changed very little in the years since he had first visited, except for the rather surprising prosperity evident in the newly repaired and painted houses and the number of shining new gigs in the High Street. Somehow or other, the village had managed to survive the Depression of the last decade and in recent years seemed to have stumbled upon good times. But there was still at the back of Kipling's mind an uneasy foreboding, and he mulled it over as he sat and smoked and gazed southward, over the Channel.

The problem, to put it bluntly, was England's infernal complacency. While the nation basked in the golden glow of Empire and celebrated itself in the Queen's Diamond Jubilee, these were latter days, and few had the wisdom to know it. This was not an ideal world but a nest of burglars, as he himself had written to his friend Jack Mackail, and England had to protect itself against being burgled. There had been trouble in South Africa after the Jameson Raid, and he had a sense of something like a wind going in the tops of the mulberry trees, of things moving into position, as troops move into place before a battle. The big smash was coming one of these days, and it would be the Germans they would have to go up against. He had warned against hubris in *Recessional*, the poem he had written for the Jubilee. But as usual, his caution had been largely misinterpreted, especially by the Liberals, who did not like to be reminded that England was the last, best hope of the civilized world. So there was nothing for him to do just now but wait and watch, as he watched now, across the Channel.

"Are you catching anything, sir?"

Kipling turned with a start. The boy with the fishing rod was named Patrick—Pat, he was called in the village, a slender, wiry boy with the freckled face and coppery hair and dancing green eyes of the Irish. Kipling understood that he had come from good family fallen on hard times; that his mother, a clergyman's daughter, was dead these last three years; and that his father, stationed in India with an Irish regiment, paid the Aunt's laundress to board the boy. It was a common practice. Kipling himself had been boarded for close on six years in Southsea, next to Portsmouth, in a small house that was little better than Mrs. Higgs's cottage. He hoped Patrick was happier than he had been.

"Catching up on my thinking," Kipling said. "The fish seem to be occupied with their own affairs. They certainly have paid no attention to me." He grinned up at the boy. "Sit, why don't you, Patrick? There's room in this ocean for another hook."

"Yes, sir," the boy said, and sat, casting his line into the water with scarcely a ripple.

Kipling liked children, for they had none of the duplicity of adults. They demanded nothing and returned all honest affection with an open and innocent affection of their own. But while this boy spoke with the seemingly earnest respect that a schoolboy might use to the headmaster, he did not have the easy trustfulness of other children his age. Kipling had met him under the copper beeches in the pleasant garden of North End House, where Aunt had gathered Josephine and Elsie and the children of the houses around the Green to hear him tell stories of the cat that walked by himself and the bad-tempered rhinoceros with cake-crumbs under his skin. The boy had crept round the gooseberry bushes to listen with the others, but he was not like them. He was older, of course, eleven or so, and well-spoken for his age, perhaps because he read books. But there was more—a wariness, a certain calculating shrewdness that made him seem alert and almost adult. He made free of the village, for he carried laundry to and from the houses around the Green, and Kipling had seen him hanging about the stables and in the taproom at the White Horse Inn. An intriguing boy, Kipling thought, puffing on his pipe and watching him out of the corner of his eye. A boy worth knowing.

Patrick turned and caught his glance. "Sir," he said, "I wonder, sir—" He hesitated, looked away, and then said, with remarkable composure, "Never mind," and reeled in his line and cast again.

The silence of the next ten minutes was broken only by the raucous shrilling of the gulls and the lapping of the waves on the shingle as a wooden skiff was rowed jerkily to shore beside the pier, towing something—a large fish, perhaps, too large to land into the small boat—at the end of a hempen line. The fisherman clambered out and lurched drunkenly up the beach in the direction of the bathing machines.

"Trunky!" he bellowed. "Trunky Thomas, where the devil be ye?"

A stout gray-haired man in a heavy woolen sweater emerged from a frame building on the cobbled ledge that the villagers called the Quarter Deck. He leaned over the stone wall. "Wot's the matter, Jack?" he called down, in a gravelly voice.

"Wot's the matter,'e asks," Jack replied, as if to himself, and raised his head. "The matter is," he said loudly, "that I've fished up a dead man. Ye'd best send for the constable."

"A dead man!" Kipling exclaimed. Beside him, Patrick hunched his shoulders, staring fixedly at the water.

"A dead man!" Trunky Thomas cried. He straightened up. "'Oo is it, Jack?"

"'Oo is it, 'e asks," Jack muttered, shaking his head. "'Tis the coast guard," he said. "The coast guard from Black Rock. 'E bobbed up 'gainst my boat like a blasted cork."

"George Radford, is it?" Trunky cried. "Well, I'll be blowed!"

Beside Kipling, Patrick cleared his throat. "Excuse me, sir," he said quietly, "but there's a story I should like to tell you, if you wouldn't mind listening."

5

"May no ill dreams disturb my rest,
Nor Powers of Darkness me molest."

—Rudyard Kipling,
The Phantom Rickshaw

Kate shivered into her woolen jacket as she and Charles stood on the windy height above the shingle, watching as a pair of men and one small boy stoutly hauled the body of a dead man out of the water and onto the beach, as if it were a harpooned whale that the sea was loath to yield.

"Drowned, it would seem," said the gentleman on the other side of Charles. He was dressed in gray tweed knickerbockers and jacket and a gray bowler, and was holding a small box camera. He aimed it carefully, pushed a button, and took a photograph of the scene on the beach. "I have heard it said that the natives along this coast, when they turn despondent, are driven by the powers of darkness to jump off the cliff and into the sea." He spoke somewhat stiffly and with a pronounced accent. Perhaps he was French, or Belgian, Kate thought. French, most likely, with those pale blue eyes.

Kate shivered again, and Charles put his arm around

her. "If you're cold," he said, "we can go back and warm ourselves."

"No," Kate said, but she was grateful for the shelter of Charles's arm, and leaned against him, looking sadly at the sodden bundle on the beach. "I was just wondering what might drive a man to take his own life in a place so beautiful and peaceful."

"Beautiful and peaceful it is indeed, ma'am," said the photographer, and bowed with a smart flourish, clicking the heels of his polished black boots. "In truth, this quaint little village is of such beauty and peace that I think an extended stay might be rewarding. I beg your pardon for the inquiry, but I wonder if you know of suitable accommodations in the vicinity—a house to let, perhaps?" And he bowed again.

"I'm afraid not," Charles said, his eyes on the scene at the beach. "We just arrived yesterday."

The man seemed to be unaffected by what was going on. "You are here on holiday?" he asked Kate.

Kate did not answer. She looked down toward the beach. "Charles, that man coming up from the pier," she said. "He's waving at us."

"Ah, Kipling!" Charles exclaimed, and went to the top of the stairs to greet the man. "Kipling, my dear old chap, how very good to see you again!"

"And you, too, Sheridan," the man said. He was short and slender, with gold-rimmed eyeglasses perched on a firm nose, under bristling black brows, over a mustache as black as a bootbrush. He was rather dark-skinned, as if he had a touch of Indian blood. He smiled. "Pardon, please. I understand that you are now to be addressed as Lord Somersworth."

Charles grinned. "Charles will do nicely, thank you, Rud. And I have decided to retain my family name, which has served me quite well for my lifetime."

"You are not changed by your elevation, then," Kipling said, returning the grin. "Uncle Ned told me you'd be down, and is sorry he is detained in London. I trust you are well settled. Seabrooke House, is that where you are?"

"Yes, and it's quite comfortable. How many years has it been since Lahore, Rud? Ten?"

"Twelve, I make it," Kipling replied. "Mian Mir in '85, where the Fusiliers were stationed. I was turning out articles on army life, and you were—"

"Tying up the loose ends of my military career," Charles said. He turned to Kate. "Kate, I should like you to meet Mr. Rudyard Kipling. Rud, my wife, Kathryn."

"Lady Sheridan," Kipling said, and bowed.

"Kate, please," she said happily. It wasn't every day that she was privileged to meet an author as famous as Mr. Kipling, and as highly respected. Everyone who had read *Recessional* was loud in its praise, although she much preferred the stories. "I do so admire your work, Mr. Kipling. Of your stories, 'The Phantom Rickshaw' is my favorite." She paused, then quoted, in a low voice, "'It is an awful thing to go down quick among the dead with scarcely one half of your life completed. It is a thousand times more awful to wait as I do in your midst, for I know not what unimaginable terror. Pity me, at least on the score of my delusion, for I know you will never believe what I have written here. Yet as surely as ever a man was done to death by the Powers of Darkness, I am that man.'"

"Good heavens," Kipling said, startled. "You have it by heart. How extraordinary."

"My wife is a writer, as well," Charles said, and Kate felt herself going red.

"Hardly 'as well'," she said quickly. "No one in the entire world writes as well as Mr. Kipling."

Kipling threw back his head and laughed uproariously. "Clever," he said. "Very clever, Kate. But you must call me Rud, or Ruddy, for I see that we are going to become friends very quickly. Pardon me, but what sort of writer are you?"

"A pseudonymous writer," Kate replied. "It would hardly be to Charles's advantage for his opponents in Parliament to know what his wife does for amusement."

"She writes murder stories," Charles said, sotto voce.

"Charles!" Kate exclaimed. But it was true. Before she came to England, she had earned her living writing penny dreadfuls for the American popular press. Now, she wrote what she liked to think of as "suspenseful fiction" for the British press, with rather more psychological interest than blood and violence.

"Murder stories!" Kipling said. "Well, well. You must allow me to read one or two of them."

"Perhaps you have," Charles replied. "Her pen name is Beryl Bardwell."

"Charles!" Kate exclaimed again, more loudly. "I thought we agreed—"

But Kipling was shaking his head. "Beryl Bardwell," he said with a chuckle. "I have read your stories in *Blackwell's* and enjoyed every one—and the Aunt, too! Aunt Georgie—Lady Burne-Jones—will be pleased beyond words to know that you are here, and will absolutely insist on meeting you. You really must come up to The Elms. This evening, shall we say? We are not in a situation to invite guests to dinner, but I can at least promise dessert."

Kate could feel her face reddening once again. Although her stories had a wide readership, she was not accustomed to hearing them admired, and wondered fleetingly if Kipling was having fun at her expense. "Oh, but I—" she began.

"I shall not take no for an answer," Kipling said. "Our family has recently been joined by a new young person by the name of John. He has rather a loud voice and vehement manner, but we would be quite pleased to introduce him to you, if you have no objection to infants. In any event, there is nothing else to do in Rottingdean but count your blessings and admire the children. Dessert at The Elms offers about as much temptation as you will find anywhere in the village." He paused, looking reflective. "Although there is this body on the beach. And speaking of mysteries, I have just been told something in which you might have a professional—"

There was a clamor from below, and Kate turned to see that the trio on the beach was on the point of being joined by a fourth, a stout, red-faced constable dressed in a blue serge uniform and a tall helmet. He was hurrying down the beach, waving his arms and hailing them angrily.

"What is he saying?" Kate asked.

"I imagine," Charles replied, "that he is telling them to leave the body alone until he is there to see to the matter. There might be clues."

Kipling gave Charles a swift glance. "Clues? What are you thinking?"

"I understood the fisherman to say that the body is that of the coast guard from Black Rock," Charles said. "Since he was an official of the Crown, the constable will want to make sure that he died by drowning, and not from some other cause."

Kate frowned, wondering what Charles had in mind. "What do coast guards do?" she asked, curious.

"They are supposed to guard against smuggling," Charles said, "although I doubt that there are many smugglers hereabouts. It has been a long time since the repeal of the excise."

"Perhaps," Kipling said, looking thoughtful. "But the traditions of smuggling die hard. There are tunnels, you see, and ghosts. At least, there is one ghost. He lives in our cellar."

"A ghost!" Kate exclaimed.

Kipling smiled. "Of course. Smugglers are not the sort to lie quietly in the grave. Do come this evening and I shall see if we can entice our ghost to manifest himself. And the boy has told me a story about—"

Kate had been watching the scene on the beach, and now she turned to Charles, plucking at his sleeve. "Charles," she said, "I think you should offer your services to the constable." She glanced at Kipling with mischievous intent. "Charles is a photographer, you see, Rud—a very skilled photographer. His camera has helped to solve several important crimes."

"Is that a fact?" Kipling inquired, looking interested.

"Yes," Kate said with exaggerated emphasis. "And it is a quite well-known fact that he is remarkably skilled at unraveling mysteries, and has been the means of bringing several killers to justice." She lifted her chin, glad to be even with her husband for revealing her secret identity. "In this case, Charles, it might be useful to photograph the dead man. There might be clues to his demise. But you'd best hurry, because it appears that the constable is about to—"

"Kate," Charles said gently, "don't you think you're overdoing it, my dear? The constable has his own methods of criminal inquiry. He would surely resent the intrusion of someone else, especially someone in an unofficial capacity."

"No, no, I quite agree with your wife, Sheridan," Kipling said briskly. "It would be a pity to waste your investigative skills." He turned toward the stairs.

"Constable Woodhouse may be a trifle hardheaded, but I'm sure he'll be glad of your services. Come, I'll introduce you and suggest that proceedings be delayed while you send for your camera. And while we're at it, perhaps you should like to hear something else of interest concerning this body."

"Something else?" Charles inquired, as he went down the stairs behind Kipling.

"What is it?" Kate asked, lifting up her skirts to hurry down the stairs behind the two men.

"The boy will tell you," Kipling said, over his shoulder. "He's a fair storyteller."

6

"For years they defied the law and ... plied their trade with so much caution that no real evidence could be brought against them. No doubt this was in a measure owing to the connivance of the inhabitants."

—A. Cecil Piper,
Alfriston: A History

Amelia gave a last pat to Lady Sheridan's upswept hair and stood back from the mirrored dressing table at which her mistress was seated. "There," she said, with satisfaction. "What d'ye think, my lady?"

"You have done it up quite beautifully, Amelia," Lady Sheridan said, turning to inspect the twist of her back hair with a hand mirror. "As you always do."

Amelia replaced the silver brush and comb in the velvet-lined travel case. "'Tisn't a hard job." She gave her mistress an admiring glance. "You've beautiful hair, mum. So thick and shiny."

"Thank you," Lady Sheridan said, and smiled as she stood and shook out the skirts of her green dress. "Flattery has earned you the evening off, my dear. It may be late, and I shan't be needing you when we return from the

Kiplings." She opened her glove case and began to sort through her gloves. "How do you find your room? Are you and Lawrence quite comfortable?"

"Oh yes, mum," Amelia said earnestly, "although nothing is as nice as our cottage at Bishop's Keep." In Amelia's view, her own rose-covered gatehouse cottage at Lady Sheridan's home was the most beautiful spot in all of England. But this was her first visit to the south coast, and she would have been pleased to sleep in a mouse hole, as long as it was in sight of the sea. "And Mrs. Portney seems a pleasant sort," she added tentatively.

Lady Sheridan, inspecting a button on her gloves, glanced up. "Only 'seems'?" she asked, with a lift of her eyebrow.

Amelia hesitated before she answered. Mrs. Portney was the cook-housekeeper who came with the house Lord and Lady Sheridan had taken for their holiday—Seabrooke House, it was called—a narrow, two-story house that fronted on the High Street near St. Aubyn's School, with a wrought-iron veranda and a generous back garden and roses tumbling everywhere. It was quite a lovely house and Mrs. Portney managed it adequately, as far as Amelia could tell, although their coming seemed to have taken the woman by surprise, for she did not have the beds aired nor a food supply laid in. And there was the matter of the mysterious noises belowstairs last night. If Amelia could believe her ears, the narrow-faced, long-nosed Mrs. Portney had been entertaining a male visitor in the vicinity of the wine cellar—more than one visitor, perhaps, from the energetic thumping and bumping and the sound, quite late in the night, of glass breaking. But Amelia did not like to make accusations, so she only smiled and gave a little shrug.

As she often did, Lady Sheridan seemed to understand

without being told. She smiled. "I'm sure we must all be willing to put up with a bit of unpleasantness now and then, in order to make the most of our holiday." She put a finger under Amelia's chin and raised it, studying her face with a frown. "But I am a trifle concerned about *you*, my dear. You are more pale than I like. Are you not sleeping? Are you well?"

Amelia turned her head aside. It wasn't that she wasn't well, for she was *very* well, although occasionally a bit nauseous in the mornings. In fact, she was pregnant with her first child, and so pleased for herself and Lawrence that she hardly knew how to conceal her delight. But she had hidden her condition from her ladyship for the few weeks she had known of it, because of what poor Lady Sheridan had suffered this last spring and summer.

It was a tragedy to lose a child, certainly, although women were always losing their first child and then going on to have a houseful. But to forever lose all hope of having a child—*that* was a calamity of such enormous proportions that the thought of it made Amelia turn cold with fear. She did not know how her ladyship could bear it—and indeed, it must have been very hard, for she had come upon her ladyship weeping bitterly many a time in the past months. Lady Sheridan had been so deathly ill that it was feared she might be lost as well as the babe, and it was all on account of coming to London, where there were such dirty fogs and choking air and terrible slums where ladies who went to do good works could catch the measles.

Now, however, her ladyship was smiling. "You're going to have a baby," she said quietly. "Is that it, my dear?"

"In six months' time," Amelia said, and was swept into her employer's warm embrace.

"Oh, Amelia!" Lady Sheridan cried tearfully, holding her close, "I am so *delighted* for you!"

"Thank ye, my lady," Amelia said, sniffing. "I've been wantin' t' tell ye, but I was afraid ... that is ..." And she felt her eyes fill up with tears and heard herself begin to sob, imagining the bitter pang her ladyship must feel at this news.

"There, there, Amelia," her ladyship said comfortingly, patting her shoulder. "Having a baby is nothing to cry over. And if your tears are for me, they truly are not necessary, my dear. I will take every bit as much pleasure in your child as I would in my own, and it will help me forget my own pain." She took a handkerchief from the dressing table and dabbed at Amelia's eyes. "There. We shall have no more weeping."

"Thank ye, mum," Amelia whispered, almost overcome.

"And you must promise me that you will take good care of yourself," her ladyship added sternly. "No carrying buckets of bath water up and down the stairs. If Lawrence isn't available, we shall see if Mrs. Portney can't find a strong boy for that job." She turned, beaming, as Lord Sheridan opened the door and came into the bedroom. "Charles, Charles, I have just heard the most blessed news!"

Charles Sheridan never ceased to be amazed by his wife. He knew how devastated she had been by the loss of the child and by the knowledge that she could never conceive another. And yet here she was, pretending to be absolutely delighted by the news that her maid was to have a baby, displaying not a flicker of envy or sorrow. But it was like Kate to conceal her deepest feelings so that she did not darken Amelia's joy. So Charles responded with an equal warmth, congratulating Amelia and promising himself privately to see to an increase in Lawrence's salary, now that he was to be a family man.

When Amelia had curtseyed and left the room, Kate sighed and turned away, and Charles thought what the pretense of happiness must have cost her. He put his arms around her for a moment, holding her close and thinking how brave she was, and yet how fragile. He still went cold at the memory of her long illness. The death of the child he could bear. It was the mother he cherished with all his soul, and whose loss would have meant the end of every joy.

Now, he looked down at her with concern. They had walked for a long distance on the cliff above the sea this morning, and she must be tired. "Are you sure you feel up to visiting the Kiplings tonight, Kate?"

For a moment she looked as if she might decide not to go, and Charles remembered, somewhat guiltily, that he had promised that they would keep to themselves this holiday. Then she said, "Oh, yes, I'm quite well. And I'm anxious to visit the cellar and see if I can coax the ghost to show himself." She smiled. "So, Charles. Tell me all about your investigation of the body on the beach. What happened after I left?"

Charles laughed shortly. "There's not much to tell," he said. "As Kipling remarked, Constable Woodhouse is a hardheaded man. More than that, he's very set in his ways—the old ways. He told me to go about my business. Politely, of course. But he made it plain that he would tolerate no interference in his investigation."

Kate frowned. "What did he say to the boy's story?"

"We didn't get that far," Charles said. "Kipling took the rejection personally, and did not put the boy forward. His name, by the way," he added, "is Patrick."

"But the boy—Patrick—saw the *murderer*!" Kate exclaimed. "He told us so himself. He might be able to identify him."

"*If* he is telling the truth," Charles said cautiously, "he saw the body being disposed of. It is not exactly the same thing."

"You didn't believe him?" Kate asked, sounding surprised. "I thought he seemed quite sincere—and remarkably composed for a boy of his age. And what reason would he have to lie?"

Charles chuckled dryly. "What reason do boys have to tell fanciful tales? However, the question is moot, Kate. Woodhouse refused all assistance, Kipling clamped his mouth shut like a sour clam, and Patrick prudently disappeared. I doubt," he added with a wry twist, "that he was eager to tell his story to the constable, after all. If word got about that he was a witness ..." Charles didn't finish the sentence.

Kate's eyebrows went up. "You don't suppose the boy is in danger!"

"No, not that," Charles said slowly. "But the villagers seem inordinately suspicious of nearly everything that happens. If it is known that the boy spoke to Kipling or to me about what he had seen, he might come in for a bad time of it."

"I've noticed the suspicion, too," Kate said. "Even our cook-housekeeper doesn't seem happy to have us here." She frowned. "The oddest thing, Charles. You remember that we are to have the use of the wine cellar, I suppose? Well, I went there this morning to check the bottles against the inventory Mrs. Seabrooke sent us, so that an accounting can be made when we are ready to leave. I found a damp spot where a substantial amount of brandy had been spilled—in the last few days, I'd say—and evidence that the shelves had recently held quite a few *more* bottles than were accounted for in the inventory."

"As long as there were no fewer, I don't suppose it

matters," Charles said. "It would be a pity to learn that the estimable Mrs. Portney has been indulging herself while the house stood vacant." He returned to his subject. "Anyway, Woodhouse is no different than most village constables. They all believe that cameras are best used for recording children having picnics and people playing croquet. They have no idea of using them as serious tools in a murder investigation. Why, not even Scotland Yard has thought of it."

Kate picked up her gloves. "So it is officially a murder, then?"

"The constable would say nothing," Charles replied, "and prevented me from getting a close look. But I saw evidence that the poor chap had been knifed. There were bloodstains on his jersey, and what looked to be a puncture wound." He paused. "No doubt there will be a coroner's inquest, however, and the truth will be learned." He gave her a narrow look. "This is none of our affair, Kate. You do know that, don't you?"

But Kate did not appear to hear him. "Who would murder a coast guard?" she asked musingly. "A smuggler, do you think?"

"In one of your sensational fictions, perhaps," Charles said with a laugh. He adored his wife and admired her shrewd logic, but she was prone to flights of fancy. "This is the modern era, Kate. There's very little money to be earned in smuggling, and hence very little incentive to take the risk."

"Oh?" Kate asked archly. "Then why do I see that small army of blue-coated and brass-buttoned functionaries lined up at Charing Cross station when the Continental express is due? I once watched them apprehend a lady who was concealing a large case of cigars in her hatbox."

"That's a different thing entirely," Charles said. "The

smuggling that went on along this coast sixty years ago was wholesale smuggling, designed to evade the excise. Entire shiploads of spirits, tobacco, tea, lace—goods that were heavily taxed—were ferried onshore here, and at Hastings and Cuckmere Haven. Dozens of men were used to move the cargo off the boats, and many others to convey it to Brighton and Falmer and Lewes, and thence to London. It was a major source of commerce."

Kate looked at him in wonderment. "But how was all this activity kept from the villagers?"

"It wasn't," Charles said. "They connived in it."

"Ah." Kate picked up her hat and turned it thoughtfully, straightening the silk roses around the brim. "Of course. They must have concealed the contraband until it could be freighted to the cities."

"And profited thereby," Charles said. "But now that the excise laws have been changed, there is little profit, less smuggling, and nothing to connive at."

"But it would make a marvelous novel," Kate said.

"So it would," Charles replied encouragingly. "The very thing for you to work on while we are here." He hoped that Kate could go back to her writing, for she was always happiest when she was engaged with one of her stories. He took out his watch and glanced at it. "If we are going to arrive at The Elms when we promised, we had best be going. Shall I have Lawrence fetch the motorcar? I don't want you to exert yourself if you're tired."

"Don't be silly," Kate said. "It's only a short way, and quite a lovely night." She began pinning her hat to her hair. "But if there is no smuggling," she said around the hatpins in her mouth, "who *did* kill the coast guard? And why?"

7

"As usual one goes along the line of least resistance and because the owner offered to sell us his sticks of furniture too, thereby saving us the bother of immediately hunting for new things, we have taken for three years this ex-smuggling stronghold in Rottingdean. It's small, low and old and in time we hope to make it comfy. At present its interior is what you might call neolithic."

—RUDYARD KIPLING TO THOMAS HARDY
November 30, 1897

"In due time I found my ghost."
—RUDYARD KIPLING
My Own True Ghost Story

STUCCO-FRONTED AND RED-TILED, The Elms stood in a sort of little island under several large ilex trees and behind six-foot flint walls which, Kipling would say many years later, "we then thought were high enough." On this evening, Kipling answered his own door, dressed in tweeds with leather elbow patches and knee-high boots, holding a nightgowned little girl in his arms.

"Welcome to our abode," he said warmly. "You'll find us very common here, with no ceremony." He bounced the little girl, who hid her face shyly on his shoulder. "This is Elsie, and where has Josephine gotten to? Josephine, Josephine! Come down and meet our visitors!"

A small girl flew down the narrow staircase and hid herself shyly behind her father's boots, then obeyed his command to step out and shake hands with Lord and Lady Sheridan. There was an easy familiarity between father and daughter, as if the two of them spent a great deal of time in one another's company.

"You'll find that we have a wonderfully rustic and innocent time of it in Rottingdean." Kipling took his daughter's hand. "Jam-smeared picnics on the downs, chasing ducks into the pond, finding birds' eggs—quite the thing, eh, Josie?" And upon her eager assent, he added, to Kate, "Perhaps you'd go riding with us some afternoon, Kate, when you've nothing better to do. A friend gave the wife and me a tandem some months ago, but Carrie isn't well enough to ride yet."

"There's a seat on the back for me," Josephine said. She looked pleadingly up at Kate, who saw that the little girl had her father's firmly cleft chin. "Please, say you'll go. My feet don't reach the pedals, or I'd do it."

"For sheer pace and excitement, a tandem beats a bicycle all to pieces," Kipling said enticingly. He grinned at Charles. "And I'd be glad to lend it to the two of you, so you can ride along the cliff. Now *that's* excitement for you."

"I'd love to go riding with you, Josephine," Kate said. She glanced at Kipling with his two daughters, and then at her husband, wondering what sharp envy Charles must be feeling. *He* would have been a wonderful father, she thought with a swift pang, and as swiftly turned her head to hide the painful thought that must be written on her face. But not swiftly enough, for she knew that Charles had glimpsed it.

Kipling led them into a low-ceilinged cave of a parlor, where his wife, Carrie, a sharp-jawed, brown-haired lady of about Kate's age, sat on a brown chair, under a blue-shaded gas lamp with leprous-looking white blotches all over it. In her arms was the Kiplings' new baby, John, swathed in a knitted wrap. On a nearby horsehair sofa sat another, older woman, quite tiny but erect and straight-shouldered, with an elvish face that was striking in its dynamic intelligence. As she stood, Kate saw that she was wearing a plum-colored dress with long, full skirts, serviceable but not particularly smart, which had outlasted several changes of fashion. The gaslight shone on her silver-gray hair, knotted loosely under a swath of soft ocher lace that had been pinned with a brooch. At her waist hung a large watch set with chrysolites.

Kipling introduced them all. While Charles joined their host in front of the small, smoky fire, Kate admired the baby, congratulated the mother, and then turned to the older woman with genuine pleasure.

"Lady Burne-Jones," she said, "I'm so pleased to meet you at last. I am a great admirer of your husband's painting, of course. And the Countess of Warwick has often spoken of your fine work with the London children." Kate knew that Georgiana Jones had strong socialist leanings and was an outspoken anti-Imperialist and advocate of liberal causes, including the thorny question of Home Rule for Ireland. Remembering Kipling's fierce defense of the Empire, Kate wondered how the aunt and the nephew managed to get along. But perhaps political disagreements were left at the door when the family gathered, and certainly there was no evidence of tension between them.

The woman fixed large blue eyes on Kate, smiling

humorously. "I'm called Aunt Georgie in this house, my lady. To avoid confusing the children, you must adopt our common practice." She gestured to the sofa and Kate sat down. "And I understand that you are one of my favorite writers, in disguise. Beryl Bardwell, indeed!" She laughed lightly. "I can hardly believe my good fortune in having you here with us in little Rottingdean, where our lives are so unlike the excitement of your novels. Such tales you tell! Quite extraordinary!"

"Thank you," Kate said. She put her hand on Aunt Georgie. "But you and Caroline must call me Kate."

Aunt Georgie nodded. "I hope you are at work on another story," she went on, with an eagerness that was clearly unfeigned. "The last one I read—some months ago, I think—was about a woman who went up in a balloon. A remarkable feat. It quite left me breathless." She smiled. "Which of course it was meant to do."

"It was inspired by a real event," Charles put in. "Kate takes her ideas from what goes on around her." His mouth turned down. "I fear, though, that she has had precious little time and energy to write in the months we've been in London."

Kate blushed, feeling that they should not even be talking about her work in the presence of a writer as deservedly famous as Kipling. But he was nodding. "I understand exactly, oh, I do. London offers far too many amusements, too many delightful corruptions. One is tempted in all directions and finds oneself quite too distracted, and far too excited, to write."

Aunt Georgie smiled. "Well, I fear you shan't find any excitement at Rottingdean to inspire *or* distract you, Kate. In fact, most of us have taken refuge here from the very temptations Ruddy describes. Compared to corrupt London, Rottingdean is wonderfully incorruptible."

"Oh, but she has already been distracted, Aunt," Kipling said, rising on the toes of his shiny black boots. "She was above the beach when the body of the dead man was towed in this morning and that blockhead Woodhouse refused our help with the investigation."

"That man," Aunt Georgie said disapprovingly. "I have spoken several times to the Parish Council about his unacceptable behavior." She turned to Kate. "I hope you weren't too distressed by the drowning, my dear."

"I fear, Aunt," Caroline said primly, "that this is not a fit subject for the children." She rang a brass bell and a white-aproned nurse appeared and whisked the two little girls away, in spite of their pleas to be allowed to stay.

"Young John is devilish clever, but I doubt he has yet mastered the language," Kipling said, settling himself in a green leather chair and motioning Charles to a matching chair on the other side of the fire. "We may go on without fear of offending his tender ears."

"I understand that it was the coast guard from Black Rock who drowned," Aunt Georgie remarked. "I met Mrs. Radford on the Brighton omnibus just last week. She is a sweet person, but quite helpless, I thought. And now she will be all alone with their two small children. But the parish has remedies to offer. I will visit her very soon and see what should be done."

"Is there any word as to the cause of death?" Charles asked. "Has it been put about that he died by drowning?"

"As a matter of fact," Kipling replied, "it has." He pulled his expressive black brows together. "But I also overheard our cook telling the serving maid that the poor fellow had the misfortune of running himself through with his own sword before he jumped off the cliff and into the sea."

Kate and Caroline gasped. "How dreadful!" Caroline exclaimed.

Aunt Georgie frowned. "But I thought the coast guards carried only wooden truncheons. I had no idea they were armed with swords!"

"A short sword is hidden inside the truncheon," Kipling explained. "It can be pulled out and wielded like a long knife. A quite effective weapon, I assure you."

Charles was staring at Kipling, and gave voice to the question that was loud in Kate's mind. "Ran *himself* through?" he asked. "On what evidence—"

Kipling held up his hand. "Don't look to me for explanations, Sheridan. I am merely reporting what the cook said to the serving maid while I lurked unseen in the hallway, awaiting an announcement as to dinner. I was given to understand, however, that it is the general report that is being circulated in the village, for the serving maid reported that her brother brought the same news home from the taproom at The Plough."

"But the boy's report absolutely contradicts the idea of suicide," Kate objected. "Surely an investigation will reveal—"

"The boy's report?" Aunt Georgie asked.

"Our young friend Patrick was hanging about on the cliff night before last," Kipling replied. "He saw a man in oilskins loading Radford's body into a skiff."

Aunt Georgie pulled in her breath. "Poor Paddy!" she exclaimed. "What a horrible thing for him to witness. He must have been terribly frightened!"

"I rather think, Aunt," Kipling said dryly, "that our sympathies should lie with the dead man. Patrick seems not to have been frightened at all."

Kate tried again. "It seems to me that Patrick's report shows that the coast guard could *not* have killed himself."

"Oh, I don't agree," Caroline murmured, stroking the baby's head with her finger. "Someone might have found the poor fellow lying dead at the foot of the cliff and decided to bury him at sea."

"I'm afraid I'm missing something," Charles said, frowning. "Why should anyone do something of that sort?"

"Out of sympathy with the dead man's family," Caroline replied. "Or perhaps to avoid the scandal of a suicide in the village."

There was a moment's silence, and then Aunt Georgie said, "I'm afraid I agree with Carrie. In *this* village, someone might have done just that—but not out of sympathy, if you ask me. And Patrick will do well not to give tongue to a contrary report, if he knows what is good for him."

"If he knows what is good for him?" Charles asked, in a tone of mild curiosity.

Aunt Georgie tilted her head at him. "Haven't you heard of the Rottingdean smugglers?"

"Oh, Aunt," Caroline sighed, with the dismissive air of someone who has listened to the story more often than she cared to. "That business took place long ago, in the time of King George. It may be very romantic and all that, but it's all over now."

"That is commonly said, Carrie, my dear," Aunt Georgie replied. "But Rottingdean keeps its own secrets, and even those of us who have maintained houses in this village for fifteen years are not privy to its inner workings. And even though I serve on the Parish Council and do my utmost to preserve the peace and tranquillity of the village, I don't pretend to understand all the little mischiefs that go on in its pubs and its streets. Or under the streets, for that matter," she added suggestively.

Kate leaned forward, intrigued. "*Under* the streets?"

The baby began to fuss, and Carrie held him against her shoulder. "Aunt is referring to the notorious Rottingdean tunnels that were dug by smugglers well over a hundred years ago," she said in a practical tone. "They've all been blocked up for fear of subsidence, or children being trapped. The area is entirely safe."

"That is the tale that is told to outsiders," Aunt Georgie said. "The truth may be exactly the opposite."

"Well, the tunnel that leads out of *our* cellar is certainly blocked," Caroline retorted. "The agent who let the house assured us so, and told us to ignore any stories to the contrary." Her voice was edgy, and Kate thought that if there was any tension in the family, it lay between Kipling's wife and his aunt—some jealousy, perhaps. It struck her that Mrs. Kipling might view her husband's aunt as a competitor for his affections and was looking for opportunities to discredit her. But the aunt did not seem inclined to surrender.

"For heaven's sake, Carrie," Aunt Georgie said, "house agents will tell you anything you like to hear. The Elms was built by a man who made his living in the illegal export of wool, and it is common knowledge that his cellar was a smugglers' depot. It lay at the hub of several tunnels that led to other houses. One may indeed be blocked, but who can say as to the others. And aren't you the very one who complained of noises in the cellar a night or two ago?"

Caroline responded to the challenge with a light laugh. "You're not suggesting that there are *still* smugglers in this village?"

"I am only suggesting that some intrigue or another is afoot," Aunt Georgie replied, lifting her chin. "You cannot have noticed it, my dear, for you have not lived here a sufficient time, but an unusual amount of money has been coming into this village lately. The chemist has a new horse to pull his old gig, and the money to stable it. And Mrs. Howard, who has been poor as a church mouse, somehow found the means to open a dressmaker's shop on the High Street and offer fabrics and laces as fine as any in Oxford Street. Perhaps you can suggest where the money might have come from."

Caroline looked cross and did not answer. The fire hissed and Kipling stirred uncomfortably. To ease the strain, Kate turned to him and spoke lightly. "Speaking of cellars—"

"Ah, yes, our ghost!" Kipling exclaimed with evident relief, and jumped up. "He may not be in evidence tonight, but you can at least see where he lives. Or where he walks," he corrected himself. "I don't suppose it is accurate to say that a ghost *lives*."

Caroline gave a horrified gasp. "Ruddy, you can't be thinking of taking our guests to the cellar, of all places!"

"Oh, but we *want* to go," Kate said quickly, rising.

"Don't trouble yourself to get up, my dear." Kipling patted his wife's shoulder. "You and John stay here, and we'll get a candle from the kitchen. I'll ask the maid to bring dessert and coffee while we're gone."

Aunt Georgie rose with alacrity and picked up the brown shawl that lay on her chair. "*I'll* come," she said. She draped the shawl around her shoulders and smiled up at Kate, who felt like a giant beside the tiny woman. Small as she was, though, her erect carriage gave the impression of strength and self-possession. "Perhaps I was wrong when I said you should find no excitement here, my dear. The notion has just come to me that you might think of writing a story that takes place in our tunnels."

"Now, that's an idea, Kate," Charles said warmly. "You could set the tale in King George's day and be sure of smugglers. You might even ask about the village and gather the names of some of the men who were involved. I'm sure there are many older people who have interesting smugglers' tales to tell."

"If that's your plot, you should visit the old windmill on Beacon Hill, behind North End House," Kipling suggested as they left the room and turned into a dark hallway with old-fashioned framed pictures on the wall. "It was often frequented by smugglers, who used the sails to signal boats out in the Channel."

"The old windmill!" Aunt Georgie said. "The very thing! Ruddy, you shall put the old mill into one of your poems, and Beryl Bardwell can put it into a story." She patted Kate's hand with a chuckle. "No argument, now. As I tell my nephew, those with a gift for writing stories are obliged to do so, in order to relieve those of us with an insatiable need for reading them." Turning to Kipling, she said, "What story are you working on now, dear?"

"I've begun to revisit the Irish boy I first thought of when we were at Bliss Cottage in Vermont," Kipling said nonchalantly. "I've gone as far as to make him the son of a private in an Irish regiment, born in India and mixed up with native life. I've christened him Kim, although I haven't been able to think of anything for him to do except trek around India having adventures."

Aunt Georgie chuckled. "Fashioned after our very own Paddy, I wonder? Well, if you observe the child for very long, you won't lack for things for your Kim to get up to. But shouldn't you have a plot of some sort?"

"What was good enough for Cervantes—" Kipling began, but his aunt cut him off.

"Don't Cervantes me," she said tartly. "I remember your mother remarking once that you couldn't make a plot to save your soul." She smiled sweetly at him. "Now, dear, hadn't you better fetch the candle?"

A few minutes later, the four of them—Kipling, Charles, Aunt Georgie, and Kate, were making their cautious way down a narrow flight of worm-eaten wooden stairs into a large, irregularly shaped, cavelike cellar carved out of the gray-white chalk on which the house was built. At the foot of the steep stairs, Kipling held the flickering candle over his head, and Kate saw that the walls, which were not at all square or straight, went back a long distance into the gloomy shadows.

"The tunnel entered at this point," Kipling said, going to a tier of wooden shelves. "But there is no access, you see—it is entirely blocked."

Behind the shelves, Kate could make out the arched outline of an opening that had been filled in with bricks and plastered over. She turned and looked around, thinking that Aunt Georgie was entirely right. The setting suggested all kinds of ideas for a story, or perhaps even a book. The present cellar contained only the detritus of previous households—broken chairs, a dirty piece of carpet, rusty tools—but she fancied she could see it as it must have been a hundred years before, filled with wooden kegs of fine brandy and boxes of cigars and French lace. She could imagine, as well, a gang of crafty smugglers, led by the man who had built the house, gathering to celebrate their latest success by tapping into one of the precious kegs.

"You've explored all the nooks and crannies, I suppose," Charles said thoughtfully. Kate looked at him curiously. He seemed to be sniffing the air.

"Actually, no," Kipling said. "We've been here less than a month, and with John's arrival..." The candle guttered and he shielded it with his hand. "Carrie's right, y'know," he said uneasily. "This place is in no fit state. P'rhaps I'd just better lock up the door and declare the cellar out of bounds."

At Kate's elbow, Aunt Georgie spoke firmly. "The tunnel is blocked *here*," she said, wrapping her shawl more securely around her. "But that does not mean that there are no other openings in this cellar—or that all the openings are blocked. The tunnels are said to have led from the cliffs to every consequential house in the village. To the vicarage, where the Reverend Dr. Hooker was the watchman for the local smuggling ring—and to Seabrooke House, of course," she added, turning to Kate. "I was told that one of the Seabrookes—Richard, I think it was—earned quite a good living by hauling goods to Falmer and Lewes. His brother was in league with the Hawkhurst Gang, and was responsible for arranging capital to finance their endeavors."

"That's very interesting," Kate said, thinking of the cellar below Seabrooke House, almost as large as this one, and the spilled brandy and evidence of bottles that had been taken away. "I shall have a look for evidence of a tunnel in our cellar."

"And the ghost?" Charles asked lightly, turning to Kipling. "You say you heard him recently?"

"A few nights ago," Kipling said. In a mischievous tone, he added, "We can extinguish the candle and wait, if you like," and suited the deed to the word.

Kate gasped as the chill dark closed suddenly around them. Beside her, Aunt Georgie shivered. They stood for a moment huddled tensely together, listening to the muffled footfalls of the servants moving around in the kitchen over their heads. Then even that noise ceased, and all Kate could hear was the low sound of their communal breathing. And then, just as she was feeling that they had waited long enough, she heard something else: a heavy, echoing thud on the other side of the wall, but very distant, as if it were miles away—or years ago. A second later, there was another thud, and a low rumble.

"There!" Kipling exclaimed in a jocular tone, out of the

dark. "Is everyone satisfied that we have heard the ghost, or do we prefer to wait for the rattling of chains?"

"I believe I am quite persuaded," Aunt Georgie replied. She spoke with a self-possessed air, although Kate could feel her trembling.

"I too," Kate said quickly.

"And I," Charles replied. "You have shown us your ghost, Rud."

"Well, then," Kipling said, and struck a match. "Shall we adjourn to the parlor and report our adventure to Carrie, and see if the serving maid has provided us with dessert and coffee?"

Walking back to Seabrooke House along the silent, moonlit street of the little village, Kate thought that it did not take much imagination to see the place as it must have been in the time of King George, when mothers and children shut themselves up in the dark houses while the men and boys were busy on the beach and in the tunnels, leaving the deserted street and the treacherous, windswept path along the cliff to the patrolling guard. She was deep in reflection, thinking that Rottingdean would indeed be a marvelous setting for one of Beryl's stories, when Charles spoke. His voice was amused.

"Well, my dear, what did you think of Kipling's ghost?"

Kate matched his light tone. "He made an impressive thud or two, but I should like to have seen him."

He smiled down at her. "You caught a whiff of him, didn't you?"

Kate was surprised. "A whiff?"

He nodded. "I should have thought that the cellar, so long closed up, would be musty. But I caught the distinct odor of a sea breeze. The ghost must be an old salt, fresh from the briny depths." His voice became sepulchral.

"Fifteen men on a dead man's chest. Yo-ho-ho and a bottle of rum."

Kate laughed, then stopped, intrigued. "But if you could smell the sea breeze, that means that the tunnel is *not* entirely closed up!"

"I should think so," Charles said. "Interesting, isn't it?" He paused, looking down at her, his eyes concerned. "I hope the evening wasn't too trying for you, Kate."

Somewhere in the distance a dog barked, and a cloud veiled the moon. "The children, you mean," she said.

"Yes." He pulled her arm under his, and matched his step to hers. "You were very brave."

Kate cast a sideways glance at her husband, loving the strength of his face, the firm nose and sensitive mouth, the kind brown eyes. But it was a shuttered face. Charles Sheridan was a true British gentleman, reserved, stoic, naturally reticent. He had never spoken to her of the bitter disappointment she was sure he must feel, knowing that there would never be a son to carry on the traditions and responsibilities of Somersworth. And he had never even hinted that the whole thing might have been her fault for being so reckless as to risk her health for the sake of a few good deeds. Often, when his glance lingered on her, then moved away, she feared he *would* say it, and that it would be a revelation from which they could never retreat, which would slice them apart like a red-hot blade. Almost as often, though, she wished he would speak, for what lay unsaid and unacknowledged was as hurtful as any accusation.

But tonight she did not want to risk hearing what was hidden in his heart, for it might mar the few weeks they had to spend in this idyllic place. So she murmured something that sounded like "Thank you," and looked up at the waning moon, half hidden in a wreath of silver clouds.

"It is a glorious night, isn't it?" she said. "It is so wonderful to be *alone* with you, my dear, with no one to watch or criticize what we are doing, and no one to please but ourselves."

Charles bent to kiss her, then put his arm around her shoulder and they walked together down the quiet street. But Kate was wrong. They were not alone—and they *were* watched.

8

"One of the outrages [perpetrated by smugglers] was the death of a patrolling customs man at Cuckmere Haven. Fearing that his attentions would interfere with their landing, the gang moved the lumps of white chalk that the officer used as way-markers for his moonlight sorties along the cliff-edge. Instead of leading him safely along the coast path, the stones lured the poor man over the parapet. Hearing his cries as he tumbled over the precipice, the gang emerged from hiding, only to find the man desperately hanging by his fingertips. Deaf to pleas for mercy, one of the gang cynically trod on their adversary's fingertips, sending him tumbling to the rocks below."

—RICHARD PLATT
Smugglers' Britain

AT LONG LAST, Patrick was beginning to appreciate Mondays. For the three years he had boarded with Mrs. Higgs, he had attended the village school, handing over his obligatory threepenny bit to Mr. Forsythe each Monday morning and suffering through endless, sleepy recitals of sums and spelling words with the other village children, some as young as three, who shared the single classroom with him. Patrick had an innate curiosity and was quick to learn, and he soon wrote and read skillfully. Under other circumstances, he might have been an able young scholar. But Mr. Forsythe's tedious instruction was hardly inspiring, and the warmth of the classroom and the monotonous murmurs of the children set him dozing. He much preferred the freedom of the village and the downs to confinement behind the gates of learning.

That confinement was at an end, at least for now. Patrick had expected that he would be sent from the village school to prep at St. Aubyn's, which had been established some sixty years before by the many-talented Dr. Thomas Redman Hooker, Master of the Hunt, vicar of St. Margaret's, and reputed lookout for the Rottingdean smugglers. Now, the school was taught by a less colorful team of masters, Mr. Stanford and Mr. Lang, and was made up of seven sallow-faced boys, sons of wealthy and distinguished men. But Patrick's father, neither distinguished nor wealthy, had unfortunately failed to send his son's tuition. He had, as well, failed to pay his son's boarding bill, which was now some ten months in arrears. As a consequence, Patrick had escaped confinement at St. Aubyn's and was more gainfully employed.

"Ye're t' fetch a basket from Mrs. Ridsdale, at Th' Dene, and another at North End 'Ouse," Mrs. Higgs said as they sat at the small table in the kitchen, over steaming bowls of breakfast porridge. "Then ye're t' go t' The Elms, where they 'ave th' new babe, an' fetch wotever's been got ready. But first, ye're t' carry six buckets o' water from th' tap, an' fire up th' copper i' th' wash'ouse."

"Yes, ma'am," Patrick said, wolfing down his toast and tea and wishing fervently that Mrs. Higgs's cottage was on the mains that came in from Brighton, so he wouldn't have to haul water all the way from the village tap. "Is that all?"

"Until lunch, when I'll need six more buckets." Mrs. Higgs tore pieces of bread into a saucer of milk for the calico cat. "Off wi' ye, now. I've a big laundry t'do today."

Patrick didn't need any special urging. The hours since the body had been towed in had been uncomfortable ones, and he had several times wished that he'd not told Mr. Kipling what he had seen. Mr. Kipling had required him to tell the man in the brown beard—Lord Charles Sheridan—and if Constable Woodhouse hadn't proved himself a pigheaded fool, he might have been required to tell him, as well. And *that* would certainly have created difficulties, for the constable was not to be trusted. In the event, he was glad that Mr. Kipling had gotten annoyed and decided to let dundering old Woodhead discover his own clues.

Having dutifully delivered six buckets of water and seven baskets of dirty laundry, Patrick was free for his chief employment, at the Hawkham Stables behind North End House. He worked there for Harry Tudwell four hours each morning and five each afternoon, and paid half his earnings to Mrs. Higgs against the delinquent board bill. What Mrs. Higgs did not know, however, was that Harry Tudwell often employed Patrick on other errands in the late evenings, when the boy was supposed to be abed, and that Patrick hid those secret shillings under a stone in the abandoned windmill at the top of Beacon Hill. In the event his father was never heard from again—which was quite likely, in Patrick's estimation—those shillings would be the only key to his future.

Patrick's work at the Hawkham Stables was far more interesting than his work in the classroom. The stables had been built in the 1860s by a wealthy lord who raced at White Hawk Down, a little way to the west and north. Since then, they had passed to a consortium of owners, most of them residents of Brighton, who raced at White Hawk and hunted with the Brookside Harriers under the direction of the well-known Rottingdean Master, Steyning Beard. This made for a continuous coming and going of gentlemen between Brighton and White Hawk and Hawkham and the kennel, and plenty of odd jobs for eager Rottingdean boys.

The stables were built around three sides of a graveled yard, in the lee of Beacon Hill. On one side was the coach house, which now sheltered the rickety coaches that plied the Rottingdean-Brighton coach run. The other two sides were enclosed by stalls for fine horses, each stall equipped with an iron manger for grain, a hayrack on the wall, and a door opening into the brick-paved walkway. At one end of the walkway was the red-tiled tack room with its saddle racks and gear hanging on the wall, and next to that the chaff room with its lethal chaff-cutting machine—a vicious blade on a big wheel—which Patrick and the other stable-boys treated with respect. Trusses of hay were stacked nearby and more could be pushed down through a trapdoor from the loft above, where the stableboys could be found taking their leisure on a lazy afternoon.

At the other end of the walkway was the stablemaster's office, with a scarred wooden table that served for a desk, a wooden chair, and windows from which Harry Tudwell, who had been stablemaster for over a decade, could oversee the gravel yard on the one side, the exercise paddock on the other, and the smithy beyond. The smell of Harry's room was delectably compounded of tobacco, saddle soap, and metal polish, and on its wooden walls were hung framed newspaper clippings, including one that described the remarkable Derby of 1863, run in torrential rain and preceded by thirty-four false starts. The favored horse, Lord Clifden, slipped on an orange peel near the finish line, lost the race by a head, and beggared half the English peerage. Not Harry Tudwell, however. Patrick had overheard him telling one of the grooms that he had been clever enough to bet on the winner—but not rich enough to bet very much.

Of all the men Patrick knew, he admired Harry Tudwell the most. Mr. Tudwell had befriended him when he was deserted by his father, had taken him fishing and taught him to shoot, and in other small ways had been a father to him. Patrick felt a strong affection for the stablemaster, believing him to be the most astutely intelligent man in the entire village, a genius, even. But Patrick's judgment was hardly objective, and perhaps it should be said merely that Harry Tudwell's was an entrepreneurial genius. He was not only competent in managing the stables—which required long discussions with nervous owners on acquiring, training, breeding, and disposing of valuable horses—but in a variety of other business undertakings as well. By somewhat circuitous means, he had acquired a share in Gerald Pott's smithy, another in John Landsdowne's chemist shop, and still another in Mrs. Howard's dress shop. Probably, if one investigated more fully, one would have discovered Harry Tudwell's dexterous finger in most of the pies of the village. Further, as an elected member of the Parish Council, he had supported Magnus Volk's ambitious scheme to build the Brighton and Rottingdean Seashore Electric Railway from the Banjo Groyne to Rottingdean Gap. The railway, a quite extraordinary undertaking, was now completed. It may have been Magnus Volks's idea, but it would never have succeeded if Harry Tudwell hadn't talked over the Parish Council, and everybody in the village knew it and appreciated what Harry Tudwell had done for Rottingdean.

As he always did when he reached the stables, Patrick

reported directly to Mr. Tudwell. The stablemaster was sitting with his shiny boots propped up on the wooden table, reading yesterday's London *Times*, which had come down to Brighton on the train and been carried to Rottingdean in the pack of a courier who brought certain other news.

"Good morning, Mr. Tudwell," Patrick said, taking off his knit cap and turning it in his hands. If he was nervous, it was with good reason. Mr. Tudwell, who knew everything that went on in the village, was bound to know about the coast guard's death, and he might also know that Patrick had seen something he shouldn't.

The *Times* came down, but the boots stayed up. "Mornin', Paddy," Mr. Tudwell said with a stern look. Somewhere in his lineage there lurked a Scot, for he was a sandy-haired, ruddy-cheeked, clean-shaven man with bright blue eyes and pale lashes. He took a gold watch out of his plaid waistcoat and glanced at it.

Patrick read the glance, and responded with relief. "Seven baskets of laundry, sir." If Mr. Tudwell could be angry at him about the small matter of being late, he must not have discovered the larger. "And six buckets of wash water," he added. "It took longer than I expected."

"Ah," said Mr. Tudwell, and put his watch away. But surely the stablemaster was troubled about something, for his face was drawn and there was a worried frown between his eyes. "Well, 'tis late enough, boy, an' ye'd best get t' th' stalls. A thorough cleanin', if ye please. Mr. Battersby will be 'ere t' inspect 'is new 'orse this afternoon. 'E' as a strict eye for detail, 'e does."

At that moment, Mr. Landsdowne, the village chemist, opened the door and stepped into the office. He was a tall man, stooped and painfully thin, wearing a rusty old black coat that contrasted incongruously with highly polished new black boots. Patrick knew that he should leave to clean the stalls, but he gave in to his curiosity and faded into the corner, as if he were waiting to be dismissed.

"Mornin', 'Arry," Mr. Landsdowne said. He took off his black hat and shifted his weight nervously. "Some of the men wanted me t' ask you about—"

"About George Radford's killin' hisself, I s'pose ye mean, John," Mr. Tudwell said, and leaned back in his chair. A somber look replaced the frown. "Sad business, ain't it? Poor boy, so young, an' with a wife an' children at 'ome. 'E's to be pitied, not blamed, is wot I sez."

Mr. Landsdowne swallowed and his adam's apple bobbed up and down. "'Twas def'nitely suicide, then?"

Mr. Tudwell nodded. "George was giv'n t' black moods, y'know. One evenin' at Th' Plough, I 'eard 'im say 'e'd thought many times of throwin' hisself off th' cliff. Tom Brown was there when 'e said it. 'E 'eard it too, an' will testify to it." Mr. Tudwell looked up at Mr. Landsdowne. "Mebbee there're some others who've 'eard somethin' of th' like—yerself, mebbee?"

There was a pause, and then Mr. Landsdowne replied, "Well, now that you mention it, t' be sure, I 'ave. George killed himself, no doubt about it." Then he stopped to chew on a corner of his lip. "But the coroner'll come over from Brighton, and there'll be an inquest."

"T' be sure," Mr. Tudwell said, in a careless tone. "But Constable Woodhouse 'as those matters well in hand. You c'n tell th' others there's nothin' t' worry about. Just to be on th' safe side, though, it might be as well to postpone some of our ... activities."

Mr. Landsdowne hunched his rusty shoulders, scowling. "Postpone? I don't like th' sound o' that, 'Arry. There's too much involved, far's I'm concerned. An' I'm sure others'll feel the same way."

"We'll talk it over," Mr. Tudwell said soothingly. "Tonight, at th' Black Horse. But it's my judgment that we 'ave t' postpone. In fact—" He glanced up and saw Patrick. "Ye're still here, boy? Thought I told ye t' get t' those stalls." Then he held up his hand. "But come back later. I'll want ye t' go on an errand this afternoon."

"Yes, sir," Patrick said with his customary alacrity. But he went to do the dirty job of mucking out the stalls chastened and deeply perplexed. He was sure now that Mr. Tudwell knew exactly what had happened on the beach, and the thought sorely troubled him. Patrick had known the dead man scarcely at all, but it was sad to think that he had left children behind—boys, perhaps, who would have to grow up without a father. And Patrick was no fool: he knew from the tone of the conversation that neither Mr. Tudwell nor Mr. Landsdowne believed that the coast guard had killed himself, no matter what they said. But Mr. Tudwell was his friend, and the friend of all the village, for he was the man who had brought it prosperity. Patrick owed him loyalty—and anyway, what would be changed if he spoke about what he had seen? The coast guard was dead, and nothing would bring him back.

With these perplexing thoughts filling his mind, Patrick worked doggedly through the morning, returned at noon to Mrs. Higgs's to refill the copper, hurried through his lunch, and ran back to the stable for his commission.

Mr. Tudwell was pacing up and down in front of the table in the office, hands behind his back, head down, clearly troubled. But when Patrick came in, his worried look vanished and he put on a smile.

"Ah, there ye are, Paddy," he said briskly. "Ye're to locate a Mr. Maurice Burke, at th' 'ove Tobacconist in Church Road, just above Kingsway. Mr. Burke asked me t' take a look at a certain gray 'unter he 'eard was for sale, an' tell 'im whether it'ud suit 'im. 'Ere's th' message: 'Th' gray hunter isn't presently available. Mebbee in a few weeks.'" The stablemaster regarded Patrick narrowly. "Let's 'ear it now, Paddy."

"'The gray hunter is not presently available. Maybe in a few weeks,'" Patrick repeated. He had delivered messages concerning the availability of various horses to other merchants in Brighton and Hove, and did not for one moment believe that a mere tobacconist was in the market for a gray hunter. But Patrick did not need to inquire into the true meaning of the message. As to that, he was already quite clear.

"Very good," Mr. Tudwell said. He put his hand on Patrick's shoulder with a fatherly benevolence. "An' since ye'll likely linger along th' sea front an' lie t' me an' say ye went lame or lost yer way, ye may as well take th' rest o' th' afternoon for th' job an' buy yerself some sweets when ye're done." And he gave Patrick a pat on the shoulder and a coin in the hand.

With a grin, Patrick shoved the coin in his pocket and ran out of the office. When he had gone, Harry Tudwell sank into the chair behind the table and buried his face in his hands. But even though his burning eyes were squeezed shut, he could still see the pale, drowned face of the young coast guard. No amount of village prosperity, no number of shiny new horses in the stable or well-stocked dress shops on the High Street could repay the wife for the loss of her husband or the children for their father. And he, Harry Tudwell, whose intentions had been of the best, who had worked hard to bring a lasting prosperity to the village through its various enterprises, could hold only himself responsible for the way things had gotten out of hand.

9

"When all the world would keep a matter hid,
Since Truth is seldom friend to any crowd,
Men write in fable as old Aesop did,
Jesting at that which none will name aloud."
—RUDYARD KIPLING
The Fabulists

NOW, IT COULD be argued that Patrick should not have carried a message for a man he believed to be involved in another man's death. But he was only a boy, with a boy's judgment and a boy's ordinary need for a man's affection and approval. So he took the coin, pocketed his reservations, and hurried off to the White Horse, where The Coffin (as the odorous old coach was known) was about to begin its afternoon run to Brighton. He begged a ride from Old Hennessey, whose Jack Russell terrier shared the box with them, barking like a banshee at every passing vehicle.

Patrick thus went in fine style as far as the coach terminus on Madeira Drive, then caught a ride on a passing omnibus when the conductor was distracted by an old woman with several large parcels and a parrot. As the bus passed Queen's Road, he hopped off and walked the rest of the way to Burke & Sons Tobacconists in Church Road, Hove—a pleasant walk on a bright, crisp Monday afternoon. He found Mr. Maurice Burke, a gray-faced, hunchbacked little man, at work behind the counter.

"Not havailable, did 'e say?" Mr. Burke asked with a frown, when he had delivered his message.

"Perhaps in a few weeks," Patrick repeated.

"Haltogether hunacceptable," Mr. Burke said. He scowled at Patrick. "Did 'e say why?"

Patrick shook his head. "No, sir. Just that it's not available."

"Well, tell 'im I sez I expect 'e'll locate another," Mr. Burke growled, "an' th' sooner, th' better, I sez." For Patrick's trouble, he gave him two Turkish cigarettes out of an orange cardboard box on the counter, and pushed him out the door.

Patrick would rather have had money, but the cigarettes were an acceptable substitute and he smoked as he sauntered in a leisurely manner eastward along the bustling sea front, glad to have his errand done with. He might have thought about what the message meant, and how it was related to the coast guard's death. But he put those thoughts aside and stopped to listen to an organ grinder with a red-hatted monkey rattling his chain, then loafed along in front of the imposing steel frame of the new Palace Pier, his hands in his pockets, whistling a beer hall tune.

Had anyone looked attentively at him, they would have seen only a thin young boy with curly red hair, dressed in a knit jersey with too-short sleeves, red suspenders, and brown corduroy trousers, truant from his employment and out on an afternoon's lark. Patrick's own view of himself, however, was rather more fabulous. He was by turns a daring pirate from *Treasure Island*, enjoying shore leave before taking to the high seas for more raids on rich merchant ships. Then he was Mr. Kipling's Mowgli, Master of the Jungle, gliding through a twilit thicket of trees with the rock python Kaa draped in a friendly fashion across his shoulders. And then he was a smuggler, carrying a tub of the finest French brandy through the tunnels under Rottingdean's High Street to—

"Look where ye're walkin', boy," a voice shrilled, and Patrick, recalled to reality, jumped back smartly to avoid being struck by a wheeled chair in which sat a wizened old man bundled up in an overcoat, propelled by a sullen male attendant wearing a checked suit and bowler hat. He did not jump back soon enough to avoid the old man's ebony cane, however, which dealt him a numbing blow on the arm. He hopped up and down, cursing and rubbing his arm, as the old man rolled on through the crowd, giggling hysterically and poking his cane at pink-faced nurses with babies in prams and fat wives with paper-wrapped packets of fish.

But Patrick's pain was short-lived, and he was soon whistling again. It was getting on to teatime, and he stopped at a street vendor's cart to buy three fresh oysters for a penny, and a little further on, finding himself still hungry, a baked potato and a tin cup full of steaming China tea. He was tempted by the ginger-beer stand, with its polished mahogany frame and bright gold taps, but held firmly to the last of his coins, which he still had in his pocket when he arrived at the electric railway's jetty at the Banjo Groyne. The coast road to Rottingdean was only three miles long, but he was tired and would far rather ride than walk, if it could be managed without cost.

Twenty minutes later, he had smuggled himself aboard the *Pioneer* in the company of a man and woman with such a large flock of children that the conductor could not be bothered to count them. Once on board, he climbed the stairs to the open deck on top of the salon for a better view of the cliffs and the Channel and the sea gulls clamoring overhead. Locally, the *Pioneer* was called the Daddy Long-legs, for it was built on 24-foot stilts so that it could make the journey in high tide as well as low. An ungainly affair, it looked like a cross between a well-appointed railway carriage, a pleasure steamer topped with a pilothouse and one of Jules Verne's flights of fancy.

For Patrick, the trip on the electric railway was the perfect end to an altogether satisfactory day, and by the time he disembarked from the *Pioneer* in the voluminous shelter of a woman's skirts, he had already forgotten his anxiety of the morning. He climbed the steps to the Quarter Deck and made his way up the High Street, past the White Horse Inn and the Black Horse pub, then sharply left, as if he were going to the stables. Instead, he took the path up Beacon Hill.

The black-tarred smock windmill that stood at the brow of the hill, overlooking the Channel, had long since ceased to grind corn and the canvas of its sails had disappeared before Patrick was born. Few people came up here except on the occasions when the village beacon fire was lit—such as Her Majesty's Jubilee, just a few months before. That had been a night Patrick would remember for the rest of his life, capping a day of parades and prayers and feasting that ended with the whole village gathering around the beacon fire, with answering fires ablaze from hilltops all up and down the seacoast, and flares sent up from ships far out in the Channel, and fireworks, and the Brighton Military Band playing at Queen's Park. Indeed, such were the celebrations all around the globe that it was unlikely that any of the Queen's subjects anywhere in her empire would forget where they were on that particular night in 1897.

But Beacon Hill was dark and silent now, and the windmill was the same shadowy and secret place it had been for the past fifty years. According to local legend, it had been much used by smugglers, who employed the mill proper to store their booty and the sails, which carried their canvas then and could be turned by hand, to send messages to ships waiting in the Channel. Now, no one used it—no one but Patrick, and the pigeons that roosted high up in the rafters, and the field mice that found it a warm and dry place to spend the winter. And since local legend also had it that the mill was haunted by the ghost of a smuggler who had been hanged there many years before, no one was likely to use it, which suited Patrick perfectly and made it a fine hideaway for his precious cache of secretly saved coins.

But still, despite its usefulness to Patrick, the mill was a gloomy place at twilight, and he felt, as he always did, a shiver of apprehension as he entered. Outside, the sea shone with a pearly luminescence that signaled a gathering storm. Inside, it was dusky and quiet, except for the low moan of the wind in the bare sail frames and the faint squeaking of the main shaft, which still turned as the sails turned, although the millstone and the spur wheel, dismantled, lay against the stone foundation. Indeed, it was so dark within that Patrick reached up above the low door and took down a stub of a candle and a match, fetched from Mrs. Higgs's cupboard. He lit it, striking the match against a stone and shielding the flickering flame from the cold wind that came through the open door. He turned to go to his cache, which was concealed behind a loose stone.

Then he saw it, and his breath froze in his throat. A man

was sitting upright, legs stretched out, his back against one of the ancient grinding wheels that had been tilted up along the opposite wall. He was staring accusingly at Patrick, his eyes like pale glass balls in a face as white as marble, his mouth open as if to charge Patrick with some horrible crime. But the man could no longer accuse anyone of anything. There was a small round hole in the front of his brass-buttoned coast guard jacket, and the wool was sodden with congealed blood. He was quite, quite dead.

10

"She [my grandmother, Georgiana Burne-Jones] was absolutely fearless, morally and physically. During the South African War [1898-1900] her sympathies were with the Boers, and ... she never hesitated to bear witness, without a single sympathizer. When peace was declared, she hung out of her window a large blue cloth on which she had been stitching the words: 'We have killed and also taken possession.' ... Single-minded people can be a little alarming to live with and we children had a nervous feeling that we never knew where our grandmother might break out next."

—ANGELA THIRKELL,
Three Houses, 1931

WHEN LADY BURNE-JONES had learned that both Charles and Rudyard were to go into Hove for cards at Mr. Sassoon's, she sent a note asking Kate to come for supper at seven that evening at North End House, with Caroline Kipling.

"If the men mean to desert us for a party," she had written, "we ladies shall entertain ourselves with a small party here at home. Nothing difficult or formal—but we shall be very gay, just we three." But Caroline declined, pleading a cold, so there were only two.

North End House was painted a sparkling white and divided from the road by a low white fence and a euonymus hedge. The original dwelling had been a three-story cottage called Prospect House, which was later joined to Aubrey Cottage next door and renamed North End House, partly because the Burne-Joneses' London home was in North End Road and partly because this house stood at the north end of the village street. Aunt Georgie had welcomed Kate into the parlor—"too small to be called a drawing room," she declared, but full of drawing-room treasures nonetheless, all beautifully artistic. Burne-Jones's paintings for William Morris's Sangraal tapestry hung on one wall, and on either side of the fireplace hung his paintings of the six powerful archangels: Gabriel, Raphael, Uriel, Azrael, Chemuel, and for Lucifer, a black opening with tongues of flame. Beside the deep window seat was a large oak bookcase filled with Aunt Georgie's books: William Morris's *A Dream of John Ball*, which described an ideal socialist society, and his new and very beautiful *Kelmscott Chaucer*, inscribed "with love to Ned and Georgie"; John Ruskin's *Fors Clavigera*, a treatise on social reform for the British working class; and *The History of Trade Unionism* by Beatrice and Sidney Webb, whom Aunt Georgie proudly said were friends of hers "and colleagues in the cause of social reform." And behind the parlor door stood a little brown cottage piano that Burne-Jones had delicately painted with girls playing in a garden and Death, scythe in hand, knocking at the garden gate.

Aunt Georgie played and sang several of Schubert's songs and some English songs from Chappell's *Popular*

Music of the Olden Time, while Kate sat on a dreadfully uncomfortable pre-Raphaelite sofa and listened with delight, looking about her at the works of art that adorned the walls. Had she been able to look into the future, she might have seen the little painted piano in the South Kensington Museum, where it was removed in later years, or glimpsed the archangels' images in countless books of art history, or read about the drawing room itself in a delightful memoir called *Three Houses*, written by Aunt Georgie's granddaughter, Angela Thirkell, some thirty-four years later. The book would have on its cover a tinted photograph of Angela and her grandfather Ned—the very same photograph which sat at this moment on top of the piano with dozens of other Burne-Jones family likenesses.

And had she been able to read Angela Thirkell's reminiscences, she would probably have chuckled at the insightful truth of the writer's affectionate observation that "my grandmother was curiously removed from real life":

> She had a great deal of natural self-possession and dignity and a power of accepting everyone—no matter what their social position—entirely for what they were in themselves. She could talk to working people in their cottages with as much ease as she received royal princesses who came to look at pictures.... There was no condescension in her visits and no familiarity, though the child who accompanied her was ready to cry with confusion as she sat with her large blue eyes fixed on some gnarled unlettered old woman and telling her tidings of comfort from *Fors Clavigera*.... She would have a worthy carpenter or wheelwright to the house once a week to discuss socialism in which she so thoroughly and theoretically believed.

Kate's chuckle would have been all the more understanding because, when they sat down to supper, Aunt Georgie began to discuss her work on the Parish Council in terms of socialist theory—a subject in which Kate herself had begun to have a recent interest but which she found a bit difficult to follow when she was hungry. Aunt Georgie spoke with such a passionate enthusiasm, however, that Kate could limit her responses to murmured yeses and noes, while paying the right sort of attention to the delicious little supper prepared by Mrs. Mounter: hot Chantilly soup, cold tongue sandwiches on buttered bread, and apple-ginger compote, made with Ribstone pippins from the orchard behind the garden.

They were finishing their compote, and Aunt Georgie was reviewing for Kate an essay that George Bernard Shaw had written for *Fabian Essays in Socialism,* when they heard voices outside the dining room window.

"But he's not at The Elms," a boy said desperately. "If he isn't here, where *is* he?"

A man's voice replied. "If ye must know, Paddy me boy, Mr. Kipling's gone t' Mr. Arthur Sassoon's 'ouse. 'E won't be back till late." The man laughed heartily. "That is, if 'e comes back at all. They went in a motorcar, an' I wudn't be a bit surprised if they din't drive right off th' cliff. Motor cars be beastly things."

Aunt Georgie rose from the table and went swiftly to the window beside Kate's chair. She threw open the casement, and Kate turned to see the boy she had met on the beach, confronting a man carrying a hoe in one hand and a basket of weeds in the other.

"Mr. Mounter," Aunt Georgie snapped, "what do you mean by speaking so dreadfully? Go on about your work, please. And you, Patrick! What is your need of Mr. Kipling?"

The man gave a muttered apology and went off, boots

crunching on gravel, and Patrick came up to the window. The freckles stood out on his white face, and his hands were balled into fists. "I must fetch him," he said urgently.

"Fetch him!" Aunt Georgie said with a light laugh. "But that's ridiculous. Mr. Kipling and Lord Sheridan have gone to spend the evening with the—"

"It wouldn't matter if he'd gone off t' meet the Queen," the boy said recklessly. "An' if his lordship's with him, all the better. They must be got back at once!"

Kate rose from her chair and stood beside Aunt Georgie. In his determination, the boy seemed more mature than she had remembered. "Why, Patrick?" she asked mildly.

The boy hesitated for a moment, his eyes searching her face. Something he saw there seemed to make up his mind, and he spoke. "'Cause," he said bleakly, "the Rottingdean coast guard's up there in th' mill." He jerked his head in the direction of Beacon Hill, rising behind the garden. "Captain Smith has been shot. Murdered."

"Murdered?" Kate whispered. A chill passed through her as she stared at the boy's set face. The second murder of a coast guard in two days!

"Murdered!" Aunt Georgie cried. "But it's nothing to do with my nephew! Why should he be involved? It's a matter for the constable! You are to stay here, Patrick. Do you understand?"

"Goodbye," Patrick said. "And *don't* tell the constable!" He was gone before the women could open their mouths to protest.

Aunt Georgie turned to Kate, consternation written on her face. They stared at one another for a moment; then Aunt Georgie seemed to pull herself together. "Something is going on here, Kate," she declared, "something unspeakably dreadful. But this is *my* village. I serve on the Parish Council, and I tell you that I will not allow evil to corrupt this beautiful place! I am inclined, on reflection, to agree with the boy. Constable Woodhouse has taken little interest in the one death. It is not likely that he will take any more interest in another. I shall send Mr. Mounter to the post office with a wire to the chief constable at Brighton, Sir Robert Pinckney, with whom I am acquainted. I shall beg him on behalf of the Council to bring his men to investigate these murders." Her eyes took on a determined gleam. "Early in the morning, you and I shall drive to Black Rock to visit poor Mrs. Radford, and when we return, I shall personally call at every house in this village, asking the inhabitants to tell me what they know about this wretched, wretched business."

Kate was silent for a moment. She did not like to contradict Aunt Georgie, but she did not think it likely that the truth, whatever it was, would be rooted out by a door-to-door canvas. More, the matter could not be let go until the chief constable from Brighton put in an appearance—whenever that might be.

"I am sure that those are all good measures," she said at last, "but there is something more immediately pressing. The scene of the murder cannot be left unattended until the chief constable arrives from Brighton or Charles and Rudyard return from Hove. Someone may stumble on the body and disturb or destroy important evidence."

Aunt Georgie frowned. "Perhaps we could send Mr. Mounter, with instructions not to allow the scene to be disturbed."

"Are you sure," Kate asked quietly, "that Mr. Mounter can be trusted?"

Aunt Georgie looked aghast. "You can't think—"

"I don't know what to think," Kate replied honestly. "I believe, however, that it is best for me to go. Our manservant, Lawrence, and his wife have gone walking along the cliffs toward Saltdean this evening, and I don't expect them back for some time. But I will send a note to Seabrooke House asking Lawrence to come to the windmill as soon as he returns. Meanwhile—" She smiled ruefully. "I am sorry for this end to a delightful evening, but I fear I must ask you to excuse me."

"Well, I hope you don't think I should allow you to go up there all alone," Aunt Georgie said firmly. "I will find a jacket and the lantern and we shall be off immediately. But first we must find Mr. Fisher and ask him to open the post office so we can send a telegram to Brighton. I hope, at least, that we can trust our postmaster!"

And so it was that The Right Honorable Baroness of Somersworth and Lady Edward Burne-Jones spent an interminable evening keeping watch over a dead man. With an involuntary shudder, Kate held up the lantern and glanced hurriedly at the body to make sure it had not been disturbed. Then she and Aunt Georgie sat just inside the door of the old windmill, waiting as the last light faded over the Channel and a pale sliver of waning moon rose over the silent, fog-shrouded downs, speaking only in whispers, as if their voices might wake the man who had been hastened so rudely to his eternal sleep.

"The dead coast guard," Kate said. "What is his name?"

"Captain Reynold Smith," Aunt Georgie replied. "He was assigned here several years ago, from Dover. He managed the coast guard office on the High Street and lived in the cottage behind."

"Was he married? Did he have children?"

"I believe not," Aunt Georgie said. "I met him occasionally on business for the Parish Council. I did not find him an altogether pleasant man. Insolent, I thought him, and quite assertive in his manner. When I spoke to him of Mr. Ruskin's ideas on social reform, I am sorry to say that he was almost belligerent in his refusal to hear me out." She shook herself. "But I will not speak ill of the dead. I am sure that Captain Smith was a good man, and merely uneducated as to the need for improved sanitation and health care in villages such as ours."

Perplexed and sad, Kate thought about the two human lives that had been taken in this placid village and wondered to herself who might be responsible. Had the same person killed both men? Why had it been done? What evil was hidden in the dark heart of this peaceful village by the sea, so serene in its seeming innocence and calm?

Sometime around ten, the fog suddenly grew more dense—not like the thick, yellow pea-soupers of London, but a gray, cold mist that curled and hissed over the downs like smoke. When Lawrence Quibbley hurried up the hill to take the women's places, they did not see his lantern until he emerged from the cloud directly in front of them. Cold, weary, and perturbed, they returned to the drawing room at North End House for a cup of hot black tea and a few moments of conversation, Aunt Georgie describing to Kate her efforts (unsuccessful, so far) to persuade the Parish Council to build a public bath and wash-house for the village, and to hire a nurse who could make daily rounds, attending to the sick and elderly.

And then Kate, so tired she could scarcely think, walked back to Seabrooke House. Her route took her past the Black Horse, a whitewashed alehouse, on the High Street. Lamplight spilled in golden puddles out of its windows and onto the cobbled street, and from within could be heard the sound of murmuring voices, sometimes breaking into loud shouts. If Kate had paused to listen, she might have saved a great deal of time and effort in the investigation of the deaths of the coast guards. But she was too tired to stop, and hurried past, and so went home to bed.

11

"Foxes Made in Germany. Considerable indignation
is being aroused in the hunting districts ... in
consequence of the importation of foxes bred in
Germany. Farmers are loud in their protestations
against the practice, and allege that they are sustaining
frequent and heavy losses by Reynard's nightly visits
to their homesteads. The German fox is described as
being even more vicious than his English namesake."
—*The Daily Telegraph,* August 30, 1897

CHARLES AND KIPLING stepped out of Kate's Panhard in
front of the stately stone-fronted residence in King's
Gardens, Hove, a little before eight. The liveried footman
was occupied in directing a carriage to a spot at the side
of the street. He turned, one eyebrow raised, to stare at the
car with a disdainful hauteur.

"I beg your pardon, sir," he said stiffly, "but I must ask
you to drive your machine around to the back. This space
is reserved for guests' horses and carriages."

Kipling, always a little hot-tempered, opened his mouth
to retort, but Charles motioned him back into the motorcar.
"This happens frequently," he said with a crooked grin,

piloting the noisy vehicle in the direction the footman indicated. "People hardly know what to do with an automobile, so they treat it as if it were a tradesman's vehicle."

Kipling grinned. "Well, let them," he said. "But this ride has made a convert of me, I must say. You must show me how all its mechanisms work. I am rather keen on that sort of thing, you know. When it's time to look for another residence, I will see about hiring a motorcar."

"But I thought you had taken The Elms for three years." Charles stopped the Panhard and they got out. "You're not settling in Rottingdean, then?"

It was Kipling's turn to be rueful. "The house is not an ideal residence. Rottingdean is too close to Brighton, for one thing, and already the daytrippers have become a nuisance. They ride past in a disreputable old charabanc and gawk at me through the study window. Or they cluster outside the gate and pester our legitimate callers. I'm afraid we'll be obliged to have the gate boarded over."

"Perhaps that's the price you must pay for fame," Charles said with a laugh.

"Not I," Kipling said determinedly. "Anyway, I think it is better to put some distance between Carrie and Aunt Georgie. It is easier just now, when Carrie is occupied with little John. But both are strong-willed women, and one is not entirely comfortable in the midst of them. If we do not locate another residence by spring, I believe I shall take Carrie and the children off to South Africa for a time."

They had come around the front of the Sassoon house, under the nose of the haughty footman, and were greeted at the door by the butler and ushered into a grand, marble-floored hall, where they surrendered their motoring coats and hats to a black-gowned maid.

"The gathering is in the library, my lord," the butler said

to Charles and led them down the hall to a double door, which he opened with a stately flourish. They stepped into an opulent, oak-paneled room lined with books and fine paintings and filled with small groups of men in black coats and white ties. Several tables lavishly decorated with hothouse flowers were laden with food suitable to a fashionable standing supper: beef and ham sandwiches, fresh whole oysters, lobster patties, sausage rolls, potato rissoles, cheeses, fruit, sweetmeats, sponge cakes, the Prince's favorite Scotch shortcake, and plates of petits fours. Green felt-topped tables for cards had been set up in an adjoining room and a quartet of musicians was playing a Strauss waltz in a corner, hidden behind a cluster of potted palms. The air was already blue with the smoke of cigars, and the conversations were occasionally punctuated by bursts of laughter and the clink of champagne glasses. At the announcement of their names, the Prince, stout and affable, his nautical beard neatly trimmed, turned and came toward them.

Charles was not an intimate of the Marlborough House set, but he had met the Prince of Wales on several other occasions. In fact, he and Kate, prior to their marriage, had helped to resolve an embarrassing and politically dangerous situation at a house party at Easton Lodge, the home of the Countess of Warwick. The Prince, the target of a potentially damaging blackmail plot, had been so impressed with Charles's forensic skills that he had declared himself ready on the spot to lend royal support to a national independent forensic laboratory, headed (of course) by Charles himself. It was a suggestion that Charles firmly resisted, and he was glad that the idea seemed to have slipped the Prince's mind. While he enjoyed the challenge of an occasional criminal investigation, Charles did not intend to make a career of it. He had far too much else to do, now that he had been obliged to take on the daunting responsibilities of Somersworth and the unpleasantness of Parliament.

"Sheridan, good to see you!" the Prince exclaimed, and extended his hand. Charles took it with a bow, greeted their host, Arthur Sassoon, then introduced Kipling.

"Mr. Kipling, sir!" the Prince exclaimed, beaming. "Splendid to meet you at last! I can't tell you how much we all admired the poem that appeared in the *Times* this summer. Her Majesty was quite pleased."

"I am delighted to hear it, sir," Kipling said, with what Charles thought was uncharacteristic modesty. "Glad to have been of service. I fear it was not your customary Jubilee Ode, however."

The Prince laughed. "There was a ghastly crop of 'em, wasn't there?" A footman held up a silver cigar box, and he took out a cigar and held it to be lit. "Yes," he said, more soberly, "amidst the pomp and circumstance of the Jubilee, *Recessional* gave one something to think about. Put the whole affair into a different perspective, as it were." He puffed.

Charles accepted a glass of wine from a silver tray, smiling to himself. If the Empress of India had been pleased with Kipling's *Recessional*, it was probably because she had not fully understood it. The phrase "Lest we forget" cautioned rather than celebrated the accomplishments of imperialist England. He rather thought the Prince had taken Kipling's point, however. In the next moment, he was sure of it.

"Yes, well, I speak for us all when I say the poem was entirely appropriate to the occasion," the Prince said, lingering on the subject. "We must not allow ourselves to become complacent."

"Your Royal Highness speaks a solemn truth," said a

tall, pale goateed man at the royal elbow. "Great power must be forever vigilant lest it be overtaken."

"Captain Pierre Gostarde, of the French Navy," Sassoon murmured to Charles. "He is in England to participate in maneuvers with Her Majesty's fleet."

The Prince turned to Kipling. "I understand that you have spent some time with the fleet this summer, sir."

"Yes, a fortnight," Kipling said warmly. "Took part in the steam-trials of a prototype destroyer. A devil's darning needle, she was, twenty-foot beam, two hundred ten overall. The little witch jumped from twenty-two knots to thirty like a whipped horse. She'll not be overtaken, I warrant, once she's into production."

"But that will take some time," growled the French captain. "Meanwhile, the Germans are building up their navy with an almost frightening speed." He glanced at the Prince. "You will forgive me, Your Highness, for talking of such things, but I learned just yesterday that a new ironclad, the *Kaiser Wilhelm II*, was launched recently at Kiel. Another—an armored cruiser of fourteen thousand horsepower—is to take to the waves shortly. And I am told that the Kaiser has carefully studied Admiral Mahon's book on the influence of sea power, and is determined that Germany shall be supreme on the world's oceans."

The Prince flicked his cigar. "Quite so, quite so," he murmured. "Nephew Willie has always wanted to be thought superior. Now that he's been bested in yachts and horses, he's taken to navies. Unfortunately for him, he will have to spend a great deal of money to catch up. Even Italy has more warships."

This remark elicited chuckles all around, but Charles knew that the Prince was not being entirely truthful. The royal yacht *Britannia*, the joy of the Prince's heart, had won every yacht-racing prize there was—until the

Kaiser commissioned her designer to build a yacht his uncle could not defeat. But when the superior German *Meteor II* appeared at Cowes, the Prince simply refused to compete. He sold the *Britannia* and concentrated instead on his racing stables, winning the Grand National, the Two Thousand Guineas, and the Newmarket Stakes. Just last year, his horse Persimmon had brought him a first Derby. A thwarted Wilhelm, meanwhile, vented his spleen by building bigger and better warships.

"Perhaps, Mr. Kipling," said a slim, elegant gentleman with a gold-rimmed monocle, dark hair parted fashionably in the center, "you should send a copy of your poem to the Kaiser. Humility is a virtue to be practiced under all flags."

"Well said, Your Excellency!" the Prince exclaimed with a shout of laughter, and slapped the man's back. "Very well said! I'll have a copy posted immediately, with my compliments. Willie won't know what to make of it. You know the poor fellow has no sense of humor."

"None whatsoever, Your Highness," the gentleman murmured and bowed, clicking his heels together.

The Prince glanced up as a handsome, blond young man approached. "Ah, Cornwallis-West," he said cordially, "my dear boy, how *are* you? The Princess of Wales was asking if I had seen you, just the other day."

"Lord Sheridan, Mr. Kipling, may I present Count Ludwig Hauptmann of Germany," Sassoon said, as the Prince stepped aside to talk with the young man.

"Actually, I prefer to think of myself as a Bavarian," the monocled count said, and Charles heard the faint accent in the man's English. "It was inevitable that Bavaria be united with Prussia, since we share a common frontier and language. Still, ever since Bismarck forced the alliance upon us, I have felt it an uncomfortable relationship." A smile flickered in his blue eyes, so pale as to be almost glacial. "I suppose it may come down finally to temperament. We Bavarians are not so rash as our Prussian neighbors. We are more deliberate."

"Rash is exactly the word," Kipling said, taking out his pipe and lighting it. "The Kaiser's congratulatory telegram to Kruger after the Jameson Raid—the reckless, Prussian way, wouldn't you say? Didn't give a thought to the effect on other governments."

"Are you sure?" Charles asked, sipping his wine. "Perhaps the Kaiser gave it a great deal of thought, and achieved exactly the effect he intended."

"Entirely correct," the count said. He adjusted his monocle. "And therein lies the difference. We Bavarians would not dream of interfering with British interests in South Africa, or anywhere else."

Charles took note of the man's narrow patrician face and pinched nose, and wondered whether he was speaking the truth.

The French captain snorted. "Would that your Prussian confederates held the same view," he said, and puffed out a cloud of cigar smoke. "The Continent is too small for new powers to flex such large muscles."

"Exactly," Kipling said, squinting through the tobacco haze. "The big squeeze. The Kaiser's bullying may seem merely childish braggadocio to some, but there's trouble ahead, mark my words."

"We are being challenged on several fronts," Charles agreed. "I had the opportunity to visit the Krupp arms works at Essen several years ago. The Germans' technological advances are quite impressive."

"True, true," Kipling replied, stabbing the air emphatically. "And they'll use that technology to harass their neighbors."

"That's not entirely fair," Sassoon objected. "The Germans have used their technology to produce scientific equipment, advances in chemistry, and fine motorcars—the Benz and the Daimler, for example."

The French captain raised one eyebrow. "Ah, but the Panhard motorcar Lord Sheridan and Mr. Kipling arrived in is of French manufacture," he observed with a slight smile. "What do you say to that, Monsieur Sassoon?"

Sassoon laughed. "Actually, my taste runs more to horses than horsepower." He turned to Kipling. "I keep a pair of hunters at the Hawkham Stable, very near Rottingdean. There is excellent hunting in the downs, and the Brookside Harriers are exceptionally fine." He frowned. "Unfortunately, the area is in danger of being overhunted, and the Master is faced with the prospect of encouraging the importation of foxes or of riding farther afield than many would like."

"The importation of foxes!" Kipling exclaimed. "I've never heard of such a thing."

Sassoon shrugged. "But where there are no vermin, there is no hunt. What is one to do?"

Charles, never having been a fox hunting man, was tempted to suggest that there might be other worthy forms of sport, but thought better of it.

"Well, sir," Kipling said, "the stable is within a stone's throw of my house. When you are there, you must join Mrs. Kipling and me for tea."

Charles turned to the count. "I read recently of the work of one of your fellow Bavarians—Professor Roentgen, at the University of Würzburg. He is a scientist."

The count raised one shoulder carelessly. "I'm afraid I don't know the man, my lord. I prefer the arts to the sciences. The theater is one of my great loves. Actually, I am in this country as my government's cultural representative.

The virtues of Teutonic culture are under-appreciated here. However, I cannot offend British sensibilities by a showing of too much enthusiasm. I work, shall we say, in a subterranean way." He gave a self-deprecating smile. "Who is this professor?"

"Roentgen discovered the X-ray," Charles said. "It has made him world-famous. The Kaiser is quite pleased to count his discovery among German technological achievements."

"One does not always have the time to keep up," the count said ruefully.

"Sheridan," Sassoon explained to the count, "is something of a scientist himself. These X-rays—" he remarked to Charles, "they're quite the thing, aren't they? Hold all sorts of promise for medical advancement, I understand. Dr. Barriston was speaking to me about them."

"Dr. Barriston!" Charles exclaimed. "Yes, I have corresponded with him on the topic, several times. He is using the X-ray to set fractures."

"Pardon?" the French captain asked quizzically. "How is that so?"

Charles smiled. As a photographer, as well as an amateur scientist, it was a subject in which he had a great interest. "X-rays are a very powerful type of radiation," he said. "Where light rays reflect off the skin, these pass through the skin and soft tissues and reveal an image of the skeleton. A surgeon might place photographic film under a broken bone—a forearm, say—and use an X-ray apparatus to determine the nature and location of the fracture. They could be used to equal advantage to explore for other dense material—a bullet lodged in the body, for instance."

The count's monocle fell from his eye. "Are you telling

me that a bullet can be viewed *inside* a body?"

"It can indeed," Charles said. "If you like, I am sure that Dr. Barriston would be glad to give you a demonstration. He is quite keen on—" He was interrupted by the sound of a commotion in the hallway. A footman scurried up behind Sassoon and spoke urgently in his ear. Their host frowned, then turned to Kipling.

"There is a—ah, a young person in the hallway who claims to have a message for you, Mr. Kipling. He will not say what it is—insists on seeing you in person."

Kipling looked alarmed. "I hope it is not a family emergency. I left Mrs. Kipling at home with our new son." He looked around. "I wonder if His Highness will excuse—"

The Prince was standing nearby with a glass in one hand and a cigar in the other. "For heaven's sake, man," he exclaimed loudly, "don't wait on ceremony." He gestured toward the double doors. "By all means, go if you must."

But at that moment, the doors burst open and a small boy hurtled through, a footman still grasping the sleeve of his knitted jersey. With some astonishment, Charles recognized him as the tousle-haired, freckle-faced Irish boy who had told them what he had seen on the beach.

"Patrick!" Kipling exclaimed anxiously. "Were you sent? Is something wrong at The Elms?"

"Not at The Elms, sir." The boy twisted out of the footman's grasp. He looked around, seeing for the first time the crowd of staring, silent men. His face flamed. "I know it's cheeky. But it's awf'lly important, or I wouldn't have—"

"Well, if it's not Mrs. Kipling or the children," Kipling snapped, "what the devil is it?"

Patrick stared down at his shoes. "It's ... it's another dead man, sir," he said in a small voice. "The coast guard from Rottingdean. Captain Smith, sir. I found him in the windmill. He's been shot."

The Prince strode forward and put a hand on the boy's shoulder. "Her Majesty's coast guard has been shot?" he demanded imperiously. "Who would have the audacity to do such a thing?"

The boy looked up at him, his eyes widening. "Sir?"

"His Royal Highness, the Prince of Wales," Kipling said, and added, not unkindly, "Answer the question."

The boy swallowed hard, then lifted his chin. "I don't know, Your Royal Highness, sir," he said. "I don't know who did it."

"Your name, boy?" the Prince asked.

"Patrick," the boy said.

"You say, Patrick, that this is another dead man? A *second*, you mean?"

"Yes, sir."

"But surely not *two* dead coast guards?"

"I ..." The boy gulped. "I'm afraid so, sir."

The Prince looked at Charles. "You're staying at Rottingdean, aren't you, Sheridan? What do you know of this?"

"Nothing of *this*, sir," Charles replied uneasily. He had the sense that he knew what was coming. "But yesterday morning, the body of the Black Rock coast patrol, a young man named George Radford, was fished out of the Channel. Village gossip has it that he committed suicide. Patrick, however, witnessed the body being hauled from the beach into the sea under the cover of darkness, so there would seem to be some question about it."

"Ah," the Prince said. He was scowling. "I trust that the local police are handling the matter expeditiously."

Kipling's chuckle was mirthless. "The local police, sir, are a local joke."

"I didn't tell the constable," the boy said earnestly to Kipling. "I didn't think he would ... that is ..." He let the sentence die away.

The Prince looked from the boy to Kipling. "Do I gather from this," he asked, narrowing his eyes, "that the local constabulary are incapable of investigating these serious crimes?"

"I suggested to the constable that his lordship be involved, Your Highness," Kipling said, pushing his lips in and out. He paused delicately. "The suggestion, unfortunately, was not well received."

Charles gave an inward sigh. He was more and more certain of what was to come, and he did not like it. But there was nothing he could do. When royalty spoke, it was accustomed to being obeyed.

The Prince's scowl deepened and his voice grew more gruff. "Two of the Crown's coast guards murdered in two days, and the local police are refusing assistance? This will not do. It will not do at all!" He turned to Sassoon. "Arthur, you know the chief constable here at Brighton, do you not?"

"I do, Your Highness," Sassoon said with alacrity. "Sir Robert Pinckney. An excellent fellow, quite forward in his methods."

"Good, good. Send a message to him forthwith, letting him know what has happened. Tell him that I have taken a personal interest in the case and that I am authorizing Lord Sheridan to conduct an investigation on behalf of the Crown. Have him send his best men to assist."

Charles felt he owed it to Kate to make an effort to resist, although he knew very well the outcome. "Sir, her ladyship and I—"

"Ah, Lady Sheridan is with you at Rottingdean?" the Prince returned. "Splendid! Let her know I asked after her health, will you? Now, is there anything else you might need for your investigation, other than the chief constable's assistance?"

Charles sighed. "If there is, sir, you can be sure I shall not hesitate to ask for it."

"Good," the Prince said warmly. "I am off in the morning for a week's shooting at Abergeldie Castle. I shall expect you to telegraph your report to me." He reached into his pocket and turned to the boy. "Patrick, you have done well to bring this situation to my attention. This sovereign is for you." And he took out a gold coin and pressed it into the boy's hand.

The boy blinked. "Yes, sir. Thank you, sir."

With a satisfied smile, the Prince turned to Sassoon. "Well, now that the matter is settled, Arthur, I believe it is time for our game. What do you say to a small wager, eh?"

12

"You may be certain that the Black Horse was a meeting place for the village smugglers, who must often have come together in secret in its small taproom and discussed their plans. It was a dangerous game the villagers were playing, for not everyone was in it. Enemies of Rottingdean acted as informers, and watched when contraband was being hidden in cottages, stables, the churchyard, tucked away in the machinery inside the Mill or in the furze bushes in Saltdean Vale. These informers were called 'ten-shilling men,' which is what they were paid for their services. They, too, played a dangerous game, for like all spies they could expect no mercy when they were caught."

—HENTRY BLYTH
Smugglers' Village: The Story of Rottingdean

HARRY TUDWELL HAD called the meeting in the small back room of the Black Horse for eight o'clock on Monday night, to discuss what should be done in the event—the likely event, it seemed now—of an official inquiry into the unfortunate death of the young coast guard. "Official," in this instance, meant an investigation conducted by someone other than the tractable Fat Jack Woodhouse—the Queen's coroner, for instance, Dr. Paul Barriston, or the chief constable, Sir Robert Pinckney. Both were from Brighton, and both had reputations for persistently sniffing out information. And neither would be nearly so obliging as the complicitous Fat Jack, who was nervous as a compass needle about the possibility that outsiders might come poking their noses into Rottingdean business.

Harry knew all about Fat Jack's feelings on the matter, because the constable had been on his doorstep not thirty minutes after the coast guard's body was hauled onto the beach, inquiring apprehensively about what was best to be done.

"Wot's best?" Harry had answered, somewhat hollowly. He recovered himself and, in a stouter voice, replied: "Well, I'll tell ye, Jack. Wot's best is t' put it about that th' fellow threw hisself off th' cliff in a fit o' despair, an' th' corpse went out wi' th' tide."

God knows, it could be true. Harry himself had felt many black moments after his wife abandoned him for a baker and a brick house in Lewes three years before, and the cliffs had seemed to offer a certain remedy. Every year, the coroner was called down twice or thrice to inquire into the deaths of men and women found huddled at the foot of the cliffs or washed up on the beach, with the bleak and invariable ruling of "Death by Suicide." Several such were buried along the northern perimeter of the church graveyard, up against the stone fence of Farmer Hartletop's muck-yard. One stone was marked with only a woman's name and the bleak word OBLIVION.

But Fat Jack, scratching his head and screwing up his fleshy mouth, was not reassured by Harry's suggestion. "'E was stabbed, too, 'Arry, right through from front to back." He paused and added mournfully: "Drownded *and* stabbed. Somebody did 'im, 'Arry, wi' 'is own knife."

Stabbing made it more difficult, but not impossible. "Well, then," Harry said shortly, "put it about that 'e tumbled onto 'is knife on th' way down."

"Well, yes," Fat Jack said slowly. He blinked his small eyes, piglike in his pink moony face, and his mustache worked back and forth. "I 'spose that'll answer. But 'oo d'ye *really* think did 'im, 'Arry?"

Harry frowned, suspecting that Fat Jack suspected him. After all, if Radford had been sniffing too close, Harry was the one most likely to know it and to take prompt action against the intruder. But whether Harry did it or not, he would never have admitted it to Fat Jack, who could not be trusted with such a dangerous piece of information.

"One o' th' men, I s'pose," he said with a shrug, "fearin' that Radford had turned up somethin' on 'im."

Fat Jack closed one eye thoughtfully. "Trunky, mebbee?"

"Could've been Trunky," Harry agreed with alacrity. "Where's th' corpse?"

"Laid out i' th' guardroom at th' coast guard station on th' 'Igh Street. Foxy Smith said t' take it there an' 'e'd look out for it."

Of course. Captain Reynold Smith of the Rottingdean Coast Guard Station had not been granted his nickname without earning it. He looked out for everything. "'Ave ye telegraphed Brighton yet?" he asked.

Fat Jack shook his head. "Foxy thought I should talk t' you first," he muttered.

"Well, do it," Harry snapped. He was irritated because Fat Jack should have been able to think of these things for himself, without being told. And if he could not—if he had to be primed and drilled with a ready answer to every conceivable question—how would he reply to Barriston when it came to the inquest? This latter question concerned Harry deeply, but he could not linger over it just now. There were more pressing matters to attend to, such as the plan that must be hammered out at tonight's meeting at the Black Horse.

As to the nature of this plan, Harry had a firm opinion, and since he was the acknowledged leader of this organization—his official position was that of the lander, who was assigned to organize the transportation and arrange for the security of the merchandise once it reached the beach—he was confident that he would have no difficulty persuading his fellow free-traders to subscribe to it. Clearly, they should lay off the work until the inquest was over and the investigation had come to an end. Like it or not, Wednesday night's shipment would have to be postponed.

"Temporarily suspended," as he put it, in his argument to the group that night. "Until th' next dark o' th' moon. Then it will be safe to get on wi' our business." He had turned to the barman with an ingratiating grin. "Perry, my fine man, go out t' th' bar an' fix us up wi' another pint all round, will ye? We'll drink t' our 'ealth an' th' next shipment, as soon as 'tis safe."

But Perry, the owner of the Black Horse and one of their number, was not to be so glibly patronized.

"Temporarily suspended!" he exclaimed. He took a bottle from a table and brandished it angrily. "This is th' very last bottle of brandy, an' not another drop i' th' cellar. I was countin' on two tuns from Wednesday night's shipment, 'Arry, an' I don't intend t' wait, coast guard or no coast guard."

Mrs. Howard was equally contentious. She shook her gloved forefinger in Harry's face and shrilled: "And I am depending on the cambric and eyelet lace, Mr. Tudwell. How am I to finish Miss Strumpshaw's trousseau without it, I'd like you to tell me. The girl is to be married a fortnight hence, and I have not begun the petticoats. To wait until the next dark of the moon is impossible, and the expense of purchasing the materials in London would be … why, it would simply be ruinous!"

Harry was attempting to formulate a reassuring response to Mrs. Howard when Curly Knapton, the proprietor of the village's only tobacco shop, loomed over him. Curly was the size of a bear and one of the best keg-men Harry had ever known, capable of carrying two tuns, each weighing about forty-five pounds, one on his chest, the other on his back, while climbing a cliffside ladder.

"And wot 'bout my 'baccy?" Curly grunted, glowering down at Harry. "I din't git all that wuz comin' t' me i' th' last shipment, 'cause a bale of it went t' Hove, t' Burke, that scaly rascal. I'm tellin' ye, 'Arry, I need it *now*. I'm as sorry as th' next 'bout young Radford, God luv 'is soul, but I sez we get on wi' th' game!"

Curly spit out the last words emphatically, and a man in a crushed green felt hat, who drove one of the wagons that was used to haul goods to Brighton and Lewes, picked them up and hammered them home.

"Right, 'Arry. On wi' th' game. I got a wife an' babes waitin' on my haulin' pay. Wot's th' matter? D'ye think Fat Jack is goin' t' blab on us? On wi' th' game, I sez! On wi' th' game!"

There was loud applause, more shouts of "On wi' th' game!" and a round of sarcastic sniggers at the mention of Fat Jack.

"Fat Jack a ten-shillin' man? Not bloody likely," muttered Curly, and Perry Stiles agreed. "Not if 'e knows wot's good fer 'im," he growled in a surly tone. He looked around. "Where's Trunky Thomas? I want t' 'ear 'ow Trunky feels about suspendin' Wednesday's shipment."

"Trunky'll land it," said a short, sallow-faced man with his hair parted in the middle. He was Grantly the grocer, recently elected to the Parish Council and therefore a man whose opinions might be thought to count for something. "Trunky's a brave man, not one to dodge a risk. An' I'm wi' th' rest o' ye—I got a big order comin' wi' th' next lot." He cast a meaningful look at Harry and added judiciously. "Mayhap we should vote Trunky t' be our lander, since 'Arry's feelin' gingerly."

There was a mutter of agreement among the crowd, and Mrs. Higgs the laundress, a close friend of Fat Jack, raised her voice. "Ye've said a true thing there, Gabriel Grantley. Trunky Thomas wud be glad enough t' bring th' ship in Wednesday night, investygashion or no."

"An' don't forget Cap'n Smith," Mrs. Higgs's sister, Iris Portney, chimed in. "The cap'n is 'ere t' take care o' us and 'elp us get the job done."

"That's right, Iris," Mrs. Higgs agreed. "Cap'n Smith won't let an investygashion get i' th' way." She looked around. "Where th' devil is Trunky?" she demanded, "an th' cap'n, too. Somebody fetch both o' 'em, an' let's vote."

Harry himself had been looking forward to the arrival of Foxy Smith, whom he had tried several times that day to contact. Foxy usually made it a point to show his face at these meetings, if only to remind the villagers that they owed their present affluence and their future prosperity to him. Harry was confident that he would agree as to the need for caution and delay. Foxy was in close and frequent contact with the investors and understood the larger situation in a way the villagers could not.

But Harry was not at all pleased to hear the group calling for Trunky Thomas. Trunky was an out-and-out troublemaker, in Harry's opinion, and would not be above exploiting the group's unhappiness to wrest its leadership from him. In fact, Harry had known for some time that Trunky had designs on his position of leadership and would try almost anything to take control of the operation. Not to put too fine a point on it, Harry didn't trust Trunky as far as he could heave a tun of brandy. If he had things his own way, Trunky would have been out of the game altogether.

But the choice hadn't been left to him, for the investors insisted that every important citizen of the village be included—with the exception, of course, of the nobs who lived around the Green and came and went as the whim struck them: the Burne-Joneses, the Ridsdales, and the new residents of The Elms. But while Harry chafed at this stipulation, he certainly saw the wisdom in it. Exclusion led to disaffection, and disaffected men easily become informers. And these days, informers with the right sort of intelligence to sell could earn a great deal more than ten shillings.

Harry jumped up on the bench and raised his voice, striving to regain control of the unruly crew. "Ye've got t' think straight about this," he cried. "Wot 'appens if Trunky lights th' ship in on Wednesday night, an' th' chief constable from Brighton is waitin' wi' th' Brighton police? Wot 'appens if there's a pitched battle, an' some o' ye don't return 'ome?"

That got their attention and the room quieted somewhat. They all remembered the bloody stories of the fierce fights between the smugglers and the Crown's preventative forces, less than a century before. He lowered his voice. "It's a coast guard 'oo died," he said, slowly and with emphasis, "not some poor drunken sod 'oo 'appened t' stumble off th' cliff one dark night." He looked around the group, challenging one pair of eyes after another. "There's no doubt about it. Somebody did young Radford, an' th' Crown is goin' t' want t' know 'oo. Th' Crown is goin' t' want *satisfaction*."

That reduced the objections to mutterings, at least momentarily, and gave Harry time to consider his strategies. It was a sticky wicket, to be sure. Trunky was threatening on the one hand and the coroner and the chief constable on the other, and there was the inquest into Radford's death to be got through. But equally important, and equally difficult to know how to handle, were the investors—the men who had put up the capital to purchase the merchandise from the French suppliers and pay the villagers of Rottingdean to smuggle it into the country.

The romance of smuggling had died several generations ago, and with it the knowledge of how most smuggling operations worked. But central to all of them, Harry knew, had been the need for money to purchase the imported goods. This meant that somebody—often a consortium of wealthy merchants—would advance the funds. A London draper, for example, might stock his shop with smuggled silks and gloves, or a publican would readily pay good value for a constant supply of duty-free wines and spirits.

Harry did not know the identity of the current investors, but he suspected that they were just such wealthy merchants, concerned that a change in the excise laws might make it difficult for them to obtain their goods and anxious to establish an alternate trade route, as it were—another way to move their merchandise into the country, in the event they were not able to use the accustomed avenues.

In fact, the investors had made it very clear, according to Foxy Smith, that this was not a short-term arrangement. They had investigated several villages along the southeast coast before they determined on Rottingdean, choosing the village because of its superior beach, its established tunnels, and its proximity to the London, Brighton, and South Coast Railway, just a few miles up the Falmer Road. They wanted to establish a regular, reliable organization that they could count on for the long term, and were willing to invest sufficiently so that the whole village would profit. They had paid very well for the improvement of the old system of tunnels, including the addition of three new tunnels to the cliffside and the excavation of a huge underground storage depot far larger than was presently required. Indeed, in Harry's opinion the tunneling project was substantially overbuilt, and he had told Foxy that he couldn't imagine bringing in enough merchandise to fill even half of the new capacity.

But Foxy had just grinned and shrugged his narrow shoulders in his usual sardonic fashion, which led Harry to suspect that the investors had financed the tunneling operations out of a different motive; that they intended to put as much money into as many pockets as possible, thereby purchasing the villagers' cooperation and ensuring Rottingdean's eagerness to continue the business arrangement in good times and bad.

Well, if that was the investors' hidden motive, Harry thought sourly, they had certainly achieved it. The honest folk who for years had been accustomed to live frugally on the weekly shillings brought in by the family breadwinners had immediately begun to savor their new affluence. They were spending every ha'penny of their increased income on new gowns and coats and horses and gigs, repairing their old cottages and building new ones, expanding old businesses and investing in new ones, such as Mrs. Howard's dress shop and Curly Knapton's tobacconist shop, which depended on the very goods they were bringing in. Now, they were willing to risk the enterprise, their investments, and perhaps even their lives to keep the merchandise and money flowing—which did not seem to Harry like a very sound plan.

Harry frowned. Where was Foxy Smith? He was the

only one who could tell him how the investors had reacted to the news that a local coast guard had died in suspicious circumstances. He was the only one who could endorse Harry's plan to postpone Wednesday night's landing. Without Foxy—

There was a thump-thump in the taproom in front. The double doors flew open and Trunky Thomas burst through. His right leg was shorter than his left and stiff, so that he walked with a peculiar rolling motion, like an old salt home from the sea. His jowled face was flushed with exertion, his cap half off, his knit jerkin hanging open.

"Well, it's about time, Trunky," Mrs. Higgs cried cordially. "We been talkin' 'bout ye an' wonderin' why ye weren't 'ere. Come in an' 'ave a drink."

"Yes, Trunky," Gabriel Grantly said, pouring a mug of ale for the new arrival. "Where's Foxy?"

Trunky rocked to a halt. "Where's Foxy?" he repeated in a gruff, grim voice. He ignored the mug Gabriel Grantly was holding out to him and waited until the whole room was quiet and all eyes were on him. "Where's Foxy? I'll tell ye where 'e is. 'E's i' th' old mill. An' 'e's *dead*, that's 'ow 'e is. Dead as a door knocker."

"Dead!" Mrs. Higgs cried, open-mouthed.

"Dead?" Gabriel Grantly gasped, staring at Trunky. The mug of ale dropped from his grasp and splashed over his new black trousers. He didn't notice.

"Dead?" Harry whispered. His heart was pounding, his breath coming fast. Without Foxy, he could not contact the investors. Without Foxy, he was like a ship adrift in a fog, unsure of its heading, unclear of its destination. Without Foxy—

"Aye, dead," Trunky said. "Shot through th' chest, 'e were." He turned to glare at Harry. "An' I've got a pretty fair idee 'oo dun it."

13

"The smugglers used her dusty lofts
And dozed there through the day,
Or waited signals from the sea
To bring 'moonshine' away.
Now owlets roost in her cupola,
And pigeons peck her stones;
But the corn she ground, the corn
    she ground
Has passed into our bones."

—R. THURSTON HOPKINS
Rottingdean Mill

K ATE SLEPT FITFULLY and wakened the minute Charles stumbled into their room and began taking off his clothes. The hands of the clock stood at five minutes to one.

"The boy found you?" she asked, getting up to light the gas lamp on the wall beside the bed. "You've seen the poor man in the mill?"

"Yes," Charles said wearily, stepping out of his trousers. "Patrick found us at Arthur Sassoon's. And yes, I've seen the body—at the insistence of royalty."

"Of royalty? You can't mean—"

"Yes." Charles was grim. "I'm afraid I do mean. His Royal Highness has taken it as a personal affront that two of the Queen's coast guard have been murdered, under the royal nose, as it were. I have been assigned to investigate the matter, and Sir Robert Pinckney, the Brighton chief constable, is to assist." He took off his collar and unbuttoned his shirt. "I'm so sorry, Kate. I hope this matter won't take too long, and we can get back to our holiday."

"It can't be helped," Kate said philosophically. "What did you discover at the mill?"

"It was too dark to discover anything, and I couldn't risk disturbing the scene by poking around without sufficient light. Anyway, I was much too tired to do more than glance around the place. We had a great deal of trouble on the return from Hove. We're lucky to have gotten back safely."

She looked at him, concerned. "Trouble?"

He drew back the blankets and climbed into bed. "I'll tell you about it in the morning," he said, in a muffled voice. "Let's go to sleep, shall we? There's much to do tomorrow, and I'm going to need your help at the mill. I will also want you to keep an eye on the boy."

"The boy." She put out the light and lay down beside him. "Do you think he's in danger?"

"Patrick knows far more than he has told us so far. In fact, he may hold the key to both these murders. If you can keep him with you and befriend him, you may be able to gain his confidence." He lifted his hand to her cheek and touched it tenderly. "I hope it's not too … difficult for you, my dear."

He was thinking, she knew, that it might be trying for her to be with the boy. She thought for a long moment before she answered, wanting to tell him that she mourned the loss of their infant for *his* sake and not for her own. That she could go through life in great contentment as long as they were together, never mind having children. And that if the deepest, most secret, most wretched truth be told, it was that she was sure she would *not* have been a good mother, by the standards he held. She did not believe in the English way of raising children: confining them with their nanny to the nursery until they were old enough to have a governess or be sent off to school. She would have felt it necessary to have her children always with her, which meant that she could not so easily travel with Charles and do the other things she hoped to do, and that she might have come to resent the child.

But while she chose the careful words she needed to tell Charles what was in her heart, his breathing slowed and became more regular, and he began to snore a little. After a moment, she put out her hand and let it rest on his shoulder, feeling the warmth of his body under the cambric fabric of his nightshirt. Somehow, soon, the words would have to be said, or they would always hang in the air between them.

Patrick was grainy-eyed when he arose the next morning, for he had not gotten a great deal of sleep. The return journey from Hove in Lord Sheridan's motorcar had held a great many excitements, not the least of which had been the three tires that had gone flat, one after the other, before they passed Kemptown and the French Convalescent Hospital. His lordship carried a supply of compressed air but it was quickly exhausted, and Patrick had earned several extra shillings for reinflating the tires with the awkward hand pump. Then both headlamps had failed just as they reached the road to Ovingdean, due (as his lordship explained) to the dampness that had partially spoiled the carbide that fueled them.

But the headlamps wouldn't have been of much use anyway, Patrick reminded himself, for a dense fog had blown in off the Channel and quickly had become so thick that it was impossible to see any distance ahead. At last, Lord Sheridan had directed him to get out and walk ten paces in front, carrying a lantern, while the motorcar crawled along behind. Away to the right, the sea muttered and chuckled among the rocks at the foot of the cliff. Picking his way, Patrick had thought unhappily of the stories he had heard of coast guards lured over the cliff's edge by smugglers who had moved the white rocks that were supposed to mark the road, and tales of carriages that had lost their way, horses and passengers tumbling to a dreadful death. He made sure of every foot of their journey.

Delayed as they were by these difficulties, they had not reached Beacon Hill and the old windmill until just before midnight. Mr. Kipling and Lord Sheridan had talked briefly with the man they encountered there—his lordship's servant, he had proved to be, whom Lady Sheridan had apparently dispatched to guard the place. Then his lordship and Mr. Kipling had gone inside with the lantern and come out again in a few minutes, as grim-faced as Patrick himself must have been when he looked upon Captain Smith, dead as a stone, and with a hole in his chest.

"There is nothing more we can do tonight," Lord Sheridan said wearily. "Whatever is to be learned will have to wait until morning. Lawrence, you will stay here, and turn away anyone who might come." He put his hand on Patrick's shoulder and his voice softened. "And you must go home, lad. Your mother will be very anxious. Shall I come with you and make some explanation?"

"Mrs. Higgs only looks out for me, sir," Patrick said. He

grinned wryly. "Anyway, she went to the Black Horse and won't've missed me. I'll be glad to stay here," he added, eager for more adventure.

Mr. Kipling shook his head. "Straight home with you now, Paddy," he said firmly. "And not a word to Mrs. Higgs about what's happened."

"Before you go," Lord Sheridan said, fixing him with those piercing brown eyes, "I wonder if you would like to tell us what you know about this killing, or about the death of the other coast guard." He had spoken almost conversationally and now paused, as if to give Patrick time to think about what he had said. "It will help us, you know, a very great deal."

Patrick pressed his lips together and shook his head numbly.

"Very well, then," his lordship said, sounding disappointed. "You must promise not to speak of this matter to anyone— not of this man's death, not of the Prince's interest, not of anything that has happened tonight." He paused, stern but not unkind. "If you cannot take us into your confidence, can we at least trust you to be silent, Patrick?"

Patrick chewed his lower lip, thinking of all he owed Mr. Tudwell and feeling that by swearing himself to silence he was casting his lot for these two outsiders and against the man who had been to him what his father had not. But there was Captain Smith, with a bloody bullet hole in his jacket, and the other dead coast guard, and two young children orphaned and a wife left without a husband.

"Yes, sir," he said, looking down.

"Thank you, Patrick," Lord Sheridan replied with grave courtesy. "I shall be here at sunrise tomorrow morning. I could use your help, if you are not afraid to be near the dead man, and if the hour is not too early for you."

"It's not too early," Patrick said.

"I shall depend upon you, then," his lordship said, and shook his hand as if he were a man. "Sleep well, Patrick. And thank you for your good work tonight."

But for all his exhaustion, Patrick had not gotten to sleep as soon as he might have liked. He had just slipped into his bed when Mrs. Higgs, definitely in her cups, returned from the Black Horse in the company of Mrs. Portney. They made a pot of tea, sat down at the kitchen table, and talked, more loudly than they might have done if they had been quite sober.

The first few words drew Patrick from his bed and down the narrow stairs. Out of sight, he listened intently until he heard Mrs. Portney's chair scrape back and the door close behind her. But before she left, he learned most of what had transpired at the Black Horse—the important part, anyway. It troubled him so deeply that he could scarcely sleep. When he did, he dreamed of Captain Smith, cheeks as white as alabaster and eyes like huge glass marbles, who seemed to glower at him out of the darkness in the corner. When he pulled the blanket over his head and turned to the wall, he saw in his mind's eye George Radford's dead face, and the bloody stain in the front of his jersey.

He dreamed of meeting Harry Tudwell and a crew of fierce-faced villagers in the tunnel that ran under the High Street. When he turned and fled the other way, he ran straight into the clutches of an unholy creature in a cloak that rustled like bats' wings. He woke, sweating and shivering, and lay awake for a long time staring at the ceiling.

But dawn, a pale, gray dawn, came at last. Still troubled, Patrick dressed and stole down to the cold, silent kitchen. Mrs. Higgs was asleep with her head on the kitchen table, her mouth open, snoring loudly. He snatched a piece of bread and washed it down with a cup of cold tea, then climbed the hill to the windmill. The grass was covered with sparkling beads of dew and the damp soaked the legs of his trousers. A hundred yards behind him, most of the village still slept in the cottages and houses nestled in a fold of the great green downs. And to the south, the Channel brooded in the mist which hid the southern horizon.

Lord Sheridan was already there, unpacking a large camera and other sorts of photographic paraphernalia. Lady Sheridan was with him, looking very pretty in a tweed suit the exact shade of her windblown auburn hair. She smiled at Patrick.

"His lordship tells me that he was very glad of your decision to go to Hove to fetch him," she said. Her mouth quirked and her gray eyes twinkled. She leaned forward and spoke in a whisper, as if for his ears alone. "Sometimes —but just sometimes, mind—it pays to do what you think is right, rather than what you are told to do."

Patrick felt the warm flush rising in his face. "Th—thank you, my lady," he said shyly. He looked around. "Where is Mr. Kipling? I thought he would be here."

"He sent a note saying that both Mrs. Kipling and the new baby are seriously ill with colds and he is needed at home," Lady Sheridan said.

"I have deputized her ladyship to help me with the camera," Lord Sheridan said, "and you are to be my investigative assistant."

Lady Sheridan put her hand on his shoulder. "If you don't feel quite comfortable going inside," she whispered, "you must say so."

"It's all right, really," Patrick said, standing up as tall as he could. "I've already seen him, and that was the big shock." He looked at her. "But shan't *you* be afraid?" His experience of ladies was limited, but he had thought that most were delicate and would certainly faint at the sight of a corpse.

"To tell the truth," Lady Sheridan admitted candidly, "I am a little nervous." She smiled at him, and he thought once again how pretty she was. "But you and his lordship will be with me, so I shall be quite brave."

Patrick smiled. He liked this lady, although her firm mouth and sharp eyes somewhat belied her soft voice and he suspected that she was only pretending to be nervous.

"Shall we begin?" Lord Sheridan said in a businesslike tone. "I intend to first photograph the scene, and then we three shall do a thorough search of the interior of the mill. We need to be finished before Sir Robert Pinckney and his officers arrive from Brighton and the villagers become aware that something is going on. Kate, you can help me set up the camera." He handed Patrick an alcohol lamp. "You shall manage the flash lamp while I take photographs, Patrick. This is how you light it." He showed him how to do it.

"What about footprints the killer might have left in the dirt floor?" her ladyship asked, frowning. "Won't we disturb them?"

Patrick gave Lady Sheridan a respectful look. Of course—footprints. He should have thought of that earlier. "I'm afraid I've already mucked up any there might be," he said apologetically. "I'm sure I did a good bit of scuffing around when I was looking at him."

Lord Sheridan nodded. "I've already had a look around, and there appear to be no distinctive prints. But we must exercise care. Walk lightly, and don't scuffle. Come now, let's get started."

A few moments later, Patrick was standing not far from the rigid body of Captain Smith, holding the lamp in his hand. His lordship was stationed a few feet away, under the hood of a large camera set up on a wooden tripod, not very different from the camera used by the beach photographer to take pictures of the daytrippers who wanted to show their friends that they had visited the seashore. But that photographer worked with a painted scene, a lady and gentleman in bathing dress and holes to put a face through and the sea for a backdrop. Here, there was only a dead body in a dark mill, and Patrick could not imagine why his lordship should want photographs of such a grisly scene.

Lord Sheridan adjusted something on the camera. "Now, then, Patrick," he said in a muffled voice, "let there be light!"

Patrick struck a match against the stone wall and lit the alcohol flame of the strange-looking lamp, then squeezed the rubber ball, as he had been instructed. A puff of magnesium powder flew into the flame. For an instant the shadowy interior of the old windmill was illuminated by a blinding white light, brighter than any Patrick had ever seen, and the pallid face of Captain Smith seemed to leap at him out of the darkness.

"Very good, my lad," Lord Sheridan said, and repositioned his camera. "Now, shall we do it again?" His lordship took a dozen photographs, handing each exposed plate to her ladyship to be stowed in a leather bag. A dozen times Patrick flashed the magnesium lamp, each time turning his head to avoid seeing the awful glare of white light, like the light of the Resurrection, on the dead man's face.

With the last flash, a reflection on the floor by the wall, not far from the spot where his shillings were hidden, caught Patrick's eye. It was a shiny brass cartridge casing, almost an inch long and perhaps a third of an inch in diameter. He was about to pick it up when Lady Sheridan stopped him.

"There might be fingerprints," she cautioned.

"Fingerprints?" Patrick asked dubiously.

"Marks made by the tip of someone's finger, and visible only with special inspection. It is a new means of identifying criminals." She raised her voice. "Charles, come and see what Patrick has discovered. It's a bullet!"

Patrick was still not quite sure what a fingerprint might be, but he knew a casing when he saw it, thanks to the hours he had spent shooting with Mr. Tudwell. "It's a casing, not a bullet," he said. "And it was not here two days ago, when I came to—" He was about to say, *to put two shillings behind the stone,* but thought better of it. "When I came to look at the pigeons."

"Patrick is correct. It is a casing." Lord Sheridan knelt and studied the shiny brass cylinder where it lay, not touching it. "But it's very odd, I must say."

"What's odd about it?" Lady Sheridan asked, bending over for a closer look.

"Well, for one thing," his lordship said, "the size and nature of the wound led me to assume that the coast guard was killed by a pistol."

In spite of himself, Patrick's eyes were drawn to Captain Smith's bloody jacket. The hole, just above the dead man's silver watch-chain, was small and neat. He had seen birds and rabbits peppered with shotgun pellets. This was different.

"But this cartridge would not fit any pistol with which I'm familiar," Lord Sheridan went on. "If indeed the weapon was a pistol, it is of a very unusual type." He stood, hands on hips, surveying the scene. "And notice the distance between the casing and the body." He took out and unfolded an ivory rule and measured it off.

"Eight feet, four inches," he muttered. "Remarkable. Quite remarkable."

"I'm afraid I don't understand, Charles," Lady Sheridan said apologetically. "What is so remarkable about the distance?"

"Look here." His lordship went back to bend over Captain Smith's body. "There are powder burns on the victim's jacket," he said, pointing, "where the bullet entered. This would suggest that he was shot at very close range—a foot, no more." He cocked his head, speaking half to himself. "Why, then, is the casing *there*, by the wall, a full seven feet from the point where the gun was fired?"

"I don't see any great difficulty," her ladyship returned. "The killer likely picked up the cartridge from the point where it fell and tossed it there."

But Patrick was beginning to see the direction of Lord Sheridan's observations, and the logic behind them. "That's not the way it would have happened," he said excitedly. "A man using a revolver would have left the mill with the casing still in the cylinder. He would not have broken it open, ejected the cartridge, and tossed it away. And if by some chance he broke open the pistol, he would have put the spent cartridge in his pocket, or let it fall where he stood."

"Very observant, Patrick!" his lordship exclaimed. "We shall make a detective of you yet. But should we exclude a rifle as the murder weapon? Some modern rifles do have an ejection mechanism that could have tossed the cartridge casing that distance."

"I have never handled a rifle," Patrick said thoughtfully, "but my father once shot an Afghan at three hundred yards with his, so it must be a very powerful weapon. Wouldn't a rifle bullet have gone right through him, and hit the wall?" As he said the words, he shuddered.

"Bravo!" Lord Sheridan said. "Indeed it would. But it did not, for I have looked. There is no sign of an exit wound."

Patrick reflected for a moment. "I don't think Captain Smith would have let anyone with a rifle get close to him."

His lordship nodded. "In his line of business, he would probably have developed strong suspicions where weapons were concerned. A pistol, however, can be hidden."

"Yes," Patrick said. "If Captain Smith thought the man was his friend ..." He stopped. He had occasionally seen Mr. Tudwell and Captain Smith in conversation at the Black Horse, or walking on the High Street. They had certainly seemed to be friends.

"You say, Charles," Lady Sheridan mused, "that there is no exit wound. So the bullet remains in the victim's body?"

"Yes," his lordship replied. "Until the autopsy, when it will be extracted. That will give us more information about the gun that fired it. And there are several other things. Look at this." He bent over and pointed to a closely smoked cigarette butt. "One might think that Captain Smith had been sitting here for some time, waiting. And there is this, too." From the dusty floor, close beside the dead man's thigh, he carefully picked up a small piece of green pasteboard, holding it by the corner.

"It looks like a ticket," her ladyship said. "A ticket to what, I wonder."

Patrick knew the answer to that, and he felt a strange relief as he said, "It's a ticket to the bathing machines on the beach. Trunky Thomas owns them. You have to pay him before you can use one. Everybody complains that he charges too much."

"Something tells me," Lord Sheridan said dryly, "that the victim would not have been in the habit of frequenting the local bathing machines."

"No," Patrick said thoughtfully. "He wouldn't." Now

that he thought of it, he realized that Harry Tudwell was not the only man he had seen walking and talking with the coast guard. Trunky Thomas knew him, too. In fact, he had seen the two of them huddled together, talking, not long after the first coast guard's body had been dragged onto the beach.

"Ah," Lord Sheridan said, "I think, then, we should have a talk with Mr. Thomas." He went back to the cartridge casing, inserted a stick in it, and placed it carefully in his handkerchief, wrapping it up. He glanced at Patrick. "You know this village, Patrick, and you must have some information about what is going on here. Is there anything you can tell us about this crime?"

Patrick half turned away, wondering how much his lordship knew about Rottingdean's nocturnal enterprise. All things considered, he himself didn't know very much for certain, beyond the fact that the villagers—almost all of them, as far as he could tell—had been involved in digging out the old tunnels and were now engaged in the smuggling business. He couldn't, for example, say where the goods were coming from or where they were going, or what besides spirits, wine, tea, tobacco, and fancy dress goods might be involved. And he certainly didn't know who had killed Captain Smith, although he had to admit to feeling grateful to whoever had dropped the ticket, for it opened the way to at least one other explanation of what had happened here. And although he had run his share of errands for Mr. Tudwell and carried his share of messages, whatever he said would be a guess, and Lord Charles was asking for information, not guesses. Besides, there was no need to tell more than was necessary at any one time, and he had already told quite a lot. He shook his head.

Lord Sheridan looked disappointed, but only nodded. "Let's go over the floor carefully, then. When we are finished, we'll go outside to wait for the constable from Brighton."

They searched in silence for ten minutes or so but discovered nothing else, and when Patrick stepped into the morning light, he wasn't sure whether he should be glad or sorry. Even for someone as intelligent as his lordship, it must not be easy to discover who had killed a man when the only clues were a cartridge casing and a ticket to a bathing machine. It was entirely possible that the killer of Captain Smith would go forever undiscovered. But whether that would be a good thing or a bad, he was not yet sure.

"Lady Burne-Jones and I should like to drive to Black Rock this morning, Patrick," Lady Sheridan said, interrupting his thoughts. "We hope to visit the widow of the young coast guard who died earlier. But neither of us are sure of the way to the cottage. Will you go with us and point it out?"

Patrick was silent for a moment, thinking of Harry Tudwell, to whom he owed so much and who counted on him, and weighing out the consequences of doing this or that, or saying the one thing or the other. But surely there was no difficulty in pointing out the Black Rock Coast Guard Station to such a lovely lady.

"It's not hard to find," he said. "You can't miss the white cottage and the flagpole. But I'll go with you, if you like."

Lady Sheridan put her hand on his shoulder. "Very good. This morning air has made me hungry. Shall we walk down to North End House and see if there might be some breakfast waiting for us there?"

Patrick was glad enough to oblige.

14

"A German colleague in Natural History asked an old Spanish lawyer [in Chile] what he thought of the King of England sending out a collector [Charles Darwin] to his country to pick up lizards and beetles and to break stones. The old gentleman thought seriously for some time and then said, 'It is not well ... No man is so rich as to send out people to pick up such rubbish ... if one of us were to go and do such things in England do not you think the King of England would very soon send us out of his country?'"

—CHARLES DARWIN
The Voyage of the Beagle

"Here begins the Great Game."
—RUDYARD KIPLING
Kim

KATE HAD THOUGHT of taking the Panhard for the trip to Black Rock, but Charles wanted it to drive to Brighton to attend the autopsy, should it be held that day. So when Aunt Georgie suggested that they take her dog cart, Kate readily agreed.

It was an early hour for calling, but Aunt Georgie was energetically determined to inquire into the welfare of the young widow, and as equally determined, when they returned, to begin her canvas of the village in order to discover what might be learned about the murders. And Kate, for her part, was also anxious to talk to Mrs. Radford. She might know something that could shed some light on the questions left by the two deaths. It was a pity to intrude on her grief, Kate thought, but better that the questions were asked by two sympathetic women than by one unfeeling man.

Aunt Georgie chirped to the pony that Mr. Mounter had brought round, Patrick leapt up behind in the four-wheeled cart, and they were off. As they drove up the High Street in the direction of the sea, Kate saw small clumps of people talking together, and she guessed that word of Captain Smith's murder was beginning to make its way around the village. One trio of gossiping women included her own cook-housekeeper, Mrs. Portney, who had a basket over her arm and was animatedly discussing something with the other two. Mrs. Portney glanced up, a look of consternation crossing her pinched face when she saw Patrick. She elbowed one of the others, who turned to stare, narrow-eyed, as they drove past. Patrick himself sat with hunched shoulders, his head down, and Kate hoped that she had not put the boy into some further difficulty by asking him to come with them.

Black Rock lay on the Dover Coach Road on the way to Brighton, about two and a half miles to the west of Rottingdean. When they came to the steep climb up the shoulder of Beacon Hill, just outside the village, Patrick jumped out to walk and spare the pony his weight. Once at the top, they could see almost to Brighton, where the shining groins reached out long fingers into the ocean.

Before them, between grassy banks, stretched the white ribbon of narrow road, its surface powdered to a fine chalk by horses' hooves and wagon wheels. On the left was the heaving ocean, stretching to the southern horizon, on the right, the rolling downs lifting to the north. The early mist had given way to a bright blue sky, dazzling sunshine that turned the ocean to a silver glitter, and a clean salt breeze. It was a fine day for a drive, Kate thought—or it would have been, if their purpose had not been so gloomy.

Aunt Georgie, her shoulders straight, her mouth set in a firm line, guided the pony past Beacon Hill, where a small knot of uniformed men and several horses and wagons stood in front of the windmill. "Those must be the men of Brighton's chief constable," she said. "I'm glad to see that Sir Robert received my telegram and came so promptly."

Kate did not correct Aunt Georgie's mistaken impression, for she had not told her that the Prince had assigned Charles to the case and had instructed the Brighton chief constable to assist him. She also refrained from telling her of the investigation that she and Charles and the boy had made that morning, not because she did not trust Aunt Georgie but because she could not be sure of the servants. Mr. and Mrs. Mounter were villagers, and Kate was beginning to wonder just how many of Rottingdean's inhabitants might be involved, one way or another, in this mysterious affair.

Patrick had jumped back into the cart and the pony was about to start the downhill slope of Beacon Hill when they were met by a comical-looking man with fuzzy gray sidewhiskers, wearing a waterproof cloak, wide-brimmed canvas hat, and drab breeches. He had a knobbed walking stick in one hand, a map in the other, and a bulging knapsack on his shoulder, from which hung a rock hammer, a telescope case, a large silver compass, a drinking cup and paired fork and spoon, and a closed wicker basket. He was wearing smoked-glass eye preservers against the ocean's glare, and had a meerschaum pipe in his mouth. He waved at them to stop, and Aunt Georgie reined in the pony.

"Good morning, dear ladies," the man said humbly, stuffing the pipe into his pocket and snatching off his hat to reveal hair that was darker than his whiskers. He spoke in a Continental accent, with an almost droll lift at the end of each sentence. "Pardon, but may one inquire whether you are acquainted with the cause of the commotion there by the windmill?"

"It is the chief constable from Brighton," Aunt Georgie said importantly, "Sir Robert Pinckney. He is investigating the death of the captain of the coast guard."

"A death?" the man said, and shook his head sadly. "An accident, one must presume?"

"A murder," Aunt Georgie replied.

Kate could not see the man's eyes, which were hidden behind his smoked lenses, but his mouth seemed to take on a wry twist. "Good heavens!" he exclaimed, and replaced his hat. "A coast guard captain murdered, in so pure and virtuous a village? And how was the poor chap killed, pray tell?"

Kate frowned, wondering at the man's odd interest. But everything about the fellow struck her as absurd, as if he were some sort of caricature. Aunt Georgie, on the other hand, who accepted people as they came, answered with perfect sincerity.

"He was shot," she replied. "It is the second death in only a few days. The other was a coast guard, as well."

"Then coast-guarding would seem to be a most hazardous occupation," the man remarked. "One wonders whether the other was murdered too?"

"That is not clear," Aunt Georgie said. "The inquiry has yet to be held." She cocked her head to one side. "Your occupation, sir, and your business in our village?"

"I?" he replied. He stroked his side-whiskers. "I am an antiquarian with a deep interest in the early settlements of this region. I have been making a survey for a paper I am preparing for the *Journal of Antiquarian Investigations*. Specifically, I am searching for antiquities and artifacts of the Celtic Iron Age." He unrolled the map. "Yours is not the first village situated at this location, dear ladies. The earliest settlements were of the Neolithic period, about two and one half centuries before the present era, but they continued through the Bronze and into the Iron Age. After a rain, one can still see the trace of the mounds and ditches and walls of the Flint People. And I must tell you"—he gestured toward the windmill—"that your unfortunate coast guard is not the first to die upon that hill. According to my researches, it is also the site of a burial pit from the late Iron Age, containing the skeletons of four adults and—"

"Indeed," Aunt Georgie said, lifting the reins. "Well, that is all very interesting, sir, but I am afraid we cannot linger. However, if you will call at North End House some afternoon, I shall be glad to hear more of what you have learned. I am a member of the Parish Council and could arrange for you to address the entire village, if you like. Our school house is available for lectures of general interest."

The man whipped off his hat again and bowed gallantly. "I should be delighted to make such an address, Madam Council Member. May one humbly inquire as to your esteemed name?"

"I am Georgiana Burne-Jones," Aunt Georgie replied, "and this is Lady Charles Sheridan."

"And your name, sir?" Kate asked quickly, thinking that she would mention the encounter to Charles. Despite the man's whimsical appearance and manner, his questions struck her as having some purpose at which she could not guess.

"I am Professor Waldemar Hertling," the man said. "Please do not allow me to detain you further." And he bowed again, so smartly that Kate almost expected him to click his heels together.

"What an odd man," Kate remarked, when they had driven on. "I don't think I've ever seen anyone like him before."

"Well, I've seen *him* before," Patrick said scornfully. "He comes around every few months, digging and poking and measuring in the oddest places."

"I doubt he is much of an antiquarian," Aunt Georgie declared. "Those four skeletons he mentioned—they were dug up some thirty years ago, and I'm sure he had nothing to do with the digging. Certainly it is no news to any of us who have lived in this area."

"I wonder," Kate said thoughtfully, "why he was asking about the coast guard." She turned halfway around in the seat to speak to Patrick, who was sitting sideways in the cart. "You seemed to have been acquainted with Captain Smith. What kind of man was he?"

Patrick looked at her, and she saw the furrow between his eyes and heard the hesitation in his voice, as if he were choosing his words. "I only know what people have said of him, really. He came here just after I did—that would be three years ago. I don't think he was much liked in the village."

"Why?"

Patrick shrugged. "He liked to have things his own way. I don't know much about it. He was above the other coast guards, though."

"That's right," Aunt Georgie said, using the brake to slow the cart's descent, so that it would not injure the pony. "The coast guard at Rottingdean is a captain. The coast guards of Black Rock and Saltdean take their orders from him."

"And what do coast guards do, exactly?" Kate asked.

They had reached the steepest part of the hill, and Patrick jumped out of the cart and walked alongside. "They patrol the cliffs every night. The coast guard from Black Rock walks to the east and meets the Rottingdean captain at an appointed spot along the cliffs, and then walks back again. The captain walks to the east and meets the Saltdean coast guard and walks back again. That's their job—patrolling the coast. Each has a three-mile stretch, more or less."

"But if there is no more smuggling," Kate asked curiously, "why do they patrol? Are they supposed to watch for sailors in distress?"

Patrick gave a short, hard, curiously adult laugh. "No more smuggling?"

Feeling that they were close to getting somewhere at last, Kate was about to ask him what he meant. But just at that moment, they heard the blare of a motorcar horn behind them, and Aunt Georgie, making soothing noises, hastily guided the pony to the verge. It was Charles in the Panhard, with a portly, frock-coated man—Sir Robert Pinckney, the chief constable of Brighton, according to Aunt Georgie. Patrick ran to hold the pony's head and they waited until the motorcar had passed, Charles and his passenger waving at them. When Patrick climbed back into the cart, he seemed to have regretted his ironic remark, and Kate could get no more out of him.

Black Rock was a terrace of small villas facing the sea, one of them doing duty as a post office. Beyond the villas with their banked-up gardens was a prosperous-looking farm with a sign announcing that it was owned by Charles Cowley, and then Patrick pointed out the whitewashed, slate-roofed Black Rock Coast Guard Station. The station stood on the downs side of the road behind a hedge of tamarisk bushes, a flagstaff topped with the coast guard's white ensign set just inside the gate. On the worn stone doorstep, under a bower of late-blooming red roses, sat a forlorn boy of five or six, a twig broom beside him. His head was down, his shoulders sagging dejectedly. Two solicitous white geese stood guard beside him as if to ward off intruders, and a trio of white chickens was pecking at the dirt.

Aunt Georgie stopped the cart, took a cloth-covered basket from beneath the seat, and they all got out. Patrick stood by the pony's head while Kate and Aunt Georgie went up to the boy. The geese stretched out their necks, hissing, but Aunt Georgie ignored them.

"Is your mother at home, child?" she asked gently.

The boy lifted his tear-stained face. "In there, mum," he said, jerking his head. "Me dad's bin drownded. She's cryin'."

"Well, don't *you* cry," Aunt Georgie commanded. "Your mother needs a man to help her about the house, my lad, and you must fill your father's shoes."

"Fill me dad's shoes?" The boy's eyes widened. "Oh, no, mum. They're too big fer me. But I kin 'elp me mother." And he jumped up and began to sweep the path, tears raining down his face.

Kate felt the unutterable pathos in the child's words and longed to comfort him. But she knew she could not. Only time would heal the loss of the father he had loved—and perhaps not even that. Perhaps he would carry the scar to his dying day.

The door was ajar, and they knocked and entered at a woman's bidding. After the brightness of sea and sky, the inside of the cottage was so dark that it was a moment before Kate could see. There appeared to be two rooms, side by side, with a third smaller one behind—a kitchen, perhaps, or a pantry—and a loft above. The brick-floored room into which they had entered was fitted with a small writing desk in the brightest corner, beside a casement window curtained in checked gingham, a paraffin lamp on a shelf above it. A cheaply framed print of the Queen and the Prince Consort hung on the wall, and a man's black oilskins hung from a peg beside it. A table and two benches were arranged in front of the fireplace, which held the cold ashes of a small fire. An earthenware teapot and three empty plates puddled with grease—the remains of breakfast—lay at one end of the table, and through the door into the other room, Kate could see a small child, a boy, asleep on a narrow cot, his blond hair rumpled, his thumb in his mouth. To one side of the fireplace, in a stuffed chair that was the only comfortable piece of furniture in the room, sat a woman in a dark woolen dress, a shawl drawn tightly around her. She looked up.

"Good morning, Mrs. Radford," Aunt Georgie said cordially. "I am Lady Burne-Jones, and this is Lady Sheridan. We have come to offer our heartfelt condolences at the loss of your husband." She put the basket on the table. "I have brought some elderberry wine, a kidney pie, and some jam puffs."

"Thank 'ee," the woman said, in a voice that was scarcely more than a whisper. "Yer more'n kind, I'm sure, milady." She was slight and very young, barely above twenty-one or -two, Kate thought, with chestnut hair pulled back severely from her child's face. She struggled to rise but could not, and was taken by a fit of coughing that shook her slender shoulders.

"Please, don't get up, Mrs. Radford," Kate said. Impulsively, she went to the child-woman and knelt beside the chair. "We know this is a terrible time for you and your children. If there is any way that we can help, you must allow us to try." But the words, so conventional, seemed paltry and thin to her own ears. Mere speech could not comfort a woman who had lost her husband in such a terrible way. Words could not recompense the children for the loss of their father, who would have guided them to manhood by his own manhood's example. Kate thought briefly of Charles, sorrowing for the son he would never have, and knew that the sorrow of these sons for their father must be equally sharp.

But Aunt Georgie was not at a loss for words. "Yes, my dear," she said crisply. "As a member of the Rottingdean Parish Council, I speak for the entire parish when I say that we will be glad to offer you whatever assistance you may require. You shall have to leave this station, as it will be wanted for the man who will take your husband's place. But I shall see that housing is arranged in one of the village's poor-relief cottages for you and your children, and food and clothing provided as well. Of course the boys shall be put to school, and some sort of work shall be found for you. We have recently appointed a new group of Poor Law Overseers who are responsible for the village charities, and I can guarantee you that even though you may have no money, you will not go hungry nor homeless. Our village has a good heart, and is compassionate toward the needy." She opened her purse and drew out a piece of paper and pencil, looking around the room as if she were assessing the condition and value of its furnishings. "Now, then. Shall we make a list of what you have and what you need so that I can report your requirements to the Overseers?"

Kate knew that these offers stemmed from Aunt Georgie's compassionate conviction that society should take care of those who could not care for themselves, and from her own sympathetic kindliness. But she couldn't help cringing at the older woman's tone, which to her ears sounded patronizing and disrespectful.

If Mrs. Radford was offended, however, she did not show it. She merely said, "Oh, ye're too kind, to be sure," and even the quietly spoken words brought on another fit of coughing which quickly turned into weeping. Aunt Georgie, truly soft-hearted beneath her officious exterior, dropped her pencil and paper and gathered up the young woman into her arms with a murmured "There, there, now, my dear. Cry if you must."

Kate took the teapot into the tiny but immaculate kitchen, which proved to contain a coal cooker with the remnants of a fire. She poked it until it blazed up, filled the kettle with water from a bucket on the wooden sink, and in a few minutes had produced a pot of fragrant tea.

A few moments after that, sipping her tea gratefully, Mrs. Radford was calm enough to say, with a quiet dignity, "I'm obliged to ye fer yer 'elp, but me and the childern wudn't like to go on the poor-relief. Me brother is comin' t'morrer, to 'elp me bury George, if they gives me 'is body back. Arterwards, he'll fetch us to Manchester, to live wi' me mum. I'll go out to char, and she'll look arter the boys." She looked around at the dark room. "'Tis a sad thing to leave this fine, big cottage and the garden and the chickens an' geese. The boys wuz 'appy 'ere, in the clean air. 'Tain't so clean in Manchester, and me mum's 'ouse is none so fine." Her voice took on a firmer tone and she gave Aunt Georgie a sideways glance. "But the boys'll go to school. I'll make sure o' that."

Kate drew one of the benches near Mrs. Radford's chair. "You and your family have lived here long?"

"Near on two years." The young woman put up a hand and pushed an escaping tendril behind her ear. A tender look crossed her face. "George loved the sea—oh, 'ow 'e

137

loved it. 'E used to go over the road and stand on the cliff and watch the ships and the fog blowin' in across the water." The tenderness turned to a sour indignation. "But 'e din't throw himself into it, as some in Rottingdean is tryin' to say."

"Who has told you that he had?" Aunt Georgie asked in a sharp voice.

"Why, th' constable's bin 'ere, o'course," Mrs. Radford said bleakly. "'E sez George flung hisself off the cliff and some'ow fell on 'is blade afore 'e tumbled into the water, and that's wot killed 'im. 'E wanted me to say that George was dark by nature, and giv'n to fits o' despair. But it's not true—that 'e threw hisself off, I mean." She took a deep breath, seeming stronger. "And 'e didn't stumble off drunk, neither. George wuz a good man 'oo loved 'is babes and me. He wuz proud and honest in 'is work as a coast guard, too—not like some 'oo cud be named. I won't 'ave it said otherwise!" The last was exclaimed with a painful bitterness, and followed by another violent fit of coughing.

"I shall speak to Constable Woodhouse," Aunt Georgie said imperiously. "Whatever the fact of the matter, he had no business speaking to you in such a manner."

Kate went quickly to the tiny kitchen to fetch a cup, poured it half full of the elderberry wine Aunt Georgie had brought, and put it to the young woman's lips. "Drink this," she commanded. "It will ease the coughing."

When Mrs. Radford was herself again, Kate took her seat again and asked, in an even, quiet voice, "Did your husband tell you that there were others who were *not* honest in their work as coast guards?"

Aunt Georgie drew in her breath sharply, but Mrs. Radford did not appear to notice. She had lifted her head and was gazing at Kate, her luminous dark eyes filled with something that might have been distress or fear or anger, or all three.

Kate met her gaze squarely and found something in it so compelling that she heard herself speaking before she had thought what to say. "Whatever you tell us, Mrs. Radford, will be entirely secure. We shan't say or do anything that could bring harm to you or the children—more harm than you have already innocently suffered, which is more than any should bear. But if you have any information, I shall ask my husband to use it to clear your husband's name of the charge of suicide. Lord Sheridan is skilled in criminal investigations and has connections at the highest levels of government. He will do what he can to see your husband exonerated."

The moment the rash promise had flown out of her mouth Kate regretted it. What gave her the right to speak for Charles, or to encourage this poor woman to pin her hope to a truth that might prove false? She had no idea what a full and careful investigation might reveal. Charles might discover that George Radford had indeed been drawn into some sort of illegal activity and had been murdered by his criminal cohorts, or had done himself to death out of guilt and shame for his dishonorable deeds. For his grieving widow, outrage would be added to anguish, and she would be justified in thinking herself and her children betrayed by someone who had promised help and friendship.

The silence was suddenly broken by the raucous gabble of the geese. Then the doorway darkened and Kate felt, rather than saw, that Patrick had come to the door. But Mrs. Radford, whose eyes were fastened on Kate's face, seemed not to see that he was standing on the stone step. She must have read some reassurance there, for after a moment she gave a slight nod and stretched out her hand.

Kate took it, feeling the fingers icy cold.

"'Tis Cap'n Smith," she whispered. "'E's the one 'oo deals in crooked goods. Remove Cap'n Smith, is wot George said 'ad to be done. Remove Cap'n Smith, and it'll all end."

"What will end?" Kate asked, suddenly recollecting that the captain *had* been removed, although Mrs. Radford could not have known it.

Mrs. Radford cast down her eyes, and Kate thought she was not going to answer. But a moment later, she raised them again, now full of a flashing anger. "Are ye blind?" she demanded fiercely. "Are ye foolish? Why, th' smugglin', o'course. The 'ole village is in on't! 'Ow d'ye think a woman as poor and lowly as Dor'thy 'Oward could open a dress shop, I ask ye?" She seemed to take courage from her own words, for she pulled herself up straight in the chair and turned her gaze, withering now, and scornful, on Aunt Georgie.

"You think yer so 'igh 'n' mighty, milady, wi' yer poor-relief cottages and yer overseers an' such. Yer village may have a good 'eart, but its soul is rotten right through. And my brave, pure 'usband, God bless 'im, knew all about it an' wuz ready to tell th' truth. So they killed 'im."

"*Who* killed him?" Kate asked sharply. "How do you know?"

But Mrs. Radford had said all she could. She fell into such a savage bout of weeping that Kate and Aunt Georgie could do nothing but wait until she had quieted a little, and then take their leave. As they left the cottage and were walking down the path to the dog cart, Kate saw a wagon passing, the team of horses driven by a uniformed constable. In the back of the wagon lay two sheet-covered corpses.

George Radford and Captain Smith might have been enemies in life, but they were making their final journey together.

15

"'I wonder,' Charles said, 'if you would like to see the X-ray photographs I made yesterday of the bones of my hand. They are really quite remarkable. Would you care to come down to the laboratory?'

The men all rose. 'Ah, science,' Hodson said with a half-bitter mockery. 'What subtle secrets it reveals! The latent pattern of the tip of the finger, the shadow of the bone beneath the flesh.'

Dr. Bassett, however, was more impressed. 'The bones of the hand,' he marveled. 'Think of the applications in medical science. And who knows? Soon we may be able to watch the very heart as it beats.'

'And soon,' Kate said, rather more somberly, 'we will have no secrets at all.'"

—ROBIN PAIGE
Death at Devil's Bridge

ARMS FOLDED ACROSS his chest, Charles watched the autopsy surgeon—who also happened to be the Queen's coroner for Brighton—at work. Dr. Barriston was experienced, precise, and methodical, although his humor took a macabre turn. Just now, he was elbow-deep in the body of George Radford, cheerfully singing a popular Gilbert and Sullivan ditty, "I Am the Very Model of a Modern Major-General." Charles pulled out his watch. Twenty of twelve. They were making good progress.

"With many cheerful facts about the square of the hypotenuse," Dr. Barriston remarked, and pulled the white sheet over George Radford's face. "Well done, old chap. You've told us as much as you're able. Pity you can't tell us who skewered you." He glanced at the chief constable. "Satisfied, Sir Robert?"

Sir Robert Pinckney, chief constable of Brighton, turned to the fair-haired, ruddy-faced young constable standing at the foot of the table, a notebook in his hand. The young constable wore a strained look and his lips were pressed tightly together.

"Your notes are complete, Soames? Do you require any further clarification?" At the shake of the young man's head, he turned back to the doctor. "Satisfied enough," he said grimly.

Barriston nodded. He was a stocky man with wild gray hair and gold-rimmed glasses, garbed in a blood-stained white laboratory smock. Singing *"I am very well acquainted, too, with matters mathematical, I understand equations, both the simple and quadratical,"* he went to a porcelain sink on one side of the room, turned on a tap, and began to scrub his hands vigorously. The water ran red.

"I take it, then, Paul," Charles said, "that you believe Radford's stab wound to be neither accidental nor self-inflicted."

Barriston left *"I quote in elegiacs all the crimes of Heliogabalus"* hanging in mid-phrase. "Neither, Charlie," he said, over his shoulder. "The gouge on the dorsal surface of the fourth rib can only have resulted from the weapon entering from behind, with considerable force, I might add. It was neither self-inflicted nor accidental—unless you wish to entertain the possibility that the deceased wedged a short sword into a tree and backed against it with sufficient strength to drive it completely through." He reached for a towel and began to dry his hands.

The fair-haired constable snorted a laugh, then quickly covered his mouth and pretended to cough.

Charles allowed himself a small smile. 'And the man was not drowned?"

"In a word, no." The doctor took off his glasses, rinsed them under the tap, and dried them on the towel. "You saw the abrasions on the wrists and ankles. The victim spent some hours in the water, roped, most likely, to some sort of weight. But he was quite dead when he went in the water. Quite dead, poor chap." He hooked his glasses over his ears. "Now, then, gentlemen. Shall we have luncheon?"

"Let's be done with it," Sir Robert growled. He jerked his head toward the sheet-draped body on the other porcelain-topped table. "I don't exactly fancy eating with that job in front of me."

The doctor sighed heavily. "Oh, very well. Although I should tell you that Mrs. McCormick, who is a very fine cook, is preparing an excellent partridge pie." He lifted his nose and sniffed the air like a hopeful dog. "Ah, I can smell it now. The kitchen is just down this passageway, you know. Are you sure you won't reconsider?"

"I think," Charles said tactfully, "that we should see what's involved in this one first. We are especially anxious to retrieve the fatal bullet."

The body of Captain Smith was lying on the other table, and they went to stand beside it. The doctor stripped off the sheet, bent closely over the body, and began a careful visual inspection, muttering *"In short, in matters vegetable, animal, and mineral, I am the very model of a modern Major-General"* After several moments he looked up at Charles. "Seems like a fairly straightforward gunshot wound to me. In at the front, with no sign that it went out at the back. Why are you so keen on digging out the bullet? D'you intend to use it again?"

Charles raised one eyebrow. "The very model of a modern Major-General has not included forensic ballistics in his curriculum?"

"Ah," Barriston said wisely. "You intend to try a few of Professor Lacassagne's parlor tricks, eh? Hope to nail our corpse's killer with a few trifling rifling grooves, do you?" He lifted his voice. *"When I have learnt what progress has been made in modern gunnery, When I know more of tactics than a novice in a nunnery—"*

"As a matter of fact," Charles said mildly, "I am following Lacassagne's example, although I don't think it is the rifling pattern we are after. The weapon is likely to be so unique that—" He shrugged. "But we will know more when we see the bullet, perhaps."

"You may, but I shall still be in the dark," Barriston replied. *"For my military knowledge, though I'm plucky and adventury, Has only been brought down to the beginning of the century.* However, since you are set on excavating for the bullet, I would suggest that we locate its exact position with an X-ray before we slice the captain open and begin burrowing like moles in his innards."

"An X-ray?" Sir Robert asked, narrowing his eyes.

"Exactly," Charles said. "A bullet often changes course radically after it enters the body, particularly if the projectile is traveling at a high velocity, or if it ricochets off a bone. An X-ray can locate it with great accuracy."

"I say amen to that," Barriston declared emphatically. "Fishing around among the organs is messy and time-consuming, and there is always the chance that one will miss the projectile amidst the mess of liver, intestines, and so forth. An X-ray can save all that bloody trouble. Besides, it is of great scientific interest—revealing the secrets of the human anatomy and all that."

Sir Robert looked at Charles. "Why do you assume that the bullet is of a high velocity?"

"Because the cartridge indicates that it is a small caliber bullet with a large powder charge," Charles replied. He nodded at the doctor. "I believe the X-ray is in order, Paul."

The doctor grinned. "Well, well. You still have an interest in this sort of thing, then? Still have your own X-ray equipment, do you?"

"Absolutely," Charles replied emphatically. "I happen to consider the X-ray one of the most promising scientific developments of the decade. I have sent for my manservant, Lawrence Quibbley. He is skilled at developing X-ray films and can manage it for us, if you like."

The doctor nodded approvingly. "Well, then, we may have an early lunch after all. If you will be good enough to position our captain's table under the Crookes tube. I'll fetch the first film. Since the wound is in the center of the chest, we'll take two overlapping X-rays. Wherever the bullet has got to, we shall be sure to spot the little devil."

While the doctor went for film, the three men shifted the heavy table under a glass bulb suspended by a chain at eye level and connected to several wires. The wires looped across the ceiling and down the closest wall to a square wooden box from the side of which protruded a lever. In a moment, the doctor returned with a heavy paper envelope, some twelve by eighteen inches.

"Now, if you'll be good enough to raise the fellow's shoulders a bit," he directed, "I'll slide this film beneath him. I've brought only this, having learned that one must

145

keep one's spare film out of the room." He chuckled wryly. "I fogged an entire pack before I learned that small detail. The rays are quite pervasive."

As Charles and the chief constable raised the dead man, the doctor slid the envelope onto the table and positioned it under the upper torso. "There," he said, standing back. "Are we ready to begin?"

"How does it work?" the young constable asked curiously. "It would seem impossible for light rays to penetrate solid flesh."

"'O! that this too too solid flesh would melt, eh?" Barriston replied. "But you see, you have made a fundamental error, my boy. These are not light rays. They are invisible rays of a mysterious and arcane nature yet unknown, created by a powerful electric current passing through the partially evacuated Crookes tube. They are capable of penetrating both vegetable and animal matter." He held up a finger. "Observe closely, while *I hum a fugue of which I've heard the music's din afore, and whistle all the airs from that infernal nonsense Pinafore.*" Whistling, he went to the box on the wall, threw the lever, and the bulb glowed briefly with an eerie green light.

"There," he said. "Did you see it?"

"See wot?" the young constable demanded. "I saw a green light, that's all."

"Ah, but therein lies the mystery, my naive young friend!" Barriston exclaimed. "Unseen by you, the invisible rays penetrated right through the captain's carcass, casting a shadow image on the photographic film placed beneath him. When it is developed, we shall see the shadow of his spine, his barrel of ribs, and the bullet that did him in. What do you think of that, eh? No more secrets—all, all is revealed. Quite, quite *parabolous*, wouldn't you say?"

The ruddy-faced constable stirred nervously. "Yes, but if

these X-rays go through dead bodies, wot keeps 'em from goin' through live ones?"

"Why, nothing at all," the doctor said. "In fact, they just went right through all of us in this room." He smiled reassuringly. "I shouldn't worry, though. They are perfectly safe. I have been using the X-ray for some months now, and I have not yet had a patient show so much as a blister or rash. On a clear day, the bright sun can do a great deal more damage to us." He rubbed his hands happily. "Now, we shall position another sheet of film under the middle to lower torso and take a second X-ray. And then, gentlemen, we can enjoy our lunch while Sheridan's assistant does his work."

Charles himself had wondered about the safety of X-rays. The materials and techniques used in photography were on the cutting edge of both chemistry and physics, and the hazards involved were often not fully appreciated. Compressed acetylene had been used for photographic lighting until just recently, and several disastrous explosions had occurred before the danger of compressing the gas became evident. But since he had no evidence of any potential danger, he chose to keep his reservations to himself.

And so, to the accompaniment of *Then I can write a washing bill in Babylonic cuneiform, And tell you ev'ry detail of Caractacus's uniform*, they completed the second X-ray and handed both films over to Lawrence Quibbley. In the doctor's dining room, Charles, Sir Robert, the young constable, and Barriston sat down to the epicurean pleasures of not just one but two fragrant partridge pies, a large apple pudding, and a bottle of excellent wine. They were still lingering over cigars when Lawrence entered the room and handed the exposed films to Charles.

"Thank you, Lawrence," Charles said. "Stay near, will

you? I shall want you to return to Rottingdean with me. We have one or two jobs to do there." He gave the films to Barriston, who took them to the window.

"Ah, yes, indeed. There's the little mischief-maker," the doctor said with satisfaction. He pointed to it with his fork. "Lodged just under the right clavicle, having been deflected from a rib."

"That's it? That's the bullet that killed 'im?" the constable whispered, awed. "That little white thing?"

"That's it," Barriston said happily. "All, all is revealed. No secrets from the prying eye of the X-ray, eh, what? Damned good thing, too. We could have missed the bloody trail and poked around for hours before we happened to stumble on it. Now let's go slice the chap open and dig out that little jewel."

Ten minutes later, they were studying the bullet itself, which the doctor had retrieved, wiped, and laid upon Charles's open palm.

Charles pulled out a magnifying lens and studied it. "Four grooves, and a right-hand twist. And it looks to be in very good condition."

Sir Robert pursed his mouth. "You said it struck a rib, Doctor. And yet the bullet shows no sign of deformation."

"That's because it is copper-jacketed," Charles replied. "Copper-jacketed with a lead core at the base."

"Ah," Sir Robert said, and put his hands behind his back. "One of the new military rifle bullets." He frowned. "And yet I thought you concluded, my lord, from the distance at which it was fired, that the weapon was a pistol."

"I hold to that conclusion," Charles said. He turned to the doctor. "Have you ever seen a pistol that fired this sort of bullet?"

"I?" Barriston asked. "Have I ever seen such a weapon?" Whimsically he answered his own question. *"I can tell undoubted Raphaels from Gerard Dows and Zoffanies, I know the croaking chorus from the Frogs of Aristophanes,* but I have not a shred of information about modern ammunition."

"And this is very modern," Sir Robert said. "I've never seen anything like it. But there's a chap in Hoggs Lane who trades in firearms. He might be able to help us."

"Ah, Reginald Barker, an old friend of mine. Give him my regards, would you?" The doctor turned back to the dead captain. "Now, then, why don't the two of you trot along and leave me to finish up our friend here. As a matter of medical curiosity, there are one or two things I want to look into while I have him open." He glanced at Charles. "Do I have to leave him tidy, or does it matter?"

"I can't answer that," Charles said. "I understand that he has no wife or children in Rottingdean, but as to parents—" He shrugged.

The doctor nodded. "I'll sew him up. If there's a funeral, he'll be presentable."

Charles dropped the bullet into a cloth bag, they took their leave, and left the doctor singing cheerfully to himself:

I know our mythic history, King Arthur's and Sir Caradoc's;
I answer hard acrostics, I've a pretty taste for paradox.
In short, in matters vegetable, animal, and mineral,
I am the very model of a modern Major-General.

16

Eggs with Truffles

"Break eight new-laid eggs into a stewpan, to these add four ounces of fresh butter, two ounces of truffles (cut up in very small dice, and simmered in a little butter), a gill of cream, a small piece of glaze, a little nutmeg, mignonette-pepper, and salt; stir this quickly with a wooden spoon over the stove-fire until the eggs, etc., begin to thicken, when the stewpan must be withdrawn; continue to work the eggs with the spoon, observing, that although they must not be allowed to become hard, as in that case the preparation would be curdled and rendered unsightly, yet they must be sufficiently set, so as to be fit to be dished up: to this effect it is necessary to stick the croûtons or fleurons round the inner circle of the dish with a little flour and white-of-egg paste; dish up the eggs in the centre of these, and serve."

—CHARLES FRANCATELLI
The Modern Cook (1896)

IN THE FEW days they had been at Seabrooke House, Kate had come to enjoy the place very much. It was a far cry from the huge, chill London house, suited to Kate's taste and appropriate for a retreat to the seaside. Seabrooke was a large two-story brick residence built in the middle of the last century, with a wide bow window that looked onto the High Street in the front, and a handsome wrought-iron veranda overlooking a generous walled garden in the back, whose stone walls were covered with a medley of pink and red late blooming roses. Beyond the wall were the downs, sweeping eastward in a tranquil harmony of golden grasses and earth and sky.

The drawing room, at the front of the house, had a pretty ceiling in low-relief plasterwork and a white-manteled fireplace topped with an ornate gilt-framed mirror. Oriental carpets were spread on the parquet floor, and on them were arranged a high-backed sofa and two large armchairs, covered in a light damask. In the bow-window recess stood a pretty Pembroke table, topped with a tray on which rested the remains of the luncheon that Amelia had carried to Kate—a plate of cold chicken, a bowl of hot vegetable soup, a custard, some cheese, and a glass of wine, arranged on a lace napkin.

And against the wall beside the recess was a desk, the top pulled down to reveal Kate's Royal typewriter, which she had brought, boxed, in her luggage. It was meant to encourage her to undertake the latest Beryl Bardwell novel, which (as her publisher reminded her, lately with growing impatience) was long overdue. Perhaps, now that she was out of London and away from sad memories, she could begin. She not only had Rud Kipling's encouragement to write a story about Rottingdean's smugglers, she had as well, delivered from The Elms this morning, the draft of a poem from Kipling. The accompanying note said,

"Perhaps these lines will inspire you, Kate. And I quote to you from the old Law: as soon as you find you can do anything, do something you can't."

This was the first verse of Kipling's poem:

If you wake at midnight, and hear a horse's feet,
Don't *go* drawing back the blind, or looking in the street.
Them that asks no questions isn't told a lie.
Watch the wall, my darling, while the Gentlemen go by!
Five and twenty ponies,
Trotting through the dark—
Brandy for the Parson,
'Baccy for the Clerk;
Laces for a lady, letters for a spy,
And watch the wall, my darling, while the Gentlemen go by!

Kate had been intrigued by the lines, but they had not sent her to work on Beryl Bardwell's story. Still holding Kipling's poem in her hand, she sat idly in the recess, her feet pulled up and her arms clasped around her knees, gazing out the window at the peaceful, picturesque scene in the High Street: pedestrians hurrying to Mr. Grantly's grocery or Knapton's tobacco shop, or to the post office or Landsdowne's chemist shop, or to Mrs. Howard's Ladies' Fashions for Fashionable Ladies, several doors down on the opposite side. A young boy in a rough smock herded a half-dozen noisy geese up the middle of the cobblestone street, headed for the pond on the Green, and a shawled woman with two water buckets suspended from a wooden shoulder yoke visited the village pump. Two pretty young nursemaids pushed perambulators toward the beach, and from the opposite direction came the man Kate had met earlier this morning, the self-styled antiquarian. He was still bearing his heavy pack on his back and wearing his smoked-glass eye preservers, even though heavy clouds had come up from the southwest and darkened the sky. He touched the brim of his canvas hat to the blushing, giggling nursemaids, then strode purposefully onward, up the High Street. Where was he going? Kate wondered. Would he call at Aunt Georgie's, since she had invited him to drop in? Or was he off into the downs in search of more antiquities?

It was not quite an hour since Kate and Aunt Georgie had returned from their visit to Mrs. Radford. Lady Burne-Jones, who was usually full of observations and recommendations about everything, seemed to have been considerably chastened by the young widow's bitter outburst. She announced that she had changed her mind about a house-to-house canvas of the village, at least for the moment. Kate herself had been shaken by Mrs. Radford's indictment of the village and profoundly saddened by the sight of the lonely sheet-covered corpses on their way to Brighton in the back of the wagon, and she could not summon much in the way of conversation. Patrick, too, had said very little on the drive back to Rottingdean and had followed Aunt Georgie without a word when she remarked that she could use his help in the garden.

Kate had felt increasingly certain that Patrick knew more than he had told them and she worried that his knowledge, whatever it was, might put him in serious jeopardy from whoever had killed the two coast guards. Privately, out of Patrick's hearing, she had told Aunt Georgie what she feared and suggested that they keep a close eye on him. Aunt Georgie, who seemed genuinely fond of the boy, had readily agreed, adding that she would also see if it would be possible to move him out of Mrs. Higgs's cottage and into North End House, where his comings and goings could be better governed. Kate smiled a little at Aunt Georgie's confidence, since she had the feeling that Patrick was the kind of boy who would resist governing. But it was a step in the right direction. Kate planned to have a serious talk with him once she had thought things through.

That might be some time, however, for a great many questions were tumbling about in Kate's mind in the same confused, inchoate way they often did when Beryl Bardwell was turning over the plot of one of her stories. But these events weren't part of a light, frivolous entertainment created to fill an idle reader's empty hour. They were agonizingly, irrevocably real. A family had been destroyed, a husband and father lost forever, his widow and children forced to leave their home. Two coast guards were dead—one, the captain, a trafficker in smuggled goods. At least, that was Mrs. Radford's claim. What was more, she had implicated the entire village, and her passionate words had rung with the urgent truth of her belief. "Are you blind? Are you foolish?" she had cried. "The whole village is in on it!"

Suddenly struck by the awful significance of the woman's words, Kate half rose from her seat. She must find Charles and tell him what she had heard! But he had not yet returned from Brighton, where he had gone with the chief constable. She would have to watch for him, and when he arrived, tell him the news as quickly as possible. He would want to question Mrs. Radford himself before she left for Manchester, and discover whether her claims had any substance. Perhaps her accusations sprang from her bitter grief.

Kate sank back on the window seat, turning over more questions in her mind. Mrs. Radford had claimed that her husband was not involved in the smuggling. What, then, was the connection between the two murdered coast guards? Had the same person killed both the guilty man and the innocent? And *why* were they killed? George

Radford might have been stabbed in a moment of rage or fear, or in a desperate, hand-to-hand fight. But Captain Smith's relaxed posture—the man had been seated beside a wall of the abandoned mill, smoking—suggested that he had been waiting for his killer. There had been no signs of a scuffle in the dirt floor; no indication that he had attempted to defend himself, the only clue the green pasteboard ticket that Patrick said had come from the bathing machines. What of the man whom Patrick claimed to have seen taking George Radford's body out to sea? Was he the killer, or someone trying to dispose of the body? And what was to be made of Constable Woodhouse? He was the authorized representative of the Queen's law, yet he had not done his duty where George Radford's death was concerned. Why? Was the constable involved as well?

Kate frowned, thinking once again of the bitter young widow in the cottage at Black Rock. "Your village may have a good heart," she had said, "but its soul is rotten right through." Was she right? Was the picturesque peace of Rottingdean a camouflage for something sinister, something evil, in which the entire village was engaged? Or was it only Beryl Bardwell's vivid imagination—the fancy of a novelist—that made her think so?

There were too many questions and not a single answer, too many mysteries and not a single clue. Kate glanced once more out the window. Very little had changed, but the scene seemed darkened. Those two men on the opposite side of the street—their faces looked pinched and anxious, she thought, and their conversation seemed furtive. The scurrying woman with the large paper parcel appeared to be glancing from right to left, almost as if she expected to be apprehended. And the man coming out of the post office, ripping open an envelope and pausing to read, suddenly turned pale, thrust the letter into his pocket and hurried off. What had happened to Rottingdean's calm tranquillity? Or was she merely seeing with new eyes?

Kate stood. There *was* something she could do while she waited to share her news with Charles. She could talk with Mrs. Portney, who was probably in the kitchen making plans for tea and the evening meal. The cook-housekeeper might be able to shed some light on some of these events, or offer some insight into the affairs of the village. And there was the business of the brandy spill in the cellar, which had made Kate very curious. Kipling had mentioned brandy in his poem about smuggling, as well as tobacco and lace.

Kate frowned. Was Mrs. Portney involved in whatever was going on now? Well, there was only one way to find out, and that was to talk with her. She picked up the luncheon tray. When the lady of the house wanted to speak to one of her employees, the servant was usually summoned abovestairs, for it was considered beneath the lady's dignity to appear in the lower regions—and even, in some households, an intrusion on the servants' privacy. But baroness or no, when Kate was at home at Bishop's Keep, she was accustomed to having regular conferences with her cook beside the comfortable warmth of the kitchen fire. And her unexpected appearance in the Seabrooke House kitchen would have the advantage of surprise. She might catch Mrs. Portney off guard, or encounter one of the other servants—the timid little tweeny or the upstairs maid—who might be willing to tell her something.

The green baize door in the dining room opened onto the back stairs, which descended to a flagged passageway across the rear of the house. Carrying her tray, Kate went down the dark stairs, avoiding the filled coal-shuttles at the bottom and the row of clean chamber pots waiting to be carried to the upstairs bedrooms. On the wall, on pegs, hung a variety of brooms and mops and buckets, along with several lanterns, a weeding hoe, a spade. Ahead of her, a heavyset man burst out of the door she assumed led to the kitchen and strode angrily to the outer door at the end of the passage, which he slammed behind him. She stared after him for a brief moment, wondering who he was. Then she remembered why she was there, and pushed the door open, her tray in one hand.

Mrs. Portney was standing at a huge black Eagle range, reaching for the iron kettle that was steaming on the back of the stove. She whirled around, eyes blazing, chin thrust forward. "I told ye not to come 'ere again—" she began furiously, and broke off.

"Oh! Lady Sheridan!" she cried, and fumbled a hasty curtsey. "I didn't know … I thought …" Her eyes narrowed at the sight of the luncheon tray. "That lazy Molly! I *told* her to listen fer yer ladyship's bell an'—"

"No, no, Mrs. Portney," Kate said soothingly, setting the tray on the well-scrubbed pine table. "I didn't ring for Molly. I wanted to bring the tray down myself." She smiled. "After all, we will be staying here for several weeks. I thought it might be well to let you know about some of Lord Sheridan's favorite food and drink, so that you may take his tastes into account when you are planning menus."

A look of momentary perplexity crossed Mrs. Portney's narrow face. "O' course, milady, but… but wudn't ye rather I come upstairs?" She twisted her hands in her white apron. "Th' Mornin' room is where Mrs. Seabrooke always give me orders. Th' kitchen ain't a fit place fer—"

"I find it a very fit place indeed," Kate replied firmly, but with a smile. "Quite warm and homey and familiar, in fact. You know, I'm an American, and we have quite different ideas about things."

"Well, yes," Mrs. Portney said cautiously. "I did know from yer ladyship's talk that ye weren't quite..." she colored. "Quite so formal as some."

"That's because I grew up in New York," Kate said. "I was an orphan, and my aunt and uncle O'Malley raised me. Uncle was a policeman, and I had six younger cousins to look out for. There wasn't money for hired help, of course, so I spent a great deal of time in the kitchen." She rolled her eyes. "I can swing a fine broom, I tell you! And the floors I have scrubbed—why, they would stretch from here to Westminster."

"Lor!" Mrs. Portney exclaimed, her mouth a round O of astonishment. "A real, true Cindereller story! Out of th' ashes an' off to th' ball, so to speak. 'Oo wud've thought it?" Then, thinking of who Kate had become, she reddened. "Oh, milady, I didn't mean—"

"That's perfectly all right, Mrs. Portney," Kate said, with a sisterly laugh. "It *is* a Cinderella story. I can hardly believe that I actually came to England and married a baron! So you see, I *do try* extra hard to please his lordship by making sure he has just what he likes to eat and drink." She pulled out a wooden chair and gestured at the teapot on the table. "While we talk, *dear* Mrs. Portney, I'd love to have a cup of the tea you were about to make."

Having heard the story of Kate's humble beginnings (for the most part true, although it omitted any mention of her own inherited fortune), Mrs. Portney was a great deal more relaxed and easy. She poured boiling water over the tea in the china pot—a fragrant imported tea flavored with sweet orange peel and cloves—then set out cups and a plate of biscuits. Rummaging in one of the drawers, she found a torn piece of wrapping paper and a stub of a pencil. When the tea had properly steeped, she poured steaming cups of it and took a chair on the other side of the table.

"Now, milady," she said comfortably, "wot was it ye wanted me to make fer 'is lordship? I do 'ope ye remember that we're a small village, an' not smart. Mr. Grantly, the grocer, don't 'ave much in the way o' fancy food, so if it's somethin' special ye're wantin', we'll 'ave to send to Brighton. An' as fer drink, wot's in the wine cellar belowstairs is the best there is in the village."

"Oh, I imagine we'll do wonderfully well out of Mr. Grantly's stock," Kate said. "His lordship is quite fond of fish of any sort. Veal cutlets always suit him, and roast partridge, and he is especially partial to a bit of lobster salad." She sipped her tea thoughtfully. "And if this tea is any indication of what you are able to obtain here in the village, I am sure his lordship will be very pleased. It is truly delicious, and quite unique. Is it imported?"

A little frown showed between Mrs. Portney's thick brows, and she stirred uncomfortably. "That's good about the lobsters," she said. "We've very fine lobsters 'ere, straight out of our waters and much better'n wot ye'll find in Lunnun. They're much admired by all the vis'tors."

"Then let us have lobster often," Kate said with enthusiasm. "Breakfast, of course, can be quite simple: any broiled fish will do, or broiled kidneys, not fried, and bacon. His lordship prefers his eggs scrambled, occasionally poached, and as to fruit, he favors apples above strawberries. You might poach the apples, perhaps with a little cinnamon, and serve them with cream."

Mrs. Portney scribbled busily with her pencil. "Well, then," she said, as she wrote down the last, "we should get on, for there are delicious apples round about. Soups, I s'pose. An' reg'lar custards."

"Yes, but not pea soup or celery soup, I am sorry to say." Kate looked up and added, as if it were an afterthought, "Oh, by the way, I should have mentioned that his lordship is in the habit of adding a sum in compensation to the cook who pleases him." She paused, and gave Mrs. Portney a conspiratorial glance. "Quite a handsome sum, I should add."

The tip of Mrs. Portney's nose grew pink. "That's very gen'rous of 'is lordship."

"He can be a very generous man when his wishes are accommodated," Kate said. "Now, as to drink, I have surveyed the wine cellar and found it quite adequate—except for brandy, of which, unfortunately there is none. There *had* been, recently, from the evidence of a broken bottle, but it is gone. What do you suppose—" She left the sentence dangling.

Flustered, Mrs. Portney pretended to study her list. "I'm sure I don't know, mum," she muttered. "Mrs. Seabrooke always saw to the cellar her own self."

"Well," Kate remarked, "it is a great pity, for if there is anything Lord Sheridan fancies when he is relaxing in the evening, it is a glass of fine French brandy. If my nose told me correctly, the brandy that was spilled in the cellar was fine indeed. If more could be got, Mrs. Portney, I'm sure his lordship would be delighted to pay."

Mrs. Portney hesitated.

"Whatever the price," Kate added significantly.

"P'rhaps," Mrs. Portney ventured, "I could make inquiries."

"That would be lovely." Kate said. "As for me, my tastes are modest. But there *is* one dish I truly love above all others, and now that I can afford it—" She gave a little shrug. "Of course, it *is* an indulgence."

Mrs. Portney's brows went up. "And wot's that, milady?"

"I hate to confess it." Kate laughed lightly. "You'll think me quite silly and extravagant."

Mrs. Portney shook her head vigorously. "Oh, no,

milady! If it's in me power, yer ladyship shall 'ave wot ye likes."

"I hesitate to mention it," Kate said, "for it involves a very great delicacy, difficult to procure and unimaginably dear—although if you were able to find it, I should be delighted to pay whatever is required, and add a substantial sum for your trouble."

Mrs. Portney's nose was growing even pinker. "What is it, milady?"

"It is eggs beaten with cream and cooked to soft curd," Kate said, "with a topping of sautéed truffles." She clasped her hands and raised her eyes. "It is a simple dish, but oh, quite heavenly! And I should be very glad to give you my recipe."

"Truffles?" Mrs. Portney frowned.

"Yes," Kate said. "They are imported from France, you know, and the duty one must pay is simply exorbitant." She laughed again. "I told his lordship that he should enter a motion in Parliament to repeal the excise on truffles—and that if he were not successful, I should go to smuggling. I am sure there are smugglers somewhere who would be glad to see what a fine profit could be made from such a delicacy."

There was a space of silence. At last, Mrs. Portney said, cautiously, "It's possible that truffles might be got fer yer ladyship. Arrangements might be made. Not straightaway, mind ye, but soon. P'rhaps I can speak t' Mr. Grantly today—it's my half-day off, ye know. I'll leave a cold supper."

"Indeed," Kate said. "If you find the truffles, I shall be content." Leaning forward, she patted the cook's hand. "And *you*, my dear Mrs. Portney, shall be very well rewarded. Mr. Grantly too, I might add."

"I shall be grateful, mum," said that worthy, with a

little bob of her head. "Most, most grateful. An' if there's anything else I can do, ye've only to ask."

Kate picked up her cup and sipped her tea. "There *is* one more thing," she said. "I have it in mind to look for some lace that Amelia might add to the throat of my dressing gown. I don't suppose, in a village the size of Rottingdean, that I shall find what I'm looking for. Where in Brighton would you recommend—"

"Oh, but ye *will* find it in Rott'ndean!" Mrs. Portney exclaimed eagerly. "Mrs. 'Oward 'as quite nice lace in 'er dress shop just down the 'Igh Street, as fancy as any ye'll find in Brighton. I know, fer I've seen it meself, and even bought a piece or two. Do 'ave a look, mum."

"Why, I believe I shall, Mrs. Portney," Kate said, smiling, and set down her cup. "And thank you again. You cannot know just how very helpful you have been."

17

"A weapon is an enemy, even to its owner."

—Turkish Proverb

I<small>T WAS PAST</small> two in the afternoon when Charles and the chief constable crossed The Steine and made their way up North Street, then through the South Gate of the Royal Pavilion Estate and along a wide gravel walkway that bisected the western lawns. They passed in front of the huge domed building that had been erected in the early 1800s to accommodate the royal stables, then let as cavalry barracks in the fifties and sixties and later reconstructed as a concert hall. In Church Street, they walked several blocks in a westerly direction, and turned right into a narrow lane. Several doors up, Sir Robert stopped before an unassuming brick-fronted shop with a painted sign board that read simply R. W. Barker & Son. The mullioned window was protected with iron bars, curtained with gray draperies to deter prying eyes, and topped conspicuously with a burglar alarm. A discreet brass medallion beside the door bore the Royal Lion and Unicorn and the inscription *Armorer, by Appointment to Her Royal Majesty.*

"The family has been in business here for at least half

a century and is considered very reputable," Sir Robert said. "They provided arms for the cavalry officers when the company was stationed in Brighton. If there is any knowledge in Brighton of a new type of firearm, my lord, we should find it here."

Charles nodded, hoping that Sir Robert was right. He did not want to take the time to make a trip to London, especially when he had promised Kate that this holiday was to be theirs alone, a retreat from the pressures that had made life so difficult for the past few months, a time to heal whatever rifts had opened up between them. At the thought of Kate, sitting alone at Seabrooke House waiting for him, Charles felt resentful of the task that was taking him away from her, and yet—and yet, there was a certain compelling excitement in it, too. The thrill of the chase, was that it? he asked himself, with a kind of self-mockery. The scent of danger on the wind, the exhilaration of the game? Well, if that was it, he could forget all that heroic silliness. He squared his shoulders. The hunt for a killer was not a schoolboy's lark but a very serious affair. Two of the Queen's officers were dead, and unless he was mistaken, the net of treachery that had snared them had been flung very wide indeed.

Sir Robert pushed open the door and Charles followed him into the narrow shop. It smelled richly of gunpowder, machine oil, and leather, and was lit by a row of gaslights along each long wall. The gaslight gleamed softly on the polished wooden butts of the rifles and shotguns that filled the wall racks, and on the glass tops of the oak cases on either side of the narrow aisle down the middle of the shop, in which a wide selection of handguns was displayed. Behind the cases there was a clutter of shooting equipment: gun cases, slings, cartridge belts and holsters, cartridge-filling machines, cartridge magazines.

"Ah, Sir Robert!" A short, slight man with gold spectacles and gray hair came toward them, dressed in an old-fashioned long-tailed coat. "So good to see you!"

Sir Robert smiled cordially and the two men shook hands. He turned. "Lord Sheridan, I should like to present Mr. Reginald Barker. Reg, my friend, his lordship has come down from London on holiday. He has a question for you with regard to a certain new type of ammunition."

With a slight smile, Mr. Barker rubbed his hands together. "New ammunition, eh, my lord? Shotgun, perhaps? If you're doing a bit of shooting in the downs, I'm sure you'll be interested in the smokeless powder cartridges we have just received. A very significant improvement, I must say, over the black powder we are all accustomed to use." He turned. "Let me show you—"

Sir Robert intervened. "Forgive me, Reg. I should have been clearer. Lord Sheridan was holidaying in Rottingdean, you see, when a pair of the local coast guards unfortunately managed to get themselves murdered. The Prince of Wales—he was down for a visit with the duchess—got wind of the killings and commissioned Lord Sheridan to look into the situation on behalf of the Crown. So you might say—in fact, I suppose we *must* say—that this is an official visit." He cocked his head. "If you'll save me some of those smokeless cartridges, though, I'd be more than pleased to give them a try the next time I'm out shooting."

"To be sure," Mr. Barker murmured. "How can I help you, my lord?"

"We believe it is pistol ammunition we are concerned with, Mr. Barker," Charles said. "An unusual cartridge was recovered at the scene of one of the murders Sir Robert mentioned, and what we assume to be the corresponding bullet was removed from the body of the victim."

"Removed, that is, by your old friend Dr. Barriston," Sir

Robert put in, "who sends you his regards."

"Ah, yes. A fine man, Dr. Barriston. Up on the latest medical advances." Behind his spectacles, Mr. Barker's eyes gleamed with interest. "An unusual cartridge, you say? You have the specimen with you?"

"He does," the chief constable said. "Although what can be learned from a spent cartridge, I'm sure I can't say."

Charles took the two cloth bags from his pocket and shook out the cartridge and bullet onto a nearby counter. "The diameter is right at thirty-hundredths of an inch," he said. "Thirty caliber, I assume." He pointed. "But look here, sir, at this oddly pronounced shoulder."

"You're confident that this is pistol ammunition?" Mr. Barker asked. "I have never seen a shouldered pistol cartridge." He picked the cartridge up and turned in his fingers, studying it carefully. "Most remarkable," he muttered. "Most, most remarkable. Yes, this casing seems too small for a rifle, although it does have characteristics which call to mind certain modern military rifles." He turned up the base of the cartridge and inspected the number pressed into the edge. "Four-oh-three. Perhaps the caliber, in the metric system?"

Charles shook his head. "I think not, sir. Thirty-hundredths of an inch is just over seven millimeters."

"Of course. Quite so." Mr. Barker tapped his forefinger against his teeth. "Well, then, four-oh-three is undoubtedly a manufacturer's designation. If that is the case, it should shorten our search."

"You don't immediately recognize it?" Charles asked, disappointed.

"I'm afraid not." Mr. Barker studied the cartridge again, more carefully. "I must say, this is most peculiar, my lord. As you have noticed, the ridge at the base is equal to the diameter of the casing. This is not typical of most pistol cartridges, where the protruding rim limits the round from sliding into the cylinder or barrel and catches on the extraction mechanism so that the spent cartridge is ejected." His voice had become excited. "But *this* cartridge is rimless, with only a groove for extraction."

Charles caught his enthusiasm. "Indeed. No doubt the shoulder of the casing performs the positioning function. It is also a clever method of increasing the powder charge which can be used with a bullet of a given diameter, without increasing the length of the cartridge."

Mr. Barker nodded. "Indeed. It is a technique used with rifle ammunition, as is the full copper jacketing of the bullet."

"One more remarkable point," Charles said. "This casing was found approximately seven feet from the point where I believe the weapon was fired, as if it had been thrown there by the weapon. Are you aware of any pistol that operates in this fashion?"

The other man paused for a moment, thinking. "I have heard," he said slowly, "that one or two German firms are experimenting with self-loading pistols. As I understand the concept—and this is only what I have been told, mind you, I have not seen it for myself—a strip of cartridges is loaded into the pistol's magazine. When the bullet is fired, the recoil forces the pistol bolt backward and the extractor drags the empty casing with it. When the casing clears the chamber, it is ejected."

"Ah," Charles said.

"Indeed. The bolt is then propelled forward by a spring, which in turn forces a new round into the chamber while another mechanism holds the hammer back until the trigger is squeezed again. If the concept could be made to work, the weapon would fire with each squeeze of the trigger until the magazine was emptied—without the operator having to manipulate the hammer or rotate the cylinder."

Sir Robert's eyes opened wide. "And *that* would be revolutionary!" he exclaimed. "It would increase both accuracy and rate of fire to a phenomenal degree. Is it… is it *possible*?"

"More than possible," Charles said gravely. "It is quite feasible, and a very sound design." He looked at Mr. Barker. "If such a self-loading weapon had been developed, where in this country might one obtain it?"

"It would be the sort of weapon a military officer would covet," Mr. Barker replied. "It would make an ideal personal side arm. I know of several firms in London that specialize in the outfitting of army officers. Shall I make inquiries?"

"If you would be so kind, sir," Charles replied, and replaced the bullet and the cartridge in their bags and the bags in his pocket. "Given a weapon so unique, its identification and discovery might very well reveal its owner."

Out in the street, Sir Robert turned apologetically to Charles. "I'm afraid this was something of a wild-goose chase, Sheridan. I'm sorry Barker couldn't do more to help us pin down the weapon."

"Don't apologize," Charles replied. "These things take a great deal of time. It is only in Conan Doyle's fanciful stories that the Great Detective can announce that the game is afoot on page one and cry checkmate on page six or seven, with Dr. Watson applauding from the wings." He chuckled wryly. "One or two happy observations, a few spectacular deductive twists, and—" He snapped his fingers. "*Voila!* the solution, as if by magic!"

Sir Robert gave a bitter laugh. "Well, if you ask me, such stories only make my work more difficult. People who read them get the idea that every crime has a solution, if only the police were clever enough to see it. But the police don't have some sly author setting up a trail of clues for us to sniff out. We have to do the sniffing ourselves." He shook himself. "But enough of that. What is your next step?"

"As much as can be done has been done here," Charles said. "I have several calls to make in Rottingdean and the surrounding area. I'd best get to it."

"D'you want me with you, or one of my men? I stand ready to provide whatever manpower you need. Were you satisfied that we've covered the crime scene thoroughly?"

"Very thoroughly, thank you, although I may make another visit there this evening. For the moment, what has to be done in Rottingdean is best done by someone unconnected with the police, I think. You'd better contact the Home Office and let them know what we're up to. We don't want officials of the coast guard hot-footing it down here to begin their own investigation. They would only get in the way."

"I'll telegraph London immediately."

Charles nodded. "If Lady Luck is with us, though, a time will come when I shall require your help. Where can you be reached?"

"Ah, yes, Lady Luck." Sir Robert sighed, fishing in his pocket. "The Great Detective may repudiate her entirely, but the rest of us know that she's responsible for apprehending most of the criminals brought before the bar."

"In the future," Charles replied, "science will give Lady Luck a hand. But we're not there yet. In the meantime, perhaps you would be good enough to loan me a side arm. I'd prefer a Webley, if you have a spare."

Sir Robert eyed him. "Expecting trouble?"

"The killer was armed with a formidable weapon. It

would be prudent to have insurance." Charles pocketed the card the chief constable had handed him. "I will send you word of my progress. Let us hope that Mr. Barker's inquiry brings us some useful bit of information."

18

"Shopping is very demonstrative."
—Lord Melbourne To Queen Victoria

"A woman's guess is much more accurate than a man's certainty."

—Rudyard Kipling
Plain Tales from the Hills

IT WAS HARDLY the usual thing, Kate thought, as she put on her tweed jacket and pinned her felt walking hat securely to her massed hair, that a seaside village so small as Rottingdean and so near to a major city should have a dress shop. Most ladies able to afford a smart gown would travel to London to buy it ready-to-wear in one of the large department stores in Regent Street, or hire a local dressmaker to construct it for her from a pattern in *The Ladies' Monthly Review* or *The Metropolitan Catalogue*. But having talked to Mrs. Portney, Kate was coming to suspect that there were many unusual things about Rottingdean, and she was curious to investigate this one.

Ladies' Fashions for Fashionable Ladies had a wide bow window level with the street, which displayed a sample of the wares to be found within. Kate paused in front of the window, surprised by what she saw. At the left stood a handsome mannequin figure with wax head and wax hands, dressed in an elegantly tailored green moire gown with huge leg-o'-mutton sleeves and a fashionable gored skirt trimmed in black ribbon, every bit as fine as a similar gown Kate had recently seen at Harrods. Beside it stood a milliner's hat stand with an elaborate blond coiffure, on which was displayed a delectable green hat trimmed with an ebullience of green and black feathers. And in the folds of the velvet window draperies stood a pair of fetching black boots, black elbow-length kid gloves, a pair of black cashmere ribbed hosiery, and a green moire-covered purse.

Kate lingered for a moment, thoughtfully calculating the total cost of the items and weighing the probability that such fashionable goods might be found so elaborately displayed in an ordinary seashore resort. But as there was more to be learned within than without, she pushed the door open and went in.

A slender, brown-haired woman in a simple blue merino dress was standing behind a counter to the left of the door, folding the length of fabric she had just cut from a bolt of gray watered silk. Scissors in hand, she looked up with a smile that, Kate thought, seemed anxiously hopeful. Perhaps she had not had many customers today, or this week.

"Good afternoon, madam," the woman said, and smoothed her hair back with her hand. "May I help you?"

"Good afternoon," Kate said, going to the counter. "I am Lady Sheridan. Mrs. Portney, at Seabrooke House, where my husband and I are holidaying, has told me that Mrs. Howard has a selection of laces here. I am looking for something that might be suitable for a dressing gown—Chantilly, perhaps, or Valenciennes."

"Of course, my lady," the woman said, and Kate caught the overtone of eagerness. Yes, there could not have been many customers today, and the woman was anxious for a sale. She turned to put up the bolt. "I am Mrs. Howard. If your ladyship would be pleased to step to the rear, you may see my laces. I have quite a fine variety."

As Kate followed the woman toward the back of the shop, she looked around. The shop itself did not quite have the elegance promised by the front window, but it came very near. Along one wall were shelves that held bolts of practical cottons, warm tweeds, smart wools, and stylish silks, artfully arranged to disguise the fact that the selection was quite small. Pinned to the shelves were drawings illustrating the latest fashions in skirts, waists, and sleeves, and another wall displayed trimmings of braid, fringe, fur, and feathers. On a counter nearby were several hats, including a narrow-brimmed white straw boater trimmed in green silk cord, with a single green tulle rose.

"Oh, what a *sweet* hat!" Kate cried, although in truth she was not terribly fond of boaters. "I simply must have it!"

"It suits you very well, my lady." Mrs. Howard smiled. "I am glad you like it, for I made it."

"You are the milliner, then?" Kate asked. She took off her own hat and set the straw one on her head at a rakish angle.

"*And* the dressmaker," Mrs. Howard said, handing Kate a mirror. "Oh, how becoming!" she exclaimed. "If your ladyship will forgive the presumption, your hair is so lovely and so warm a color that a fussy hat would detract from it. You should always wear something simple."

"Well, I shall certainly wear *this*," Kate said, turning her head to admire herself in the mirror. "I must say, Mrs. Howard, that I am quite surprised to find a shop of this quality in such a rural village."

Mrs. Howard smiled, showing uneven teeth. "It was opened just last month. Rottingdean has seen an increasing number of daytrippers down from London and over from Brighton, now that the electric railway is in operation. Frankly, I thought to take advantage of the growing number of shoppers who are visiting the village."

"You must not apologize for having good business sense," Kate replied. "A great many women would envy you your courage in striking out on your own. I wish you every success."

"Thank you, your ladyship," Mrs. Howard said. "Although I must admit—" She bit her lip. "But you are looking for laces." She gestured at a display of samples. "I have narrow edging lace for hems, embroidered lace for insets and sleeves, gathered and pleated lace—and some quite fine Valenciennes and Mechlin laces, imported from France. And here is the Chantilly, and here a lovely Maltese guipure."

"What a selection!" Kate cried admiringly. She fingered the samples at length, although she had never had much interest in such things and hated to spend money frivolously. "I shall of course have the Chantilly—it is exactly what I am looking for. Ten yards, please."

"Ten yards!" Mrs. Howard's eyes widened. "But—"

"I shall, of course, wish to pay you today," Kate said smoothly. "I find that it is such a nuisance to ask his lordship to handle my dressmaking accounts." She waved her gloved hand with a confiding little laugh. "You know how husbands are, Mrs. Howard. They make such a fuss over little extravagances like laces and ribbons and gloves, although they spend twice or three times as much on their favorite tobacco and brandy." She trilled another laugh.

"To be sure," Mrs. Howard said warmly. "Oh, I fully

agree with you, your ladyship. It is far better to handle one's personal accounts oneself."

"And I am tempted by this charming Valenciennes," Kate went on, "although I should like it in black, rather than ivory, and I shall require, oh, say, fifteen yards." She glanced up. "Do you have it in black?"

Mrs. Howard seemed taken aback, but recovered quickly. "Not... not in stock, I'm afraid, your ladyship. That is, not in the shop. But I know where it is to be had. That is, if you wouldn't mind waiting a few days—"

"Oh, not at all!" Kate said. "In fact, I shouldn't object to paying a little extra for a special order, and paying ahead of time in order to ensure prompt delivery." She paused, and touched the delicate lace pensively. "And if the price were right, I might also have some of this Maltese guipure. Later, of course, after I have seen the quality of the other laces."

Mrs. Howard's frown cleared. "Then I shall be delighted to obtain what you want," she said. There was something beseeching about her smile. "I cannot say how deeply honored I am by your patronage, your ladyship. I have hoped that the ladies from the Green—Lady Burne-Jones and Mrs. Ridsdale and now Mrs. Kipling—might be enticed to visit my shop and see for themselves that my goods are as fashionable as any they can purchase in Brighton. Perhaps," she added delicately, "you would do me the honor of recommending me to them, and to other ladies of your acquaintance?"

"I shall be more than pleased to do so, Mrs. Howard," Kate said with enthusiasm, and drew forth her purse. "Now, shall we reckon up how much I owe you? I promised his lordship that I would shop for a supply of his favorite tobacco this afternoon, although I am afraid I shall have to disappoint him. In such a small village—"

"Oh, but you should ask Mr. Knapton across the way," Mrs. Howard said, picking up her receipt book. "I happen to know that he has several very good tobaccos, and is able to obtain others upon notice."

Kate beamed as she took out her pound notes. "Well, then," she said, "both lace *and* tobacco! My little shopping expedition has been quite an amazing success."

19

"It is the duty of responsible citizens of means to look to the proper schooling of the children. Too many of these poor unfortunates are turned out into the streets at an early age to fend for themselves without education, without purpose, and without hope. While one should be mindful of the pride of the benighted poor, their needs must be met, often in spite of their unenlightened resistance."

—ROBERT CHARLES DOBEST
Toward a More Perfect Society (1893)

As HE ALWAYS did, Patrick followed Aunt Georgie with alacrity when she asked him to spend the afternoon doing odd jobs for her in the garden at North End House. He took pleasure in the frequent garden work, for Aunt Georgie usually stayed to supervise and would often read to him in the intervals, bits from grown-up books by men like Ruskin, or from Mr. Kipling's *Jungle Books*. But today, he was especially glad to retreat to the garden. He did not want to go to the stables, where he would surely be confronted by Harry Tudwell; and he did not want to be met by any who might have been at the Black Horse the night before and be asked a question he could not answer.

In fact, Patrick would have run off to hide in the old windmill if he hadn't feared he might be discovered by someone who wanted to poke around the site of Captain Smith's murder.

The garden at North End House was not much larger than a tennis court, but it had been laid out as a series of little garden rooms contained by walls and corridors of shrubbery, so that it seemed to go on forever. Each of the little rooms had a particular kind of interest: roses, or herbs, or ferns, or plants mentioned in Shakespeare or the Bible, or plants loved by bees or valued for their fragrance. Beyond the pergola planted with climbing roses was a small trellis-fenced plot where each of Aunt Georgie's grandchildren had a place to sow their penny-packets of mustard and cress and nasturtiums. The whole thing was surrounded by a flint wall and was quite private—as secret a place as the windmill to spend a hidden afternoon, and much more pleasant.

Aunt Georgie was a skilled gardener, but she had one special adversary to combat: snails, some quite tiny, some as large as florins. They left their slimy trails on the window panes, roosted under the roof of the wooden pergola, and a party of them could always be found under the overturned pots. Patrick's usual job was to harvest these creatures and deposit them into the large porcelain pan under the rain butt, then add a handful of salt and watch them curl. When they were adequately pickled, he tipped them onto the rubbish heap.

Today, Aunt Georgie gave him a berry bucket and set him to picking snails from the dahlias, while she went into the house. Glad for the work, he went straight to it, eager to forget what he had heard and seen at the Black Rock coast guard cottage. But although he resolutely shut the widow's accusations out of his mind, he kept hearing her voice and seeing the little boy hunched on the step, crying for his father—a cry with which he could certainly sympathize. These recollections pulled him one way while old loyalties tugged him another, and he felt torn between them, like a piece of meat yanked at by a pair of hungry village dogs. If only he knew what he should do! But surely he couldn't do much because he didn't *know* much, at least not for certain. All he had were guesses, and he had already decided that nobody would want those. But that didn't lighten his guilt

Patrick had dumped his second bucket into the snail-pot when a tray of ham sandwiches and a pitcher of lemonade appeared on the table in the pergola. He had breakfasted early, so he sat down on a wooden bench and began to eat eagerly. He was finishing the second thick, meaty sandwich when Aunt Georgie sat down in the wicker chair opposite, clearly intent on carrying on a conversation. But her opening remark did not bring him any comfort.

"Patrick," she said, settling her shawl around her shoulders, "I have been giving serious thought to your future."

"Yes, ma'am," Patrick returned warily. The last time Aunt Georgie had opened a similar conversation, she had ended by giving him a copy of a political tract which argued for the establishment of trade unions for the working class.

She cocked her head to one side and regarded him gravely. "You are an intelligent boy and clearly much above the other village children in your potential for improvement. What have you heard from your father recently?"

Patrick looked away. "Nothing, ma'am."

"He is still in arrears to Mrs. Higgs?" At Patrick's reluctant nod, Aunt Georgie pressed her lips together and gave a disapproving shake of her head. "I do not suppose, then, that he has sent your tuition to St. Aubyn's, as he promised to do."

"No, ma'am," Patrick said, feeling a chilliness in his stomach that was not attributable to the lemonade he had just drunk. Aunt Georgie liked to take charge of other people's affairs, and he had the feeling that she was about to take charge of his. He set down his glass. "Thank you for the lunch," he said, and stood. "I'd best get back to work now. There are *buckets* more snails."

Aunt Georgie lifted her chin. "Sit down, Patrick," she commanded. "We have not finished our talk."

Unwillingly, Patrick sat on the edge of the wooden bench.

"Now," she said, in a stern tone. "I have it on reliable authority that you are no longer attending Mr. Forsythe's school. Instead, you are spending your days frequenting the stables, and your evenings running through the village and over to Brighton."

"No, ma'am," Patrick said. "I work for Mr. Tudwell at the stables, and I do errands for him." He took a deep breath. She wouldn't stop until she had dug it all out of him, so he might as well tell her. "The money goes to Mrs. Higgs, to pay my board bill."

"To pay—" Aunt Georgie began in a half-horrified tone, and then stopped. "I see," she said, after a moment, and in a kindlier voice. "Yes, yes, I *do* see." There was another silence, and then: "Well, I cannot say that I believe Mr. Tudwell to be a good influence upon you, Patrick, nor Mrs. Higgs a fit guardian of youth. You need someone who can direct you toward a productive life. And a boy of your promise most certainly *should* continue his education, whatever his father's regrettable failings. I have therefore—"

Alarmed, Patrick started to speak, but she held up her hand and continued, in a magisterial tone, "I have therefore determined, Patrick, to become your guide and sponsor and undertake to support you at St. Aubyn's."

Patrick gulped "Oh, but I couldn't—that is, I don't want—" He stopped, faltering under the dreadful sense that his earlier dilemma, wrenching as it was, had taken on a new and even more threatening dimension. He could not for the life of him imagine being confined to a dreary life of scholarship at gloomy St. Aubyn's, with only those seven sallow boys and two lackluster masters for company. But he could not imagine returning to the tender mercies of Mr. Tudwell—not after what he had seen and heard. What *was* he to do?

"I understand that you don't want to accept anyone's help, my boy," Aunt Georgie was saying in a now quite kindly tone. "This speaks very well of your sense of responsibility. Your father may not be much, but you must have had a decent mother who taught you to stand up for yourself." She gave him a beneficent smile. "Surely you can see, however, that you must be properly educated if you are to make anything of yourself in the world. I have the means, and I wish to help, and you must allow me to do so." Her voice took on a ringing quality, and he began to hear echoes of the trade union tract she had given him. "It is my duty to society to prevent the destruction of a perfectly good life. It is *my* responsibility as a laborer in the vineyard, as Sidney Webb tells us so clearly, to help a fellow-laborer in distress. I am confident that you will repay this debt many times over, Patrick, as you grow to manhood and turn your own hand to the betterment of the world in which we dwell as fellow-creatures."

Patrick felt that Aunt Georgie must be speaking allegorically, for he knew that he had never labored in a vineyard and he was pretty sure she hadn't either. He tried to reply, but nothing would come out.

"It is decided, then," she said, obviously pleased with herself. "I will speak with Mrs. Higgs this evening and write straightaway to your father, telling him what is to be done, and why. I will also inquire of Mr. Stanford and Mr. Lang how soon you may be admitted to St. Aubyn's as a boarding scholar. In the meanwhile, there is the matter of clothing and shoes." She glanced with distaste at his corduroys. "You must have a new wardrobe, of course. And it would be much better if you were to come at once and stay with me until we have heard from the masters. I am quite adamant that you should not return to Mrs. Higgs. I shall explain this to her myself, of course."

By this time, Patrick was entirely speechless with dismay, which Aunt Georgie interpreted in quite another fashion.

"I see that you are overwhelmed with gratitude, dear boy," she said gently. "Perhaps no one has ever offered to help you before." With a gesture of unconscious condescension, she smiled and patted his head exactly as if he were a small dog. "Well, then. Since you cannot find your tongue to thank me as you might wish, perhaps you will be glad of a little more fruitful labor. Come, and I will show you the refuse that is piled up to be burned. I have calls to make in the village regarding this unfortunate affair of the coast guards' deaths, but I am quite sure that this is a task you can manage for yourself."

A half-hour later, Patrick was standing at the brick incinerator just outside the flint wall, poking the last sticks into the fire, when Mr. Kipling joined him, hands thrust into the pockets of his trousers, a troubled look on his face. Without preamble, he said:

"Look here, Paddy. The Aunt tells me she is planning to

school you at St. Aubyn's. What do you think of the idea?"

His eyes watering from the acrid smoke, Patrick turned to Mr. Kipling. "It's what my father wants," he said. "But I..." He brushed his eyes with his sleeve. "I don't s'pose I have much of a choice."

Mr. Kipling regarded him gravely, his mouth working under his brush of a mustache. "Well," he said at last, "the best we can do, young or old, is to play the cards as they are dealt. But it does seem to me that a fellow ought to have a choice." He was silent for a moment longer. "It is true that there has been no word from your father in nearly a year?"

Patrick nodded wordlessly.

Mr. Kipling fell silent again. Then he said, "I was boarded myself, you know, as a young person. My mother and father lived in India, and I was sent to a house in Southsea, to a woman who took in children. She was married to an old Navy captain who had been entangled in a harpoon-line while whale fishing, and had a terrible scar on his—" He shook himself, as if to cut loose from a painful memory. "It was a house of desolation. I hope Mrs. Higgs treats you a good deal better."

Patrick felt a warmth within him, where before had been only an icy chill. "She's not a wicked woman," he said.

Kipling smiled faintly. "I doubt you would tell me if she were. Ill-treated children have a notion of what they are likely to get if they betray the secrets of a prison-house before they are clear of it." He cocked his head, his eyes sharp and searching. "But you don't fancy St. Aubyn's?"

"No, sir," Patrick said.

"Well, I can't blame you for that," Kipling replied. "I have met Masters Stanford and Lang, and found them wanting. Can't say much for the boys, either. But that's not the only public school in the country, you know. I went to

Westward Ho! and it was great fun. I'm currently writing a story about some of the things that went on there." He chuckled. "Dead cats and the like."

Patrick wanted to say that Aunt Georgie had offered no choices, but feared to sound ungrateful. Whatever other possibilities there might be, they seemed as remote as a trip to the South Seas or a journey to the moon.

Mr. Kipling stood for a moment longer. "Well, cheer up, old man. We'll see what's to be done." He turned on his heel and left, going back through the apple orchard toward The Elms.

And this was why Patrick was standing alone at the brick incinerator when the fuzzy-whiskered antiquarian came striding resolutely up the path toward the stables, his eyes masked with his smoked-glass eye preservers, his pack clanking like medieval armor, his waterproof flying out behind him like a magician's cloak. He did not see Patrick, who stared after him, frowning perplexedly, until the man disappeared around the corner of the stableyard in the direction of Harry Tudwell's office. He walked with the air of a man who knew exactly where he was going, who he expected to see, and what he aimed to accomplish.

Patrick watched for one minute more. Still frowning, he turned back to the brick incinerator, gave the fire a last poke to be certain that it was safely contained, and left it to burn by itself.

20

"The game is afoot!"
—Sir Arthur Conan Doyle
The Adventure of the Abbey Grange

FOR THE BETTER part of the last hour, Harry Tudwell had been sitting at his desk in the office of Hawkham Stables, first drumming his fingers, then twiddling a pencil, then twirling his watch chain, all quite unconsciously. Harry was lost in thought. After what had happened the night before, he had a great deal to think about.

The most urgent matter, of course, was Foxy's murder, which was difficult enough to deal with in itself, never mind the other complications. Harry had taken his orders from the coast guard captain, who was in close communication with both the investors and the suppliers and knew precisely when each shipment would arrive, what it would contain, and where it was bound once it left Rottingdean. Now that Foxy was dead, where would Harry's instructions come from? How would he know when to expect the shipments? How would he know what to do with the goods? Troublesome complications in what had been an otherwise sublimely smooth operation.

With a dark look, Harry picked up the pencil and threw it, hard, across the room. There were other complications, as well, even more troublesome. Trunky Thomas's indictment of him was utter nonsense, and Harry was fired by the righteous wrath of a man who has been maliciously and wrongfully accused of a murder he did not commit. But at the Black Horse last night, the sheer volume of Trunky's accusations had overridden Harry's surprised protestations of innocence, and Harry knew that some of the others were inclined to side with Trunky. They were bound to talk among themselves and with other villagers, and Harry would soon become the *de facto* killer—not only of Foxy Smith, but also of George Radford as well. When the authorities came to investigate, it would be very easy to offer him up, a convenient scapegoat for the sins of the village. It would be very easy, in fact, to put forward an eyewitness, somebody who claimed to have seen Harry do the deed.

This thought made Harry shudder, and he got up and began to pace back and forth in front of his table. To forestall such a disagreeable eventuality, he had to find out who had shot Foxy Smith. Was it Trunky, attempting to insinuate himself between Harry and Foxy, or Harry and the investors? Was it one of the others, angry at Foxy's highhanded way of doing business, or at the captain himself, who had never gotten along with anybody in the village? Or had the killing been arranged by the investors, who were frightened by Radford's death and anxious to back out of their arrangement with the village? And how was Foxy's murder connected to that of the younger coast guard? Had the same person killed both men? To protect himself, did he have to discover *two* murderers?

Harry went to stand before the window, hands behind his back, staring at the bustle of men around the smithy, behind them a boy leading a pair of horses to exercise. The most pressing problem of all, unfortunately, had to be solved immediately. What was he to do about tomorrow night's shipment, which Harry felt had to be signaled off, and which Trunky and the others insisted on signaling *in*? How could he determine what the investors expected him to do? How might he—

The door opened with a creak and Harry turned. A slender man with fuzzy gray side-whiskers, so tall that he had to duck his head to clear the doorjamb, had entered the room, without the formality of knocking. The staff in his hand and the canvas pack on his back, from which hung a variety of clanking implements, gave him the appearance of an old-fashioned peddler of pots and pans. His smoked-glass eye preservers, in conjunction with his waterproof cloak, made him look like a masked black bat.

"Good afternoon, Mr. Tudwell," the man said, in a deep voice colored by a slightly gutteral Continental accent.

"Good afternoon," Harry returned, feeling that he knew the man but unable, momentarily, to recall his name. Then, in the same instant, he remembered: this was the eccentric whom he had seen wandering about the downs on occasion in the last several summers, a foreigner with a peculiar taste for odds and ends of stones and bones. He had never known the vagabond's name, for the man seldom came into the village and had never required the stable's services, obviously preferring to do his perambulating on foot. Well, Harry thought, measuring him with an expert eye, it would not be advisable to hire out any of the better animals to the fellow. If he wanted to ride, he would have to be satisfied with old Jupiter, who was not so nimble-footed that he could get anyone into trouble. He was about to ask if a horse was what was wanted when the stranger surprised him with an unusual question.

"Are you expecting any other visitor? I do not wish that we should be disturbed."

"No," Harry said, nonplussed. "That is, I—" He frowned. "Look here, sir," he said, "can I help you?"

The stranger seemed amused. "No, no, I rather think it is the other way around, my good Mr. Tudwell. I am here to help *you*."

The mysterious visitor waited while Harry digested this unexpected remark, then touched the fingers of his left hand to his forehead, as a magician might, pretending to see the unseen. As he raised his hand, his implements jangled.

"Just now," he said, "just as I entered, you were asking yourself how you might contact certain gentlemen—gentlemen who have invested a great deal of money in this village, gentlemen with whom you have lost contact as a result of the untimely demise of one of your confederates. You were wondering how you should deal with a certain business transaction which has been scheduled for tomorrow evening." He lowered his hand and smiled, stretching thin lips across his teeth. "I am here to answer those questions, Harry Tudwell, and to inform you of your good fortune."

Harry recoiled, dumfounded. This clanking apparition obviously knew more of his business than he did. "What ... what good fortune?" he demanded. He smelled a trap. But if it was a trap, Harry knew with a sinking heart, he was already well and truly caught.

"Why, your advancement in rank," the man said. He gave Harry a jovial grin, the effect of which was partially compromised by the fact that the expression in his eyes could not be read. "The unfortunate death of Captain Smith has left a gap, shall we say, a broken link in the chain. You, sir, are to fill that gap. You have moved one link up the chain. You have been promoted, as it were."

Harry pulled in his breath. "'Oo the devil *are* you?" he cried, trying to disguise the stark fear that clutched at his innards. "Wot business do you have, coming in here and—"

"I?" The stranger laughed with genuine amusement. "I am the next link in the chain, Mr. Tudwell. You will report to me."

"Your name?" Harry was conscious that his voice was not too steady. "Wot's your name?"

"My name, sir," the man said, "is unimportant. Perhaps more to the point, it would be dangerous for you to know it. What one does not know, of course, one cannot reveal, even under extreme duress." The light glinted from the smoked lenses that masked his eyes.

Harry was beginning to feel like a small chip of wood being sucked willy-nilly into a drain hole. His ears were roaring. "But ... but if I don't know your name," he managed, half-gasping, "or where you may be reached, 'ow am I to ... to contact you?"

"You are *not* to contact me." The man spoke sternly, as if he were a schoolmaster and Harry a disobedient boy. "It would be hazardous to try, and this is a game where the risks run high. Your advancement, Mr. Tudwell, is of more consequence than you can know, and the game is larger than you can think. When it is required, I shall contact you. Is that clearly understood?"

Harry closed his eyes, trying to think it through logically. Obviously, the investors, whoever they were, were no fools. They had a system, well worked-out, well-organized, carefully scheduled. He had to try to understand their system so that he could use it rather than be used by it. But he must not allow himself to be rushed into any agreements. He firmed his voice.

"I'll need time to think about this. I can't commit m'self at th' moment. There are other factors to be considered, other—"

"There is no time," the man said. His tone was conversational but the words knife-edged. "If you are not inclined to accept immediately, I shall walk down the High Street to call on a certain Mr. Thomas, who, I am reliably informed, has already expressed a great deal of enthusiasm for this particular position. If Mr. Thomas should be pleased to step up in rank, you will become, shall we say, superfluous."

Harry stared at him.

"Superfluous, yes," the man repeated, with a melancholy sigh, as if he rather liked Harry and wished it were otherwise. "In the same way that your unfortunate predecessor became ... superfluous."

Harry gulped. A sudden intuition, as sharp and persuasive as the point of a dagger, told him that this man was Foxy Smith's killer, and that if he failed to do as he was told, he would go the way Foxy had gone. He felt himself being pulled into the vortex of the drain, the light closing down to a pinpoint over his head, the roaring in his ears almost deafening.

"I ... see," he said weakly. "Well, in that case—"

"You have chosen very wisely, Mr. Tudwell." The man lifted his head. "I am pleased that we have arrived at a meeting of the minds." His voice became brisk. "Now, about the transaction that has been scheduled for tomorrow evening. The investors have decided that, under the circumstances, there is a very great danger of detection."

"Yes," Harry said. "Right." His mouth was dry, and his voice came out in a squeak. He swallowed, and put more force behind his words, anxious to recoup any status he might have lost by appearing tentative. "I told 'em at last night's meeting that we should suspend operations. I said it wasn't safe, with th' possibility of an inquiry an' all."

The smile came and went quickly, although the smoked lenses hid the man's eyes. "A very intelligent caution, Mr. Tudwell. However—"

"They didn't like it," Harry said, "They want t' go ahead with th' landing."

The man sighed. "Unfortunately, we *must* go ahead with the landing. The arrangements have been made, the ship has sailed, and we cannot alter our plan. However, I must emphasize the importance of caution. Be certain that you have people you can trust."

"That's th' trouble," Harry muttered. "I don't know as I can trust anybody."

"It is time," the man said severely, "that your troops learned to follow orders. You must see to it that they understand and obey. Whatever Captain Smith's faults, he was not a man to brook any disobedience in his subordinates. In that way, he was quite satisfactory. He may have gone too far, but—" He broke off. "But that is neither here nor there."

Harry frowned, seeing another difficulty. "Th' trouble is, they're not troops. I'm not sure exac'ly 'ow I can force 'em to—"

"The method, Mr. Tudwell, is not important. I leave it to you to find an appropriate way to compel their complete cooperation, bearing in mind that the operation is everything." He pulled himself up. "*Everything*, you understand."

"Yessir," Harry said, although for the life of him, he could not think how he could compel Trunky Thomas to cooperate.

"Well, then. You will take your party to the position

on the cliff tomorrow night. When the ship appears and shows the signal, you will answer with the appropriate designation for a landing at Rottingdean. You know the code?"

"Three lanterns," Harry muttered.

"Very good. Three lanterns it is. One more thing. Tomorrow morning, a traveling case will arrive here in your office. Guard it well, for it is of great importance. After dark has fallen and before you take your position on the cliff, stow the traveling case in the first bathing machine and apply this lock to the hasp. I have the second key." He handed Harry a padlock and a key. "Further, I wish you to see that a skiff is pulled up on the beach, near to the bathing machines."

"A skiff?" Harry asked, puzzled.

The man did not answer the question. "You will not see me, but I shall know what transpires and evaluate your performance accordingly." He smiled grimly. "This will be, as it were, your first test. Do you understand?"

Harry understood all too well. A vast and desperate anxiety began to rise up in him.

"Very good. I will contact you when it is safe to resume our operation. Until then, you must carefully monitor the course of the official investigation. You should particularly keep your eye on a certain party by the name of Sheridan, who is staying here in Rottingdean. He may prove meddlesome."

Harry nodded.

The man pulled his waterproof around him. "It would seem, then, that the game is afoot. And that, Mr. Tudwell, is all I have to say today." He turned toward the door.

"Wait!" Harry cried, feeling that his lifeline was about to be cut. Fear him or not, this man was his only contact with the investors—his only contact beyond the village. And the village itself, and the villagers, now seemed terribly threatening.

The man turned, frowning. "Yes?"

A dozen questions were turning in Harry's mind. He grasped at one. "Wot ... wot's t' be done with the goods we've got squirreled away down below? Where are we t' haul 'em?"

"Nowhere, for the moment. Until you hear from me again, you are simply to store the merchandise. Except for small lots that may be used for local consumption, discreetly and with proper accounting. No more questions. I am off."

The door closed and the man was gone before Harry could try once again to detain him. He sank helplessly into his chair, beaten, utterly exhausted, trembling uncontrollably. The man was Foxy's murderer, of that he was certain. And that he could be the next victim, of that he was certain, too.

Harry's visitor, on the other hand, strode powerfully down the brick-paved walkway, his cape rustling, his gear clanging at every step. If he saw the boy shrink quickly out of sight into the first loose-box, he gave no visible sign of it. But who could know, masked as he was, what he had seen?

21

"Honesty is for the most part less profitable than dishonesty."

—PLATO
The Republic

"It is an honest town ..."

—MARK TWAIN
"The Man that Corrupted Hadleyburg"

DEEP IN THOUGHT, with Lawrence on the seat beside him, Charles piloted the Panhard up the cobbled High Street of Rottingdean. He was oblivious to the delirious shouts of small children and the stares and head-shakings of pedestrians who had never before seen a motorcar, and he was startled into a full awareness of his surroundings only by the furious shout of a man who was herding a flock of half-a-dozen nervous sheep across the street. He pulled on the brake and brought the motorcar to a shuddering halt just in front of Seabrooke House, leaving the engine idling noisily.

"Ah, Lawrence," he said, pulling his goggles up. "We have arrived."

"Yessir," Lawrence said. "Want me t' put 'er in th' carriage 'ouse, sir?"

"Yes, yes, please do," Charles said distractedly, and took off his duster. "Let her ladyship know that I have returned, but that I have one or two important errands in the village." He lifted his tweed motoring cap and smoothed his wind-ruffled hair. "I shall return by teatime, I expect."

"Very good, sir," Lawrence said, and slid into the driver's seat. The Panhard chugged off up the street, and Charles turned to walk down the street, toward the Gap.

The constable's office occupied the front half of a narrow wooden building on the Newhaven Road, the back half of which was taken up by the jail. One of the cells had been occupied for the night by Rafe Hawkins, whom Constable Woodhouse had reluctantly imprisoned on a charge of wife-beating on a warrant sworn out by Rafe's angry mother-in-law. But after a night's cooling off, the young wife, babe in her arms and both eyes purpled, had appeared to plead for her husband's release so that he could go to his employment. The constable had willingly complied, sending Rafe off with a compassionate pat on the back. It gave Jack Woodhouse a great deal of satisfaction when the minor domestic misunderstandings that made up such a large part of his work could be resolved with so little effort.

Now, seated comfortably in his chair, a steaming cup of tea at his elbow and the sporting page of the weekly *Brighton Herald* spread out on the desk in front of him, Constable Woodhouse—Fat Jack to his friends and acquaintances—was the very image of a comfortable and contented man: plump, rosy-cheeked, slow of movement. A lazy man, some might also add, and they would have been right. But Fat Jack Woodhouse had long ago discovered that, where the business of life was concerned, idleness offered greater rewards than industry, and honesty less profit than dishonesty. Watching the wall, as the old adage had it, paid off. This revelation had certainly made Fat Jack's tenure as the constable of Rottingdean much easier and more comfortable than it might otherwise have been. As he contemplated his declining decades, he had little to complain or worry about.

But anyone who knew the constable well would see the unwonted furrows between the eyes, notice the nervous chewing of the black mustache and observe that, despite the favorable conclusion of this morning's domestic drama and the larger satisfactions of his life in general, Fat Jack Woodhouse was deeply worried. Even as he digested the fine steak-and-kidney pie that had been his luncheon, the constable was already feeling the first twinges of a nervous stomach, brought on by the workings of an unquiet mind.

A shadow darkened the open doorway, and the constable looked up from the cricket results. The gentleman standing easily before him had a neat brown beard and was dressed in a brown tweed walking suit, brown boots, and tweed cap. He inclined his head and spoke in a deep, cultured voice.

"Good afternoon, Constable Woodhouse."

With a sharp misgiving, the constable recognized Lord Sheridan. He had appeared with that meddling Kipling fellow on the beach when the constable was trying to handle the business of the body, and offered to take photographs of the whole sordid mess. A bother, as far as Fat Jack was concerned. Anyway, it wasn't a good idea to have pictures. Sometimes they showed more than you'd like, and they got handed around for others to look at.

"M'lord," he growled, folding the newspaper and pulling out a sheaf of papers, making it as plain as he could that he was occupied with official business and that his lordship was intruding upon his valuable time.

The visitor stepped into the room and stood in front of the desk, ignoring the chair meant for visitors. He brought the conversation directly to the point. "I am here at the request of the Crown to ask you a few questions concerning the deaths of George Radford and Captain Smith."

Fat Jack felt his mouth fall open, and he shut it with an audible click. His stomach lurched. "The Crown?"

"The dead men were Her Majesty's coast guards," Lord Sheridan replied. "If you feel it necessary to verify my authority for this inquiry, you may telegraph the chief constable at Brighton." His expression was bland, but his eyes were challenging. "I shall be happy to accompany you to the post office and wait with you until you receive Sir Robert's reply."

Fat Jack swiftly weighed the likelihood that the gentleman was lying against the effort required to walk to the post office and send a telegram, and decided to take his lordship at his word. He sighed. "That won't be necess'ry," he said. "Sit down, sir."

But Lord Sheridan preferred to stand. Fat Jack, feeling that to look up at his questioner would put him at a schoolboy's disadvantage, reluctantly stood, hitching up his sagging trousers.

"Well, then," he said loudly, trying to sound like a man with no troubles at the back of his mind, "what questions was yer lordship wantin' to ask?"

Lord Sheridan met his eyes. "I understand that you examined George Radford's body. What did you determine to be the cause of his death?"

Fat Jack hastily reached back in his mind to his conversation with Harry Tudwell and the explanation they had concocted. At the time, Harry had persuaded him that it was their best course of action—indeed, their only course of action. Now, he wondered why they had ever thought such a bizarre story would satisfy anyone who seriously inquired. But it was too late. He had nothing better to offer. He swallowed.

"Th' young chap killed 'isself," he said lamely.

"And how did you come to that conclusion, Constable Woodhouse?" Lord Sheridan asked in a conversational tone.

Fat Jack chewed on his mustache, trying to ignore the sharp teeth gnawing at his innards. "Well, m'lord," he said reluctantly, "there was a bloodstain on the front of 'im, an' 'e was drownded. It seemed to me that 'e flung 'isself off the cliff an' 'appened to fall on 'is knife on the way down. Anybody'll tell ye that the boy suffered black moods, and was given to drink. A despairin' sort 'e were, m'lord."

Lord Sheridan gave him a thoughtful look. "I just came from the performance of George Radford's autopsy, Constable Woodhouse. I must inform you that the young man neither fell on his sword nor drowned."

Fat Jack's stomach cramped. "M'lord?"

"The surgeon found a nick on the dorsal surface of the fourth rib."

Fat Jack stared blankly. "M'lord?"

Lord Sheridan spoke in a crisp, factual tone. "The victim could have received such an injury only if the blade that killed him was thrust from the rear. What is more, the abrasions on his wrists and ankles—which you might have seen, constable, had you looked closely—suggest that the body was bound to a heavy weight. And further, a man was observed putting the body into a skiff and rowing it out to sea." He paused, letting the words sink in. "Mr. Radford was murdered."

A burning sensation arose in Fat Jack's gullet. He swallowed. "Well, I..." He felt sweat bead out on his forehead and his cheeks go pale. "If ye say so, m'lord. I'm sure it's a surprise to me m'lord." He licked his lips and asked the dreaded question. "'Oo was the man wi' th' skiff?"

"The witness could not see him plainly."

He let out a small breath, feeling relief flood through him. He placed the flat of his hands on his desk to support himself. "An' 'oo was th' witness?"

"I cannot answer that. Are you quite all right. Constable?"

"Just a lit'le indigestion," Fat Jack said, and burped. "Too many onions." A witness? Who was the witness?

"Yes. Well, then, now that you know the facts, Constable Woodhouse, and since you know the village, perhaps you can tell me who might have had a reason to kill Mr. Radford." Lord Sheridan's eyes were as hard as two brown buttons. "Who might have wanted the man dead?"

Fat Jack's mind, unbidden, flew back again to his conversation with Harry Tudwell. Of course any of the men in the village could have killed young Radford, and might've done so, under the circumstances. But Tudwell was the cleverest and the most resolute of the lot and, next to Foxy himself, had the strongest reason to resent Radford's nosing into village affairs. If he offered Harry Tudwell as a suspect, would this insistent man go away? But if he offered Tudwell and the killer turned out to be someone else, what would happen when word got about that he had slipped the stablemaster's name to the investigator? It was not the ethics of betrayal that troubled him—Fat Jack, like everyone else in the village, recalled with great clarity what fate had befallen the ten-shilling men.

"'Oo wanted 'im dead?" The constable made his face

blank and shook his head, "I'm sure I don't know, m'lord. This is a 'onest an' a law-abidin' village."

"Honest and law-abiding?" Lord Sheridan's mouth quirked. "And yet you've just had two murders."

Fat Jack frowned, thinking that perhaps he should have gone to the bother of sending that telegram. What if this man wasn't who he claimed to be? What if he were one of the investors, making a private inquiry into the two deaths? He cleared his throat.

"I don't know anything about th' second killin'," he said defensively. "By the time I 'eard Cap'n Smith was shot an' went up to th' windmill to 'ave a look, the lot from Brighton was already there, pokin' about." He frowned again, conscious that he was telling a lie—several lies, in fact—and added, in a surly tone, an honest truth. "I didn't take it none too lightly that they came on my turf wi'out doin' me the curt'sy o' lettin' me know."

"I'm sure you didn't," Lord Sheridan replied pleasantly. "Well, then, since you are aware that Captain Smith was also murdered on your turf, as you say, let us put the question another way. Who, in your opinion, might have had reason to kill these two men?"

Fat Jack, struggling against his insubordinate stomach, tried to think of some halfway intelligent response. "Well, sir, since they was both coast guards and both murdered, I'd say it was likely that one man killed both of 'em."

Lord Sheridan shook his head, frowning. "That assumption is unwarranted, Constable Woodhouse. They could have been killed by different people."

Fat Jack felt himself to be at a great disadvantage. He could say hardly anything without revealing what he knew, and what little he could say made him sound like the village idiot. "Well, m'lord," he said finally, "the coast guard at Black Rock was not much liked round 'ere. 'E could've been done in by almost anybody."

"Not much liked? Why not?"

"B'cause, sir, 'e … well, 'e poked about." Fat Jock wanted terribly to sit down. "'E didn't just stick to coast guardin' along 'is section o' cliff."

"What sort of thing did he poke into?" Lord Sheridan asked sharply.

Fat Jack knew he had gone too far. "'E was just … nosy," he said. "'E liked to know wot was goin' on."

"Captain Smith, on the other hand, *was* well liked?"

The constable nodded, relieved at the change of subject.

"He was friendly with the villagers? A congenial sort?"

"Well," the constable said cautiously, "I don't know about congenial. Most coast guards keep to themselves. But 'e got along wi' folks."

"How long had he been here? Where did he live?"

"'E came 'ere three years or so ago from Dover, I 'eard 'im say. 'E lived in the cottage behind the old customs office on the 'Igh Street. 'E had no wife."

"Did he have any enemies?"

Harry Tudwell's name trembled on the tip of the constable's tongue and threatened to fall off. Fat Jack closed his mouth and shook his head. Whoever this man was, whatever his real business, it was not safe to name names.

"What about Mr. Thomas?"

The constable blinked. Trunky Thomas? Yes, he'd thought about that possibility. Trunky had a skiff, several, in fact. Trunky had just as much reason as anybody, maybe more, to want George Radford dead. And Trunky was keen to displace Harry Tudwell—had, in fact, gotten the backing of the more prominent villagers. Perhaps he had told Foxy that he was taking over as lander, and they had argued. Perhaps …

"What about Mr. Thomas, Constable?" Lord Sheridan repeated, watching him narrowly.

"Forgive me, m'lord," Fat Jack muttered, feeling pinned. He couldn't suggest Trunky as a suspect any more than he could suggest Harry, and for exactly the same reasons. "Ye caught me off guard, m'lord, an' I had to think about it." He looked up, trying to meet Lord Sheridan's eyes. "But I doubt Trunky's yer man, sir. I don't know of a reason 'e'd 'ave to kill anybody." He paused and added, cautiously: "Why d'ye ask, sir?"

Lord Sheridan pulled out a gold pocket watch and consulted it. "I should like to talk with Mr. Thomas before the hour grows later. Would you care to accompany me, Constable Woodhouse, or are you too"—his lordship's mouth quirked again—"too busy?"

Fat Jack sighed and cast one last, longing look at his cold tea and folded newspaper. "I s'pose I can spare th' time," he said grudgingly.

"Good." Lord Sheridan turned toward the door. "I don't imagine it will take too long, or prove too taxing."

22

"The last of the Rottingdean smugglers was probably 'Trunky' Thomas, who was the uncrowned king of the Gap at the turn of the century, as he was the proprietor of Rottingdean's four bathing machines as well as being owner of several fishing boats."

—Henry Blyth
Smugglers' Village: The Story of Rottingdean

"So," said Mr. Landsdowne crisply, "it is decided? Ye'll carry th' third lantern and work wi' me t' see that everything falls out accordin' t' our plan?"

Trunky Thomas folded his hands over his belly and sat back in his wooden chair, regarding the village chemist, whom he did not like and certainly did not trust, with suspicion. In fact, truth be known, Trunky had got where he was in life by suspecting everyone and not trusting anyone. He and Foxy Smith had been alike in that much, at least. But he had to admit that Landsdowne had brought him a clever idea, and that with the proper direction and under the proper leadership it could work to everyone's advantage, including his own.

"Right, then," he growled. "Tell 'Arry I'll do it." He

narrowed his eyes. "But if ye cross me in this, John, I'll have yer—"

"I won't cross ye, Trunky," the stoop-shouldered chemist said emphatically. "I speak fer th' village when I say ye're our man. We're tired o' 'arry's shilly-shallyin', 'is caution-this an' caution-that. We're countin' on ye t' keep us movin' forward." He stuck out his thin hand. "'Tis a bargain, then?"

"A bargain," Trunky said.

"Good. I'll go back an' tell 'arry that we've agreed to be 'is two signal-men."

They shook hands, the chemist took his leave, and Trunky settled his bulk in his chair and put his boots on the square deal table that served as his desk, looking out the window to the ocean. The sky was cloudless and a brisk wind blew out of the south, ruffling the Channel. If this weather held until tomorrow night, they should be all right. And after that, it would be clear sailing.

Trunky smiled to himself, clasped his hands behind his head, and tilted his chair on its back legs. If he were judged by what he was thought to own, he was not the most prosperous man in Rottingdean. Three small fishing boats, two skiffs, four bathing machines and a broken-down old pony to turn the capstan that hauled them up and down the beach, this frame shack perched at the edge of the cliff, that dilapidated cottage on the Whitehaven Road where he lived. Not much, by most accounts, to show for a lifetime of hard work.

Which was exactly the way Trunky liked it. He didn't want anyone to know that he was a rich man—houses in Newhaven, a valuable acreage on the outskirts of Brighton, notes in a bank vault, a cache of sovereigns hidden in a wall. These secret holdings were the fruits of his years of diligent effort as a one-man free-trade entrepreneur.

He had been smuggling long before the investors had appeared and seduced the villagers with an offer they could not refuse. But if you asked anyone in Rottingdean to name the village's most respected man, he'd be up there, top of the list, well above Harry Tudwell.

Trunky's lip curled at the thought of Tudwell. He had warned Foxy Smith that the man was a bandy-legged little coward and not to be trusted to manage the landward side of the operation. It was too bad that the captain hadn't listened to reason and gotten rid of the troublemaker long ago. If he had, he might be—

Trunky's thoughts were interrupted by a tenative knock at the shack door. He raised his head and tipped his curly-brimmed bowler back with a grimy thumb. "'Oo's knockin'?" he called gruffly.

"Jack Woodhouse," came the reply.

Ah, Fat Jack, the laziest man in Rottingdean. But a reliable man, a cooperative man. A man who knew when to watch the wall. Trunky raised his voice. "Come in, Fat Jack, an' mind th' door, that th' wind don't take it off!"

The constable stepped inside, a tall, brown-suited gentleman at his heels. Fat Jack, with an oddly fearful glance that Trunky could not read, fumbled his way through introductions. "'Is lordship 'as some questions," he said. "'Bout young Radford an' Cap'n Smith."

"That so?" Trunky asked, not getting up, and not taking his heels from the table. Since there were no other chairs in the shack, his visitors, perforce, had to stand. He spoke with a barely disguised insolence. "Wot does yer lordship want t'know?"

"To begin with," Lord Sheridan said mildly, "who stabbed George Radford, who bound him to a heavy weight, and who rowed his body out to sea in a skiff?"

Trunky dropped his hands and rubbed a finger over his

chapped lips. "Stabbed, eh?" he muttered. "Trussed up an' towed out t' sea?" He cast a contemptuous look at the constable. "'E didn't fall on 'is knife as 'e jumped off th' cliff t' drown 'isself, th' way Fat Jack told it to us?"

Fat Jack opened his mouth to remonstrate, thought better, and closed it.

"No," his lordship said. "He did not."

Trunky narrowed his eyes and picked out the most relevant point. "Whose skiff?"

"That, Mr. Thomas," his lordship said thoughtfully, "is a central question. I wonder if you would mind our taking a look at yours."

Trunky *did* mind, as a matter of fact. He minded very much, but it was safer not to show it. "Wot else d'ye want to ask?"

"Who might have wanted to kill George Radford?"

Trunky was by nature a slow and deliberate man who thought questions through before he attempted to answer. This question, however, afforded an opportunity he could not resist. He responded before he reflected. "Ye might talk t' 'Arry Tudwell. 'E's the stablemaster at 'Awk'am Stables."

"Is he? And what might have been Mr. Tudwell's motive?"

Trunky shrugged. "Radford got too close t' 'is business, mebbee."

"What business?"

This question, sharply put, gave Trunky pause. Perhaps he should not have been so quick to implicate Harry. After all, that particular sword could cut both ways. "Ye'll 'ave t' ask 'Arry," he said evasively. "'E's a close-mouthed man. I don't know much about 'is business."

"Let us go on, then," Lord Sheridan said. "What do you know about the murder of Captain Smith?"

Trunky's eyes narrowed. They were now treading more

dangerous ground. "I know wot I 'eard," he said cautiously.

"Then you did not see the body?"

Trunky said nothing.

His lordship reached into his pocket and took out a green pasteboard ticket. "This was found beside the body, Mr. Thomas. It is similar, is it not, to those used to enter your bathing machines?" Fat Jack, looking on, coughed anxiously.

Bugger the ticket! Trunky started to speak, stopped, started again. "Lots ... lots o' people use th' bathin' machines," he said finally. "'Alf th' people in Rottingdean's got tickets."

His lordship held it up. "With the stub still attached?"

Trunky swallowed. He must have dropped the ticket when he pulled out his handkerchief to mop his forehead. But it didn't mean anything, anyway. He had come straight from the old windmill to the Black Horse with the announcement of Foxy's murder. Half the town knew he had been there.

"Well, yes," he said, "now that ye mention it, I prob'ly *did* drop that ticket. 'Twas a real shocker t'see th' cap'n sittin' there wi' a bullet 'ole in 'is middle, dead as a doorknocker. I pulled out me 'andkerchief t' mop me brow. Prob'ly lost it then."

"And that was what time, Mr. Thomas?"

Trunky knew exactly what time he had been there, but he scratched his head, pretending to think. "Oh, mebbee eight o'clock or after. 'E was cold," he added helpfully. "'E'd been dead a good long time when I saw 'im."

"And who do you think might have killed him?"

Trunky gave the nosy lord a long stare. Two-edged sword or not, he now had no choice. "Talk t' 'Arry," he said.

"I shall," his lordship replied. He fixed Trunky with his

sharp brown eyes. "Do you have a gun, Mr. Thomas?"

Trunky's throat closed over his quick denial, and it was a good thing, too. Too many people—including Fat Jack, standing there with his eyes bulging out, and Harry Tudwell, who would be glad enough to incriminate him—had seen his gun.

"I do," he said at last. "No law against 'avin' a gun. A man wi' proppity needs a gun t' defend hisself."

Lord Sheridan glanced around the shack as if to question Trunky's claim to property, but said only, "I should like to see it, please."

Trunky shot an apprehensive glance at the constable. He could say that he kept it at the cottage, but Fat Jack, who had been in the shack one day when he took it out, would likely betray him. The constable looked away. Trunky sighed. Opening the drawer, he took out his Webley revolver, the gun his brother had brought back from the Zulu wars, fifteen years before. He laid it on the scarred wooden desk.

Lord Sheridan picked it up and sniffed the muzzle. "Recently fired," he murmured. He worked the catch and broke the gun open, then held the barrel up to the light and sighted through it while Trunky cursed himself for not having cleaned the weapon. Then he snapped the action shut and placed the gun on the table, saying nothing. Trunky put the gun back in the drawer and closed it. "I used it fer target practice last week."

"Is that right?" his lordship replied, one eyebrow raised. "Several of you shooting, were there?"

Trunky swallowed. "No, just me. I got a butt set up behind me cottage." His tongue felt thick and his hands had gone clammy. "I didn't shoot 'im." He swallowed and said it again, louder. "I didn't shoot Foxy, ye 'ear?"

Lord Sheridan looked at the constable. "Please see that

Mr. Thomas does not leave the village before the coroner's inquest, Constable Woodhouse. I am likely to have other questions for him after I have talked to Mr. Tudwell."

Fat Jack cast a miserable glance at Trunky. "Yessir," he said. His face was slick with sweat, as if he were suffering the pains of the grippe. "Wotever ye say, m'lord."

His lordship looked back at Trunky, his expression flat and unrevealing. "Now, shall we have a glance at those skiffs?"

The examination of the skiffs took the better part of a half-hour, but if it yielded any evidence, Lord Sheridan said nothing of it to Trunky or the constable. When the two men had left, Trunky returned to his shack and resumed his accustomed posture, feet up, hands clasped behind his head, eyes searching the inscrutable ocean.

But Trunky was not smiling, nor was he reflecting on his houses or land or bank notes or gold sovereigns. Rather, he was thinking with despair about the impending inquest and wondering how in God's name he was going to persuade the twelve men of the coroner's jury to believe his story.

23

"Kipling suspected it."

—Ezra Pound
The Cantos

"… Not twenty paces away a magnificent dog-fox sat on his haunches and looked at the children as though he were an old friend of theirs.

'Oh, Mus' Reynolds, Mus' Reynolds!' said Hobden, under his breath. 'If I knowed all was inside your head, I'd know something wuth knowin'. Mus' Dan an' Miss Una, come along o' me while I lock up my liddle hen-house.'"

—Rudyard Kipling
Puck of Pook's Hill

KATE WALKED SWIFTLY down the High Street toward the Gap, glancing into every green byway and peering into every windowed shop—the chemist's, the tobacconist's, the grocery, the alehouse, the post office. Lawrence had reported that Charles had one or two important errands and would be home by teatime. But teatime had come and gone, and Kate felt her information could not wait on his return. She had put on her jacket, pinned on her hat, and walked out into the bright clear afternoon, looking for him.

The village street was busy, but once again it seemed to Kate that there was something sinister about its activity. A hatless gypsy woman with long black hair, carrying a woven basket of rabbits, turned surreptitiously and slipped into a lane. A ruddy-cheeked man with a scythe over his shoulder stepped into the gutter so she could pass, averting his eyes from hers and muttering something she could not catch. A cluster of men on the corner turned their backs as she walked by, as if they did not want her to see their faces.

Kate felt a shiver of apprehension. With its perfection of whitewashed slate-roofed houses, its quaintly cobbled street, its green gardens and golden downs and wide views of the sparkling, sun-ruffled sea, Rottingdean was just as lovely as it had seemed the day she and Charles arrived. But now, under the picture-book loveliness, Kate felt something dark and somber brooding. "Its soul is rotten right through," the young widow had cried. And Kate shivered once again as she realized that Rud, who had not even heard the woman's story, suspected it: "Laces for a lady, letters for a spy," he had written. "Watch the wall, my darling, while the Gentlemen go by." How many men, women, and children in this village had turned away from the truth, closing their eyes and ears to a venture that turned honest men into something else altogether?

"Kate!"

Kate started. In front of her, turning the corner from Newhaven Road, was Charles. In her haste, she had all but collided with him.

"Charles!" she said, clutching at his arm. "I've been looking for you. There is something you need to know—

several things, in fact, and they're all important. Is there somewhere we can talk privately?"

A few minutes later, Charles having procured a glass of sherry for each of them, they were seated at a table in the large taproom of the White Horse Inn, with its curious carvings and half-paneled walls. From the evidence of the painted wooden signs that hung above the wainscoting, the inn must once have been an important coaching station. One sign, with a date of 1808, announced a new coach called the Royal Charlotte, which would make the forty-mile journey between Brighton and Hastings in ten hours. Another trumpeted the opening of the Falmer Road in 1822, the "new coach road" that linked Rottingdean to the county town of Lewes. Kate wondered, fleetingly, how much smuggled contraband, how many clandestine communications, had been carried by those coaches.

Charles listened thoughtfully to her story, frowning at the widow Radford's bitter accusation of Captain Smith, smiling a little when Kate told about her conversation with Mrs. Portney, and shaking his head over the tale of the Chantilly and Valenciennes lace that she had ordered from the dressmaker.

"And here," Kate said, drawing a tobacco tin out of her handbag, "is a little present I purchased for *you,* my dear. I hope you enjoy it, for it is very good. Or so the tobacconist assured me." She smiled, remembering Kipling's verse. "Brandy for the parson, tobacco for the clerk."

Charles took the tin, opened and sniffed it. "So it is," he said admiringly, turning a pinch between his fingers. "A very fine Turkish tobacco, which I should rather have expected to find in one of the best shops in London. Thank you very much, Kate. Your resourcefulness never fails to amaze me." He began filling his pipe. "But what's this about a parson and a clerk?"

"It's a poem Rud sent me this afternoon," she said. "It's called 'A Smuggler's Song.'" She drew it out of her handbag and read the first verse.

"'Five and twenty ponies,
Trotting through the dark—
Brandy for the Parson,
'Baccy for the Clerk;
Laces for a lady, letters for a spy,
And watch the wall, my darling,
while the gentlemen go by.'"

"Mmm," Charles said, striking a match and touching it to his tamped tobacco. He drew appreciatively. "Yes, fine."

"Of course it's fine!" she exclaimed. "But listen to *this* verse, Charles—it's even finer. Rud has it exactly right.

"'If you do as you've been told, 'likely there's a chance,
You'll be give a dainty doll, all the way from France,
With a cap of Valenciennes, and a velvet hood—
A present from the Gentlemen, along o'being good!'

"You see?" she said excitedly. "Everyone in the village is either involved or knows what's going on, but they've closed their eyes and kept their mouths shut because they're benefiting from it."

"Ah," Charles said, as a wreath of smoke curled over his head.

"Don't *ah* me, Charles Sheridan!" Kate leaned closer, frowning. "And don't tell me I'm imagining things, either. I'm certain that George Radford was killed because he threatened to reveal what was going on. In fact, he may even have been killed by Captain Smith, who was the leader of the smugglers!" She put her finger on Charles's chest, tapping for emphasis. "This is not a poet's fancy or one of Beryl Bardwell's inventions. This is the *truth*."

"You're very likely right, Kate," Charles said. He clasped her hand and closed his eyes meditatively. "By Jove, this is a *very* fine tobacco."

She pulled her hand back, surprised. "I'm ... right?"

He opened his eyes again. "The evidence you have assembled fits the story that has emerged so far from my own investigations." He raised his glass of sherry and sipped it. "This is very fine sherry, as well," he said, leaning back. "Don't you think so?"

"Charles!" Kate exclaimed impatiently. "Tell me about your investigations. What have you learned?"

"I will tell you later, my dear," Charles said, and smiled. "But we have a small matter to attend to first—a social call, as it were, although our host will not be at home. Drink up." He lifted his glass to hers.

Charles's "small matter" turned out to be a search of the cottage just off the High Street in which Captain Smith had lived. Kate was nervous as they stood before the closed door as if they were about to call on the occupant of the building. She felt only slightly reassured by the fact that Charles had a key, obtained when the late captain's personal effects were surrendered to him. She knew that the man whose house this was could not come upon them, but that did not keep her from feeling that he was watching behind the rosebush, or on the other side of the door. She felt rather better once they were safely inside the empty cottage and the door shut and latched against any challenge.

"Well," Charles remarked, looking around, "I shouldn't think a search would take long. There isn't much here to search through."

The cottage was a single large room with a wooden floor, heavy beams supporting a low ceiling, and a fireplace of laid-up stone. A narrow bed stood against one wall, a trunk at its foot. A wooden sink-and-cupboard arrangement ran under a casement window on a second wall, and a table and chair stood against a third. A stuffed chair sat before the cold fireplace, which contained a small black kitchen range that had not been cleaned recently. One corner of the room was curtained off as a closet, and in another stood a wooden cupboard of books. The room was spare and tidy, the only decorations a wall-hung gold-framed photograph of a dark-haired woman in the hoop skirts of thirty years before, signed "To Reynold, from his Loving Mother." Beside it, in a matching frame, hung a photograph of a smiling man in a coast guard's uniform—the man Kate had seen, dead, in the old mill. His eyes, bright and curious, seemed to follow her as she moved, as if he were about to ask what they wanted from him.

There was a paraffin lamp on the table, but the sun through the window brightened the room. Charles made for the desk, instructing Kate to look through the trunk and the closet, and the next few minutes passed in silence, the only sound the twitter of a robin outside the window. Kate, still feeling the dead man's eyes on her, took the photograph from the wall and laid it face down on the bed, then began with the closet. She found nothing remarkable there: a thick blue overcoat, a woolen uniform jacket with gold buttons and braid, a tweed shooting jacket, a pair of tweed trousers, boots. She went through all of the pockets, discovering nothing but a wrapped peppermint candy and a telegram, still folded in its yellow envelope, which she glanced at and put on the table for Charles to read. She opened the trunk and lifted out neat stacks of clothing—woolen trousers, a uniform jacket, folded shirts, cotton stockings—finding nothing of any interest. Quickly, she searched the bed, lifting the thin mattress and peering beneath it. Then she straightened and went to the wooden sink. A mug filled with assorted knives, forks, and spoons caught her eye, for one of the knives was quite unusual. It looked like a small sword, actually, with a hilt...

She looked at it closely and gasped. "Charles, I think there's *blood* on this knife! And here are initials—GR!"

It was indeed blood, and after a moment's study, Charles spoke grimly. "Well done, Kate. I think you've found the weapon that killed Radford—his own knife." He shook his head. "I'm not sure I should have thought to look for it among the kitchen utensils."

"Then you knew it was here?" Kate cast a glance at the wicked knife and shuddered, thinking of the family it had ripped apart.

"I thought it might be—if Smith killed him, and I believe he did. If we question the boy closely, we may find that he recognized the captain, taking the body out to sea." He held up the telegram. "You found this in a pocket?"

"Yes. Is it important?"

Charles handed it to her. "What do you think?"

"MEET AT HIGH POINT 4 PM SIGNED WILLY," she read slowly, and shook her head. "I don't know, Charles." She handed back the telegram. "The only Willy I can think of is the Kaiser, but I hardly imagine a coast guard captain would be receiving telegrams from heads of state. What else have you found?"

"These were in a ledger in the cupboard," Charles replied, indicating several items he had laid out on the table. "When I have time to study the ledger, it may also prove useful."

Kate bent over a sketch, crudely drawn free-hand in pencil on a torn and wrinkled scrap of brown paper. "It's a map of Rottingdean. Look, Charles, at these little squares—they are houses! There's the pond on the Green, and that little square is The Elms, and that one is North

End House. This heavy line has to be the High Street, and this dotted line ..." Her mouth went dry.

Charles finished the sentence for her. "This dotted line must represent the tunnel."

She stared at him. "Charles, we've solved the mystery. This is *proof* that Captain Smith was involved with the smugglers!"

"Not necessarily," Charles said cautiously. "He might have been investigating their activities."

"But that doesn't account for George Radford's knife!"

"Someone might have put it here, with the intention of incriminating Foxy Smith."

Kate frowned. "You can't really think—"

"No. I believe Smith killed Radford to keep the smuggling operation from being discovered. But we can't rule out other possibilities, Kate. After all, we can't get into Smith's head and find out what he knew, and we don't have any evidence that Radford was killed to keep him quiet. And there are still several puzzles. For instance, look at these." He pointed to two sheets of onionskin paper covered with penciled compass bearings, lines, and arcs.

"What are they?"

"Map overlays. They're used in the Army, where one can't forever be annotating one's map with the latest tactical information. These appear to match an inch-scale Ordnance Survey map."

"Which map? A map of what area?"

Charles shook his head. "I can't tell. The registration marks aren't designated by coordinates."

"They won't be of much use, then." Kate, thinking that the sketch of the tunnel was far more interesting than sheets of onionskin that might or might not tell them anything, went back to the drawing. She put her finger on one of the squares. "You know, I believe this is Seabrooke

House, Charles. And look—the tunnel is right *there*, just behind the house!"

Charles was still studying the overlays. "I might be able to guess the area, if I could find the appropriate Ordnance Survey sheet." He paused. "What's puzzling me, though, isn't the *what* but the *why*. I'd use a map overlay to plan something dynamic—an invasion, perhaps, not a simple smuggling operation." He frowned. "And then there is that gun ... yes, the gun," he muttered, more to himself than to her.

Kate looked up. "The gun? You've found the gun that killed Captain Smith?"

Charles began gathering up the overlays and sketch and putting them into the ledger. "Not yet. But we will, Kate, we will—it's just a matter of time." He wrapped the knife in a clean cotton cloth and gathered everything up, then looked at her, grim-faced. "And while we may not be able to get inside Foxy Smith's head and learn all that he knew, what we've found in this room tells us something very much worth knowing."

His mouth relaxed into a smile and he put his arm around Kate's shoulders. "Let's go back to Seabrooke House, shall we? We can talk there—and now that Foxy's no longer around to tell the chickens what to do, perhaps we can unlock the hen-house."

Kate frowned. "I don't think I understand that."

"I'm not sure I do either, Kate—at least, not all of it. But guessing is better than closing our eyes, or watching the wall. Isn't it?"

24

"I'll tell you a tale, an' you can fit it as how you please."
—RUDYARD KIPLING
Puck of Pook's Hill

"In the course of a landing, a newcomer to the parish arrived and was horrified to find that goods were being illegally landed. 'Smuggling! Oh, the shame of it! Is there no magistrate to hand, no justice of the peace? ... Is there no clergyman, no minister?' The innocent man's enquiries were silenced when one of the locals pointed out the vicar holding a lantern."
—RICHARD PLATT
Smugglers' Britain

PATRICK SQUATTED DOWN in the corner of the empty loose-box in the stable for a long time before he began to move about. Harry Tudwell might step out of the stable office at any moment and collar him, and he wasn't at all sure that the man with the rattling pack and batwing waterproof hadn't caught sight of him stepping hastily away from the door and might turn back to search for him. And the loose-box—dark and smelling of horses and sweet summer hay—was as good a place as any to think things through from beginning to end and all in between, a project which took a great deal of time because Patrick had a great deal to think about.

He had to think about the errands he had done for Mr. Tudwell, about the nighttime enterprises of certain villagers and the routes they took to do their work, and about the lantern lights on Beacon Hill. He had to consider what and whom he had seen on the beach on the preceding Friday night; what he had heard Mrs. Higgs and her sister Mrs. Portney discussing in the kitchen the night before; and what he had overheard in the stable office between Mr. Tudwell and the chemist and—just now—between Mr. Tudwell and the odd-looking man with the smoked-glass eye preservers, who could be anything but was certainly *not* an antiquarian.

But Patrick's attempt at logical consideration was repeatedly interrupted by the frightful memory of Captain Smith sitting bolt upright and stark dead in the old mill, and the wrenching anguish of the family in the coast guard cottage at Black Rock. He hadn't much liked the captain, and he hadn't known Mr. Radford except by sight. But not to see the sky or smell the ocean or feel the shingle under your feet—that would be a terrible oblivion, and Patrick caught himself shivering whenever he thought of it.

By the time he managed to sort through everything, Patrick realized that he probably knew more about what had happened and what was going to happen than Mr. Tudwell himself—more than anyone else in the entire village, maybe. This realization might have made another boy feel puffed up and important, but it only made Patrick apprehensive. He was not a particularly moral child—as for most boys of his age, morality was a matter of what served most handily—but he knew that his dilemma was essentially a moral one. Mr. Tudwell had been a father to him when his own father had turned his back—wasn't it right that he should tell him what the villagers were planning so that he could take steps against the conspirators? But if Patrick told and Mr. Tudwell fixed things for now, the eventual catastrophe—for it *would* come, of that Patrick was certain—could hurt a great many people. And whatever loyalties Patrick owed the stablemaster, Mr. Tudwell had led the village into the valley of temptation, as the vicar would put it—shouldn't he pay for what he had done? Patrick was seized with another fit of shivering at the thought of a third death. There had to be a better way out.

The boy sat on his haunches for another ten minutes, pondering alternatives. Since he had come to Rottingdean, Mr. Tudwell had been the most important man he knew. That was no longer true, however. Patrick knew two other important men, and they might be able to help sort this thing out. He stood, looked cautiously out of the loose-box, and surveyed the passage in both directions, then slipped out and headed down the path. The story whose beginning he had seen that night on the beach now had a middle, and perhaps even an end. It was time to tell it to Mr. Kipling.

Kate was glad that today was Mrs. Portney's half-holiday, for that meant she and Charles could talk without fear of being overheard. It was well after six o'clock, and the informal but generous supper laid out on a white cloth on the drawing-room table was more than welcome. Amelia had lighted the gas lamps, the fire was burning cheerfully, and Kate, having changed into her favorite yellow silk dress, was pouring tea. Charles came into the room wearing a smoking jacket, his brown hair freshly combed.

He sat down beside the fire with a tired sigh. "And this was meant to be our holiday! I'm sorry, Kate. I didn't intend—"

"Sshh," she said. "It's no matter. There will be time for our holiday." She took him his cup of tea. "You've had a very long day. You must be exhausted."

"I'm tired," Charles admitted. "But I feel we are making progress." He grinned ruefully. "Although I'm damned if I know what we're progressing *toward*. Just when I think I understand it, something else presents itself." He shook his head. "Like those blasted overlays," he muttered.

Kate put a cold tongue sandwich on a plate, added several small egg-and-anchovy sandwiches and a generous spoonful of potato salad and dressed cucumbers. "I hope you don't mind a cold supper," she said, putting the plate on the small table beside his chair. "Mrs. Portney is out."

Charles caught her hand and kissed it, then let it go. "I was well fed at luncheon. Barriston insisted that Pinckney and I share his partridge pie and apple pudding while we waited for the X-rays."

A few silent moments passed while Charles ate and Kate prepared her own plate. When she had sat down on the other side of the fire, her plate in her lap, he said, "Would you like to hear what went on in Brighton—besides the partridge pie, that is?" He regarded her, his head on one side. "Although some of it is a bit grisly. Perhaps the story should wait until we've finished our suppers."

"No, tell," Kate commanded, and listened while he related the outcome of the two autopsies and his conversation with the gun shop owner. "It's lucky that Dr. Barriston was able to take the X-rays and retrieve the bullet," she said, when he had finished.

"Lucky indeed. The bullet would have been found, most likely, but the job would have taken a great deal more time." He frowned at the fire. "I don't know, though, that we learned anything from the bullet that we had not already surmised from the cartridge. We shall just have to wait and see what can be found out from Mr. Barker's inquiries in London. If it is true that there are very few guns of that type, we might have something."

"What about your errands here in Rottingdean?"

Abstractedly, Charles picked up his napkin and blotted his lips. "Yes. Well, I stopped for a visit with the constable, who is up to his ears in all of this." He gave her a halfsmile. "His nickname, by the way, is Fat Jack."

Kate looked up at him, startled. "The constable is involved in the smuggling?" Then, more thoughtfully, she remarked, "Well, I suppose he would have to be in on it, in one way or another, This is a small village. The constable would certainly have to know what was going on. And then of course he'd have to pretend not to, or he'd have to arrest people, or report them, or something."

"Precisely. Fat Jack is a lazy man with a very simple philosophy: people who don't ask questions are never told any lies."

Kate was thinking that Charles's reply was remarkably like Kipling's line, "Them that asks no questions isn't told a lie," when the door opened and Amelia stepped in. "A Mr. Kipling is 'ere t' call," she said, "wi' a young boy—Patrick, I b'lieve."

Kate turned, surprised, as Rud and the boy—dressed in the same coarse shirt and green corduroys he had worn that morning, and still without a jacket—came into the room.

"Forgive us for interrupting your supper," Rud said. "We wouldn't have come at such an hour, but it seemed rather ... well, urgent."

"It's no interruption," Charles said. "We've finished, although there is plenty left for those who are hungry."

Kate smiled at Patrick, who stood shyly behind Rud. "Would you like a glass of milk and a sandwich, Patrick?"

The boy pushed back an unruly lock of hair. "Thank you," he said, and took the chair Kate pulled out for him at the table. She sent Amelia for milk and heaped a plate with food, which the boy began to devour hungrily.

"You've eaten, Rud?" she asked.

"Yes, thank you," he replied. "We had a late, large tea, and Carrie is off to bed with a flannel brick at her feet and a magazine in her hand—containing one of Beryl Bardwell's stories, if I'm not mistaken. Her cold is troublesome, and the house is beastly damp. I dare say bed is the best place for her." He eyed the decanter of port on the table. "I'd be grateful for a glass of something, though. If you've the time to listen, Patrick has a story to tell, and stories do go better with a glass."

"Well, then," Kate said, pouring a glass for Kipling. "When Patrick has finished eating, we can all listen."

"Meanwhile, Rud," Charles said to Kipling, "I have one or two things to tell you about today's inquiries. Shall we go into the garden for a smoke?"

When Patrick had finished and the men had come back, the three of them joined Kate at the fire. "A story?" she asked, looking expectantly at Patrick, sitting in a large chair that made him look like a very small boy. "Well, tell away, then, Patrick. We are all ears."

Patrick told the story simply and straightforwardly, with very little nervousness. When he came to the end, he lowered his head and said to Charles, "I'm sorry, sir, really I am. I expect that if I'd told earlier, Captain Smith might not have gotten killed."

"Because he would have been in jail for murdering George Radford, you mean?" Charles asked dryly.

"Something like that," Patrick said. Kate heard the

unhappiness in his voice and impulsively reached out to touch his hand. "The trouble was," he added, "I wasn't sure it was really Captain Smith rowing the skiff that night—although the coast guards always wear black oilskins, while everybody else wears yellow. Almost everyone else," he amended.

"That's right!" Kate exclaimed. "George Radford had black oilskins. I saw them hanging in the cottage today."

"Who else has black oilskins, Patrick?" Charles asked. The boy hung his head. "Mr. Tudwell," he said, after a minute.

"Harry Tudwell," Kipling said, "has been a good friend to Patrick. Given him work and taken him shooting and the like."

"I see," Charles said.

Patrick bit his lip. "I was sure that it was the coast guard skiff, too—but then, anybody could have borrowed it. It's kept on the beach, right there at the Gap. So I didn't tell, because I didn't ... well, I wasn't sure just who to tell, or whether telling was right. I didn't want to get anyone in trouble, and I was really only guessing."

"Sometimes guesses are all there are to go on," Charles remarked.

"The part I really don't understand, though," Kipling said, pulling at his mustache with a frown, "is that man—the antiquarian, you called him?"

"Yes, but he isn't," the boy said. "That's only what he *pretends* to be, sir. I've seen him out among the downs poking around and sighting with his compass and marking up his maps, but he's always miles away from the burial sites and the old settlements. And I've seen him talking to Captain Smith." Patrick frowned. "I think I've seen him somewhere else, too, only he didn't —" His voice trailed off and he shook his head as if he were puzzled.

"It sounds as if he reports to the men who are financing this enterprise," Kate said thoughtfully. "What was it he called them? Investors? They must make a huge profit when all the goods are sold."

"They haul it all to London, I suppose," Kipling remarked. "That's where they're likely to get the best price."

"Some of the goods go to Brighton," Patrick put in. "Mr. Tudwell sends me with messages which are supposed to be about horses but which are really about tobacco and brandy." He smiled self-consciously. "It's like a game, you see. Everybody knows it's not horses, but everybody pretends not to know anything."

"The Great Game," Charles said reflectively.

"What doesn't go to Brighton or London is sold in the High Street," Kate said, and told about her afternoon's shopping expedition and Mrs. Portney's offer to find brandy and truffles.

"My word." Kipling beetled his thick brows in mock dismay. "The dressmaker, the tobacconist, *and* the grocer? Oh, Rottingdean, innocent Rottingdean, to what depths have you descended? I daresay we'll soon be hearing that the vicar is holding the lantern."

"Actually," Patrick said, "this vicar is new, and too proud to hold a lantern for anybody." He looked puzzled at Kipling's chuckle and added, earnestly, "But the very oldest tunnel under the village goes to the vicarage, and the Reverend Hooker was a lookout man for the old Rottingdean gang. *He* probably held the lantern."

"Look here, lad," Kipling said sternly, "how do you know where the tunnel goes? And about Hooker, too, for that matter?"

"I know about the Reverend Hooker because Mr. Forsythe—he's the village schoolmaster—told me. And I know about the tunnels because I go..." He corrected himself. "I mean, I used to go down there with the other boys."

"Used to?" Charles asked.

"When I first came here. Now, though, we're not supposed to. Mr. Tudwell told me to keep clear, and Ernie Shepherd got an awful beating from his father for going down there."

"Because it's dangerous?" Kate asked. "I suppose there might be cave-ins, or you could get lost."

"Because we're not supposed to know that the men are working down there," Patrick replied off-handedly. "Last year, you see, they repaired the old tunnels and dug some new ones and made the underground cellar much bigger."

"'They'?" Charles asked. "Who was in charge of the excavation?"

The boy bit his lip. "Mr. Tudwell." He raised his eyes. "But he's a *good* man," he burst out. "Good to me, anyway. He ... he's looked after me."

"I see," Charles said. "Well, then. You were saying that you weren't to go into the tunnel."

"Right. We weren't to know anything about it, but the end of it comes out in the cliff. It's behind a rock fall, but we found where they tipped the spoil out on the beach so that the waves could wash it away."

"I don't suppose," Charles said pensively, "that you did as you were told. About the tunnels, I mean." He looked straight at Patrick, and there was a twinkle in his eye. "If I were your age, nothing would keep me out of them."

"Yes, m'lord," Patrick said, unblinkingly. "I daresay that's true, m'lord."

Kate suppressed a giggle.

Charles took out the scrap of paper on which the tunnel was drawn and showed it to Patrick. "This is a sketch of the tunnel system, isn't it? Is this accurate?"

The boy studied it for a moment, then nodded. "More or less, sir. This is where it comes out on the beach. And this"—he pointed—"is the new section."

"Where's the underground cellar?" Charles asked.

"Here." Patrick put his finger on the map, at a point not far from Seabrooke House. "Where this circle is."

"How big is it?"

Patrick looked around. "Bigger than this room. The ceiling is a lot lower, though."

"What are you getting at, Charles?" Kipling asked.

"I'd like to see this tunnel for myself," Charles said. "Where can we get in without attracting any attention?"

"How about my cellar?" Kipling offered. "We'd have to unblock the passage, but it probably wouldn't be very much work. We'd have to do it, though," he added ruefully, "without waking Carrie. She wouldn't be quite easy if she knew we were larking about in the old smugglers' tunnel."

Patrick shook his head. "It would be easier from the cellar here, sir. There's an entry behind that big wooden rack where they keep the wine bottles. All you have to do is unhook a wire and push the rack to one side. There's a hasp on the door, but it isn't locked."

"Of course there's an entry there!" Kate exclaimed, thinking of the broken brandy bottle. "But how do *you* know about it, Patrick?"

"Mrs. Portney is Mrs. Higgs's sister," Patrick said. "I've helped her carry things up and down the stairs." He looked at Charles. "If you want to see the tunnel and the cellar, sir, I could show you. We'd need lanterns, though." He glanced at Charles's smoking jacket. "And you'd need to wear something else. It's filthy down there."

"There are lanterns hanging on the wall in the back passage," Kate said, standing up. "I'll get them, and we can all go."

Charles gave her a firm look. "Not all of us," he said. "You must stay here, Kate."

"But that's not fair!" she protested. "I *want* to go. I've never been in a tunnel. And besides, Beryl Bardwell is considering putting the tunnels into a story, and she can't do that if she hasn't seen them." She looked down at her full yellow skirt. "Wait while I change. It will only take a moment."

"When this is all over," Charles said, "you can climb into a pair of my trousers and you and Beryl can explore as much as you like. But tonight, we need someone to stand watch for us, in case there's difficulty."

Patrick gave her a sympathetic look. "I'll be glad to go with you and this Beryl person," he volunteered helpfully. "I can show you all kinds of interesting things. If you don't mind rats," he added. "And bats, at the beach end."

"Good," Charles said. "Now, where will we find those lanterns?"

And with that, Kate had to be satisfied.

25

"I warned the old fox and his neighbours long ago that they'd come to trouble with their side-sellings and bye-dealings; but we cannot have half Sussex hanged for a little gun-running."

—RUDYARD KIPLING
Puck of Pook's Hill

"ARE WE READY?" Charles asked, checking his trousers pocket for his compass, the map, and a small notebook. Patrick seemed confident enough, and Charles doubted that either compass or map would be necessary, but it might be good to get a sense of where they were with reference to the aboveground features.

"Ready, by heaven!" Kipling exclaimed, lifting the lantern to peer into the dark opening in the cellar wall. "Yo-ho-ho and a dead man's chest. How Stevenson would have loved this adventure!"

As the boy had said, the wine rack was easily pushed aside and the plank door readily opened to reveal a narrow, low-ceilinged passageway.

Charles turned to Kate. "We'll leave the door open," he said, "and one of the lanterns here with you. When do you expect Mrs. Portney to return?"

"I don't know," Kate said, her worried look giving her away. "Do you really think this is a good idea? What if you're discovered? What if you meet some of the villagers in the tunnel?"

"We won't," Patrick said in a reassuring tone. "It's such a beastly place that nobody ever comes down unless they're hauling or digging or something. And if they were doing that, we would hear 'em. Sound carries a long way in the tunnel. Sometimes you can hear people talking all the way at the other end."

"Then I'll hear you," Kate said, "if you call out."

"You will," Charles promised her. He suspected that they were in greater danger of discovery by Mrs. Portney than by anyone else. But he patted his jacket just the same, making sure that he had the pistol that the chief constable had lent him. He did not think there would be trouble, or he would not have allowed the boy to lead them; on the other hand, it was well to be armed.

By the time they had gone fifty yards or so in the direction of the beach, Charles had decided that the boy was right: the tunnel was a beastly place, indeed, a place for gnomes and earth-people. It was scarcely wider than Charles's shoulders, and too low for him to stand erect. The chalk walls were grayish-white and bore the marks of picks and chisels, like the toothmarks of some ancient beast, and here and there clusters of embedded flint nodules, glinted in the lantern light. The ceiling was covered with soot, where it had been blackened by the burning pitch of long-ago torches. At one point, a date had been hacked roughly into the rock, with soot rubbed into it so that it stood out against the whiteness.

"Seventeen-forty," Charles read, and whistled to himself, thinking back to a time, a century and a half before, when desperate, angry men had cut this passageway, foot by laborious foot, through the solid chalk. He shivered, feeling ancient eyes on him, and thought that the rumors of ghosts in the cellars of Rottingdean might not be just idle gossip. The air was damp and still and cold, like the air in an icehouse. Somewhere in the distance, water dripped, the sound magnified by the rock walls.

"There's a section that crosses the drain along the High Street," Patrick said, just above a whisper. Being shorter, he was walking more comfortably. "That's where the water is running. But mostly it's dry."

"I must say," Kipling whispered hoarsely, from the rear, "there's not much in the way of elbow room. How do they move the goods in such a tight space?"

"In pushcarts and on sleds," Patrick said. "They've built wood ones that just fit. You'll see them in the big cellar." They walked in silence for a moment, then he added, "There's a sort of junction just ahead. We go to the left. It's not far after that."

Walking behind Patrick, Charles felt himself fascinated by the boy, who seemed to know everything and moved so effortlessly and without fear in this dark place. There was more to this bright, inquisitive lad than there was to the average village boy, that was certain. It was a damned shame that Patrick's father was so far away and took so little interest in his son. The boy deserved better. What's more, he was at a vulnerable age, in a vulnerable position. Without further formal schooling and under the influence of these enterprising village fellows with their get-rich schemes, it was likely that he would follow in their footsteps. Better to get him out of the village, into something more settled and with greater promise. He would talk to Kipling. Perhaps, between them, they could come up with something suitable.

Patrick held up his hand, halting their forward progress. "Here's the junction," he said. "The big cellar is to the left. If we keep straight on, we will come to the beach."

Charles peered ahead. The tunnel was wider and more obviously traveled, and there were deep scratches in the chalk walls and gouges in the floor, as if something heavy had been shoved along. He looked down at the crude map. "There seem to be several branches. Are they still open?"

"Only one," Patrick said. "The branch that goes to the cellar of the White Horse. It's used quite often, as it is the only entrance at that end, except for the opening onto the beach."

Charles took the lantern from Kipling and held it up, looking to the right. That tunnel was narrower and much lower. He would have to bend double to enter it.

"Where does that lead?"

"To the cellar at the Black Horse," Patrick said. "Mostly what goes that way are small wooden barrels of spirits. They rope them together and drag them." He grinned knowingly. "Perry organizes that part. He owns the Black Horse."

No doubt Perry organized that part very expeditiously, Charles thought—moving the liquor straight from the ship to the cellar of the alehouse, where it was let down. As he understood it, spirits were usually smuggled over-proof, and were diluted to bring them to a strength that was both drinkable and profitable. Perhaps some letting down had occurred in the cellar at Seabrooke House, and might account for the spilled brandy.

"And who organizes the rest of it?" Charles asked.

"Captain Smith always managed the ship—signaling, and all that."

"Who oversees the transfer of the goods?"

The boy looked cornered. "Mr. Tudwell," he muttered at last.

"And the distribution? That is, moving the goods to their final destination."

The boy did not answer.

Charles nodded. "Well, then, shall we carry on?"

They turned to the left. Fifty paces later, the tunnel widened suddenly into a square, cavelike room, carved out of the chalk. The lantern flickered eerily against the white walls, casting grotesquely misshapen shadows, and the flint nodules winked like wise eyes. Boxes, crates, and small barrels were stacked against the walls, the lids stamped with their contents, although there were no attached bills of lading. Charles stooped to read. Tobacco, fabric, lace, tea—it was no wonder Kate had been able to purchase in Rottingdean the same goods she might have bought at an exclusive shop in London. All this merchandise, stored here against the day when it would be hauled out and distributed for sale. He glanced around. Still, though, it was a very large room, not even partially filled, and obviously constructed at great effort.

"This is newly excavated?" he asked Patrick.

"Most of it. There was a smaller cellar here to start with, maybe twelve feet by twelve feet or so. The rest was dug last summer."

"How many people were involved?" Kipling asked. "It looks like it would take an army to dig it out."

"Most of the men in the village were in it one way or another, either digging or hauling the rock to the beach."

"Last summer," Charles said thoughtfully. "Is that when the smuggling began in earnest?"

The boy nodded. "Trunky Thomas did some before then, but he was the only one. His father was a smuggler before him, you see."

Kipling was looking around. "What strikes me as strange," he said in an amazed tone, "is the sheer *size* of this room. Imagine the rock that had to be moved. And think of the appalling work involved!"

"And yet," Charles said, "it's not much used." He turned to Patrick. "Has it ever been filled to its capacity?" The boy shook his head.

Charles spent the next few moments looking at the crates of stores and finding very little of real interest. At the back of the room, however, he came on something vastly more intriguing. A dozen empty crates were stacked precariously high, and behind them, there was a shadowy opening in the wall.

"Give a hand here, Kipling," he said. "Let's move these."

A few moments later, they had uncovered a shallow alcove, empty except for three small wooden crates. They had been hidden, Charles thought. Why?

"I should like to pry these open." He looked around. "I wonder whether..."

"I'll get a crowbar," Patrick offered quickly. "They keep one with the carts." In a moment he was back, a short iron bar in his hand. Charles lifted the smallest box from the alcove, put it on the floor next to the lantern and looked at it. On the cover were printed several words in large black-letter type.

"What does that say?" Patrick asked.

"In German, it says Blasting Caps, Handle With Care, Do Not Drop," Charles translated. *German?*

"Maybe we shouldn't open it," Kipling said nervously. "They might blow up in our faces."

"Detonators can deteriorate with age," Charles agreed, "and there's no telling how old these are. We'll leave them."

"What are these people intending, do you think?"

Kipling asked in a puzzled voice. "To undermine the entire South Downs?"

"I'd be surprised if they aim to do any blasting in the vicinity of the village," Charles said. "It would certainly give away the game. And it might cause some structural damage up above. They'd hate to bring down their landlord's walls." He looked at Patrick. "Do you recall any blasting?"

The boy shook his head. "It was all picks and shovels and men sweating and cursing."

Kipling chuckled. "Well said, my boy. Sweating and cursing comes with picks and shovels as certainly as blood comes with bullets."

"But I suppose," Charles said reflectively, "that someone might have *thought* they would have need of blasting. Let's see what else we have. Maybe it will resolve the mystery."

But the second box, when opened, did nothing to enlighten them. Instead, it gave Charles something new to puzzle over. "Telegraph keys," he muttered, feeling baffled. "Coil buzzers."

"Like the telegraph key in the post office," Patrick said. "For sending messages out of town." Then he frowned. "But where, I wonder. If it's just Brighton, Mr. Tudwell dispatches me, or one of the other boys."

Charles wondered too. As he had understood the smuggling operation—at least, as he had *thought* he'd understood it—it was a small-scale, self-contained, local enterprise, relying on local people to unload the ship and distribute the merchandise. But these telegraph keys suggested something much larger, some sort of coordinated activity that required communications with distant points—and quick, clandestine communications, at that, achieved by climbing a pole and tapping a telegraph wire. Their investigations were beginning to assume a larger dimension. But what did it all mean?

"Well," Kipling said cheerfully, "at least we know that in the event of a national emergency, Rottingdean will be able to communicate with the outside world."

There was one last box left in the alcove, a stout wooden crate some two feet long with rope handles on each end and the designation "M/96—*Ein Dutzend*" stamped on the lid, and under that the word *"Obendorf."* Kipling bent over to pick up the crate.

"Beastly heavy for its size," he grunted, and set it down on the floor beside the other boxes. He straightened. "I say, Sheridan. Can this box be what I think it is?"

"I believe so," Charles said, and squatted, considering the box for a long moment. Yes, it almost certainly was. But why? The blasting caps, the telegraph keys, and now— He frowned. The pieces of the puzzle were beginning to fit together, but he did not like the look of it. He did not like it at all.

Patrick picked up the crowbar. "Well, if nobody else is going to open it—"

"Don't be cheeky, my young sinner," Kipling said, and took the crowbar. *"I'll* do the honors." He pried up the lid and laid it aside. A strong smell of metal lubricant arose from the box.

"Well, I'll be blowed," Kipling said, dropping the crowbar with a clang and staring. "It jolly well *is."*

"Yes, indeed. It most certainly is." Charles took a heavy oilpaper package from the crate, and began to unwrap it.

"I still don't..." Patrick began perplexedly, and then, with great interest, "It's a gun!"

"A dozen guns, actually." Charles held the pistol up, admiring the ingenuity of its design. The long, slender barrel, coated with jelly, gleamed in the light of the lantern. The checkered wood grip fit the palm of his hand. He hefted it, considering. Just a shade under four pounds. Heavy, by some preferences, but considering its firepower—

"Well, well." Kipling whistled between his teeth. "Nothing like my trusty old target pistol. Wicked-looking thing, I'd say." He bent closer. "What the devil do you make of that rectangular body, Sheridan? I've never seen anything like that before."

"That," Charles said, "is the magazine where the ammunition is stored. It's a self-loading pistol, Kipling."

"A self-loading—" Another whistle.

Charles nodded. "According to the gun-shop owner I talked with, this gun can fire off the whole magazine as fast and as easily as you can pull the trigger. The recoil of the firing opens the breech and ejects the empty cartridge case as it loads a fresh cartridge."

He looked down at the pistol with an odd mixture of admiration and sadness, realizing that its capacity for automatic reloading enormously amplified the handgun's killing power and transformed it from a defensive to an offensive weapon. After this, close combat would never be the same.

"Very ingenious," he said, half to himself. "And very, very deadly."

"It ejects the cartridge?" Patrick looked at Charles, a frown between his eyes. "Then it is the same sort of gun that killed Captain Smith?"

"Indeed, Patrick," Charles said. "Yes, it is almost certainly the same sort of gun." He squinted at the pistol. "By Jove, this rear sight appears to be adjustable! Take a look at this, Kipling."

Kipling studied the sight. "The graduations are marked off in hundreds," he said, "up to seven hundred. Feet, d'you suppose? Yards?"

Charles took the gun back. "Sights on military weapons are marked in yards or meters," he said, "but seven hundred? That's a normal range for a rifle—almost unbelievable for a pistol. There's some sort of chamber marking here. Let's see if I can make it out." He took out his magnifying lens and held the gun closer to the light to peer at it.

"What does it say?" Kipling asked. "Is it a British weapon? Or French?" He hunched his shoulders. "You don't suppose these men are running guns and explosives to the Irish, do you? By damn, if they are—"

Charles looked up. "I don't know about that, but this gun is neither British nor French." The chamber was stamped SYSTEM MAUSER. "It's German."

But the box, which advertised itself as containing a dozen such guns, contained only eleven. They did not require the assistance of the Great Detective, Charles thought, to conclude that the twelfth Mauser was the one that had killed Captain Smith.

26

"TO R W BARKER HOGGS LANE BRIGHTON RE QUERY THIRTY CALIBER JACKETED BULLET AND SHOULDERED RIMLESS CASING WITH FOUR ZERO THREE HEADSTAMP STOP SPECIMEN IS SEVEN POINT SIX THREE MILLIMETER MANUFACTURED BY DEUTSCHE WAFFEN UND MUNITIONSFABRIKEN USED IN NEW M96 SELFLOADING MAUSER PISTOL STOP HAVE EXCLUSIVE FRANCHISE UK STOP EXPECTING FIRST CONSIGNMENT SHORTLY STOP HAND BILL WITH PARTICULARS TO FOLLOW VIA POST STOP REGARDS WESTLEY RICHARDS NEW BOND STREET LONDON"

KIPLING PUT DOWN his coffee cup and read the telegram that Charles handed him across the breakfast table.

"Well!" he said, when he had finished. "What do you make of it, Sheridan?"

Kate took the telegram from the table and read it herself. From what Charles had told her on his return from the expedition through the tunnel, the gun was a critical key—not only to solving the murder of Captain Smith, but to unraveling the mystery of the smuggling. It was a revolutionary gun, he had said: a weapon that in fifty years would no doubt be in the possession of half the armies of the world, supplanting the revolver as a military side arm and enormously expanding the shooter's individual firepower. But why was this gun—why was a whole *box* of these guns—hidden in a smugglers' cache under the Sussex downs?

"The telegram tells us nothing that we had not already learned," Charles said.

"But it does confirm that there are no other guns of this type in England," Kate reminded him. She picked up a serving dish from the center of the table, thinking how pleasant it was to breakfast without a servant hovering nearby. "Would you like more of the broiled kidneys, Charles?"

"Yes, it does confirm that," Charles said, taking the dish and spooning out the kidneys. "Kate, please give my compliments to Mrs. Portney on the breakfast. Kidneys, scrambled eggs, even poached apples with cinnamon and cream. I could have wished for nothing else."

"It also confirms," Kipling said in a harsh tone, "that the guns came from Germany. I tell you, Sheridan, our government had better have a close eye on those Germans. They're up to no good over there. Commissioning warships, building munitions factories, designing guns—we're in for trouble, mark my words." He leaned forward, eyes gleaming, one thick forefinger jabbing the air. "They're meddling in South Africa, where we're heading for a big row. And if they take a hand in the Irish Question, or fall in with the anarchists, there'll be hell to pay." He shook his head darkly. "Still, though," he muttered, reaching for the jam jar, "I wouldn't half mind owning one of the guns in that box. Seven hundred yards? If they just weren't *German*—"

"That does complicate the matter," Charles remarked. "Their being German, I mean. It is all rather difficult to piece together."

Kipling smacked the table with the flat of his hand. "Don't you see it, Sheridan? These Rottingdeaners have gotten hooked into something bigger than they know. It's all so beastly clever—and obvious too, now that we've found those Mauser pistols. They think they're smuggling innocent goods, when in truth, they're running guns."

"But wouldn't they *know* what they're smuggling?" Kate asked doubtfully. "After all, guns weigh a great deal more than tobacco or dress goods. And they *are* bringing in merchandise. Charles and I had some of the very best sherry yesterday at the White Horse."

"Not necessarily," Kipling said. "They could receive just enough goods to satisfy them, and the rest ..." He shook his head, scowling. "I'll lay you twenty quid that those guns are aimed at the Empire, one way or another."

"Kipling's right about the possibility of the villagers being deceived," Charles said. "And it would account for some of the details that are puzzling me. The size of that newly enlarged cellar, for instance. And the fact that some of the goods they're bringing in could be imported without duty."

Kipling nodded wisely. "You'll see," he said. "Somebody's pulled the wool over these Rottingdeaners' eyes."

"Perhaps I will know more after I've talked to Tudwell," Charles said. "He's on my list for this morning." He looked at Kate. "Then I will speak to George Radford's widow, and after that, Kipling and I will go on to Brighton. Is there anything I can get for you?"

"Anything I should want is probably here, at a discount," Kate said, with a little laugh. "I wonder whether Mrs. Portney is making progress toward the truffles."

Kipling looked puzzled. "Truffles?"

"A test of the local system of domestic supplies," Kate replied.

Charles grinned. "Have you made arrangements for the boy?"

"Yes," Kate said. She and Charles had talked late the night before about Patrick. Given what the boy knew, she felt concerned for his safety and proposed that she and Aunt Georgie keep him occupied and out of mischief for the day. "I sent a note to Aunt Georgie, suggesting that she find Patrick some garden employment this morning and that we take a picnic to the downs this afternoon. I thought Patrick might drive the pony and look after us."

"Then perhaps the three of you will look after Josie as well," Kipling said. "Carrie is still in bed with her cold— although if you ask me," he added, "it's just an excuse to finish Beryl Bardwell's story."

"Of course," Kate said warmly. "I'd love to take her along. She's a delightful little girl."

Kipling leaned on his elbows. "Speaking of the boy, I've been wondering what's to be done with him. The Aunt has offered to put him into school at St. Aubyn's. But I'm opposed to leaving him here in the village, where he will be under the influence of these fellows. The boy is bright and inquisitive. Perhaps we can think of something else."

"What would you say to making inquiries as to the whereabouts of the father?" Charles asked. "It would be good to know whether Patrick is an orphan, or merely abandoned."

"*Merely* abandoned?" Kate murmured.

Charles sighed. "Sorry. But before we begin meddling in his life, we ought to know whether there's a parent somewhere who should be consulted."

"Very good," Kipling said. "I'll inquire of my contacts in

India and see what's to be learned." He pushed back his chair and stood up. "Thanks for the breakfast. I'd best get back to The Elms and look in on Carrie and young John." He glanced at Charles. "I am going to Brighton with you later, after you've seen Tudwell. And we *are* joining forces this evening, aren't we?"

"You still want to be in on it?" Charles asked. "I can't promise that there won't be difficulties—especially in view of what the boy told us last night. Of course, that need not trouble us. We're only to observe and take notes. Still—"

"Do I want to be in on it?" Kipling grinned jauntily. "I'm always up for a jolly good adventure. But I checked the glass this morning, and it was beginning to fall. There may be a bit of a blow later this evening—not in time to spoil the picnic, however," he added, with a little bow to Kate. "I'll tell Josie she's been invited. It'll please her mightily, and she can spend the morning in the kitchen, making her own sandwiches." He went off whistling.

It was a busy morning at the stables. In the yard in front of the smithy, under the beechnut tree, a farrier bent over a horse's hoof, setting a new shoe. Behind him another smith hammered noisily at a bar of hot iron on his anvil while the smith's boy worked the bellows. Two whiskered gentlemen were studying the configuration of a large gray hunter, a uniformed trainer was working a recalcitrant colt in the exercise paddock, and a barefoot, ragged boy was dragging fouled hay out of the loose-boxes. The boy pointed the way to the stablemaster's office, and Charles took the liberty of opening the door without a preliminary knock.

Harry Tudwell was seated behind a scarred wooden table, gazing out the window in the direction of the smithy. He turned at the sound of the opening door, ready to lash out angrily at the interruption. But when he saw that the intruder was a gentleman, he got hastily to his feet and put on an amiable smile, which, Charles noted, did little to disguise the lines of worry that crossed his freckled forehead. The office smelled of tobacco and horse liniment, and the walls displayed old newspaper clippings. The London *Times* lay in a heap on the floor, a mug of tea sat on the table, and a cheap glass dish, a souvenir of Brighton, was overflowing with cigarette butts.

"G'mornin', sir," Tudwell said with as much cheer as he could muster. His sandy hair was tousled and his pale blue eyes, rimmed with light lashes, were red. It appeared that the stablemaster had not slept well. "'Ow can I 'elp ye? Are ye in th' market for stablin' or is't a 'orse ye're lookin' for?"

"Neither," Charles said, and extended his hand with a show of great politeness. "I am Lord Charles Sheridan, Mr. Tudwell. I am here at the request of the Crown to look into the murders of the two coast guards."

At the sound of the name, an anxious furrow appeared between Harry Tudwell's eyes. "Lord Sheridan?" he said. "The ... Crown?"

"Exactly so." Charles sighed. "These deaths are a sad matter, of course. As you might imagine, there is a great deal of concern about the affair at the very highest levels. I have already spoken to several other people in the village, who suggested I talk with you."

"They did, did they?" Harry Tudwell's eyes narrowed. "'Oo was it? 'Oo told ye to talk to me?"

"I'm afraid I can't disclose the names of my informants, Mr. Tudwell. May we sit?" Charles pulled out a chair and sat down, crossing one leg over the other, being ostentatiously careful not to destroy the crease in his trousers. He took off his Homburg hat and perched it carefully on his knee, pulled out his pipe, and began to light it.

Eyes fixed on Charles, Harry Tudwell slowly lowered himself into his chair, reaching for a crumpled pack of cigarettes. He pulled one out and lit it with a hand that was trembling noticeably. "Well, I don't know why anybody'd send ye to me," he muttered. "Ye're wastin' yer time. I don't know a thing."

"I was informed that you might be able to say why the two men were killed," Charles said, in a conversational tone, sitting back with his pipe.

Harry Tudwell's ruddy face was growing redder. "Why they was killed!" he exclaimed hotly. "'Ow should I know a thing like that? I 'ardly knew either of 'em. Anyway, I 'eard George Radford killed hisself. Are ye tellin' me 'e was murdered?"

"Regrettably, yes," Charles murmured. He glanced up. "I have been given to understand that Captain Smith was a particular friend of yours, Mr. Tudwell. I was hoping that you might have some knowledge of his personal affairs."

"A partic'lar friend!" Tudwell snorted. "I don't know 'oo ye've been talkin' to, but that's wrong. I knew 'im to talk to, o' course, but as for 'is pers'nal affairs—" He paused and his mouth took on a calculating look. "I can name a name or two, though, if ye're lookin' for th' captain's friends. Or for someone 'oo might've 'ad reason to kill 'im."

Charles beamed. "Then I *have* come to the right man after all!" He pulled a leather-bound notebook out of his pocket, uncapped his fountain pen, and waited expectantly.

Harry Tudwell pushed his mouth in and out as if he were considering something. When he finally spoke, it was with a tone of finality. "Ye should talk to Trunky Thomas. Trunky owns th' bathin' machines at the Gap an' 'as 'is own fishin' fleet. 'E 'ad reg'lar dealings wi' the captain." Charles was writing busily. "And what sort of dealings would those be?"

There was a fractional pause, and Harry Tudwell's sandy eyebrows came together. "Now, that's none o' my business, is it?" he said. "I don't go round th' village nosin' into people's affairs. I give a 'and 'ere and a 'and there, when I see a need, and I keep a eye out to make sure things is goin' good. I *am* an elected member o' th' Parish Council, y' know." He allowed himself a small smile. "But I keep my business to myself an' I don't ask questions about other folks' business." Having delivered this speech, he sat back, more at ease.

Charles studied his notes. "A very commendable attitude, Mr. Tudwell. But, I fear, without benefit to the Crown."

"I can't 'elp that, now, can I?" There was a barely disguised edge of triumph in Harry Tudwell's voice. "But Trunky'll be glad to 'elp th' Crown. As I said, 'e was close t' th' captain."

"Thank you," Charles said. He looked down at the notebook for a moment, then glanced up. "Perhaps, though, you *can* tell me about the tunnels."

Harry seemed to catch a lungful of smoke and began to cough violently. It took him a few moments to recover, with the assistance of a gulp of cold tea from the mug at his elbow. "The tunnels?" he asked, when he could speak again. "You mean, those ol' smugglers' tunnels that was dug under the village, way back, which've been closed off for years an' years?"

"Yes," Charles said. "Those tunnels."

Harry's jaw worked. "There ain't much to tell. Ain't anything left of 'em, either. It'd be dangerous to 'ave something like that open for children to lose theirselves in, now, wouldn't it? Why, there was a little boy, over in Kent, got into a tunnel an' got lost an' died. I read about it in th' *Times*, not six months ago."

"So the tunnels are no longer in use?"

"O' course not," Harry said, in a voice that implied that Charles was a fool to ask the question. "Wot'd they be used *for*, I'd like to know."

"Storage, perhaps. I understand that some of the cellars in the village open onto the tunnels."

Harry returned a hollow laugh. "Storage! This is a *poor* village. Nobody's got much t' store, short of winter provisions."

Charles spoke in an even tone. "Weapons, perhaps."

Harry stared at him blankly.

"Explosives as well," Charles added.

Harry blinked. "Ye're talkin' about guns? Ye' mean … rifles?"

"Then you know nothing of weapons and explosives being stored in the tunnels?"

"Rifles an' dynamite?" Harry exclaimed, incredulous. "Why, that's ridiculous, that's wot it is!" He half rose out of his chair. "'Ooever told you there's guns down there is lyin' through 'is teeth. Why, there's nothin' down there but—" He stopped. "There's nothin' down there at all," he said. "Tell me 'oo said it, and I'll—"

Charles sat forward, emptied his pipe into the glass dish, and stood. "I believe I have taken enough of your time, Mr. Tudwell," he said briskly. "If you think of anything else that might be of help, you may reach me at Seabrooke House. Good day."

Harry sat for a moment after the gentleman had gone, shaking his head. "Rifles an' dynamite," he muttered to himself. "Rifles an' dynamite. Why, I never 'eard such foolishness."

27

"A mask tells us more than a face."

—Oscar Wilde

The photographer, dressed in gray tweed knickerbockers and a gray bowler, stood behind his camera and tripod on the high down, his head under the black cloth hood. Delicately, he adjusted the focus of the lens, perfecting the inverted image of the scene below on the ground glass screen at the back of the camera—a wide view from Beacon Hill to Saltdean, including the quiet village drowsing in the sun and the sea beyond. A beautiful view, one that would delight any sightseer and charm any number of viewers at home. A view so beautiful, in fact, that it almost distracted him from his present compelling difficulties and made him forget his purpose.

But the photographer was far too well disciplined to lose himself in the beauties of nature. Recalling himself to his task, he slipped the plate box into the camera and squeezed the pneumatic bulb that worked the shutter. Quickly, he took another shot of the same view, then ducked out from under the hood and searched through his camera bag until he found his compass. He noted the bearing of St.

Margaret's church in the middle of the scene, and then took careful bearings on the abandoned windmill to the west and a barn on the cliff to the east, laying the compass on the stone wall beside him as he finished his notations. Without these measurements, the photographs would be merely pretty, like the snapshots the daytrippers took of the picturesque Sussex shore to show their friends and relations at home. With them, the view was not only pretty but immensely useful, for it allowed the features of the landscape to be precisely positioned on the most recent Ordnance Survey map and used for strategic purposes, rather than for mere entertainment.

For the past year, off and on, the photographer had been engaged in taking pictures of the entire South Sussex coast from Seaford to Worthing. Watching him, observing the care with which he planned his photographs and documented their position, someone might have thought that he was preparing these views for publication in a magazine or book. But these photographs would never be published, and only a handful of people would ever see them. They would be filed away against that future day when they would become vital to the national interest. And in the meantime, anyone who saw him at work would believe him to be an eccentric tourist engaged in an earnest, endless search for scenic beauty, doggedly seeking to capture on film the great, wide sweep of the downs and the sea.

He allowed himself a brief, secret smile. It suited his purpose that real sightseers thought him oddly eccentric and kept their distance, while the local folk knew he was not one of theirs and left him alone. But he was no more a tourist than he was any of the other identities he adopted from time to time. Who was he? Except on the rare occasions when he received news from home—from his mother or one of his sisters, say, imposing on him an unwelcome sense of familial obligations—he seldom thought of his real identity. In fact, if the truth be told, he had all but forgotten who he was, for over the many years he had worked at his profession he had developed the useful faculty of totally losing himself in his current identity, as an actor might lose himself in a role and become one with the characters he played on stage.

For a moment, the photographer allowed a flickering reminiscence to distract him. In his youth, he had had a great interest in the arts, especially in the theater, and had spent long hours studying the methods of actors, the way they absorbed themselves in their roles. To this day, he spent whatever time he could at the theater, taking special delight in the plays of Gerhart Hauptmann, like that wonderfully wicked comedy, *The Beaver Coat*, which he had seen recently. In fact, he would dearly have loved to become an actor, but his father had put an end to that nonsense. He had become a cadet, graduating just in time to serve as a young lieutenant in the last great war. It was not without serious misgivings that he had undertaken this service, because his mother had been born in an area that was then France.

But he had served with courage and distinction in a particularly challenging assignment, and his achievements were noticed in high places. That had been more than twenty-five years ago, and since that time he had been given the freedom to design and pursue a number of projects more or less of his choosing, developing as it were his own entrepreneurial schemes and recruiting a cadre of hand-picked men to carry them out. These projects had been for the most part successful, one or two of them stunningly so, and had won the admiration of his superiors.

The photographer's current mission, however, was far

more daring than any he had proposed and carried out in the past. Some even called it reckless and foolhardy and warned that failure or discovery (the two were synonymous) would seriously set back any similar efforts on the part of others in his division. Even the skeptics, though, had to admit that his idea, if it succeeded, would pay unimaginable dividends. If it succeeded, it would change the course of empires.

But the success of this venture was now in grave doubt, and his experience told him that there was little he could do but watch as events played themselves out. There was no point in self-recrimination, of course, but it was good to know where one stood. Objective as always (for objectivity was one of the essential skills of his trade), he acknowledged that he had made one, perhaps two, fundamental miscalculations. Those he might have survived, had it not happened that he had also suffered one or two bits of infernally bad luck. Taken together, his mistakes and his ill fortune could very likely add up to catastrophe—but it was not necessarily so. When all was concluded, he would choose which of two plans to execute. He would—

He was jolted back to the present by the unwelcome sound of voices and the noise of an approaching wagon. More daytrippers, he supposed, on an errand something like his own, and began to pack up his gear. But a moment later, as the wagon came into full view, he recognized the occupants. They were the two women he had seen yesterday on the other side of Rottingdean, with a little golden-haired girl—and the boy, who was driving the wagon.

Yes, it was the same boy, the photographer thought with irritation. The damned ubiquitous nuisance of a boy, who seemed to turn up everywhere. On the road to Black Rock, in the stable passageway after his conversation with Harry Tudwell, and even at—

The photographer frowned, thinking back through the occurrences. Was it possible? Had this boy seen him in *all* of his disguises? And was it also possible that he had been listening outside the stablemaster's office, when the photographer had been giving instructions to Harry Tudwell? Still, even if that were true, the boy was surely not quick or perceptive enough to identify—

But at that instant, the boy looked up and caught his eye, and the photographer saw the clear and sudden start of recognition flash across his face.

It was true. The boy knew him.

28

"Few can see
Further forth
Than when the child
Meets the Cold Iron."

—RUDYARD KIPLING
Puck of Pook's Hill

IT WAS, KATE thought as they rode along, a perfect day for a picnic, and she was very glad that she and Aunt Georgie had thought of the idea. Josie had been delighted too, when she had brought her little basket, already packed, to North End House.

"We're going on a picnic, a picnic, a picnic," she had chanted happily, her blue eyes sparkling. She pushed her fists into the pockets of her white pinafore and looked up at Kate. "Who else is going with us, Lady Sheridan? Daddy has gone to Brighton and Mummy has a frightful cold, but can't we take Nanny and Elsie and John? They'll be lonely if they're left."

"John is still a little young for picnics," Kate said, putting a basket into the wagon. "Nanny is staying behind to mind him and Elsie to amuse him, so there will be only the four of us. Anyway, we'll be back by teatime."

Aunt Georgie bustled down the path, giving instructions. "Kate, please put that basket under the seat. Patrick, I hope you haven't forgotten the rugs." She looked around, a bit abstracted. "Where did I put my shawl? Patrick, did you remember the lemonade?" To Kate, she said, "I simply cannot believe the price of lemons these days, Kate. They are so *dear!*" Then, "Patrick! Where is my knitting? If the rest of you go running off to explore, I shall want something to amuse me."

But at last they were off, behind a pony who seemed to know that this was a holiday jaunt, and not a bit of workaday travel. They went up the rising road, Patrick with the reins loose in his fingers, letting the pony have its head up the rutted lane through the curving chalkland, pulling them along beside a low flint wall daubed with the muted colors of moss and lichen. In the distance, flocks of sheep shone white, like constellations of stars on the flanks of the hills. Off to the left, stubble lay silver in the sun, with a few fiery poppies still blazing among the corn stooks, and behind them Kate could see the Brighton race course, and the old windmill standing at arms on the top of Beacon Hill.

Then they were on the open downs, driving across the short, springy grass that was trimmed and kept so beautifully by the sheep. Kate could smell the wild thyme and marjoram crushed by the pony's hoofs, and hear the sharp *killy-killy-killy* of a kestrel and the bright tumbling notes of skylarks, and catch an occasional glimpse of chalkhill blue butterflies clustering around a late thistle. She sighed happily. The downs were clean and innocent and so beautiful that she could almost forget the sordid adventure that lay behind them in Rottingdean.

"There it is," Patrick said after a while, pointing to a large flint barn with tiled roof. It was built on a prominence that gave it a commanding view of the downs and the sea beyond. "That's Height Barn. If you look out from the loft, you can see all the way to the valley of the River Ouse, and back to Brighton. On a moonlit night, you can count the ships far out in the Channel by counting their lights."

"Is that where we're to picnic?" Kate asked.

"In Wedding Hollow, behind the barn," Josie piped up. "There's a dew-pond there, and fairies. It's my favorite place in all the world."

"It looks like someone else is enjoying the area too," Aunt Georgie said with interest. "Look. There's a man taking pictures, there by the stone wall."

"It's a beautiful vantage point," Kate said. "Perhaps I'll ask Charles to bring one of his cameras and shoot it. The photographs would be a perfect souvenir to take home with us." She put her hand on Patrick's shoulder. "Perhaps you'll come with us, Patrick, and show us the best place from which to shoot."

But Patrick didn't answer. His eyes were fixed on the man with the camera, who stood on the hill beside the grassy lane. Then he seemed to shake himself, and turned.

"That's the best place," he said. "Where that man is."

"But we don't want to go to the barn," Josie insisted. "Drive us to the Hollow, Patrick. I want to look for fairies!" She sobered. "But we must be careful when we look for fairies, my father says, for the fairies might be looking for us, although they don't like to be called fairies but People of the Hills, who can do real magic, not just wave silly little wands around in the air. And they might carry us off."

There might well be fairies, Kate thought, as she climbed out of the wagon in Wedding Hollow and gazed around, for the place had the look of enchantment. There was a small, clear pond, surrounded by a thicket of gorse and blackberry and wild roses. Patrick, who seemed subdued, took Josie off to explore. Aunt Georgie and Kate spread the rugs and put out sandwiches and hard-boiled eggs and potted meats and little cakes, and after a while the children came back and they all sat down and ate. Afterward, Patrick packed the food into the baskets and Aunt Georgie settled down with Josie in the curve of her arm to read one of the stories from *The Jungle Books*. Kate lay down in the dry grass and meadowsweet beside them, the sun warm on her face, listening drowsily until she fell asleep.

It was nearly an hour later when she awakened. The sun had disappeared behind a bank of gray clouds and a wind was stirring in the tops of the beech trees. Aunt Georgie and Josie sat up, too, rubbing their eyes.

"My goodness," Aunt Georgie exclaimed, "I believe I've been asleep."

"I'm cold," Josie said, rubbing her arms. "Where's the sun?"

"It's gone under a cloud," Aunt Georgie said. "The glass was falling this morning, so perhaps we will have a bit of rain." She got to her feet and shook the dry grass out of her skirts. "Kate, why don't you find Patrick, and we'll start home."

"Of course," Kate said, and went off to look in the beech grove, and then in the blackberry thicket, and finally at the empty barn on the hill, shouting the boy's name all the while. But there was no answer to Kate's calls, nor to Aunt Georgie's peremptory summons, nor to Josie's piping wails. After an hour's searching and shouting, they had to acknowledge the truth.

Patrick had disappeared, and Josie could not be persuaded that the People of the Hills had not carried him off.

29

"All is riddle, and the key to a riddle is another riddle."
—RALPH WALDO EMERSON
The Conduct of Life (1860)

AFTER CHARLES'S INTERVIEW with Harry Tudwell, he and Kipling drove into Brighton to talk to the chief constable. On the way, Charles stopped at Black Rock and, leaving Kipling to wait in the motorcar, went into the cottage for a brief talk with the widow Radford. She was waiting with all her belongings piled about her for her brother to come and take her and the children to Brighton, where they planned to bury her husband. She did not weep. Worse, she regarded Charles with a long, bitter look and replied to his questions with a torrent of scathing words, as hot and fierce as a fountain of molten rock.

Feeling depressed and hollow, Charles climbed back into the Panhard. Kipling looked at him searchingly, as if to ask him how the conversation had gone, then thought better of it and, pulling his motoring goggles over his eyes, sat back in the seat.

They drove for a while in silence. It was a pretty day, but a low band of gray clouds to the south, over the Channel, presaged a change in weather. At Kemptown, they met the Rottingdean omnibus on its return trip from Brighton, and pulled over to the grassy verge to keep from spooking the horses. Charles stopped the car.

In the sudden silence, Kipling said, "You're thinking that you've solved Radford's murder, then?"

Charles pulled up his goggles and rubbed his eyes. Goggles or no, the fine grit from the roads seemed to filter through every crevice. "Judging from the evidence in Smith's cottage and from what Mrs. Radford told me just now, it seems pretty clear that Captain Smith killed him. Radford apparently let Smith know that he planned to inform the officials about the smuggling operation at Rottingdean. Mrs. Radford claims that he wanted to persuade Smith to abandon his evil ways." Charles sighed. "He might just as easily have wanted to blackmail Smith for a share of the ill-gotten gains. I don't suppose we'll ever know which it was."

"Give him the benefit of the doubt," Kipling said.

"Yes, I suppose," Charles replied. "However it was, we have the weapon—Radford's knife, which Kate found among the cutlery in Smith's cottage. Smith must have run him through back to front, and then hauled him out for burial in the Channel."

Kipling nodded. "So, Radford was killed by Smith. But who killed Smith?"

"Someone with access to the guns we found in the tunnel last night," Charles said. "I am willing to wager, however, that it was neither Trunky Thomas nor Harry Tudwell. I've spoken to both, and while they have plenty to hide, I don't think they're concealing murder."

Kipling looked grim. "Plenty to hide, indeed. To my way of thinking, those guns and explosives are tantamount to murder, all by themselves. In the hands of anarchists—"

He shook his head angrily. "And to think that Rottingdean has gotten itself involved with gunrunning! It's a bloody disgrace, that's what it is! The village will never recover from the dishonor."

Charles gave him a questioning look. "So you're convinced that's what's going on?"

"What else can it be?" Kipling demanded. "You said yourself that the bit of smuggling they've done or are likely to do scarcely warrants the cost of those underground works. And in today's market, smuggling makes no economic sense—not on a large scale, in any event."

"I've got to agree with you there," Charles said. "And the guns are critical—there's no getting around that. But still—" He frowned.

"Still what?" Kipling asked. "You're thinking there's something else?"

"It's the map overlaps," Charles said. "They don't fit a smuggling venture—nor a gunrunning operation, either. That's the one piece of the puzzle that makes no sense to me at all."

"Well," Kipling said darkly, "all I can say is that we had better find a way to keep this out of the papers. Life in Rottingdean won't be worth a shilling if the story gets out. The village will sink under the shame of it."

"I agree to that, too," Charles said. The omnibus safely past, he drove back onto the road and they finished the journey into Brighton in silence, stopping for lunch at an inn on the east side of the town.

Their visit took longer than expected because Sir Robert had been called out to a robbery at the home of a prominent citizen, and they had to wait over an hour for his return. While they waited, Kipling read the *Times* and Charles reviewed the notes he had scribbled in his notebook over the past two days, making sure he had all the details straight in his mind. It was those map overlays that puzzled him so, as he had told Kipling, and the telegraph equipment. Everything else, he could fit comfortably into one or another scenario. But those two pieces were out of place, unless—

Kipling rattled the newspaper furiously. "Another blasted German warship commissioned at Kiel!" he exclaimed, "and according to the *Times*, the Germans are looking to the Philippine Islands for new coaling stations to serve their fleet." He shook his head darkly. "Mark my words, Sheridan. This is serious business. We'll find ourselves at war with them one of these days—no matter that the Kaiser is the grandson of the Queen."

But Charles was scarcely listening. He sat very still, beginning to get a glimmering of a possibility—a fantastic-seeming possibility, a very faint glimmer, a will-o'-the-wisp luring him down a dark road, overhung with truly frightening shadows. Like a riddle, with another riddle as its key. But however fantastic this explanation might seem, there was surely something to it. He studied his notes once again, seeing no flaw in his hypothesis and shivering as he thought about the eventuality. Well, tonight's venture, however it turned out, would surely yield more information. It *had* to. If his theory was correct, the stakes were unimaginably high, and the game was much larger than anyone had thought.

Upon his return, Sir Robert was appropriately apologetic for the delay. They began their conference by going over all of the points Charles had been arranging in his mind, one by one, from the murders of George Radford and Captain Smith to the smuggling operation that was planned for that night.

"According to the boy, the smugglers are to signal from the old house on the cliff just to the west of the village,"

Charles said. "We shall simply observe what transpires and—"

Sir Robert shook his head. "I'm sorry, Sheridan," he said gruffly. "I fear there's to be more to it than that." He pushed a yellow telegram across the desktop.

With a sinking feeling, Charles picked it up. "OBSERVE MY HAT STOP," he read out loud. "APPREHEND KILLER FORTHWITH STOP ARREST WHOLE DAMNED VILLAGE IF YOU HAVE TO STOP WALES." He looked at Sir Robert questioningly. "You told HRH?"

Sir Robert winced. "I had to, didn't I? He left explicit orders to be kept informed."

Kipling was gloomy. "To be sure. But if you bring your men down the coast en masse, it's bound to get into the newspapers. You know what a fuss they'll make of it. Underneath, the story is desperately tawdry, but on the surface it reads like a romantic fiction—smuggling, secret tunnels, hidden guns, all the trappings of a cheap adventure novel." He shook his head. "Things are bad enough now, but after this, the daytrippers and souvenir-seekers will swarm all over the village. They'll make a circus of the place. No sane person will want to live there ever again."

"Worst of all," Charles said, "a company of law enforcement officers will drive the killer or killers underground and erase any hope of discovering who's behind those guns." He leaned forward. "Maybe we can effect a compromise between your orders and the requirements of the situation."

"If we can, I'm willing to work something out," Sir Robert said. "What do you have in mind?"

Charles described the plan he had been considering. They spent the next half-hour fine-tuning their strategy. By the time they shook hands and he and Kipling took their leave, Charles was reasonably satisfied with what they had agreed to.

The question now was whether it would work as they hoped, or whether something they could not foresee would destroy their carefully laid plans.

30

"You must lose a fly to catch a trout."
—George Herbert
Jacula Prudentum (1651)

"I don't *want* to be calm," Aunt Georgie cried. "I want the boy found, do you hear me?" She thumped her hand on the constable's desk. "Turn out the men of the village! I want an immediate search."

Constable Woodhouse sighed heavily. "But Lady Burne-Jones," he said, "I am trying to tell ye that th' boy *will* be found, no doubt about it. 'E'll turn up, in 'is own good time. Boys do that, y'know? They pop off, I mean. On their own business. 'E's gone fishin', most like." He gave her what was obviously meant to be a reassuring smile. "It's near on teatime, milady. If th' young imp ain't back tomorrow mornin', come an' tell me, an' I'll 'ave a look for 'im myself."

Kate made another attempt. "I believe," she said, "that what Lady Burne-Jones is saying is that the boy did *not* pop off on his own business. He did not go fishing, because he had no fishing equipment. We do not believe he has been injured, for we thoroughly searched the area. We think

264

he has been ..." She swallowed. The idea was almost too terrible to contemplate.

The stout constable raised both eyebrows. "Been wot?" he asked.

"Kidnapped," Kate said.

"Kidnapped!" the constable echoed, his bulbous eyes opening wide with a look of utter disbelief.

"Yes, kidnapped," Aunt Georgie snapped. "Would you like us to spell the word for you, sir?"

"That'll not be necess'ry." The constable could scarcely suppress his smile. "Ye'll pardon me, yer ladyships, but 'oo would want to kidnap a worthless *boy?*"

Kate bit her lip. When she had seen the photographer standing near the barn, she had thought nothing of it. Why should she? The South Downs were crowded with photographers and painters seeking to capture the wild, sweeping beauty of earth and sky and sea, and falling all over one another in the general melee. There was nothing about this particular photographer that should have caught her attention.

So it wasn't until Patrick had vanished and she had begun the fruitless search for him that she remembered the man in the gray bowler, packing his camera equipment hurriedly, as if he wanted to make his escape. She remembered, too, that Patrick had stiffened as if he recognized the man, and that all through the picnic lunch, the boy had been nearly silent. And then, with a sudden start, she remembered something else, as well: talking with another photographer, similarly dressed in tweed knickerbockers and gray bowler, on the Quarter Deck above the beach on the morning that George Radford's body was pulled out of the ocean. That man had spoken with an accent—French or Belgian, perhaps—and had said something about the natives being driven by the powers of darkness to jump off the cliff, as if suggesting that the victim had killed himself. An intuition told her that the photographer on the Quarter Deck and the photographer near the barn were the same man. But why in heaven's name would he want to kidnap Patrick? How was this foreign photographer—if that's what he was—connected to the unhappy events in Rottingdean? And if he had the boy, what did he intend to do with him? Oh, if she hadn't fallen asleep! If she'd kept a closer eye on the boy, if she'd taken her responsibility more seriously, none of this might have happened!

But Constable Woodhouse suffered none of Kate's distress or guilt. "It's clear as day, milady," he declared cheerfully. "Since there's nobody'ud want the foolish boy, there's nobody'ud take 'im. Th' lad's got hisself lost, is all. 'E'll come draggin' back to th' village when 'e's 'ungry an' cold. Go 'ome an' 'ave yer tea an' don't fret."

But somebody *did* want the boy, and somebody *had* taken him, for some appalling purpose or another. Kate was as sure of that as she was of her own name, and the certainty made her sick with apprehension. Patrick knew too much about the village's profitable smuggling operation. Patrick knew what was going on in the tunnels, and what was planned for this very evening. He had seen the man who rowed George Radford's body out to sea and had overheard Harry Tudwell talking with one of the investors about—

"Well!" Aunt Georgie exclaimed indignantly, rising from the chair in front of the constable's desk. "I can see that we are going to gain no cooperation from the law, which is either too indolent or too inept to be of any real use." She pulled at Kate's sleeve. "Come, Lady Sheridan. We will organize our *own* search. When the boy is found, it will be no thanks to the law!" And with a last withering look at the constable, she swept out the door.

But as Kate and Aunt Georgie quickly discovered, it was impossible to organize a search. For one thing, the men to whom they spoke appeared to share the constable's view: that Patrick had simply gone off in pursuit of his own affairs and would return when he was ready. For another, there seemed to be an air of barely suppressed anticipation in the village, as if everyone were waiting for something important to happen and had no interest in anything else. Kate thought she knew what they were waiting for and wished desperately that she knew whether it and Patrick's disappearance were connected.

And now that she'd had time to consider it, she was beginning to understand that a search of the area where Patrick had disappeared was not likely to do any good, anyway. If her intuition was right and the photographer had abducted Patrick, the boy wouldn't be on the downs— he would be hidden somewhere, bound so that he could not escape and gagged so that he could not cry out. But *where*?

"My head aches so terribly that I can scarcely see," Aunt Georgie said with a heavy sigh, after they had met with their third or fourth refusal. "I must go home, Kate. There's nothing more I can do except pray for him."

Kate put her arms around Aunt Georgie. "And I'm beginning to think that there's no point in trying to search, even if we could get the men to do it," she said, feeling a great weariness. "Anyway, it will be dark soon. Charles and Rud will return from Brighton shortly, and they will surely know what to do."

But as she made her own way back to Seabrooke House, she was not at all sure that Charles and Rud would have any answers, or be able to offer any helpful suggestions. Patrick had been taken for an unknown purpose by a man who seemed to stand far behind the scenes, a man whose face she could neither remember nor describe with any clarity.

But she could remember Patrick, his freckled face, his fiery hair, his dancing eyes green as springtime. And his loss burned like a fire in her heart.

31

"Suspicion always haunts the guilty mind;
The thief doth fear each bush an
officer."

— WILLIAM SHAKESPEARE
Henry VI, 3

HARRY TUDWELL'S MISGIVINGS about tonight's undertaking
had been growing deeper and darker over the past
twenty-four hours. On the one hand, he was glad to have
been advanced in rank—"promoted," as the representative
of the investors had so agreeably put it. He could scarcely
wait to tell Trunky Thomas and the others that he had been
chosen to take over the deceased Foxy's position, and that
from now on, the instructions from the investors would
come solely through him. On the other hand, Harry could
not rid himself of the ominous suspicion that the sinister
man who had visited him was Foxy Smith's killer, and
that if he did not do as he was instructed, he would find
himself ticked off as "superfluous" as well.

Harry's misgivings had darkened even further after he
had been visited by that dandified lord in his Homburg
hat, who claimed to represent the Crown and who

wrote down everything Harry said in a fancy leather-bound notebook with a fountain pen. But even though the investors' representative had warned him that Lord Sheridan might prove meddlesome, his lordship was clearly more interested in his stylish trouser creases than in digging up the truth, and Harry hardly thought that the toff posed any real danger. It was the chief constable in Brighton who Harry feared, and although there had been no sign of him since he took away Foxy's corpse, Harry couldn't shake the feeling that he and his men might be waiting when the ship came in that night.

Taken altogether, then, Harry was not in the highest of spirits as he began tonight's work—a mood that was not brightened by the threat of a menacing storm blowing out of the southeast, over the Channel. But the leather traveling case had arrived safely, just as the investors' representative had said, and Harry had kept to his office the entire day so that it would not go unguarded. As dusk fell, he took his bull's-eye lantern and picked up the traveling case, carrying it down a seldom-used path to the beach, where he locked it into the first bathing machine. Then he located one of Trunky's skiffs and pulled it onto the deserted shingle near the bathing machines. Having managed all of this without being detected, he climbed up the stairs to the top of the cliff.

There was a light in the window of Trunky's shack and as he walked across the gravel, Harry wondered once again why the man had agreed to be the third lantern for tonight's landing. Harry was sure enough of John Landsdowne's loyalty, for their friendship went back to boyhood days, and even though the chemist had openly criticized him in that noisy meeting at the Black Horse, Harry knew John would never let him down. But Trunky Thomas was certainly no friend, and Harry had been surprised when Landsdowne had told him yesterday that Trunky had volunteered for signaling duty. It had even occurred to Harry that Trunky might have some sort of villainous intention in mind. Still, the loyal John would be there, so if Trunky meant to make a move, he would have to take on the both of them. Anyway, it seemed better to have Trunky with him and out of mischief when the ship came in. *If* the ship came in, Harry reminded himself, eyeing the waves licking at the beach and the angry lightning that flickered far out to sea. They were in for a blow, there was no doubt about it. The men would have to work fast to get everything unloaded and into the tunnel while the ship could still stand close off the shore without danger.

If Trunky had any malevolent ambitions, he gave no sign of them when he opened the door to Harry. Neither did he offer any friendly remark. They greeted one another with wary nods, took their lanterns and walked to the chemist's shop to meet John Landsdowne. As the three walked back down the High Street to the coast road, Harry's disquietude took on a new coloring. At this time of evening, the villagers should have been at table, wolfing down their suppers in preparation for the night's work. Instead, they stood in their doorways or sat in their windows, silently watching the trio pass. Something in their guarded expressions gave Harry to suspect that they knew some secret to which he was not privy, but he passed this off as his nerves playing tricks on him. They were getting what they wanted, weren't they? The ship was coming in, just as they had demanded. They had nothing to gain and everything to lose if there was trouble tonight. When the time came, in an hour or so, they'd be gathered on the beach, ready to unload the goods.

Still, Harry couldn't shake the thought of the chief

constable's men lurking somewhere on the cliff so, as the three of them turned onto the coast road and began the uphill eastward climb, he said to John and Trunky, "Best be on your guard, boys. The Queen's forces may be about tonight."

Trunky snorted contemptuously. "Ain't no forces hereabouts. Queen's or any other. If there was, my men 'ud told me."

"Trunky's right," John said. "Nobody's 'eard nothin'. It's all clear for t'night."

Harry smarted under the suggestion that Trunky's intelligence network was superior to his, but he said nothing. For all he knew, Trunky was right—but that did not dispel the nagging feeling, growing stronger by the minute, that they were being watched. They walked the rest of the way to their signaling station, the old farmhouse on the cliff, arriving shortly after eight o'clock. It was full dark.

When the flint-walled farmhouse was built two hundred years before, it had stood a safe distance from the cliff. But the ocean had eaten away the land, and half of the building had vanished into the surf below. Open to the sea on one side, with three partial walls still standing to shield the lanterns from sight, it was an excellent signaling post.

Harry shuttered his lantern so that his eyes would grow accustomed to the dark and sat down on a fallen timber, staring seaward. The wind was gustier now and the lightning flickers were brighter, and he began to wonder whether the ship captain would respond to their signal or would decide to abort the landing. The three lanterns instructed the ship to put in at Rottingdean, where the villagers were waiting to unload it; if they showed only one lantern, the ship would shift course for Saltdean Gap, a quarter of a mile to the east, and the men would hurry to meet it. Two lanterns would send it even further east, toward Newhaven.

The three of them sat in an edgy silence for the better part of an hour. Once or twice Harry thought he heard something—a footfall, a scattering of rock—and got up to investigate but found nothing. Then John pointed to a single brief flash of light perhaps a mile offshore. "There 'tis!" he exclaimed. "Ship's light."

"Good thing, too," Trunky growled. "I was beginnin' to wonder if plans 'ad changed an' nobody told us."

Relieved that the ship had gotten this far in without incident, Harry stood up and prepared to unshutter his lantern. "Ready with your lanterns," he directed briskly. "We'll flash on the count of three, all together." He began the count. "One ... two ... three." On the final count, he raised the shutter, sending out a gleam of light into the blackness.

The ship responded with another single flash. For a second, Harry stared, not quite taking it in. Then, "They've got it wrong!" he exclaimed, exasperated. "They're going to Saltdean! Didn't they see your lanterns?" He turned to his companions. "We'll have to repeat the signal."

But Trunky's and John's lanterns were still on the ground, shuttered, and their faces told the story. They had intentionally botched the signal.

"Wot d'ye think you're doin'?" Harry demanded angrily. "Why would ye send th' ship to—"

"Take him!" Trunky commanded. Lansdowne seized both of Harry's arms from behind, pushing him to his knees and swiftly lashing his wrists.

"You bastards!" Harry cried. "I trusted you, John! I—" Struggling furiously, trying to get to his feet, he felt the cold hardness of a gun barrel pressed behind his ear.

"Shut yer mouth," Trunky said. "There's a good chap." He pushed Harry over on his side. "Tie 'is feet, too, John, an' stuff yer 'andkerchief in 'is mouth. Lively now, th' men are waitin' for us."

"But why Saltdean?" Harry demanded, as John whipped a stout cord around his ankles. "It's far 'nough to th' tunnel as 'tis. Why—"

"The tunnel?" Landsdowne laughed harshly. "We ain't usin' th' tunnel tonight, 'Arry. We're takin' th' goods an' movin' 'em east, along th' coast road to New'aven. There ain't like to be any coast guards to th' east."

"John," Trunky snarled, "you're talkin' too much. 'E don't need to know our business."

"You blighter!" Harry kicked out with his bound feet. "When I get free o' this, I'll show ye wot th' business is all about! It won't just be me, neither. Th' investors will be after you."

"'Oo needs th' investors?" Trunky's tone was surly. "We'll make more on our own than wi' them."

"But they paid plenty o' money for wot's on that ship," Harry cried, "an' ye're stealin' from 'em." He appealed to John. "'Ave a care wot ye're doin', John, ol' friend. D'ye think they'll take this lyin' down? D'ye think—"

"I said *shut up*," Trunky said savagely. A second later, Harry felt the shock of a blow to his temple and he was lost in black unconsciousness.

32

"... In my heart
Lie there what hidden woman's fear there will—
We'll have a swashing and a martial outside ..."
— WILLIAM SHAKESPEARE
As You Like It

WHILE AMELIA LAID the tea things, Kate paced impatiently up and down in front of the drawing-room fire. Shortly, Charles arrived from Brighton, having dropped Kipling off at The Elms, but he had little to offer in the way of suggestions about finding Patrick, only a fierce exclamation of dismay.

"Kidnapped! But who the devil would—?"

"The photographer I saw by the barn was the same man we talked with on the Quarter Deck on Saturday," Kate said intently. "Gray bowler, gray knickerbockers—I'm sure of it. And Patrick recognized him too. I don't know how that man is connected to this awful business, Charles, but I'm sure he's taken the boy. The question is, what are we going to do about it?"

Hurriedly, Charles finished the last of his sandwich. "Describe the man to me, Kate. Tell me everything

275

that you remember about him."

Kate closed her eyes and thought back to the encounter. "Gray bowler, gray knickerbockers," she repeated. "I can't recall anything about his face, except that he had very pale blue eyes. He spoke with a Continental accent, French, perhaps. And he wore polished black boots. I remember that, because he clicked his heels when he saluted, in a military way." She frowned and opened her eyes. "Somehow, that detail seems important, but I can't think why. Anyway, he made some sort of remark about the natives killing themselves by jumping off the cliff. And he said he liked Rottingdean because it was so quaint and peaceful. He said he was looking for accommodations in this vicinity."

Charles sat silent for a moment, deep in thought. Then he leaned forward, his eyes alight. "A Continental accent? A military salute?"

"Yes," she said. "Yes, he clicked his heels together, like … like that antiquarian we met on the road to Black Rock. The same antiquarian that Patrick overheard talking to Harry Tudwell in the stable office." She stared at him. "Charles! The photographer and the antiquarian—they're the same man!"

Charles took her hand in both of his. "Kate, my dear—"

She jerked her hand back. "Charles, you've got to believe me. I know it doesn't make sense, but—"

"I *do* believe you, Kate," Charles replied. "You have given me the one clue that just might make sense out of this whole damned muddle! If this photographer-cum-antiquarian has taken Patrick, it can only be because the boy can identify him. And if his identity is *that* important to the success of the game …" His voice trailed off and he sat, thinking.

Kate bit her lip. "Charles, I'm frightened. That man—do you think he will harm Patrick?"

Charles was grim. "I won't lie to comfort you, my dear. Yes. I fear that he will harm the boy. He's already killed one man. His future success in this country depends on his real identity—whatever that is—remaining concealed. He doesn't want anyone to know his name or who he is, and if Patrick can tell—"

"Then we must *find* him!" Kate cried. "We must find the boy!"

"I'm sorry, Kate. I can't help you." Charles looked at the ormolu clock on the mantel. "I have to be on the cliffs in a half-hour. I have a feeling that tonight we'll get to the bottom of all this, one way or another, and everything will come to light." He paused, his eyes on her face. "I suppose you've told the constable that Patrick has gone missing."

"Of course, but he's useless," Kate said bitterly. "Aunt Georgie and I talked to several of the villagers, too, about organizing a search, but they refused to be involved. She has gone back to North End House with a sick headache. I think she has given up." Kate bit her lip. "How about Rud? Perhaps he could help." But help *how?* she cried out to herself. She already knew that it would be fruitless to search the downs, for she was sure that the man had taken Patrick somewhere else. Where else—?

"I need Kipling with me tonight." Charles stood and touched her face tenderly. "I am so very sorry, Kate. I know how deeply you feel about this. Please, have another cup of tea—or better yet, a glass of brandy. Try to be calm, and for heaven's sake, don't do anything rash. In fact, I am giving you an order: you are to stay in this house for the rest of the night. As soon as this venture is over, I promise we'll turn the whole village out for a search."

"But by then it will be too late," Kate said despairingly. "And it is all my fault! If I hadn't fallen asleep, if I'd kept a closer eye on him—" She began to weep.

In answer, Charles tipped up the decanter, poured a glass of brandy, and set it in front of her. Then he kissed her and was gone.

Kate was not a woman to yield easily to tears. She wept only for a few minutes, until it came to her that she was weeping more for herself than for Patrick, and more out of guilt than sorrow. Then she stopped weeping and swallowed the brandy Charles had poured for her, feeling its warmth go all through her. She sat back in the chair, leaning her head on the cushion, thinking. She refused to consider the possibility that Patrick was dead. He had to be alive, somewhere—and somewhere close by, most likely. If Beryl Bardwell had created a plot in which a child was kidnapped, where would the villain hide him? The old windmill, perhaps? The tunnel?

The tunnel! She jumped to her feet just as Amelia came into the room to clear away the tea things. "Forget the dishes, Amelia," she commanded. "You can clear up later. Just now, I need you to help me change."

"Yes, milady," Amelia said, blinking at the unexpected urgency in her mistress's voice. "You're going out this evening?"

"Yes," Kate said. "Yes, indeed. I am going out." She paused, frowning. She was not afraid to go by herself, but if there were difficulties, she might be grateful for help. And she would certainly require a light of some sort, and a weapon. And yet she needed to move swiftly, without being encumbered. "Is Lawrence available?"

"Why, yes, ma'am," Amelia said, her eyes opening wide. "'E's in th' kitchen wi' Mrs. Portney, 'aving 'is tea."

"Good," Kate said with satisfaction. "Lawrence can go with me. Now, come upstairs quickly and help me find some clothes."

"Surely, milady," Amelia said, following Kate into the

hall. "Your green silk is fresh pressed. Will you be wearing it?"

Kate smiled. "I think not, Amelia. Stout boots and woolen trousers and a dark waistcoat will be more suited to the occasion." To Amelia's gasp, she replied firmly, "Now, come, and I shall tell you what I plan to do."

33

"The truth is rarely pure and never simple."
—OSCAR WILDE
The Importance of Being Earnest

HARRY SWAM UP out of the blackness, pain hammering like an angry smith at the anvil of his skull. He was face down. His arms, pulled tight behind him, felt as if they had been wrenched out of their sockets, and his wrists and ankles were bound with fire. His nose was stopped with dirt, his mouth stuffed with a wad of cloth, and he could scarcely breathe. Under the roaring that filled his ears, he thought he heard voices. He did not open his eyes. If they were going to kill him, let them get it over and done with. He didn't want to see the gun.

"Tudwell." Someone shook him roughly, rolled him over on his back, toed him with a boot.

"Tudwell!"

Hands yanked the wad of cloth out of his mouth. A torrent of icy water spilled across his face. He choked and gasped and his eyes popped wide open.

Two faces and a lantern loomed over him out of the dark.

"Ah, he's coming around," Rudyard Kipling said briskly. "Come on, Harry. Time to wake up."

"Snap out of it, man," said a deeper voice. It was the toff with the fancy hat and the creased trousers, except now he wore a canvas jacket and a pair of old tweeds. He didn't look quite so toffish, somehow. "We want you to tell us what's going on."

Harry closed his eyes, trying giddily to sort through the dire misadventures that had befallen him. It was true that he had been deceived and double-crossed, but that was all in the line of work, so to speak, all part of the game. Betraying his betrayers to an outsider, to a representative of the Crown—that was a far darker dishonor than any that had been done to him. He could not bring himself to it. He opened his eyes. In the sky above, lightning flickered. A cold wind was blowing, bringing with it the first spits of rain.

"I took a fall," he muttered.

"And tied and gagged yourself into the bargain." Kipling sounded half-amused. "Quite a trick."

"Come, come, Harry," Lord Sheridan said sharply. "We've been watching. We saw what your two compatriots did to you, and we know it is part of a plan. We want to know what they're aiming to do."

Harry was sullenly silent.

Lord Sheridan sighed. "Look here, Tudwell. There is more to this than you know. These investors you believe to be backing your enterprise—they are not what you think them to be. In fact, if I'm correct, there are *no* investors. You have been deceived, Harry." His voice dripped scorn. "You have been a fool."

"No investors?" Harry asked, startled. "But then where did the money—" He clamped his mouth shut. They couldn't goad him into speech. "Ye'll get nothin' from me," he said.

Sheridan knelt down beside him and his voice became suddenly hard. "You have been organizing the villagers to smuggle goods into this country, under the direction of Captain Reynold Smith, recently deceased. If you will give us information that will help us apprehend his murderer, the Crown may deal more leniently with you when you are brought to justice." He paused, spacing his next words, giving them extra weight. "If you do not cooperate in this matter, you will be tried as an accomplice to the captain's murder. Now, who is the killer?"

Harry shuddered, and the sinister vision of the investors' representative rose up before his eyes. Name him, and things might go easier. But he had no name to offer—and no hard proof that the man had anything to do with Foxy's death. If he accused him and the Crown failed to gain a conviction, Harry knew full well what would become of *him*.

"I don't know 'oo killed Foxy," he growled, turning his face aside. "I got nothin' to tell ye."

Sheridan grabbed his chin and roughly pulled his head back, staring at him with narrowed eyes. When he spoke, his words were slashing. "What has been done with the boy?"

The question shook Harry. "Th' boy? Paddy, ye mean?"

"Yes, Paddy." Kipling said grimly. "Where is he?"

"'Ow th' devil should I know?" Harry swallowed, trying to pull his head free. "'E's a boy. Boys go off. Anyway, that one's too smart to get 'isself into trouble. 'E's an imp, 'e is."

Sheridan's eyes were like flint and his grip like a vise. "The boy disappeared early this afternoon on a picnic in the downs with Lady Sheridan and Lady Burne-Jones. We believe he was kidnapped by the man who is behind all of this—the same man who visited you yesterday in the disguise of an antiquarian."

Harry stared. "You ... know about that?" Damn! What *didn't* they know?

"This man has more than one identity," Sheridan said, "and the boy is the only one who can put them together. That's why he was taken." He shook Harry's chin. "Come on, Tudwell. Tell us what you know. If the man kills Patrick, his blood will be on your hands."

Harry grimaced. Paddy was far more useful than the other village boys he occasionally employed to deliver coded messages. The boy saw everything and remembered everything he saw. He used his considerable intelligence, his curiosity, his intuition. He was loyal and he was—as far as Harry could tell—without fear. That was why he was so valuable.

But there was something else, and in that moment, Harry brought himself to acknowledge it. He was fond of Paddy, very fond indeed. Since his wife had gone off to live in the baker's brick house, Paddy had become very close to him, almost like a ... yes, like a son. Harry thought of the hours they had spent among the downs, riding, exploring, shooting. And he made up his mind.

"All right," he said. "Wot d'ye need t' know?"

Sheridan's grip relaxed. "The foreign gentleman who visited you yesterday afternoon. Tell us what you know of him."

"I never met 'im before yesterday," Harry said, working his lower jaw. "Before that, 'e only dealt wi' Foxy."

"How long did he deal with Foxy?"

"A couple of years. 'E's th' one 'oo paid for th' tunnels."

"Yes, the tunnels," Sheridan said. "The new excavations are far more extensive than one might expect, given the small amount of goods you are able to bring in. Why?"

Harry would have shrugged, had he been able. "It wasn't my business to ask *why*," he said. "It was my business to see that th' work got done an' th' men got paid. Th' money came in 'andy, I'll tell ye. There ain't much other work around 'ere now." He paused suspiciously. "Wot's th' tunnel work got to do wi' th' boy?"

Sheridan persisted. "The man who paid you to enlarge the tunnels. Did he also hire you to bring in the guns?"

Harry shook his head from side to side. "I *told* ye this mornin'. I don't know nothin' about any guns."

"Paddy took us into the tunnels last night," Kipling said severely. "We found a box of blasting caps and a case of pistols—a new type. The same type that killed Captain Smith. We think you're running guns, Tudwell. Who are they for? The Irish?"

The Irish! Running guns! Harry jerked his head. "I don't know nothin' about any guns," he repeated vehemently. "An' if I don't, nobody else in th' village does, neither. All we do is unload tuns an' crates an' boxes off th' ships and carry 'em into th' tunnels. Then we send th' stuff on its way, quick as we can. Not all of it," he added hastily. "Some of it stays 'ere, for th' shops. Most of it goes out, though."

Sheridan's eyes were narrowed, his mouth grim as death. "Do you want to know what I think, Tudwell? I think your village has been had. You are the victims of a grand deception."

"Been 'ad?" Harry demanded angrily. "Deception? Wot th' devil d'ye mean?"

"The tunnels you were paid to dig," Sheridan said, "the smuggling you've been paid to do—it's all a concealment for something else. Something much larger and of much greater consequence." He turned to look at Kipling. "And it's not gunrunning, either."

"Somethin' larger?" Harry frowned, remembering the man's words. *Your advancement, Mr. Tudwell, is of more consequence than you can know, and the game is larger than you can think.* What had he meant? What did any of this have to do with Paddy's disappearance? Where was the boy? What had the man done with him? And where, in all this bloody mess, was the bloody truth?

Kipling was shaking his head. "But if it's not gunrunning, what can it be, Sheridan? What sort of organization would put this much money and effort into—"

"You said it yourself, Kipling." Sheridan's voice vibrated with a tense excitement. "As an investment, the smuggling makes no economic sense at all. Except for the villagers, nobody is going to profit financially, no matter how many shiploads of merchandise they bring in here. But what if the smuggling is a cover-up for something larger and far more sinister? What if a foreign government wants a free port on the south coast of England, and they're willing to buy a village to get it?"

Harry felt as if he had suddenly stepped into a pit of quicksand. "To buy a village?" he whispered.

"Wait a minute," Kipling said. "I don't understand. A free port? You're talking about a duty-free port?"

"I'm talking about a port that can be entered without anyone's knowledge or control," Sheridan replied. "Say that one of the great Continental powers—the Kaiser's government, for instance—wants to infiltrate men and arms into this country. What better strategy might it devise than to embroil an entire village in its scheme? And what better village than one with a proud heritage of smuggling?"

Harry felt himself go cold. "Ye're talkin' about th' Germans?" he whispered disbelievingly. "Ye're sayin' we've been dealin' wi' th' bloody *Germans?*"

Kipling's eyes were bright. Two spots of red showed on his cheeks. "By Jove!" he exclaimed. "It's too incredible for words—but yes, it fits. Willie isn't running guns. He's planning a bloody invasion!"

34

"The female of the species is more deadly than the male."

—RUDYARD KIPLING
The Female of the Species

LAWRENCE WAS WAITING in the cellar, but from the look on his craggy face, this was not an expedition he wanted to undertake. "Beggin' yer pardon, milady," he said, frowning, "but if Lord Charles was 'ere, 'e wouldn't permit—"

"I am sure you're right, Lawrence," Kate said briskly, tucking her hair under Charles's tweed golf cap. "If Lord Charles were here, he would no doubt be very upset with me. In that event, I should consider his objections and then do as I felt right. As I am doing now."

Lawrence tried again. "But milady, consider yer 'ealth! Yer not long out o' a sickbed an'—"

"Thank you for your concern," Kate said, "but I am quite well, and this is work that *must* be done. A child's life is in danger, and if I sit around waiting for the *men* to do something, it may well be lost." She bent to tuck the leg of Charles's woolen trousers into her boot. They fit loosely and not very attractively, but that could not be helped. In any event, this was a rescue, not a fashion show. She straightened and put her hands on her hips. "Now, you may agree to go with me, or you may refuse—in which case, I shall ask Amelia to put on your trousers and go with me." She narrowed her eyes. "So, Lawrence. Which is it to be? You and I, or Amelia and I?"

"Amelia!" Lawrence's mouth and hunched shoulders showed strong disapproval. "I wouldn't 'low me wife t' dress up like a man an' go muckin' around in a dark tunnel." His eyes took on a crafty look, and he made one more effort to dissuade her. "Why, there's prob'ly rats down there. An' spiders. Big 'airy spiders." He used his hands to measure out a spider the size of a washbasin. "Tunnels are ter'ble places, milady. Why, I once read 'bout a man 'oo broke 'is leg in a tunnel an' died o' starvation."

"Had he been a woman, he would have packed a sandwich," Kate said, pulling on her close-fitting leather driving gloves. Over the trousers, she was wearing a heavy woolen fisherman's sweater and a knit scarf. "Well? Are you going or staying?"

Lawrence sighed heavily. "I'm goin'. But if Lord Charles was 'ere —"

"Very good. Then I believe we are ready. Do you have the lantern and the photographic equipment?"

"Yes'm," Lawrence said. "But I don't for th' life o' me know wot ye mean t' do with—"

"And a weapon of some sort?" Kate was not about to tell him why the photographic equipment was important. She took the lantern from him. She struck a match and lit it.

Lawrence looked sheepish. "I wanted t' take a knife from th' kitchen, but Mrs. Portney was sittin' right beside th' drawer. So I found this in th' garden shed." He held up a cricket bat.

"That will serve more effectively than a knife, I believe," Kate said. "I should much prefer to bash someone over the head than to cut him up." She held out her hand. "I will take the bat and the lantern and go first. You fetch the rest, and bring up the rear."

Lawrence's mouth fell open. "Milady—"

Kate seized the bat. "Enough!" she said sharply. "We are wasting time." She put her hand into her trouser pocket to be sure she had the map. "Now, push those shelves aside. We will leave the door open. When Amelia has seen Mrs. Portney settled in her quarters for the night, she will come down here and keep watch for us."

Huffing and puffing and making a great show of difficulty, Lawrence pushed the wine rack to one side. Kate opened the wooden door and stepped through, holding the lantern. Ahead of her, the long rock corridor led into a stifling, smothering blackness. The air had a damp chill, and it smelled stale and musty.

Kate hesitated, suppressing an involuntary shudder. She would not admit it to Lawrence, but she was terribly frightened, so frightened that she was shaking under her woolen garments and her teeth were beginning to chatter. Lawrence was undoubtedly right about the rats and the spiders, and she could not bear to think what the darkness would be like if their light failed.

But her terror was not just for herself. Since Patrick had gone missing and she realized that he had been abducted, she had carried a frozen knot of fear in her stomach. The excitement of dressing in Charles's clothes and going into the tunnel had taken her mind from that fear temporarily, but now it was back. Was Patrick still alive? Was he in the tunnel, or somewhere else? The map showed that the tunnel system was a perplexing maze, a labyrinth of old and new excavations. What if he were here but hidden, bound and gagged, in some secret corner? What if the man who had taken him had already fled, and the boy could not be found? What if—

She straightened her shoulders resolutely. Patrick could die while she debated with herself. It was time to go forward. And anyway, Beryl Bardwell insisted on seeing the damned tunnel.

35

"If you wake at midnight, and hear a horse's feet,
  Don't go drawing back the blind, or looking in the street.
  Them that asks no questions isn't told a lie.
  Watch the wall, my darling, while the Gentlemen go by!"

—RUDYARD KIPLING
A Smuggler's Song

CHARLES ROSE FROM his kneeling position. A gust of wind chilled him and a streak of lightning ripped the southern sky, showing skittering clouds. An ominous roll of thunder drummed in the distance.

"An invasion?" Tudwell shook his head incredulously. "You mean, the man I talked to is a *spy*? 'E's plannin' t' send *soldiers* 'ere?"

Kipling gave him a stern look. "Aiding and abetting a foreign power—that's treason, you know. And two of the Queen's coast guards are dead. When this comes out, Harry, you'll be branded for a traitor."

"Treason!" Tudwell squeaked. His eyes were like round silver coins. "No! I swear on my mother's grave! I didn't know 'e was a spy! I didn't know nothin' about soldiers or guns! I ain't never 'eard a *whisper* of an invasion! I can't … I never … I—" His mouth began to flap and his words disintegrated into whimpers.

"We're wasting time," Charles said. "We have to find the foreigner. Where is the ship putting in?"

Tudwell was struggling desperately to get command of himself. "Trunky an' John—they … they signaled th' ship t' put in at Saltdean, a quarter mile to th' east of 'ere. But th' foreigner 'e's not with 'em."

Charles regarded him suspiciously. "How do you know?"

"Because that wasn't part of 'is plan." Tudwell licked his lips. "'E thought th' ship was comin' in 'ere, ye see. Won't 'e be bloody surprised when 'e figures out that it's 'eaded east"

"Where is he?" Kipling asked.

"Cut me loose, an' I'll tell ye," Tudwell cried.

Charles jerked Tudwell to his feet, pulled out his pocket knife, and slashed the cord that held the man's wrists. "Tell," he snapped, and pushed the point of the knife into Tudwell's gut.

"Ow!" Tudwell cringed from the knife point. "'E's gone t' th' Gap."

"The Gap?" Kipling asked, surprised. The lantern glinted off his gold-rimmed glasses. "Why would he go there?"

Tudwell was babbling again. "T' get 'is travelin' case, ye see. 'E sent it t' me this afternoon, with instructions t' lock it in one o' th' bathin' machines. 'E also said t' pull up a skiff on th' beach, so I reckon 'e's plannin' t' row out t' th' ship." He rolled his eyes, and the whites showed. "Ye don't think 'e'd take th' boy with 'im, do ye?"

Kipling picked up the lantern and turned away. "Come on, Sheridan. There's no time to lose!"

Tudwell picked up his own lantern and took several unsteady steps after Kipling. Charles put his hand on the man's shoulder and swung him around. "One more thing, Tudwell," he said grimly. "Mr. Kipling and I are both armed. If either of us even suspects a double-cross, you're a dead man. Is that quite clear?"

"Clear," Tudwell gasped. "I'm with ye. I swear!"

"Right," Charles said. "Come on, then."

The three of them started downhill toward the town at a brisk trot. In just over five minutes, they were at the intersection of the coast road and the High Street, across from the White Horse, which showed only one light in the very back of the building. They paused to catch their breath, then turned left toward the Gap.

The street was deserted and the shops and cottages dark. There was no sound but the whistle of the wind through the chimney pots, and nothing stirred save a black dog, nosing through a rubbish bin for his dinner. Charles reflected wryly that the villagers—those who were not at Saltdean, ready to unload the ship—must have gone early to bed, prudently extinguishing their lamps so that no light would be cast on the smugglers at work and turning their faces to the wall to avoid any glimpse of them.

He took the lead, and with Kipling in the rear and Tudwell between them, they slipped through the shadows down the High Street to the stone wall overlooking the beach. The four bathing machines had been pulled up almost under the cliff's overhang, and a skiff was beached on the shingle not far away.

Tudwell set down the lantern. "There!" he exclaimed, pointing breathlessly to the empty skiff. "'E's still 'ere!"

"Shutter the lanterns," Charles said. When they were dark, he waited a moment, his eyes becoming accustomed to the stormy night. Seaward, lightning danced and the angry peal of thunder echoed from the cliffs. To the right were the steps to the beach and the shadowy cat's cradle of the pilings and trusses that supported the iron pier, the terminus of the Volk's electric railway. Thirty yards out, perched on its spindly legs high above the waves, was the boxy shape of the Daddy Longlegs, moored for the night. The wind was freshening and the seas were coming short and hard, white-capped. If the man intended to row out in this weather, Charles thought, he would have his work cut out for him—particularly since the ship was lying *off* Saltdean, rather than straight out from the Gap. But perhaps the storm had decided him to abandon his plans and sent him inland, instead. If so, had he taken Patrick with him? Or had he already disposed of the only person who had seen him in three of his disguises?

Charles turned to Tudwell. "Do you have the key to the bathing machine?"

Tudwell hastily went through his pockets. "'Ere 'tis," he said, handing it over. "Th' case is in th' first machine. 'E gave me th' padlock an' kept th' other key." He frowned. "Ye're not goin' down there, are ye?"

Kipling spoke in a tense voice. "If the man is here, Sheridan, he's armed. He could be anywhere along the cliff, or in the rocks—or out there in that infernal contraption. You'll be a sitting duck on the open beach."

"Nobody's going to get a good shot in the dark. If anybody fires, you cut loose with that revolver of yours. That'll give me time to find cover."

Kipling shook his head stubbornly. "Whatever is in the traveling case, it can't be worth the risk."

"We have to know whether the case is there," Charles said. "If it is, we'll wait for him to pick it up. If not—"

If not, what then? What if the man had already retrieved his traveling case, taken the boy, and driven up to Falmer to catch the morning train? Or what if he'd picked up the case, but disposed of the boy? He could make better time and be less easily spotted if he were traveling alone. Master of disguise as he was, it wasn't likely they would ever catch up to him. Charles pushed the thought away. There was no point speculating before he checked the bathing machine.

Kipling bent close to his ear. "This could be a beastly trap," he said, low and urgent. He jerked his head at Tudwell. "How do we know we can trust this man?"

"We don't," Charles replied. "It might be a good idea to gag him so he can't give an alarm."

"Right," Kipling said, and whipped out his pocket handkerchief. "I'd better retie his hands, too, or he'll have the damn thing off."

Tudwell groaned. "I'm *with* ye," he protested.

"We'll just make sure of that," Kipling said roughly, and went to work.

Charles took out the Webley revolver the chief constable had lent him the day before and double-checked to be sure that all six chambers were loaded. "Cover me, Kipling." He nodded at Tudwell. "And keep a sharp eye on him. You're right—this could be a trap."

It had been more than a dozen years since Charles had found himself under fire, yet in this moment of stress, the training and experience all came back to him. He took the steps quickly, then dashed to his left, aiming for the shadow of the undercliff. His back to the chalk face, he moved cautiously along it, boots crunching on the rocks, gun at the ready. He reached the bathing machine and glanced both ways, up and down the beach. Nothing moved except the rhythmic waves, cresting a few feet out and breaking heavily on the shingle. But the man he was watching for could be hiding among the jumble of rock slabs farther to the left, sighting down the barrel of a repeating rifle or ready to blaze away at him with that murderous handgun. Charles had been only partially truthful when he'd assured Kipling that the dark would protect him. An alert, attentive man whose eyes were accustomed to the dark could see the shadow of a movement, even on a pitch-black night. Armed with that Mauser, he had only to aim and squeeze the trigger.

But Charles had to take the chance. In a low, crouching run, making himself as small a target as possible, he moved swiftly out of the shadows to the bathing machine, slipped the key into the padlock and turned it, lifting the lock from the hasp and swinging the door open. On the floor just inside sat a medium-sized leather traveling case with a handle. Their man was still here.

Charles slid the case out onto the shingle. It was obviously full, but not overly heavy. The gold-colored metal clasps were closed and locked, and there was no identification anywhere—no name, no initials, no shipping labels. He closed the door, refastened the padlock in the hasp, and picked up the case. With a final, quick survey of all the landward approaches, he retraced his steps. A minute later, he was with Kipling and Tudwell.

"Good show, old chap!" Kipling exulted. "What do we do now?"

"We move to a spot on the cliff just over the bathing machines," Charles said, "and wait for our man to pick up his case. I don't think it will be long—not if he means to get out to the ship before the storm breaks."

They repositioned themselves. "He surely wouldn't be fool enough to row out in this storm," Kipling said when they were settled behind the low stone wall. "It would be suicide!"

"Our man is daring," Charles replied. "In pursuit

of his dream, he's used to taking risks that would turn an ordinary man's hair white. And you know yourself, Kipling, the line between boldness and foolhardiness is hard to draw."

"Ah, yes," Kipling muttered. "Hard indeed. Hard, hard, indeed."

36

"There are some frauds so well conducted that it would be stupidity not to be deceived by them."

—CHARLES CALEB COLTON
Lacon, 1825

THEY DIDN'T HAVE long to wait. Off to the left, where the slabs of fallen chalk tumbled almost out to the tide line, Charles saw a low, bobbing light. A lantern! As the light grew closer, he glimpsed two shadowy figures, a tall, cloaked figure walking behind a smaller one. The smaller was carrying the lantern.

Charles let out an involuntary breath of relief. Tudwell grunted excitedly and swiveled his shoulders in a pantomime of speech. "It's the boy!" Kipling whispered gleefully.

Charles tensed, waiting until the pair were almost directly beneath them. Then he stood, raising his pistol. "Halt!" he commanded loudly. *"Bewegen Sie sich nicht!"*

The cloaked man stopped in midstride, as if unbelieving. Then he put out his left hand, seized Patrick's shoulder, and turned in their direction, keeping the boy between himself and them. "Lord Sheridan?" he inquired. "You are not going to make the effort to carry out this conversation in German, I hope. That would be too tedious. And silly, as well. We can transact our business quite adequately in English."

A flicker of lightning lit the scene, and Charles saw that the man held a Mauser in his right hand. The barrel was pressed against the back of Patrick's head.

"My God," Kipling exclaimed incredulously. "Count Hauptmann! The Kaiser's cultural representative. What the devil—"

"Herr Kipling, too," the count said pleasantly. "So you have both come to see me off. I am sorry to have kept you waiting, gentlemen. I had to stop and fetch a little ... insurance, shall we say." He laughed in ironic amusement.

Kipling leaned over the wall. "Patrick? Are you all right?"

"All right, sir," Patrick replied steadily. "But he's planning to make off with that skiff and—"

"That's enough, boy!" the count snapped. "Sheridan, you can see that I am armed. But perhaps you cannot see that this gun is—"

"I know about the gun," Charles said brusquely.

"Ah. So you recognize Herr Mauser's clever invention? Do you also know of the way I have put it to use?" Patrick squirmed, trying to pull free. The count collared the boy more firmly and brought the gun to his cheek. "Stand still, my young friend," he said icily, "or I shall be forced to do something you would not like." Patrick stopped struggling and stood still.

"Yes, we have seen how you used the Mauser," Charles said. "We discovered the ejected shell casing on the floor of the mill and X-rayed Captain Smith's body to locate the bullet. Given the opportunity to compare the grooves on the bullet with the rifling of that pistol of yours, we could likely prove that you used it to kill him."

"Ah, this modern science," the count said. "So up-to-date in its methods. X-rays, studies of bullets—soon there will be no escape for even the wiliest of criminals." His tone grew harder. "I take it, then, that you have spoken to Mr. Tudwell since my conversation with him?"

"Mr. Tudwell has joined forces with us," Charles said. "In fact, he is here now, although he is rather ... tied up at the moment."

The count laughed dryly. "Then you know about the investors and the smuggling. What a pity that Mr. Tudwell could not be trusted to hold his tongue. He might have enjoyed a long and lucrative employment with us."

Harry Tudwell made rude noises behind his gag.

"What we know," Charles said in a deliberate tone, "is that there are no investors, and that whatever smuggling is going on here is a fraudulent cover for another activity altogether."

There was a moment's silence; then the count said, archly, "Very clever, Sheridan. And just what might that activity be?"

"Captain Smith was not as careful an agent as you could have wished, Hauptmann. In his cottage, we found map overlays which suggest that an amphibious operation is planned for this vicinity. We also discovered George Radford's knife, which the captain used to kill Radford after he threatened to interfere with this plan. And in the tunnels, we found a supply of Mausers, explosives detonators, and telegraphy devices—equipment that could be used to expedite the infiltration of agents or saboteurs into this country. What we don't know, however, is whether you are acting in an official capacity, on behalf of the Kaiser's government and with his blessing, or whether this is a freelance project of your own devising."

He paused. "Perhaps you would care to enlighten us as to that detail. We are also curious to know why you killed Captain Smith."

"Captain Smith?" Hauptmann replied scornfully. "He was killed because he was insubordinate, of course. He was ordered to leave the handling of George Radford to his superiors. Not only did he disobey that order, but after he had killed the man, he botched the disposal of the body. Given certain remarks that Radford was making, it was virtually certain that complaints would be heard by those in authority and that Smith would be accused. His rash act jeopardized the entire operation—hence, I took it upon myself to discipline him." There was a loud peal of thunder. "Now, if you will excuse me, I shall fetch my traveling case and be on my way. My ship is expecting me."

"Your case?" Charles asked. He lifted it up onto the wall. "I believe, sir, that we have anticipated you. We have it here."

"Ah." The count was silent for the space of several breaths. Then: "Have you opened it?"

"Not yet," Charles said. "Whatever is in it is undisturbed. You may have it—in return for the boy."

"Throw in an hour's head start, and you have a bargain," the count replied.

"Don't trust him, Sheridan," Kipling whispered urgently.

"On my word as a gentleman," the count said. "And I have yours, I assume."

"Of course," Charles said. He picked up the case. Kipling pulled at his arm. "We can't give it to him, Charles. The case may be full of valuable strategic information. We still don't know whether the man is working for the Kaiser or for himself, and we know nothing about the extent of his espionage activity. If he gets back to Germany with those documents, they could be used to—"

Charles shook his head. "The game is up, Rud. We understand enough about his operation to scuttle it entirely, and he knows it. Whatever is in that case is probably more of an embarrassment to the Kaiser and to Hauptmann than a threat to the Queen's realm. And it certainly isn't worth a gun battle that would cost Patrick's life, and quite possibly ours."

"My compliments, my lord," the count said in an admiring tone. "You have stated my own conclusions quite competently. In any event, I have grown very fond of this young man in the hours we have spent together. He is a bright chap, very courageous. It would be sad indeed for him to die at so tender an age."

"Then you should be glad to let him go," Charles said. "I'm coming down with the case."

"Excellent. You will leave your gun on the wall, however."

Charles hesitated.

"Come, come, Sheridan," the count snapped. "We are gentlemen, are we not? A bargain is a bargain."

"Keep your gun on the man," Charles said sotto voce to Kipling, and picked up the case. A moment later, he was on the beach.

"Very good," the count said. "Put it in the skiff." Charles shook his head. "The boy first."

"Lord Sheridan," the count said, in a tone of rebuke, "I gave my word as a gentleman."

Charles walked to the skiff, put the case in the bow, and turned. "Now the lad."

"When I am ready," the count said. "Step away from the boat."

"You gave your word as a gentleman," Charles said angrily.

"What makes you think I am a gentleman?" The count's

301

laugh grated harshly. "A man is a fool who trusts the word of a spy. I have a use for the boy. He is going with me." Pushing the gun into Patrick's neck and keeping the boy between himself and Kipling, he walked sideways toward the skiff.

Charles clenched his hands, angry and helpless. If he leapt for the boy, Hauptmann would kill him, he was certain of that. But Patrick was dead already, for he knew too much to be set free. The moment Hauptmann stepped into the boat, he would jump for it, throw the man off balance, give Patrick an instant to flee. He tensed. But before he could move, the entire beach was suddenly and eerily lit, as if by a lightning bolt or a blue-white flare of enormous power.

The count cried something in German as he instinctively threw up his hand to shield his eyes. Charles, in a darting run, snatched the boy and dove for the cover of the nearest bathing machine.

The impression of the flash lingered long after it went out. There was a silence, and then a clear, melodic voice spoke from the rock fall. "A picture, they say, is worth a thousand words."

"Kate!" Charles exclaimed. "What the devil—"

"Lady Sheridan?" the count cried, in a strangled voice. "You have taken a *photograph!*"

On the headland above, Kipling unshuttered the lantern and held it up. Stunned, Charles saw Kate, dressed in trousers and a heavy sweater, her hair pinned up under his tweed golf cap, advancing onto the beach, a cricket bat in her hand. Lawrence, with a box camera in one hand and Charles's magnesium lamp in the other, was a step behind her.

"Surely you know something of *Lear*, Your Excellency," Kate said sweetly, and with as much self-assurance as if they were in a ballroom. "Perhaps you remember Gloucester's lines from the second act. 'All ports I'll bar; the villain shall not 'scape ... besides, his picture I will send far and near, that all the kingdom may have due note of him.'" She paused and added, regretfully: "Helpful to us, but not so to you, I fear, sir. A spy's photograph in the hands of his enemy rather spoils his game, I should think." The count sputtered something in indistinguishable German.

Charles stepped out from the bathing machine. "I believe our bargain is concluded, Hauptmann. We have the boy. You have the case. Now, take the skiff and go, before the storm makes it impossible for you to reach the ship."

There was a silence. "Very well, then," the count said at last. "Perhaps we shall meet again, in happier circumstances." He chuckled dryly. "Although next time, I should rather you left your wife at home."

He turned his back on them, shoved the skiff into the waves, and leapt into it. He seized the oars, set them in the locks, and with powerful strokes began to pull out into the angry sea.

37

"No man can calculate the effect on our delicate economic fabric of a well-timed, well-planned blow at the industrial heart of the kingdom, the great ... towns, with their teeming populations of peaceful wage-earners ... It is imperative that the invaders should seize and promptly intrench a prearranged line of country, to serve as an initial base. This once done, they can use other resources; they can bring up transports, land cavalry and heavy guns, pour in stores, and advance. But unless this is done, they are impotent ..."

—ERSKINE CHILDERS
The Riddle of the Sands, 1903

"AND THIS IS the spot where they found it?" Kate asked curiously, stepping from the front seat of the tandem bicycle she and Charles had borrowed from the Kiplings. "Down there on the rocks?"

The brisk morning breeze whipped her auburn hair into an unruly mass, but it was nothing like the fury of the storm several days before, which had left piles of debris all up and down the south coast. Although the wind made pedaling difficult and the tandem made uphill riding a challenge, it was a beautiful day for bicycling. The sparkling blue-green waters of the Channel stretched out to the horizon, and the sky was a complementing blue, punctuated here and there with wheeling flocks of white gulls. Directly below them was a small cove cut in the white chalk cliffs, and a narrow crescent of wet shingle. The tide was just beginning to ebb.

Charles laid the bicycle on the turf and joined her at the edge of the cliff, where they sat down together. "Hauptmann's traveling case? Yes, just down there, to the left, on those rocks."

Kate followed Charles's pointing finger to a pile of jagged rocks against which a gentle surf was breaking. "What about the skiff?"

"It washed up farther to the east, what was left of it."

She tucked her skirt under her knees and was silent for a moment, thinking of how it must have been, alone in a terrifying storm in a small wooden boat. "Do you suppose they will ever find the count's body?" she asked at last.

"It doesn't seem likely," Charles replied. "Of course, Hautpmann may have gotten clean away. Finding the wrecked skiff was hardly a surprise, after all. Once he made the ship, he would simply have abandoned the boat to the mercy of the storm. Finding the case—that's what makes me think he was drowned."

Kate turned to look at Charles, loving his grave, thoughtful face, the strength of his shoulders. "It is over, then."

"Over?" He chuckled wryly. "I think not, my dear. How did Kipling put it the other evening? 'The great game is over when we are all dead.'"

"But if Hauptmann himself has perished and the plan is known, the danger is past, isn't it?"

"But Hauptmann is only a single player, Kate. And this scheme of his may have been a serious plan for invasion—or it may have been merely a diversion or a contingency plan. When they learn what happened, the Kaiser's agents will no doubt consider themselves fortunate that this particular intrigue did not create an international incident. But they will try again at another place, at another time, with another strategy. That is how the game is played."

Kate turned her gaze back to the ocean, thinking about the past few days. After Hauptmann had rowed out to sea on that stormy night, Charles sent a coded message to the Brighton chief constable, who had set up a command post at the telegraph office in Newhaven. Sir Robert had directed his forces to surround and seize the villagers and confiscate the smuggled goods. The next morning, a fresh contingent of coast guards undertook an aggressive patrolling of the beach. In the flotsam of the storm, one of them had found the count's traveling case.

What Kate knew of the contents of the case, she owed to Charles's narration. In a heavily secured room of the Rottingdean coast guard station, in the presence of Charles and Kipling, the chief constable had forced the clasps of Hauptmann's case. The items they found sealed in a waterproof oilskin pouch told a story of methodical, meticulous planning for an invasion of the south coast. Photos and glass negative plates covered virtually every foot of shoreline from Newhaven to Brighton, carefully detailing each usable landing area at which troops could disembark, every avenue of advance by which the invading force could move swiftly inland, every commanding high ground upon which artillery batteries and observation posts could be established. Elaborate notes, compass bearings, and triangulations pinpointed the location of each photo. There was a collection of onionskin map overlays, a selection of railway timetables, and a manuscript composed of columns of six digit numbers, clearly an encrypted report.

After examining the contents, Sir Robert closed the case and locked it in a mail sack. The sack was taken under guard to Brighton, where Arthur Sassoon secured it in his bank vault until the Prince had conferred with the War Office and an appropriate course of action was decided upon. Charles and Sir Robert had, of course, sent their offical report to HRH that very night, by royal courier. His response was what they had expected: all involved were sworn to absolute silence and the matter was declared a State secret. In particular, the Prince insisted that the Queen not be told, for fear that she could not restrain her wrath against her grandson the Kaiser and would reveal all in an unguarded moment. A nice bit of irony, Kate thought, for Her Royal Majesty had complained for years that the Prince could not be trusted with important matters.

As for Rottingdean, the Smugglers' Village, it had been ordered that all contraband was forfeit to the Crown and that all tunnel entrances were to be sealed, including the one on the beach, which was to be hidden by a carefully contrived avalanche of rocks. To Harry Tudwell's enormous relief, no other action was to be taken against the village and its inhabitants. There was no doubt that they could be trusted to hold their tongues for all eternity. After all, none of them wanted to confess to being naive, gullible fools, easily taken in by a Trojan Horse scheme that had deceived them with its promise of glittering wealth.

And Patrick? If it had not been for him, of course, Hauptmann might have succeeded in his scheme. When the boy had seen the photographer standing by the barn in the downs, he recognized him as the antiquarian, a recognition that was confirmed when he found a compass the man had left on the wall. Realizing that the boy had seen and could identify him in all three of his disguises—the count who attended Sassoon's party in Hove, the photographer who took pictures in the downs, and the antiquarian who wandered up and down the coast—Hauptmann had seized Patrick and hidden him in the tunnel. For his courageous service in helping to foil the spy's plot, the lad was to receive a handsome royal stipend sufficient to guarantee him an education appropriate to his talents. Kipling had managed to locate the boy's father and obtain his permission to act on Patrick's behalf. Now, he and Charles were debating whether to send the lad to Westward Ho!, Kipling's school, or—

"Patrick," Kate said now, thinking aloud. "You know, Charles, there are other options for the boy."

Charles turned, startled by what must have seemed to be a change of subject. "I suppose there are," he said. His eyes lingered on hers. "I have wondered," he said after a moment, "whether you should like to bring him to live with us."

"I have thought of it," Kate said. "Since we cannot ..." She stopped and made herself say it: "Since I cannot have children, perhaps you would like to have him with us. He is a fine boy, and very brave, and he admires you enormously. Of course, he is not your son and cannot inherit from you, but—" She stopped and swallowed and then said, in a sudden burst of feeling, what had been in her heart for too many weeks. "Oh, Charles, my dear, I am *so* sorry! I have failed you. Because of me, your family name will not—"

Charles put his arm around her and pulled her against him. "Kate," he said gently, "because of you, I will never be lonely, or bored, or want for beauty or grace. Measured against the many ways you enrich my life, my concern for my name or my inheritance is—" He held up his thumb and forefinger, a fraction of an inch apart. "Is only this."

Kate bit her lip. "You're not just trying to make me feel better?"

"Look at me," he said, and lifted her chin so that she could not avoid his eyes. "I don't speak easily about such matters, Kate. But I tell you now that *you* are the joy of my life, and I want no other. And to reveal my utter selfishness, I should add that if you were a mother, your attention and your loyaltion would always be divided. As matters stand, I count myself lucky to have you, just *you*, wholly to myself." He kissed her gently and added, with a chuckle, "You and Beryl Bardwell, of course."

She leaned against him, feeling a deep peace and contentment within her for the first time in a very long time. They sat for several quiet moments, then Charles said, "There is just one thing that I must know, Kate."

"What is it, dear?" she murmured.

"Why the *devil* did you go down in that tunnel after the boy when I gave you explicit instructions to stay at home and out of danger? And why the camera?"

Kate frowned. "Have you thought what might have happened if I hadn't appeared on the beach and taken that photograph? Hauptmann would have tried to take Patrick into the skiff, and you would have leapt upon him and been shot to death by that awful gun of his. And then both Hauptmann and the boy would have drowned and—"

"Stop," Charles said, putting his finger on her lips. "I admit to all that, Kate. I am glad you were there, believe me. But I still don't understand—"

Kate sighed. "Well, it was Patrick, of course. And Beryl."

"*Beryl?*"

"Don't you remember? I told you she wanted to see the

tunnel. The plot she has in mind for the next story has a tunnel in it."

"Ah," Charles said, "I see. And the camera?"

"For Beryl's research, of course," Kate said. She shuddered, opening her eyes very wide. "You don't think I was going to go down there more than once, do you? Why, there were *spiders*!"

Historical Notes and Authors' Reflections

"Every man must be his own law in his own work, but it is a poor-spirited artist in any craft who does not know how the other man's work should be done or could be improved."

—RUDYARD KIPLING
Something of Myself

B ILL ALBERT WRITES:
As we have learned in our earlier works in this series, it is always a challenge to include a real person in a fiction. Given a man whose literary works are famous and whose political convictions are controversial, the challenge is even greater: to credibly re-create the man, and to create a credible fiction that can contain and partly explain the man. It takes luck (and often a great deal of hard work) to discover documented aspects of the person's character that can be incorporated without contradiction into the fictional plot. In the case of Kipling, we were indeed fortunate in our choice, for as our research took us deeper into the man's life, we uncovered many authentic aspects of his personality which supported our initial conception of the plot and showed us how to enhance and enlarge it.

Years ago, Kipling's poetry was the hands-down favorite among the male students of my junior-high English class. While he never served on active duty, Kipling early on developed a great passion for the military in general and, in his later years, the defense of the Empire in particular. He was the common soldier's greatest admirer, spokesman, and advocate, as he demonstrates in such poems as "Gunga Din," "Tommy," "Boots," and "Fuzzy-Wuzzy," and throughout his life he continued to call to the nation's attention the plight of the enlisted man. He was also the Empire's staunchest champion, raising an urgent warning against the Kaiser's bellicose posturings and the complacency of the British.

For the purposes of our story, Kipling's move to Rottingdean in the summer of 1897 was most fortuitous. The village has a long and well-established tradition of smuggling, and we wanted to use that aspect of its history in the plot. However, as we had learned in our research for an earlier book, *Death at Gallows Green*, smuggling in England had generally ended by the mid-eighteen hundreds, and Rottingdean seemed to have settled down to a more lawful existence. The key to this puzzle came to us when we were looking into an unrelated question: "Where and when was the first automatic pistol developed?" When we learned of the M96 Mauser, invented in Germany and first distributed in the year of our story, our double-layered plot emerged.

According to his personal correspondence, Kipling's concern over the rise of Germany began in the period of our story, and we have borrowed some of his warnings for use in his character's dialogue. In 1901, he established a firing range just outside Rottingdean because he felt the need to improve British marksmanship and raise his people's awareness in the face of this threat. The vulnerable Sussex seacoast had been invaded by the Romans, Saxons, Normans, and French, and he could see no reason why it would not be a German target as well. When his long-predicted Great War finally came, he secured a commission for his son John, who was only a month or so old at the time of our story. The eighteen-year-old boy could have avoided service due to his poor eyesight, but his father went to considerable lengths to get his son placed in the Army. In August 1915, Lieutenant John Kipling went to war, and in September he was reported missing in action. His loss profoundly affected his father.

A German invasion of England is a plot long celebrated in fiction—and in fact. In 1871, Sir George Chesney, alarmed by Germany's recent defeat of France, wrote *The German Conquest of England in 1875 and Battle of Dorking, or Reminiscences of a Volunteer*. The story, which first appeared anonymously, narrated the British Army's defeat at Dorking after a German invasion at Worthing, thirteen miles west of Rottingdean. In 1903, Erskine Childers wrote *The Riddle of the Sands*, the first important British spy novel, describing a grand plan for a German cross-Channel invasion of East Anglia. Historical sources suggest that the German High Command considered this contingency in the 1890s, and in July 1940, they drew up the plan for Operation Sea Lion. After a diversionary attack near Dover, the might of the Wehrmacht would land on the south coast near Brighton and push northward, enveloping London from the west and severing the English capital from the country's industrial heartland. This plan was never implemented, due only to the Luftwaffe's failure to wrestle air supremacy from the Royal Air Force in the skies over Southern England.

Susan Wittig Albert writes:

For me, one of the great pleasures of historical fiction involves meeting real people and exploring real places. In *Death at Rottingdean*, I met Georgiana Burne-Jones, Rudyard Kipling's "Beloved Aunt" and wife of Edward Burne-Jones, the celebrated painter. She was a woman of extraordinary power and personal charm, a socialist whose deep passion for the abstractions of social theory seemed sometimes to overtake her equally deep compassion for the poor and the sick. The Burne-Joneses came to holiday in Rottingdean in the late 1870s and stayed to purchase a house—that they called North End House.

Georgiana spent extensive periods of time in the village while her husband was still alive, and died there in 1920. She was a small woman, with plenty of ideas for the way the village should be run and the energy to put them into action. A disciple of the socialist William Morris, she served on the Parish Council, set up a Village Credit Society to make low-interest loans to the needy, brought a public-health nurse to the village, and helped to clean up the drains. And in 1900, this pacifist, pro-Boer woman, hearing of the victory at Mafeking, hung a blue banner at a window of North End House, bearing the words cited in the headnote to Chapter Thirteen: "We Have Killed And Also Taken Possession." The patriotic villagers gathered angrily on the Green, planning to storm the house, and Georgiana's pro-Empire nephew, Kipling, had to come out and soothe their ugly temper.

It was the Green, The Elms, and North End House that made such a vivid impression on me when Bill and I visited Rottingdean for the first time in 1993, with the idea of this book in the back of our minds. While the village has grown substantially, the houses and the Green are much as they were in those peaceful summer days before the turn of the century, and I could imagine our characters moving and talking and trying to understand the puzzling events with which these two upstart American authors were about to confront them. My sense of pleasure was immeasurably deepened a few months ago by my discovery of a book called *Three Houses*, written in 1931 by Georgiana's granddaughter, novelist Angela Thirkell, and re-released just in time for *Death at Rottingdean*. In it, Thirkell describes North End House, her grandmother, and the village with an attentive, affectionate intimacy. Thirkell *is* Kate, in Chapter Thirteen and in other descriptive passages, and many of the details of the book come from the granddaughter's fond recollections of her grandmother's house and garden, and her memories of Uncle Ruddy and his daughter Josephine, who died tragically in the year following our story, during a visit to America.

And of course we were impressed by the downs, with their curving skylines and plunging scarps, their combes, dry valleys, and beechwood slopes—although the landscape has been changed since the time of our story by modern farming technology. But the Old Mill still stands on Beacon Hill, its sails stretched to the wind. And before it still lies the Channel, whose waves no longer eat away at the now-stabilized chalk cliffs, but whose gray-blue waters still stretch to the far horizon. Kipling says it best, in a poem called "Sussex":

> So to the land our hearts we give
> Till the sure magic strike,
> And Memory, Use and Love make live
> Us and our fields alike—
> That deeper than our speech and thought,
> Beyond our reason's sway,
> Clay of the pit whence we were wrought

Yearns to its fellow-clay
God gives all men all earth to love,
But, since man's heart is small,
Ordains for each one spot shall prove
Beloved over all.
Each to his choice, and I rejoice
The lot has fallen to me
In a fair ground—in a fair ground—
Yea, Sussex by the sea!

References

We use both primary and secondary documents in our research for this mystery series. Here are a few books that we found helpful in creating *Death at Rottingdean*.

Belford, James N., and Jack Dunlap. *The Mauser Self-loading Pistol,* Alhambra, California: Borden Publishing Co., 1969.

Birkenhead, Lord. *Rudyard Kipling.* New York: Random House, 1978.

Blyth, Henry. *Smugglers' Village: The Story of Rottingdean.* Brighton: Carmichael & Co. Ltd., 1984.

The British Journal Photographic Almanac and Photographer's Daily Companion. London: Henry Greenwood, 1896 & 1897.

Childers, Erskine. *The Riddle of the Sands,* originally published in 1903, available as a Dover reprint.

Heater, Derek. *The Remarkable History of Rottingdean.* Brighton: Dyke Publications, 1993.

Hogg, Ian V. *Military Pistols and Revolvers.* Poole: Arms and Armour Press Ltd., 1987.

Kipling, Rudyard. *Kim.* London: Macmillan, 1901.

—. *The Letters of Rudyard Kipling, Vol. 2: 1890–99,* edited by Thomas Pinney. Iowa City: University of Iowa Press, 1990.

—. *Puck of Pook's Hill*. London: Macmillan, 1906.

—. *Something of Myself*. London: Macmillan, 1937.

—. *Stalky & Co*. London: Macmillan, 1899.

Lewis, Lesley. *The Private Life of a Country House: 1912–1939*. London: Futura Publications, 1980.

Midgley, John. *The Great Victorian Cookbook*. North Dighton, MA, 1995.

Platt, Richard. *The Ordnance Survey Guide to Smugglers' Britain*. London: Cassell Publishers Ltd., 1991.

Schellenberg, Walter. *Hitler's Secret Service* (Original Title: *The Labyrinth*). New York: Pyramid Books, 1956.

Smith, Michael. *Rudyard Kipling: The Rottingdean Years*. Brownleaf, 1989.

Times, Military correspondent. *Imperial Strategy*. London: John Murry, 1906.

Thirkell, Angela. *Three Houses*. Originally published by Oxford University Press in 1931, now available in reprint. Wakefield, RJ: Moyer Bell, 1998.

Twain, Mark. "The Man that Corrupted Hadleyburg," from *The Man that Corrupted Hadleyburg and Other Stories and Essays*. New York and London: Harper & Brothers, 1904.

For more information about Crime Books go to
> crimetime.co.uk